"Beautifully crafted, heartrending, and spine-tinglingly chilling, *The Whisper Man* is a thrilling tour de force."
—**Sarah Pinborough,** *New York Times*–**bestselling author of *Behind Her Eyes***

"A gripping exploration of father-son relationships with a propulsive plot, *The Whisper Man* is a true skin-crawler."
—***The Guardian*** (UK)

"Imagine Stephen King and Alfred Hitchcock penning a tome of nightmarish menace and dread. This would be it. *The Whisper Man* is a powerful psychological suspense debut."
—***New York Journal of Books***

"The best crime novel of the decade."
—**Steve Cavanagh, bestselling author of *The Defense***

"*The Whisper Man* is going to be huge. Dark enough to chill your blood but so beautifully written you will not be able to put it down. Utterly brilliant."
—**Ali Land,** *Sunday Times*–**bestselling author of *Good Me Bad Me***

"A riveting page-turner! Dark and unsettling, this one creeps under your skin."
—**J. D. Barker, internationally bestselling author of *The Fourth Monkey***

D0207189

Praise for *The Whisper Man*

"Works beautifully . . . If you like being terrified, *The Whisper Man* has your name on it."
— *The New York Times* (**Editors' Pick**)

"Superb." — *Publishers Weekly* (**starred review**)

"Poignant and terrifying . . . Take a deep breath before diving into this one." — *Entertainment Weekly*

"Alex North weaves a stunningly captivating narrative that's a nuanced and grounded exploration of father-son relationships. . . . A master class in genre exploration. An incredible read."
— **Joe and Anthony Russo, directors of** *Captain America*, *Avengers: Infinity War*, **and** *Avengers: Endgame*

"*The Whisper Man* is the most unsettling thriller I have read since Jo Nesbø's *The Snowman*. Much more than the sum of its parts, it is nightmarish and disturbing and, at the same time, a moving and life-affirming novel about fathers and sons, and grief, loss, and recovery." — **Alex Michaelides, author of the #1** *New York Times* **bestseller** *The Silent Patient*

"Brilliant . . . an affirmation of the power of the father-son relationship . . . will satisfy readers of Thomas Harris and Stephen King."
> —*Booklist* (starred review)

"A terrifying page-turner with the complexities of fatherhood at its core." —*Kirkus Reviews*

"A powerful and scary story that will haunt readers long after the final page is turned."
> —*Library Journal*

"First it's spooky. Then it's scary. Then it's terrifying. And then . . . well, dear reader, proceed at your own risk. An ambitious, deeply satisfying thriller—a seamless blend of Harlan Coben, Stephen King, and Thomas Harris. My flesh is still crawling."
> —**A. J. Finn, #1** *New York Times*–**bestselling author of** *The Woman in the Window*

"Get ready to be unnerved. This novel is thrilling."
> —**Brad Meltzer, #1** *New York Times*–**bestselling author**

"Beautifully written. Beautifully plotted."
> —**C. J. Tudor, bestselling author of** *The Chalk Man*

THE
WHISPER MAN

ALEX NORTH

CELADON
BOOKS

NEW YORK

For information, address Celadon Books, a Division of Macmillan Publishers, 120 Broadway, New York, NY 10271.

www.stmartins.com

ISBN: 978-1-250-80168-5

Our books may be purchased in bulk for promotional, educational, or business use. Please contact your local bookseller or the Macmillan Corporate and Premium Sales Department at 1-800-221-7945, ext. 5442, or by email at MacmillanSpecialMarkets@macmillan.com.

Printed in the United States of America

Celadon Books hardcover edition published 2019
Celadon Books trade paperback edition published 2020
Celadon Books mass market edition / October 2021

10 9 8 7 6 5 4 3 2

For Lynn and Zack

Jake.

There is so much I want to tell you, but we've always found it hard to talk to each other, haven't we?

So I'll have to write to you instead.

I remember when Rebecca and I first brought you home from the hospital. It was dark and it was snowing, and I'd never driven so carefully in my life. You were two days old and strapped in a carrier in the backseat, Rebecca dozing beside you, and every now and then I'd look in the rearview mirror to check that you were safe.

Because you know what, Jake? I was *absolutely fucking terrified*. I grew up as an only child, completely unused to babies, and there I was, responsible for one of my own. You were so impossibly small and vulnerable, and I so unprepared, that it seemed ludicrous they'd allowed you out of the hospital with me. From the very beginning, we didn't fit. Rebecca held you easily and naturally, as though she'd been born to you rather than the other way around. Whereas I always felt awkward, scared of this fragile weight in my arms, unable to tell what you wanted when you cried. I didn't understand you at all. That never changed.

When you were a little older, Rebecca told me it was because you and I were so alike, but I don't know if that's true. I hope it isn't. I'd have always wanted better for you than that.

But regardless, we can't talk to each other, which means I'll have to try to write all this down instead. The truth about everything that happened in Featherbank.

Mister Night. The boy in the floor. The butterflies. The little girl with the strange dress.

And the Whisper Man, of course.

It's not going to be easy, and I need to start with an apology. Because over the years I've told you many times that there's no such thing as monsters.

I'm sorry that I lied.

PART ONE
JULY

ONE

The abduction of a child by a stranger is every parent's worst nightmare. But statistically it is a highly unusual event. Children are actually most at risk of harm and abuse from a family member behind closed doors, and while the outside world might seem threatening, the truth is that most strangers are decent people, whereas the home can be the most dangerous place of all.

The man stalking six-year-old Neil Spencer across the waste ground understood that only too well.

Moving quietly, parallel to Neil behind a line of bushes, he kept a constant watch on the boy. Neil was walking slowly, unaware of the danger he was in. Occasionally he kicked at the dusty ground, throwing up chalky white mist around his sneakers. The man, treading far more carefully, could hear the *scuff* each time. And he made no sound at all.

It was a warm evening. The sun had been beating down hard and unrestrained for most of the day, but it was six o'clock now and the sky was hazier. The temperature had dropped and the air had a golden hue to it. It was the sort of evening when you might sit out on the patio, perhaps sipping cold white wine and watching the sun set, without thinking about fetching a coat until it was too dark and too late to bother.

Even the waste ground was beautiful, bathed in the amber light. It was a patch of shrubland, edging the village of Featherbank on one side, with an old disused quarry on the other. The undulating ground was mostly parched and dead, although bushes grew in tough thickets here and there, lending the area a maze-like quality. The village's children played here sometimes, although it was not particularly safe. Over the years, many of them had been tempted to clamber down into the quarry, where the steep sides were prone to crumbling away. The council put up fences and signs, but the local feeling was that they should do more. Children found ways over fences, after all.

They had a habit of ignoring warning signs.

The man knew a lot about Neil Spencer. He had studied the boy and his family carefully, like a project. The boy performed poorly at school, both academically and socially, and was well behind his peers in reading, writing, and math. His clothes were mostly hand-me-downs. In his manner he seemed a little too grown-up for his age—already displaying anger and resentment toward the world. In a few years he would be perceived as a bully and a troublemaker, but for now he was still young enough for people to forgive his more disruptive behavior. *He doesn't mean it,* they would say. *It's not his fault.* It had not yet reached the point where Neil was considered solely responsible for his actions, and so instead people were forced to look elsewhere.

The man had looked. It wasn't hard to see.

Neil had spent today at his father's house. His mother and father were separated, which the man considered a good thing. Both parents were alcoholics, functioning to wavering degrees. Both found life considerably easier when their son was at the other's house, and both struggled to entertain him when he was with them. In general, Neil was left to occupy and fend for himself, which obviously went some way toward explaining the hardness the man had seen developing in the boy. Neil was an afterthought in his parents' lives. Certainly he was not loved.

Not for the first time, Neil's father had been too drunk that evening to drive him back to his mother's house, and apparently also too ambivalent to walk with him. The boy was nearly seven, his father reasoned, and had been fine alone all day. And so Neil was walking home by himself.

He had no idea yet that he would be going to a very different home. The man thought about the room he had prepared and tried to suppress his excitement.

Halfway across the waste ground, Neil stopped.

The man stopped close by, then peered through the shrubs to see what had caught the boy's attention.

An old television had been dumped against one of the bushes, its gray screen bulging but intact. The man watched as Neil gave it an exploratory nudge with his foot, but it was too heavy to move. The thing must have looked like something out of another age to the boy, with grilles and buttons down the side of the screen and a back the size of a drum. There were some rocks on the other side of the path. The man watched, fascinated, as

Neil walked over, selected one, and then threw it at the glass with all his strength.

Pock.

A loud noise in this otherwise silent place. The glass didn't shatter, but the stone went through, leaving a hole starred at the edges like a gunshot. Neil picked up a second rock and repeated the action, missing this time, then tried again. Another hole appeared in the screen.

He seemed to like this game.

And the man could understand why. This casual destruction was much like the increasing aggression the boy showed in school. It was an attempt to make an impact on a world that seemed so oblivious to his existence. It stemmed from a desire to be seen. To be noticed. To be loved.

Because that was all any child wanted, deep down.

The man's heart, beating more quickly now, ached at the thought of that. He stepped silently out from the bushes behind the boy, and then whispered his name.

TWO

Neil. Neil. Neil.

Detective Inspector Pete Willis moved carefully over the waste ground, listening as the officers around him called the missing boy's name at regular intervals. In between, there was absolute silence. Pete looked up, imagining the words fluttering into the blackness up there, disappearing into the night sky as completely as Neil Spencer had vanished from the earth below it.

He swept the beam of his flashlight over the dusty ground in a conical pattern, checking his footing as well as looking for any sign of the boy. Blue tracksuit pants, Minecraft T-shirt, black trainers, army-style backpack, water bottle. The alert had come through just as he'd been sitting down to eat the dinner he'd labored over preparing, and the thought of the plate there on his table right now, untouched and growing cold, made his stomach grumble.

But a little boy was missing and needed to be found.

The other officers were invisible, but he could see the flashlights as they fanned out across the area. Pete checked his watch. 8:53 P.M. The day was almost done, and although it had been hot this afternoon, the temperature had dropped over the last couple of hours, and the cold air was making him shiver. In his rush to leave, he'd forgotten his coat, and the shirt he was wearing offered scant protection against the elements. Old bones too—he was fifty-six, after all—but it was no night for young ones to be out either. Especially lost and alone. Hurt, most likely. And scared.

Neil. Neil. Neil.

He added his own voice: "Neil!"

Nothing.

The first forty-eight hours following a disappearance are the most crucial. The boy had been reported missing at 7:39 P.M., well over an hour and a half after he had left his father's house. He should have been home by 6:20, but there had been little coordination between the parents as to the exact time of his return, so it wasn't until Neil's mother had finally called her ex-husband that their son's absence was discovered. By the time the police arrived on the scene at 7:51, the shadows were lengthening, and approaching two of those forty-eight hours had already been lost. Now it was closer to three.

In the vast majority of cases, Pete knew, a missing child is found quickly and safely and returned to his or her family. Cases were divided into five distinct categories: throwaway; runaway; accident or misadventure; family abduction; nonfamily abduction. The law of probability was telling Pete right now that the disappearance of Neil Spencer would turn out to be an accident of some kind, and that the boy was going to be found soon. And yet, the farther he walked, the more gut instinct was telling him differently. There was an uncomfortable feeling curling around his heart. But then, a child going missing always made him feel like this. It didn't mean anything. It was just the bad memories of twenty years ago surfacing, bringing bad feelings along with them.

The beam of his flashlight passed over something gray.

Pete stopped immediately, then played it back to where it had been. There was an old television set lodged at the base of one of the bushes, its screen broken in several places, as though someone had used it for target practice. He stared at it for a moment.

"Anything?"

An anonymous voice calling from one side.

"No," he shouted back.

He reached the far side of the waste ground at the same time as the other officers, the search having turned up nothing. After the relative darkness behind him, Pete found the bleached brightness of the streetlights here made him feel oddly queasy. There was a quiet hum of life in the air that had been absent in the silence of the waste ground.

A few moments later, stuck for anything better to do right now, he turned around and walked back the way he'd come.

He wasn't really sure where he was going, but found himself heading off to the side, in the direction of the old quarry that ran along one edge. It was dangerous ground in the dark, so he headed toward the cluster of flashlights where the quarry search team were about to start work. While other officers were working their way along the edge, shining their beams down the steep sides and calling Neil's name, the ones here were consulting maps and preparing to pick their way down the rough path that led into the area below. A couple of them looked up as he reached them.

"Sir?" One of them recognized him. "I didn't know you were on duty tonight."

"I'm not." Pete bent the wire of the fence up and ducked under to join them, even more careful of his footing now. "I live locally."

"Yes, sir."

The officer sounded dubious. It was unusual for a DI to turn up for what was ostensibly grunt work like this. DI Amanda Beck was coordinating the burgeoning investigation from back at the department, and the search team here was comprised mainly of rank and file. Pete figured he had more years on the clock than any of them, but tonight he was just part of the crowd. A child was missing, which meant that a child needed to be found. The officer was maybe too young to remember what had happened with Frank Carter two decades earlier, and to understand why it was no surprise to find Pete Willis out in circumstances like this.

"Watch yourself, sir. The ground's a bit shaky here."

"I'm fine."

Young enough to discount him as some old man as well, apparently. Presumably he'd never seen Pete in the department's gym, which he visited every morning before heading upstairs to work. Despite the disparity in their ages, Pete would have bet he could outlift the younger man on every machine. He was watching the ground, all right. Watching everything—including himself—was second nature to him.

"Okay, sir, well, we're about to head down. Just coordinating."

"I'm not in charge here." Pete pointed his flashlight down the path, scanning the rough terrain. The beam of light only penetrated a short distance. The bed of the quarry below was nothing but an enormous black hole. "You report to DI Beck, not to me."

"Yes, sir."

Pete continued staring down, thinking about Neil Spencer. The most likely routes the boy would have taken had been identified. The streets had been searched. Most of his friends had already been contacted, all to no avail. And the waste ground was clear. If the boy's disappearance really was the result of an accident or misadventure, then the quarry was the only remaining place that made sense for him to be found.

And yet the black world below felt entirely empty.

He couldn't know for sure—not through reason. But his instinct was telling him that Neil Spencer wasn't going to be found here.

That maybe he wasn't going to be found at all.

THREE

- - - - - - - - - -

"Do you remember what I told you?" the little girl said.

He did, but right now Jake was doing his best to ignore her. All the other children in the 567 Club were outside playing in the sun. He could hear the shouting and the sound of the soccer ball skittering back and forth. Whereas he was sitting inside, working on his drawing. He would much rather have been left alone to finish it.

It wasn't that he didn't like playing with the little girl. Of course he did. Most of the time she was the only one who *wanted* to play with him, and normally he was more than happy to see her. But she wasn't acting particularly playful this afternoon. In fact, she was being all *serious,* and he didn't like that one bit.

"Do you remember?"

"I guess."

"*Say* it, then."

He sighed, put the pencil down, and looked at her. As always, she was wearing a blue-and-white-checked dress, and he could see the hash of a graze on her right knee that never seemed to heal. While the other girls here had neat hair, cut level at the shoulders or tied back in a tight ponytail, the little girl's was spread out messily to one side and looked like she hadn't brushed it in a long time.

From the expression on her face now, it was obvious she wasn't going to give up, so he repeated what she'd told him.

"If you leave a door half open . . ."

It should have been surprising that he *did* remember it all, really, because he hadn't made any special effort to make the words stick. But for some reason, they had. It was something about the rhythm. Sometimes he'd hear a song on the radio and it would end up going around and around in his brain for hours. Daddy had called it an *earworm,* which had made Jake imagine the sounds burrowing into the side of his head and squirming around in his mind.

When he was finished, the little girl nodded to herself, satisfied. Jake picked up his pencil again.

"What does it mean, anyway?" he said.

"It's a warning." She wrinkled her nose. "Well—kind of, anyway. Children used to say it when I was little."

"Yes, but what does it *mean*?"

"It's just good advice," she said. "There are a lot of bad people in the world, after all. A lot of bad *things*. So it's good to remember."

Jake frowned, and then started drawing again. Bad people. There was a slightly older boy called Carl here at the 567 Club who Jake thought was bad. Last week, Carl had cornered him while he was building a LEGO fortress, and then stood too close, looming over him like a big shadow.

Why's it always your dad who picks you up? Carl had demanded, even though he already knew the answer. *Is it because your mum's dead?*

Jake hadn't answered.

What did she look like when you found her?

Again, he hadn't answered. Apart from in nightmares, he didn't think about what it was like to find Mummy that day. It made his breath go funny and not work properly. But one thing he couldn't escape was the knowledge that she wasn't here anymore.

It reminded him of a time long gone when he had peered around the kitchen door and seen her chopping a big red pepper in half and pulling out the middle. *Hey, gorgeous boy.* That was what she'd said when she'd seen him. She always called him that. The feeling inside when he remembered she was dead had the kind of sound the pepper had, like something ripping with a *pock* and leaving a hollow.

I really like seeing you cry like a baby, Carl had declared, and then walked away like Jake didn't even exist. It wasn't nice to imagine the world was full of people like that, and Jake didn't want to believe it. He drew circles on the sheet of paper now. Force fields around the little stick figures battling there.

"Are you all right, Jake?"

He looked up. It was Sharon, one of the grown-ups who worked at the 567 Club. She had been washing up at the far side of the room, but had come over now, and was leaning down with her hands between her knees.

"Yes," he said.

"That's a nice picture."

"It's not finished yet."

"What is it going to be?"

He thought about how to explain the battle he was drawing—all the different sides fighting it out, with the lines between them and the scribbles over the ones who had lost—but it was too difficult.

"Just a battle."

"Are you sure you don't want to go outside and play with the other children? It's such a lovely day."

"No, thank you."

"We've got some spare sunscreen." She looked around. "There's probably a hat somewhere too."

"I need to finish my drawing."

Sharon stood back up again, sighing quietly to herself, but with a kind expression on her face. She was worried about him, and while she didn't need to be, he supposed that was still kind of nice. Jake could always tell when people were concerned about him. Daddy often was, except for those times when he lost his patience. Sometimes he shouted, and said things like, *It's just because I want you to talk to me, I want to know what you're thinking and feeling*, and it was scary when that happened, because Jake felt like he was disappointing Daddy and making him sad. But he didn't know how to be different from how he was.

Around and around—another force field, the lines overlapping. Or maybe it was a portal instead? So that the little figure inside could disappear away from the battle and go somewhere better. Jake turned the pencil around and began carefully erasing the person from the page.

There.

You're safe now, wherever you are.

One time after Daddy lost his temper, Jake found a note on his bed. There was what he had to admit was a very good picture of the two of them smiling, and underneath that Daddy had written: *I'm sorry. I want you to remember that even when we argue we still love each other very much. XXX.* Jake had put the note into his Packet of Special Things, along with all the other important things he needed to keep. He checked now. The Packet was on the table in front of him, right beside the drawing.

"You're going to be moving to the new house soon," the little girl said.

"Am I?"

"Your daddy went to the bank today."

"I know. But he says he's not sure it's going to happen. They might not give him the thing he needs."

"The *mortgage,*" the little girl said patiently. "But they will."

"How do you know?"

"He's a famous writer, isn't he? He's good at making things up." She looked at the picture he was drawing and smiled to herself. "Just like you."

Jake wondered about the smile. It was a strange one, as though she were happy but also sad about something. Come to think of it, that was how he felt about moving. He didn't like it in the house anymore, and he knew it was making Daddy miserable too, but moving still felt like something they maybe shouldn't do, even though *he* was the one who'd spotted the new house on Daddy's iPad when they were looking together.

"I'll see you after I move, won't I?" he said.

"Of course you will. You *know* that you will." But then the little girl leaned forward, speaking more urgently. "*Whatever happens, though,* remember what I told you. It's important. You have to promise me, Jake."

"I promise. What does it *mean,* though?"

For a moment he thought she might be going to try to explain it more, but then the buzzer went on at the far side of the room.

"Too late," she whispered. "Your daddy's here."

FOUR

Most of the children seemed to be playing outside the 567 Club when I arrived. I could hear the mingled laughter as I parked. They all looked so happy—so *normal*—and for a moment my gaze moved between them, searching for Jake, hoping to see him among them.

But, of course, my son wasn't there.

I found him inside instead, sitting with his back to me, hunched over a drawing. My heart broke a little at the sight of him. Jake was small for his age, and his posture right then made him seem tinier and more vulnerable than ever. As though he were trying to disappear into the picture in front of him.

Who could blame him? He hated it here, I knew, even if he never objected to coming or complained about it afterward. But it felt like I had no choice. There had been so many unbearable occasions since Rebecca's death: the first haircut I had to take him to; ordering his school clothes; fumbling the wrapping of his Christmas presents because I couldn't see properly through the tears. An endless list. But for some reason, holidays had been the hardest. As much as I loved Jake, I found it impossible to spend all day, every day with him. It didn't feel like there was enough left of *me* to fill all those hours, and while I despised myself for failing to be the father he needed, the truth was that sometimes I needed time to myself. To forget about the gulf between us. To ignore my growing inability to cope. To be able to collapse and cry for a while, knowing he wouldn't walk in and find me.

"Hey, mate."

I put my hand on his shoulder. He didn't look up.

"Hi, Daddy."

"What have you been up to?"

"Nothing much." There was an almost imperceptible shrug under my hand. His body seemed barely there, somehow even lighter and softer than the fabric of the T-shirt he was wearing. "Playing with someone a bit."

"Someone?" I said.

"A girl."

"That's nice." I leaned over and looked at the sheet of paper. "And drawing too, I see."

"Do you like it?"

"Of course. I love it."

I actually had no idea what it was meant to be—a battle of some kind, although it was impossible to work out which side was which, or what was going on. Jake very rarely drew anything static. His pictures came to life, an animation unfolding on the page, so that the end result was like a film where you could see all the scenes at once, superimposed on top of each other.

He was creative, though, and I liked that. It was one

of the ways in which he was like me: a connection we had—although the truth was that I'd barely written a word in the ten months since Rebecca died.

"Are we going to move to the new house, Daddy?"

"Yes."

"So the person at the bank listened to you?"

"Let's just say that I was convincingly creative about the perilous state of my finances."

"What does *perilous* mean?"

It was almost a surprise that he didn't know. A long time ago, Rebecca and I had agreed to talk to Jake like he was an adult, and when he didn't know a word we'd explain it to him. He absorbed it all, and often came out with strange things as a result. But this wasn't a word I wanted to explain to him right now.

"It means it's something for me and the person at the bank to worry about," I said. "Not you."

"When are we going?"

"As soon as possible."

"How will we take everything?"

"We'll rent a van." I thought about money, and fought down a hint of panic. "Or maybe we'll just use the car— really pack it up and do a few trips. We might not be able to take *everything* with us, but we can sort through your toys and see what you want to keep."

"I want to keep all of them."

"Let's see, eh? I won't make you get rid of anything you don't want to, but a lot of them are very young for you now. Maybe another little boy would like them more."

Jake didn't reply. The toys might have been too young

for him to play with, but each of them had a memory attached. Rebecca had always been better at everything with Jake, including playing with him, and I could still picture her kneeling down on the floor, moving figures around. Endlessly, beautifully patient with him in all the ways I found so hard to be. His toys were things she'd touched. The older they were, the more of her fingerprints would be on them. An invisible accumulation of her presence in his life.

"I won't make you get rid of anything you don't want to."

Which reminded me of his Packet of Special Things. It was there on the table beside the drawing, a worn leather pouch, about the size of a hardback book, which zipped shut around three of the sides. I had no idea what it had been in a previous life. It looked like a large Filofax without the pages, although God knew why Rebecca would have had one of those.

A few months after she died, I went through some of her things. My wife had been a lifelong hoarder, but a practical one, and many of her older possessions were stored in boxes stacked in the garage. One day I'd brought some in and started to look through them. There were things going back to her childhood in there, entirely unconnected to our life together. It felt like that should have made the experience easier, but it didn't. Childhood is—or should be—a happy time, and yet I knew these hopeful, carefree artifacts had an unhappy ending. I began crying. Jake had come and put his hand on my shoulder, and when I hadn't immediately responded, he'd wrapped his small arms around me.

After that, we'd looked through some of the things together, and he'd found what was to become the Packet and asked me if he could have it. Of course he could, I said. He could have anything he wanted.

The Packet was empty at that point, but he began to fill it. Some of the things inside had been sifted from Rebecca's possessions. There were letters and photographs and tiny trinkets. Drawings he'd done, or items of importance to him. Like some kind of witch's familiar, the Packet rarely left his side, and except for a few things, I didn't know what was in there. I wouldn't have looked even if I'd been able to. They were *his* Special Things, after all, and he was entitled to them.

"Come on, mate," I said. "Let's get your things and get out of here."

He folded up the drawing and handed it to me to carry. Whatever the picture was meant to be, it clearly wasn't important enough to go into the Packet. He picked that up himself and carried it across the room to the door, where his water bottle was hanging on a hook. I pressed the green button to release the door, then glanced back. Sharon was busying herself with the washing-up.

"Do you want to say goodbye?" I asked Jake.

He turned around in the doorway, and looked sad for a moment. I was expecting him to say goodbye to Sharon, but instead he waved at the empty table he'd been sitting at when I arrived.

"'Bye," he called over. "I promise I won't forget."

And before I could say anything, he ducked out under my arm.

FIVE

On the day Rebecca died, I had picked Jake up by myself.

That afternoon was supposed to have been one of my writing days, and when Rebecca had asked if I could pick up Jake instead of her, my first reaction had been one of annoyance. The deadline for my next book was a handful of months away, and I'd spent most of the day failing miserably to write, at that point counting on a final half hour of work to deliver a miracle. But Rebecca had looked pale and shaky, and so I had gone.

On the drive back, I had done my best to question Jake about his day, to absolutely no avail. That was standard. Either he couldn't remember or he didn't want to talk. As usual, it had felt like he would have responded to Rebecca, which, coupled with the ongoing failure of the book, had made me feel more anxious and insecure than ever. Back home, he had been out of the car like a flash. Could he go and see Mummy? Yes, I had told him. I was sure she'd like that. But she isn't feeling well, so be gentle with her—and remember to take your shoes off, because you know Mummy hates mess.

And then I had dawdled at the car a little, taking my

time, feeling bad about what an abject failure I was. I'd trailed in slowly, putting stuff down in the kitchen—and noting that my son's shoes had *not* been taken off and left there as I'd requested. Because, of course, he never listened to me. The house was silent. I presumed that Rebecca was lying down upstairs, and that Jake had gone up to see her, and that everyone was fine. Apart from me.

It was only when I finally went into the living room that I saw Jake was standing at the far end, by the door that led to the stairs, staring down at something on the floor that I couldn't see. He was completely still, hypnotized by whatever he was looking at. As I walked slowly across to him, I noticed he was not motionless at all, but shaking. And then I saw Rebecca, lying at the bottom of the stairs.

Everything was blank after that. I know I moved Jake away. I know I called an ambulance. I know I did all the correct things. But I can't remember doing them.

The worst thing was that I was sure that, although he would never talk to me about it, Jake remembered everything.

Ten months later, we walked in together through a kitchen where the sides were all but covered with plates and cups, the little visible counter space dirty with smears and crumbs. In the living room, the toys spread over the bare floorboards looked scattered and forgotten. For all my talk of sorting toys before we moved, it looked like we'd already gone through all our possessions, taken what we needed, and left the rest dotted around like trash. There had been a constant shadow over the place for months now, always growing darker, like a day gradually drawing to an end. It felt like our home had started dying when Rebecca did. But then, she had always been the heart of it.

"Can I have my picture, Daddy?"

Jake was already on his knees on the floor, gathering his colored pencils together from wherever they'd rolled to this morning.

"Magic word?"

"Please."

"Yes, of course you can." I put it down beside him. "Ham sandwich?"

"Can I have a treat instead?"

"Afterward."

"All right."

I cleared some space in the kitchen and buttered two slices of bread, then layered three slices of ham into the sandwich and sliced it into quarters. Trying to fight through the depression. One foot in front of the other. Keep moving.

I couldn't help thinking about what had happened at the 567 Club: Jake waving goodbye to an empty table. For as long as I could remember, my son had had imaginary friends of some kind. He'd always been a solitary child; there was something so closed away and introspective about him that it seemed to push other children away. On good days, I could pretend that it was because he was self-contained and happy in his own head, and tell myself that was fine. Most of the time I just worried.

Why couldn't Jake be more like the other children? More *normal*?

It was an ugly thought, I knew, but it was only because I wanted to protect him. The world can be brutal when you're as quiet and solitary as he was, and I didn't want him to go through what I had at his age.

Regardless, until now the imaginary friends had manifested themselves subtly—more like little conversations he'd sometimes have with himself—and I wasn't sure I liked this new development. I had no doubt the little girl he told me he'd been talking to all day had existed only in his head. This was the first time he'd acknowledged something like that out loud, talking to someone in front of other people, and that scared me slightly.

Of course, Rebecca had never been concerned. *He's fine—just let him be him.* And since she knew better than me about most things, I'd always done my best to abide by that. But now? Now I wondered if maybe he needed real help.

Or maybe *he was just being him.*

It was one more overwhelming thing that I should have been able to deal with, but didn't know how. I didn't know what the right thing to do was, or how to be a good father to him. God, I wished that Rebecca was still here.

I miss you . . .

But that thought would make the tears come, so I cut it dead and picked up the plate. As I did, I heard Jake speaking quietly in the living room.

"Yes."

And then, in answer to something I couldn't hear, "Yes, I *know*."

A shiver ran through me.

I walked quietly over to the doorway, but didn't step through it yet—just stood there listening. I couldn't see Jake, but the sunlight through the window at the far end of the room was casting his shadow by the side of the couch: an amorphous shape, not recognizably human but moving gently, as though he were rocking back and forth on his knees.

"I remember."

There were a few seconds of silence then, in which the only sound was my own heartbeat. I realized I was holding my breath. When he spoke next, it was much louder, and he sounded upset.

"I don't want to say them!"

And at that, I stepped through the doorway.

For a moment I wasn't sure what I was going to see. But Jake was crouched down on the floor exactly where I'd left him, except that now he was staring off to one side, his drawing abandoned. I followed his gaze. There was nobody there, of course, but he seemed so intent on the empty space that it was easy to imagine a presence in the air there.

"Jake?" I said quietly.

He didn't look at me.

"Who were you talking to?"

"Nobody."

"I *heard* you talking."

"Nobody."

And then he turned slightly, picked his pencil back

up, and started drawing again. I took another step forward.

"Can you put that down and answer me, please?"

"Why?"

"Because it's important."

"I wasn't talking to *anybody*."

"Then how about putting the pencil down because *I said so*?"

But he kept drawing, his hand moving more fervently now—the pencil making desperate circles around the little figures there.

My frustration curdled into anger. So often, Jake seemed like a problem I couldn't solve, and I hated myself for being so useless and ineffective. At the same time, I also resented him for never offering me so much as a clue. Never meeting me halfway. I wanted to *help* him; I wanted to make sure he was *okay*. And it didn't feel like I could do that by myself . . .

I realized I was gripping the plate too tightly.

"Your sandwich is ready."

I put it down on the couch, not waiting to see if he stopped drawing or not. Instead, I went straight back through to the kitchen, leaned on the counter there, and closed my eyes. For some reason, my heart was pounding.

I miss you so much, I thought to Rebecca.

I wish you were here. For so many reasons, but right now because I don't think I can do this.

I started to cry. It didn't matter. Jake would either be drawing or eating his sandwich for a while, and he wasn't going to come into the kitchen. Why would he, when there was only me here to see? So it was fine. My son could talk quietly to people who didn't exist for a while. As long as I was equally quiet, so could I.

I miss you.

That night, as always, I carried Jake up to bed. It had been that way ever since Rebecca's death. He refused to look at the place where he had seen her body, clinging to me instead, with his breath held and his face buried in my shoulder. Every morning; every night; every time he needed the bathroom. I understood why, but he was beginning to grow too heavy for me, in more ways than one.

Hopefully that would change soon.

After he was asleep, I went back downstairs and sat on the couch with a glass of wine and my iPad, loading up the details of our new house. Looking at the photograph on the website made me uneasy on a different level.

It was safe to say it was Jake who had chosen this house. I hadn't been able to see the appeal at first. It was a small, detached property—old, two stories, with the ramshackle feel of a cottage. But there was something a little *strange* about it. The windows seemed oddly placed, so that it was hard to imagine the layout inside, and the angle of the roof was slightly off, so that the face of the building appeared to be tilted inquisitively, perhaps even angrily. But there was also a more general sensation—a tickling at the back of the skull. At first glance, the house had unnerved me.

And yet, from the moment Jake had seen it, he had

been settled on it. Something about it had utterly entranced him, to the point that he refused to look at any others.

When he'd accompanied me to the first viewing, he had seemed almost hypnotized by the place. I had still not been convinced. The interior was a good size, but also grimy. There were dusty cabinets and chairs, bundles of old newspapers, cardboard boxes, a mattress in the spare room downstairs. The owner, an elderly woman called Mrs. Shearing, had been apologetic; this all belonged to a tenant she had been renting to, she explained, and would be gone by the time it was sold.

But Jake had been adamant, and so I'd organized a second viewing, this time by myself. That was when I had started to see the place with different eyes. Yes, it was odd-looking, but that gave it a sort of mongrel charm. And what had initially felt like an angry look now seemed more like wariness, as though the property had been hurt in the past and you'd have to work to earn its trust.

Character, I supposed.

Even so, the thought of moving terrified me. In fact, there had been a part of me that afternoon that had hoped the bank manager would see through the half-truths I'd told about my financial situation and just turn down the mortgage application outright. I was relieved now, though. When I looked around the living room at the dusty, discarded remnants of the life we'd once had, it was obvious that the two of us couldn't continue as we were. Whatever difficulties lay ahead, we had to get out of this place. And however hard it was going to be for me over the coming months, my son needed this. We both did.

We had to make a fresh start. Someplace where he wouldn't need to be carried up and down the stairs. Where he could find friends that existed outside his head. Where I didn't see ghosts of my own in every corner.

Looking at the house again now on my screen, I thought that, in a strange way, it suited Jake and me. That, like us, it was an outsider that found it hard to fit in. That we would go together well. Even the name of the village was warm and comforting.

Featherbank.

It sounded like a place where we would be safe.

SIX

·············

Like Pete Willis, DI Amanda Beck knew very well the importance of the first forty-eight hours. She had her team spend the next twelve of them continuing to search the various routes that Neil Spencer might have taken, along with interviewing family members and beginning to build a profile of the missing boy. Photos were acquired. Histories were probed. And then at nine the next morning, a press conference was held and a description of Neil and his clothing was released to the media.

Neil's parents sat mutely on either side of Amanda while she made the requisite appeals and encouraged witnesses to come forward. Cameras flashed intermittently across the three of them. Amanda did her best to ignore them, but she could sense Neil's parents registering each one, flinching a little as though the photographers were jabbing at them.

"We encourage people to check any garages and sheds on their property," she told the room.

It was all kept as calm and low-key as possible. Her main aim right now, besides locating Neil Spencer, was to assuage people's fears, and while she could hardly claim outright that Neil had absolutely *not* been abducted, she could at least make it clear where the focus of the investigation rested for the moment.

"The most likely explanation is that Neil has had an accident of some kind," she said. "While he has been missing for fifteen hours, we are holding out every hope of finding him, safe and well and soon."

Inside herself, she was not so confident. One of her first actions back in the operations room afterward was to arrange for the handful of known sex offenders in the area to be brought in quietly, and then questioned more loudly.

Over the course of the day, the search area was expanded. Sections of the canal—an unlikely proposition—began to be dredged, and extensive door-to-door inquiries were carried out. CCTV footage was analyzed. She studied the latter herself; it showed the beginning of Neil's journey, but lost him before he reached the waste ground and failed to pick him up again afterward. Somewhere between those two points, the little boy had vanished.

Exhausted, she tried to rub some life into her face.

Officers went over the waste ground again, this time in full daylight, and the exploration of the quarry continued.

There was still no sign of Neil Spencer.

The boy did make an appearance of sorts, though, and increasingly so as the day wore on: photographs were circulated on the news, particularly the one of Neil smiling shyly in a football jersey—one of the few pictures his parents had of him looking happy. Reports showed simple maps with key locations marked with red circles and possible routes dotted in yellow.

Video of the press conference was also aired. Amanda watched it on her tablet in bed at home that evening, and thought that Neil's parents seemed even more beaten down on camera than it had felt at the time. They looked *guilty*. And if they weren't feeling guilty yet, then they would soon; they would be made to. At the briefing that afternoon, she had cautioned her officers, many of whom were parents themselves, that while the circumstances around Neil Spencer's disappearance might be controversial, his mother and father were to be treated with sensitivity. It went without saying that they were hardly model parents, but Amanda didn't suspect them of any direct involvement. The father had some minor offenses on his record—drunk-and-disorderlies; fighting—but nothing that raised any warning flags. The mother's record was clean. More to the point, they both appeared genuinely devastated by events. There hadn't even been any recrimination between the two of them, as hard as that was to imagine. They both just wanted their boy home.

She slept poorly and was back at the department early. With over thirty-six hours behind her, only a bare handful of them spent resting, she sat in her office, thinking about the five categories of child disappearance, forced increasingly toward an uncomfortable conclusion. She did not believe that Neil had been abandoned or disposed of by his parents. If he had suffered an accident on his route, then he would have been found by now. Abduction by a different family member seemed unlikely. And while it was not impossible he'd run away, she refused to believe that she'd been outwitted for this long by a six-year-old boy with no money or supplies.

She gazed at the photo of Neil Spencer on the wall, considering the nightmare scenario.

Nonfamily abduction.

The public at large might generally have thought of it as stranger abduction, but precision was important. Children in this category were rarely abducted by people who were completely unknown to them. More often, they were befriended—groomed by people on the periphery of their lives. So the focus of the investigation that day shifted, with the strands that had formed a more subtle part of the last day and a half now brought front and center. Friends of the family. Families of friends. An even closer look at known offenders. Internet activity in the home. Amanda loaded up the available CCTV footage again and began examining it from different mental angles, concentrating less on the prey now than on potential predators in the background.

Neil's parents were interviewed again.

"Did your son express any concerns about unwanted attention from other adults?" Amanda said. "Did he mention being approached by anyone?"

"No." Neil's father looked affronted by the very idea of it. "I'd have fucking well done something about that, wouldn't I? And for fuck's sake, don't you think I'd also have mentioned it before now?"

Amanda smiled politely.

"No," Neil's mother said.

But less firmly.

When Amanda pressed her, the woman said that actually she *did* recall something. It hadn't occurred to her to report it at the time, or even when Neil went missing, because it had been so strange, so stupid—and anyway, she'd been half asleep at the time, so she hardly even remembered it.

Amanda smiled politely again, while also resisting the urge to rip the woman's head off.

Ten minutes later she was in the upstairs office of her superior, Detective Chief Inspector Colin Lyons. Whether from the tiredness or the nerves, she was having to stop her leg from jittering slightly. Lyons himself just looked pained. He had been closely involved in the investigation and understood as well as Amanda did the situation they were now likely to be facing. Even so, this recent development was not one he'd wanted to hear.

"This doesn't go to the media," Lyons said quietly.

"No, sir."

"And the mother?" He looked at her suddenly, alarmed. "You've told her not to mention this in public? At all?"

"Yes, sir."

Of fucking course, sir. Although Amanda doubted it had been necessary. The tone of some of the press was already judgmental and accusatory, and Neil's parents had enough culpability to deal with already without deliberately copping to more.

"Good," Lyons said. "Because Jesus Christ."

"I know, sir."

He leaned back in his chair and closed his eyes for a few seconds, breathing deeply. "Do you know the case?"

Amanda shrugged. Everybody knew the case. That wasn't the same thing as *knowing* it.

"Not everything," she said.

Lyons opened his eyes and sat there staring at the ceiling.

"Then we're going to need some help," he said.

Amanda's heart sank a little at that. For one thing, she'd worked herself to the brink these last two days, and she didn't relish the thought of having to share any spoils of the case now. For another, there was also the specter that was being acknowledged here. Frank Carter. *The Whisper Man.* Assuaging fear among the public was going to get harder now. Impossible, even, if this new detail got out.

They would have to be very careful indeed.

"Yes, sir."

Lyons picked up the phone on his desk.

Which was how, as the time of Neil Spencer's disappearance ticked close to the end of that crucial forty-eight-hour period, DI Pete Willis became involved in the investigation again.

SEVEN

Not that he wanted to.

Pete's philosophy was a relatively simple one, ingrained in him over so many years that it was now more implicit than consciously considered: a blueprint on which his life was built. The devil finds work for idle hands.

Bad thoughts find empty heads.

So he kept his hands busy and his mind occupied. Discipline and structure were important to him, and after the nonresult at the waste ground he had spent most of the last forty-odd hours doing exactly what he always did.

Early that morning had found him in the gym in the basement of the department: overhead presses; side laterals; rear deltoids. He worked on a different body part each day. It wasn't a matter of vanity or health, more that he found the solitude and concentration involved in physical exercise a comforting distraction. After three-quarters of an hour, he was often surprised to discover his mind had been mercifully empty for most of it.

That morning, he had managed not to think about Neil Spencer at all.

He had then spent most of the day upstairs in his office, where the multitude of minor cases piled on his desk provided ample distraction. As a younger, more impetuous man, he would probably have yearned for greater excitement than the trivial crimes he was dealing with, but today he appreciated the calm to be found in boring minutiae. Excitement was not only rare in police work, it was a bad thing; usually it meant someone's life had been damaged. Wishing for excitement was wishing for hurt, and Pete had had more than enough of both. There was comfort to be had in the car thefts, the shoplifting, the court appearances for endless banal offenses. They spoke of a city ticking quietly along, never quite perfect, perhaps, but never falling apart either.

But while he'd had no direct involvement with the Neil Spencer investigation, it was impossible to avoid it entirely. A small boy, when missing, cast a large shadow, and it had become the most prominent case in the department. He heard officers talking about it in the corridors: where Neil might be; what might have happened to him; and the parents, of course. The latter was quieter speculation, and had been officially discouraged, but he kept hearing it anyway—the irresponsibility of letting a little boy walk home alone. He remembered similar talk from twenty years ago and walked on quickly, no more disposed to entertain it now than he had been back then.

Just before five o'clock that evening, he was sitting quietly at his desk, already considering what he would do that evening. He lived alone and socialized rarely, so his habit was to work his way through cookbooks, often making elaborate meals before eating them alone at the dinner table. Afterward, he would watch a film or read a book.

And the ritual, of course.

The bottle and the photograph.

And yet, as he gathered his things together, almost ready to leave, he realized his pulse was racing. Last night, the nightmare had returned for the first time in months: Jane Carter whispering, *You have to hurry,* down the phone to him. Despite himself, it had been impossible to escape from Neil Spencer completely, which meant the darker thoughts and memories were a little closer to the surface than he preferred to keep them. And so, as he pulled his jacket on, he was not entirely surprised when the phone on his desk began ringing. There was no way of knowing for sure, and yet somehow he already did.

His hand trembled a little as he picked it up.

"Pete," DCI Colin Lyons said down the line. "Glad to catch you. I was hoping I could have a quick word upstairs."

His suspicions were confirmed as soon as he entered Lyons's office. The DCI had revealed nothing in the call, but DI Amanda Beck was there too, sitting with her back to him on the side of the desk nearest the door. There was only one investigation she was working on right now, which meant there was only one reason his presence could have been requested.

He tried to keep calm as he closed the door. Tried—

especially—not to think about the scene that had awaited him twenty years ago when he had finally gained access to the extension Frank Carter had built on his house.

Lyons smiled broadly. The DCI had a smile that could power a room.

"Good of you to come up. Have a seat."

"Thanks." Pete sat down beside Beck. "Amanda."

Beck nodded a greeting, and gave him the flicker of a smile—an exceedingly low-wattage equivalent of Lyons's that barely even powered her face. Pete didn't know her well. She was twenty years younger than him, but right now looked much older than her years. Blatantly exhausted—and nervous too, he thought. Maybe she was worried her authority was being undermined and that the case was about to be taken away from her; he'd heard she was ambitious. He could have set her mind at rest on that score. While Lyons was probably ruthless enough to remove her from the investigation if it suited him, he was never going to pass it on to Pete instead.

They were relative contemporaries, he and Lyons, but despite the disparity in their ranks Pete had actually joined the department a year earlier, and in many ways his career had been the more decorated. In a different world, the two of them would have been sitting on opposite sides of the desk right now, and perhaps even *should* have been. But Lyons had always been ambitious, whereas Pete, aware that promotion brought conflict and drama of its own, had little desire to climb the professional ladder any further than he already had.

That had always rankled with Lyons, Pete knew. When you go after something as hard as he had, there were few things as irritating as someone who could have had it more easily but never seemed to want it.

"You're aware of the investigation into the disappearance of Neil Spencer?" Lyons said.

"Yes. I was involved in the search of the waste ground on the first evening."

Lyons stared at him for a moment, perhaps evaluating that as a criticism.

"I live close to there," Pete added.

But then, Lyons lived in the area as well, and he hadn't been out there trawling the streets that night. A second later, though, the DCI nodded to himself. He knew that Pete had his own reasons to be interested in missing children.

"You're aware of developments since?"

I'm aware of the lack of them. But that would come across as a rebuke to Beck, and she didn't deserve that. From the little he'd seen, she'd handled the investigation well and done everything she could. More to the point, she'd been the one to direct her officers not to criticize the parents, and he liked that.

"I'm aware that Neil hasn't been found," he said. "Despite extensive searches and inquiries."

"What would your theory be?"

"I haven't followed the investigation closely enough to have one."

"You haven't?" Lyons looked surprised at that. "I thought you said that you were out searching on the first night."

"That was when I thought he'd be found."

"So you don't think he will be now?"

"I don't know. I hope he will."

"I'd have thought you would have followed the case, given your history?"

The first mention there. The first hint.

"Maybe my history gives me a reason not to."

"Yes, I can understand that. It was a difficult time for all of us."

Lyons sounded sympathetic, but Pete knew this was another source of resentment between them. Pete was the one who'd closed the area's biggest case in the last fifty years, and yet Lyons was the one who'd ended up in charge. In different ways, the investigation they were circling was uncomfortable for both of them.

Lyons was the one to bring that spiral to its point.

"I also understand you're the only one Frank Carter will ever talk to?"

And there it was.

It had been a while since Pete had heard the name out loud, and so perhaps it should have delivered a jolt. But all it did was bring the crawling sensation inside him to the surface. Frank Carter. The man who had kidnapped and murdered five young boys in Featherbank twenty years ago. The man whom Pete had eventually caught. The name alone conjured up such horror for him that it always felt like it should never be spoken out loud—as though it were some kind of curse that would summon a monster behind you. Worse still was what the papers had called him. *The Whisper Man.* That was based on the idea that Carter had befriended his victims—vulnerable and neglected children—before taking them away. He would talk quietly to them at night outside their windows. It was a nickname that Pete had never allowed himself to use.

He had to fight down the urge to leave the room.

You're the only one he'll talk to.

"Yes."

"Why do you think that is?" Lyons said.

"He enjoys taunting me."

"About what?"

"The things he did back then. The things I never found out."

"But he never tells you?"

"No."

"Why bother speaking to him, then?"

Pete hesitated. It was a question he had asked himself numerous times over the years. He dreaded the encounters, and always had to suppress the shivers he felt as he sat in the private interview room at the prison, anticipating Carter's approach. He would feel broken afterward, sometimes for weeks. There would be days when he would shake uncontrollably, and evenings when the bottle would be harder to resist. At night, Carter found him in dreams—a hulking, malevolent shadow that would bring him screaming out of sleep. Every meeting with the man damaged Pete a little more.

And yet still he went.

"I suppose I'm hoping that one day he'll slip up," he answered carefully. "That maybe he'll reveal something important by accident."

"Something about where he dumped the Smith boy?"

"Yes."

"And about his accomplice?"

Pete didn't reply.

Because, again, there it was.

Twenty years ago, the remains of four of the missing boys had been found in Frank Carter's house, but the body of his final victim, Tony Smith, had never been recovered. There was no doubt in anyone's mind that Carter was responsible for all five murders, and he himself had never denied it. But it was also true that there were certain inconsistencies within the case. Nothing that could have exonerated the man: just little strands that left the investigation frayed and untidy. One of the abductions was estimated to have occurred within a certain time period, but Carter had an alibi for most of it, which didn't make it *impossible* for him to have taken the boy, just stretched the likelihood somewhat. There were witness accounts that, while not definitive, described a different individual at certain scenes. The forensic evidence in Carter's house was overwhelming, and they had witness statements that were far more concrete and reliable, but a doubt had always remained as to whether Carter had acted alone.

Pete wasn't sure whether he shared that doubt or not, and most of the time he did his best to ignore the possibility. But that was clearly why he was here. And, like any horror that had to be faced, it was preferable to drag it out into the light and get it over with. So he decided to ignore Lyons's question and get to the point.

"Can I ask what this is about, sir?"

The DCI hesitated.

"What we're going to discuss goes no farther than the four walls of this office right now. Is that clear?"

"Of course."

"The CCTV we have suggests Neil Spencer did walk in the direction of the waste ground, but somewhere in the vicinity he vanished. The search has drawn a blank so far. All the locations he's likely to have wandered into by accident have been cleared. He's not with friends or other family members. Naturally, we're forced to consider other possibilities. DI Beck?"

Beside Pete, Amanda Beck came to life. When she spoke, she sounded a little defensive.

"Obviously, we considered those other possibilities from the beginning. We've done the door-to-doors. Interviewed all the usual candidates. That's got us nowhere yet."

There has to be more to it than that, Pete thought. "But?"

Beck took a deep breath. "But I interviewed the parents again an hour ago. Looking for anything that might have been missed. Any kind of lead. And his mother told me something. She hadn't mentioned it before because she thought it was stupid."

"What was it?"

But even as he asked the question, he knew the answer. Perhaps not the exact form it would take, but close enough. Over the course of the meeting, the pieces of a new nightmare had been steadily coming together into a single picture.

A little boy missing.

Frank Carter.

An accomplice.

Beck added the final piece now.

"A few weeks ago, Neil woke his mother in the middle of the night. He said that he'd seen a monster outside his window. The curtains were open, like he really had been looking out, but there was nothing there."

She paused.

"He said it had been whispering things to him."

PART TWO
SEPTEMBER

EIGHT

Jake was excited when we collected the keys from the estate agent in Featherbank, whereas I just felt anxious as we drove to our new home. What if the house wasn't how I remembered it from the viewings? What if I got inside and hated the place now—or, worse, that Jake did?

All of this would have been for nothing.

"Stop kicking the passenger seat, Jake."

The drumming of his feet from behind me stopped, but then started up again almost immediately. I sighed to myself as I turned a corner. But then, he was excited, which was a rare enough occurrence in itself, so I decided to ignore it. At least one of us was happy.

It was a lovely day, though. And my nerves aside, it was impossible to deny that Featherbank was beautiful in the late summer sun. It was a suburb, and while it was only five miles away from a heaving city center, it felt more like the countryside here. Down by the river, on the southern edge of the village, there were cobbled roads and cottages. Farther north, away from a single row of shops, there were steep streets of pretty sandstone houses, and most of the pavements were lined with trees, the leaves thick and green overhead. With the window rolled down, the air outside smelled of cut grass, and I could hear music and children playing. It felt peaceful and tranquil here—as slow and warm as a lazy morning.

We reached our new street, which was a quiet residential road with a large field on one side. There were more trees around the edges, the sun cutting through the leaves and dappling the grass with light, and I tried to imagine Jake out there, running around just across from our house, his own T-shirt bright in the sun. Still as happy as he was now.

Our house.

We were here.

I pulled into the driveway. The house still looked the same, of course, but the building seemed to have different ways of staring out at the world. The first time I'd seen it, it had seemed forbidding and frightening—almost dangerous—and then the second, I'd thought it had character. Now, just for a moment, the odd arrangement of windows reminded me of a beaten face, with an eye pushed up over a badly bruised cheek, the skull injured and lopsided. I shook my head and the image disappeared. But an ominous feeling remained.

"Come on, then," I said quietly.

Outside the car, the day was still and quiet. With no breeze to move the warm air, we were in a capsule of silence. But the world was humming softly as we approached the house, and it felt to me as though the windows were watching us, or perhaps something just out of sight behind the glass. I turned the key in the lock and opened the door, and stale air wafted out. For a second it smelled as though the house had been sealed for far longer than it had been, perhaps even with something left rotting inside, but then all I could detect was the bleachy scent of cleaning products.

Jake and I walked through the house, opening doors and cupboards, turning lights on and off, drawing and closing curtains. Our footsteps echoed; otherwise, the silence was absolute now. But as we worked our way through each room, I couldn't shake the sensation that we were not alone. That someone else was here, hiding just out of sight, and that if I turned at the right moment I'd see a face peering around a doorframe. It was a stupid, irrational feeling, but it was there. And it wasn't helped by Jake. He was excited, moving quickly from room to room, but every now and then I'd catch a slightly puzzled look on his face, as though he had been expecting to find something that wasn't here.

"Is this my room, Daddy?"

What was going to be his bedroom was on the second floor, raised up from the landing outside, so that his window was smaller than the rest: the eye staring out across the field from above the swollen cheek.

"Yes." I ruffled his hair. "Do you like it?"

He didn't reply, and I stared down at him nervously. He was gazing around, lost in thought.

"Jake?" I said.

He looked up at me.

"Is this really *ours*?"

"Yes," I said. "It is."

And then he hugged my legs so suddenly that it

almost knocked me off balance. It was as though I'd shown him the best present he'd ever seen and he'd been worried he might not be able to keep it. I crouched down so we could embrace more properly. The relief I felt was palpable, and suddenly that was all that mattered. My son was happy to be here, and I'd done something good for him, and nothing else was important. I stared over his shoulder at the open door and the landing beyond. If it still felt like something was just around the corner there, I knew it was just my imagination.

We were going to be safe here.

We were going to be happy.

And for the first week, we were.

At the time, I stood looking at a newly assembled bookcase, marveling at my industry. DIY had never been a strong point of mine, but I knew this was something Rebecca would have wanted me to do, and I imagined her pressed up behind me now, with the side of her face against my back and her arms around my chest. Smiling to herself. *You see? You can do this.* And while it was only a small taste of success, even that was an unusual feeling recently, and I liked it.

Except, of course, I was still alone.

I began filling the shelves.

Because that was another of the things Rebecca would have done, and even though this new house was about Jake and me moving on, I still wanted to honor that. *You always put out the books,* she told me once. *That's when it starts to feel like home.* She had never been happier than when reading. There had been so many warm, contented evenings, with the two of us curled up at different ends of the couch, me writing as best I could on my laptop, her lost in novel after novel. Over the years we had accumulated hundreds of books, and I set to work unpacking them now, sliding each one carefully into place.

And then it came to my own. The shelves beside my computer desk were reserved for copies of my four novels, along with the various foreign translations. It felt ostentatious to have them on display, but Rebecca had been proud of me and had always insisted on it. So this was another gesture to her—as was the empty space I left on the shelves, ready for the ones that hadn't been written yet, but would be.

I glanced warily at the computer. Beyond turning it on to check that the new Wi-Fi worked, I hadn't really done a thing with it this last week. I hadn't written anything for a year. That was something that was going to change. New start, new—

Creak.

A noise from above me, the sound of a single footstep. I looked up. It was Jake's room that was directly overhead, but I'd left him in the living room playing while I did the building and unpacking.

I moved to the doorway and looked up the stairs. There was nobody on the landing. In fact, the whole house suddenly felt still and quiet, as though now that I was still, there was no movement at all. The silence rang in my ears.

"Jake?" I shouted upstairs.

Silence.

"Jake?"

"Daddy?"

I almost jumped. His voice had come from the living room, directly beside me. Keeping one eye on the landing, I leaned in. My son was crouched on the floor with his back to me, drawing something.

"Are you all right?" I said.

"Yes. Why?"

"I was just checking."

I leaned back out, then stared up at the landing again for a few seconds. It was still quiet up there, but the space had a strange sense of potential to it now, once again as though there were somebody standing just out of sight. Which was ridiculous, of course, because nobody could have come in through the front door without me knowing. Houses creaked. It took a while to get used to them, that was all.

But even so.

I walked upstairs slowly and cautiously, stepping quietly, with my left hand raised, ready to deflect anything that leaped out at me from that side. I reached the top—and of course the landing was empty. When I stepped into Jake's room, that was empty too. A wedge of afternoon sunlight was coming through the window, and I could see tiny curls of dust hanging in the air, undisturbed.

Just the house creaking.

I went downstairs more confidently, feeling silly but also more relieved than I'd have liked to admit. At the bottom, I had to edge past the piles of mail on the last two steps. There had been a lot so far: the usual documents that inevitably come with moving into a new house, along with innumerable local take-out menus and other junk mail. But there had also been three proper letters, addressed to someone called Dominic Barnett. All three were marked either *Private* or *Addressee Only*.

I remembered that the previous owner, Mrs. Shearing, had rented the house out for years, and on a whim I ripped one of the letters open now. Inside, I found an itemized account from a debt collection company. My heart sank. Whoever Dominic Barnett was, he owed the company on an old cell phone contract. I opened the others, and they were the same: notices for unpaid money. I scanned the details, frowning to myself. The amounts weren't large, but the tone of the letters was threatening. I told myself it wasn't an insurmountable problem and that a few phone calls would sort it out, but this move was meant to be a new start for Jake and me, not to deliver a fresh set of obstacles for me to overcome.

"Daddy?"

Jake had appeared in the living room doorway beside me. He was holding his Packet of Special Things in one hand and a piece of paper in the other.

"Is it all right if I play upstairs?"

I thought of the creak I'd heard, and for a second I wanted to say no. But again, that was absurd. There was nobody up there, and it was his bedroom; he had every right to play in it. At the same time, we hadn't seen much of each other that day, and it felt isolating for him to disappear upstairs now.

"I guess," I said. "Can I see your drawing first?"

He hesitated. "Why?"

"Because I'm interested. Because I'd like to."

Because I'm trying here, Jake.

"It's private."

Which was fair enough, and a part of me wanted to respect that, but I didn't like the idea of him keeping secrets from me. The Packet was one thing, but it felt like if he wouldn't even show me his *drawings* now, then the distance between us must be increasing.

"Jake—" I started to say.

"Oh, fine."

He thrust the sheet out at me. Now that it was being offered, I was reluctant to take it.

But I did.

Jake had never been good at drawing straightforward, realistic scenes before, preferring his convoluted, unfolding battles instead, but he'd attempted one here. The picture was rough, but it was obviously an approximation of our house from the outside, reminiscent of the original photograph that had caught his attention online. He had captured the odd look of the place well. The curved, childlike lines stretched the house into a strange shape, elongating the windows, and making it look more like a face than ever. The front door appeared to be moaning.

But it was the upstairs that drew my attention. In the right-hand window he'd drawn me, standing by myself in my bedroom. On the left, there he was in his own room, the window large enough here to include his whole body: a smile on his face, the jeans and T-shirt he was wearing right now shaded with crayon.

And beside him, he'd drawn another person in his

bedroom. A little girl, her black hair splayed almost angrily out to one side. Her dress was colored in with patches of blue, leaving the rest white. Little scrapes of red on one of her knees.

A corkscrew smile on her face.

NINE

After Jake's bath that night, I knelt on the floor beside his bed so that we could read to each other. He was a good reader, and we were currently working our way through *Power of Three* by Diana Wynne Jones. It was a childhood favorite of mine, which I'd chosen without thinking. The horrible irony of the title had only occurred to me afterward.

When we'd finished that night's chapter, I put the book down with all his others.

"Cuddle?" I said.

He slipped out of the covers without a word and sat sideways on my knees, wrapping his arms around me. I savored the cuddle for as long as I could, and then he clambered back into bed.

"I love you, Jake."

"Even when we argue?"

"Of course. *Especially* when we argue. That's when it matters the most."

That reminded me of the picture I'd drawn for him, which I knew he'd kept. I glanced down at his Packet of Special Things, which was under the bed now, so that if he were to drape his small arm out in the night he'd be able to touch it. But that in turn made me think of the drawing he'd done that afternoon. He hadn't been pleased about showing it to me, and so I hadn't asked him about it at the time. But in the warm, soft light of his bedroom, it felt like maybe I could now.

"It was a good picture of our house today," I said.

"Thank you, Daddy."

"I'm curious about something, though. Who was the little girl in the window with you?"

He bit his lip and didn't answer.

"It's okay," I said gently. "You can tell me."

But again he didn't reply. It was obvious that, whoever it was meant to be, the little girl was the reason he hadn't wanted to show me the drawing today, and he didn't want to talk about her now either. But why not?

The answer occurred to me a second later.

"Is she the little girl from the 567 Club?"

He hesitated, then nodded.

I sat back on my heels, doing my best to hide the frustration I felt. The *disappointment,* even. For the last week, everything had seemed fine. We had been happy here, Jake had seemed to be adjusting well, and I had been cautiously optimistic. And yet apparently his imaginary friend had been following us all along. The thought made me shiver slightly—the idea that we had left her behind in the old house, and ever since she had been working her way slowly across the intervening miles to find us.

"Do you still talk to her?" I said.

Jake shook his head.

"She's not here."

From his own disappointment, it was obvious that he wanted her to be, and once again I felt uneasy. It was unhealthy for him to be fixated on someone who wasn't there. At the same time, he looked so dejected and lonely right now that I almost felt guilty at depriving him of it. And also hurt that, as always, I wasn't enough.

"Well," I said carefully. "You start school tomorrow. I'm sure you'll make lots of new friends there. And in the meantime, I'm here. *We're* here. New house, new start."

"Is it safe here?"

"Safe?" Why was he asking that? "Yes, of course it is."

"Is the door locked?"

"Yes."

The lie—a white one—came automatically. The door wasn't locked; I didn't think I'd even hooked up the chain. But Featherbank was a quiet village. And anyway, it was early evening and the lights were all on. Nobody was going to be that blatant.

But Jake looked so frightened that I was suddenly conscious of the distance between the two of us and the front door. The noise of running his bath. If someone had crept in while we were up here, would I have heard it?

"You don't need to worry about that." I did my best to sound firm. "I'd never let anything happen to you. Why are you so worried?"

"You have to close doors," he said.

"What do you mean?"

"You have to keep them locked."

"Jake—"

"If you leave a door half open, soon you'll hear the whispers spoken."

A chill ran through me. Jake looked scared, and the phrase certainly wasn't the kind of thing he would have come up with by himself.

"What does that mean?" I said.

"I don't know."

"Where did you hear it, then?"

He didn't answer. But then I realized he didn't need to.

"The little girl?"

He nodded, and I shook my head, confused. Jake wouldn't have thought up that rhyme by himself, but equally, he couldn't have heard it from someone who wasn't there. So perhaps I'd been wrong at the 567 Club and the little girl was real? Perhaps Jake had just called goodbye without realizing she had gone outside? Except he had been alone at the table when I'd arrived. It must have been one of the other children, then, trying to scare him. From the expression on his face right now, it had worked.

"You're completely safe, Jake. I promise you."

"But I'm not in charge of the door!"

"No," I said. "I am. And so there is nothing for you to worry about. I don't care what somebody told you. You need to listen to *me* now. I'm not going to let anything happen to you. *Ever.*"

He was listening, at least, although I wasn't sure he was convinced.

"I *promise* you. And do you know why I won't let

anything happen to you? Because I love you. Very much indeed. *Even when we argue*."

That brought the slightest of smiles.

"Do you believe me?" I said.

He nodded, looking a little more reassured now.

"Good." I ruffled his hair and stood up. "Because it's true. Good night, sweetie."

"Good night, Daddy."

"I'll come up and check on you in five minutes."

I turned the light off as I left the room, then padded downstairs as quietly as I could. But rather than collapsing on the couch as I wanted to, I stopped at the front door.

If you leave a door half open, soon you'll hear the whispers spoken.

Rubbish, of course, wherever he had heard it. But the words still bothered me. And just as the idea of the little girl trailing us across the country had disturbed me, now I couldn't shake the image of her sitting next to him, her hair swept out to one side and that strange smile on her face, whispering frightening things in his ear.

I hooked up the chain for the night.

TEN

DI Pete Willis had spent the weekend miles away from Featherbank, walking in the nearby countryside and trailing a stick through random tangles of undergrowth. He checked the hedges he passed. Occasionally, when the fields were empty, he hopped over stiles and trawled through the grass there.

Anyone watching might have mistaken him for a rambler, and to all intents and purposes he supposed that was what he was. These days, in fact, he deliberately thought of such expeditions as walks and outings—as just another way for an old man to fill his time. It had been twenty years now, after all. And yet a part of him remained focused. Rather than absorbing the beauty of the world around him, he was constantly searching the ground for bone fragments and snatches of old fabric.

Blue jogging pants. Little black polo shirt.

For some reason, it was always the clothes that stayed with him.

However much he tried not to think about it, Pete would never forget the day he'd viewed the horrors plastered inside the extension Frank Carter had built on the side of his house. Returning to the department afterward, he had still been reeling from the experience, but as he stepped through the sliding doors there had at least been some sense of relief. Four little boys had been killed. But even though Carter had remained at large for the moment, the monster finally had a name—a real one, not the one the papers had given him—and four victims would be the end of it.

In that moment, he had believed it was nearly over.

But then he had seen Miranda and Alan Smith sitting in the reception. Even now he could still picture them clearly. Alan had been wearing a suit and sitting bolt upright, staring into space, his hands forming a heart between his knees. Miranda's hands had been pressed between her thighs, and she had been leaning against her husband, resting her head on his shoulder with her long brown hair trailing down his chest. It was late afternoon, but they had both looked exhausted, like long-distance travelers who were trying and failing to sleep where they sat.

Their son Tony was missing.

And twenty years on from that afternoon, he still was.

Frank Carter had managed a day and a half on the run before he was finally arrested, his van pulled over on a country road nearly a hundred miles from Featherbank. There was forensic evidence that Tony Smith had been held in the back of his van, but no sign of the boy's body. And while Carter had admitted killing Tony, he refused to reveal where he had discarded his remains.

The weeks that followed had seen extensive searches along the myriad possible routes Carter could have taken, all of them to no avail. Pete had attended several. The number of searchers had dwindled over time until, two decades later, he was the only one still out searching. Even Miranda and Alan Smith had moved on. They lived far away from Featherbank now. If Tony had been alive, he would be twenty-seven years old. Pete knew that Miranda and Alan's daughter, Claire, born in the tumultuous years that followed, had just turned sixteen. He attached no blame to the Smiths for rebuilding their lives after the murder of their son, but the fact remained that he himself could not let it go.

A little boy was missing.

A little boy needed to be found and brought home.

As he drove back into Featherbank now, the homes he passed looked comfortable. Their windows were illuminated in the darkness, and he could imagine whispers of laughter and conversation drifting out from within.

People together, as people should be.

He felt a degree of loneliness at that, but you could find pleasure where you looked for it, even in as solitary a life as his. The road was lined with enormous trees, their leaves lost in the darkness except for where the streetlights touched them, scattering the street with intricate yellow-green explosions that undulated in the soft breeze. It was so quiet and peaceful in Featherbank that it was almost impossible to believe it had once played host to atrocities as terrible as Frank Carter's.

A flyer was attached to the lamppost at the end of his street—one of the many MISSING posters that had been put up in the previous weeks by Neil Spencer's family.

There was a photograph of the boy, details of his clothing, and an appeal for witnesses to come forward with information. Both the image and the text had faded under the incessant beat of the summer sun, so that, as he drove past it now, it reminded him of wrinkled flowers left at the scene of an old accident. A little boy who had disappeared was beginning to disappear for a second time.

Nearly two months had passed since Neil Spencer went missing, and despite the resources, heart, and soul that had been poured into the investigation, the police knew little more now than they had on the evening he'd vanished. As far as Pete could tell, Amanda Beck had done everything right. It was a reflection of her efficiency, in fact, that even DCI Lyons, a man with a constant eye on his own reputation, had stood by her and left her in charge of the case. Although the last time Pete had passed Amanda in the corridor, she had looked so worn out that he had wondered if that wasn't its own kind of punishment.

He wished he could tell her that it would get easier.

After being summoned to Lyons's office, Pete had talked Amanda through the original investigation, but his involvement in the case had turned out to be cursory. There had been the familiar feeling of dread when he made the request to visit Frank Carter. He had imagined himself sitting across from the monster, being treated like a plaything, and, as always, he had wondered if he could do it—whether this encounter would be the one that finally proved too much for him. And yet his fear had been in vain. For the first time that he could remember, his request to talk to Carter had been met with refusal. The so-called Whisper Man, it seemed, had decided to go silent.

Pete had visited him on several occasions, and he had been prepared to do so again, but still—it had been impossible to suppress relief at that. That feeling had brought guilt and shame along with it, of course, but he had talked himself out of it. Sitting across from Frank Carter was an ordeal. It was bad for his health. And since the only connection was what Neil claimed to have seen and heard at his bedroom window, there was no reason to think it would help.

Relief was the correct response.

Back home, he tossed his keys onto the dining room table, already planning the meal he would make and the programs he would watch to fill the handful of hours before sleep. Tomorrow would bring the gym, the paperwork, the admin. Life as usual.

But before then, he performed the ritual.

He opened the kitchen cabinet and took out the bottle of vodka he kept in there, turning it around in his hands, weighing it, feeling how thick the glass was. There was a solid, protective layer between him and the silky liquid inside. It had been a long time since he'd opened a bottle like this, but he could still remember the comforting *click* that would come if he turned the top and broke the seal.

He retrieved the photograph from a drawer.

And then he sat down at the dinner table, with the bottle and photograph before him, and asked himself the question.

Do I want to do this?

Over the years the urge had come and gone, but to some extent it was always present. There were many obvious things that could jostle it awake, but there were also times when it seemed to stir at random, following its own oblique schedule. The bottle was often as dead and powerless as a cell phone without charge, but sometimes there was a flicker there. Right now the urge was stronger than he could recall. For the last two months, in fact, the bottle had been talking to him increasingly loudly.

You're only delaying the inevitable, it told him now. *Why make yourself suffer like this?*

A full bottle—that was important. Pouring a drink from a half-finished bottle was less comforting than breaking the seal on a fresh one. The comfort lay in knowing you had enough.

He gently tested the seal now, tempting himself. A little more pressure and it would break, and the bottle would be open.

You might as well give in.

It will make you feel worthless, but we both know that's what you are.

The voice could be cruel as well as friendly. Play the minor chords as easily as the major.

You're worthless. You're useless.

So open the bottle.

As so often, the voice was his father's. The old man was long dead, but even forty years on, Pete could picture him: fat and sprawled in a threadbare armchair in the dusty living room, a look of contempt on his face. Nothing Pete had done as a boy had ever been good enough for him. *Worthless* and *useless* were words he'd learned early and often.

Age had brought with it the understanding that his father had been a small man, disappointed with everything in his life, and that his son had just been a convenient target to vent his many frustrations on. But that understanding had come too late. By then the message had been absorbed and become part of his programming. Objectively, he knew it wasn't true that he was worthless and a failure. But it always *felt* true. The trick, explained, still convinced.

He picked up the photograph of Sally. It was many years old, and the colors had faded over time, as though the paper were attempting to erase the image imprinted upon it and return to its original blank slate. The two of them looked so happy there, their faces pressed together. It had been taken on a summer's day. Sally appeared full of joy, grinning in the sun, while Pete was squinting against the light and smiling.

This is what you lose by drinking.

This is why it's not worth it.

He sat there for a few minutes, breathing slowly, then he put the bottle and the photograph away and began to make dinner. It was easy to understand why the urge had strengthened since Neil Spencer went missing, and that was why it was good his involvement had come to nothing. Let the urge flare in the light of that, he thought. Let it have its moment.

And then let it die.

ELEVEN

That night, as always, I found it difficult to fall asleep.

Once upon a time, when I had a new book out, I would go to events and even do the occasional signing tour. I generally went by myself, and I would lie awake afterward in unfamiliar hotel rooms, missing my family. I always found it hard to sleep when Rebecca wasn't there beside me.

It was harder still, now that she never would be. Before, if I stretched my arm out onto the cold side of a hotel bed, I could at least imagine she was doing the same back home—that we might feel the ghosts of each other. After she died, when I stretched my arm out in our own bed I felt nothing but the cold emptiness of the sheets there. Perhaps a new house and bed should have changed that, but they hadn't. When I stretched my arm out in the old house, I had at least known that Rebecca had lain there once.

So I stayed awake for a long time, missing her. Even if moving here had been the right decision, I was aware of a greater distance between Rebecca and me than ever before. It was terrible to leave her behind. I kept imagining her spirit in the old house, staring out of the window, wondering where her family had gone.

Which reminded me of Jake's imaginary friend. The little girl he'd drawn. I did my best to empty my head of that, concentrating instead on how peaceful it was here in Featherbank. The world outside the curtains was quiet and still. The house around me was entirely silent now.

It allowed me to drift, at least after a time.

Glass smashing.

My mother screaming.

A man shouting.

"Daddy."

I jerked awake from the nightmare, disorientated, aware only that Jake was calling me and so I needed to do something.

"Hang on," I shouted.

A shadow at the end of the bed moved, and my heart leaped. I sat up quickly.

Jesus Christ.

"Jake, is that you?"

The small shadow moved around from the foot of the bed to my side. For a moment I wasn't convinced it was him at all, but then he was close enough that I could recognize the shape of his hair. I couldn't see his face, though. It was occluded entirely by the darkness in the room.

"What are you doing, mate?" My heart was still racing, both from what was happening now and from the residue of the nightmare it had woken me from. "It's not time to get up yet. Absolutely nowhere near."

"Can I sleep in here with you tonight?"

"What?" He never had before. In fact, Rebecca and I had always held firm on the few occasions he'd suggested it, assuming that relenting even once would be the beginning of a slippery slope. "We don't do that, Jake. You know that."

"Please."

I realized that his voice was deliberately quiet, as though there were someone in another room he didn't want to hear.

"What's the matter?" I said.

"I heard a noise."

"A noise?"

"There's a monster outside my window."

I sat there in silence, remembering the rhyme he'd told me at bedtime. But that had been about the door. And anyway, there was no way anybody could be outside his window. We were one floor up.

"You were dreaming, mate."

He shook his head in the darkness.

"It woke me up. I went across to the window and it was louder there. I wanted to open the curtains but I was too scared."

You would have seen the dark field across the road, I thought. *That's all.*

But he sounded so serious that I couldn't say that to him.

"All right." I slipped out of bed. "Well, let's go and check, then."

"Don't, Daddy."

"I'm not scared of monsters, Jake."

He followed me into the hall, where I switched on the light at the top of the stairs. Stepping into his room, though, I left the light off, and then approached the window.

"What if there's something there?"

"There isn't," I said.

"But what if?"

"Then I'll deal with it."

"Will you punch it in the face?"

"Absolutely. But there's nothing there."

And yet I didn't feel as confident as I sounded. The closed curtains seemed ominous. I listened for a moment, but there was nothing to hear. And it was impossible for anybody to be out there.

I pulled the curtains open.

Nothing. Just an oblique angle of the path and garden, the empty road beyond, and then the dark, shadowy expanse of the field stretching away into the distance. A dim reflection of my face was staring back into the room. But there was nothing else out there. The whole world seemed to be sleeping peacefully in exactly the way that I wasn't.

"See?" I did my best to sound patient. "Nobody there."

"But there was."

I closed the curtains and knelt down.

"Jake, sometimes dreams can seem very real. But they're not. How can anybody have been outside your window when we're all that way above the ground?"

"They could have climbed the drainpipe."

I started to answer, but then pictured the outside of the house. The drainpipe *was* just to the side of his window. A ridiculous idea occurred to me. If you lock and chain a door to keep a monster out, what choice does it have but to climb up and get in some other way?

Stupidity.

"There was nobody out there, Jake."

"Can I sleep with you tonight, Daddy? Please?"

I sighed to myself. Obviously he wasn't going to sleep alone in here now, and it was either too late or too early to argue. I couldn't decide which. It was easier right now just to give in.

"All right. But just for tonight. No fidgeting, though."

"Thank you, Daddy." He picked up his Packet of Special Things and followed me back through. "I promise I won't fidget."

"So you say. But what about *stealing all the covers*?"

"I won't do that either."

I turned the hall light off and then we clambered into bed, Jake on what should have been Rebecca's side.

"Daddy?" he said. "Were you having a nightmare before?"

Glass smashing.

My mother screaming.

A man shouting.

"Yes," I said. "I suppose so."

"What was it about?"

The dream itself had faded a little now, but it had been a memory as much as a nightmare. Me as a child, walking toward the doorway to the small kitchen of the house I had grown up in. In the dream, it was late, and a noise from downstairs had woken me. I had stayed in bed with the covers pulled over my head and the dread thick in my heart, trying to pretend that everything was okay, even though I knew it wasn't. Eventually I had tiptoed quietly down the stairs, not wanting to see whatever was happening, but drawn to it all the same, feeling small and terrified and powerless.

I remembered approaching the bright kitchen along the dark hall, hearing the noises coming from in there. My mother's voice was angry but quiet, as though she thought I was still asleep and she was trying to keep me safe from this, but the man's voice was loud and uncaring. All their words overlapped. I couldn't make out what either of them was saying, only that it was ugly, and that it was building toward a crescendo—accelerating toward something awful.

The kitchen doorway.

I reached it just in time to see the man's red face contorted in rage and hatred as he threw the glass at my mother as hard as he could. To see her flinch away, far too late, and to hear her scream.

The last time I'd ever seen my father.

It was such a long time ago, but the memory still surfaced every now and then. Still clawed its way up out of the dirt.

"Grown-up stuff," I told Jake. "Maybe I'll tell you one day, but it was just a dream. And it's fine. It all had a happy ending."

"What happened in the end?"

"Well, *you did*, eventually."

"Me?"

"Yeah." I ruffled his hair. "And then you went to sleep."

I closed my eyes, and the two of us lay there in silence for so long that I assumed he'd dropped back off to sleep. At one point, I stretched my arm out to one side and rested my hand gently on top of the covers over him, as though to reassure myself he was still there. The two of us together. My small, wounded family.

"Whispering," Jake said quietly.

"What?"

"Whispering."

His voice sounded so far away that I thought he was already dreaming.

"It was whispering at my window."

TWELVE

You have to hurry.

In the dream, Jane Carter was whispering down the phone to Pete. Her voice was quiet and urgent, as though what she was saying were the most frightening thing in the world.

But she was doing it anyway. Finally.

Pete had sat at his office desk, his heart thumping in his chest. He had spoken to Frank Carter's wife numerous times during the investigation. He had appeared outside her place of work, or arranged to find himself walking alongside her on busy pavements, always careful not to be seen with her anyplace her husband might hear of. It had been as though he had been making covert attempts to turn a spy, which he supposed wasn't far from the truth.

Jane had provided alibis for her husband. She had defended him. But it had been obvious to Pete from his first encounter with her that she was terrified of Frank—he thought with good reason—and he had worked hard to convert her: to convince her it was safe for her to talk to him. To take back what she had said and tell the truth about her husband. *Talk to me, Jane.*

I'll make sure that Frank can't hurt you and your son anymore.

And now it seemed like she was going to. Such fear had been beaten into Jane Carter over the years that even now, phoning him without the bastard in the house, she could still only bring herself to whisper. Courage is not the absence of fear, Pete knew. Courage *requires* fear. And so, even as the adrenaline hit—even as he felt the case beginning to close ahead of him—he also recognized the bravery of this call.

I'll let you in, she whispered, *but you have to hurry. I've no idea how long he'll be.*

In reality, Frank Carter would never return to the house. Within an hour it would be crawling with police and CSIs, and an alert would be out to locate Carter and the van he was driving. But at the time, Pete hurried. The journey to her house only took ten minutes, but they were the longest of his life. Even with backup on standby, he felt alone and scared when he arrived, like someone in a fairy tale where a monster was absent but might return at any moment.

Inside, he watched Jane Carter's trembling hands as she unlocked the door to the extension with the key she'd stolen. The whole house was silent, and he felt a shadow looming over them.

The lock came undone.

Step back now, please, both of you.

Jane Carter stood in the middle of the kitchen, her son hiding behind her legs, as Pete pushed open the door with one gloved hand.

No.

At once, there was the hot smell of rotting meat. He shone his flashlight inside—and then came the pictures, appearing to him one by one in swift succession, the sights and sensations illuminated as if by camera flashes.

No.

Not yet.

For the moment, he lifted his hand, moving the flashlight over the walls instead. They were painted white, but Carter had decorated them, drawing crude green blades of grass at the bases and childlike butterflies fluttering above. Close to the ceiling, there was the skewed yellow approximation of a sun. A face had been sketched on it, the dead black eyes staring down at the floor below.

Pete followed its gaze, finally lowering the beam.

It became difficult to breathe.

He had been searching for these children for three months, and while he had always anticipated an outcome like this, he had never entirely given up hope. But here they were, lying in this rank, warm darkness. The four bodies looked real and unreal at the same time. Lifelike dolls that had been broken and now lay still, their clothes intact except for their T-shirts, which had been pulled up to cover their faces.

Perhaps the worst thing about that particular nightmare was that it had become familiar enough over the years not to disturb his sleep. It was the alarm that woke him the next morning.

He lay there for a few seconds, trying to keep calm.

Attempting to ignore the memory was like shoving at mist, but he reminded himself that it was only recent events that had roused these nightmares, and that they would fade in time. He turned off the alarm.

Gym, he thought.

Paperwork. Admin.

Routine.

He showered, dressed, packed the bag for his workout, and by the time he headed downstairs to make coffee and a light breakfast, the dream had receded and his thoughts were more under control. There had been a brief interruption to his life—that was all. It was completely understandable that turning the soil over had released some pungent ghosts from the earth, but they would fade soon. The urge to drink would weaken again. Life would return to normal.

It was only when he took his breakfast through to the living room that he saw the red light on his cell blinking. He'd missed a call; there was voice mail to listen to. He dialed the number and listened to the message, chewing his food slowly.

Forcing himself to swallow it. His throat was tight.

After two months, Frank Carter had agreed to see him.

THIRTEEN

"Just stand against the wall for me," I said. "A little to the right. No, *my* right. A little more. That's it. Now give me a smile."

It was Jake's first day at his new school, and I was far more nervous about the prospect than he was. How many times could you check a drawer to make sure clothes were ready? Were there names on everything? Where had I put his book bag and water bottle? There was so much to consider, and I wanted everything to be perfect for him.

"Can I move yet, Dad?"

"Hang on."

I held up my phone in front of me as Jake stood against the only blank wall in his bedroom, dressed in his new school uniform: gray trousers, white shirt, and blue jumper—all of it fresh and clean, of course, with name tags on absolutely everything. His smile was shy and sweet. He looked so grown up in his uniform, but also still so small and vulnerable.

I tapped the screen a couple of times.

"Done."

"Can I see?"

"Of course you can."

I knelt down and he leaned on my shoulder as I showed him the photographs I'd taken.

"I look okay."

He sounded surprised.

"You look *perfect,*" I told him.

And he did. I tried to enjoy the moment, even though it was tinged with sadness, because Rebecca should have been here too. Like most parents, she and I had taken pictures on Jake's first days in a new year at school, but I'd changed my phone recently, and it was only earlier this week that I'd realized what that meant. All my photographs were gone—lost forever. To add insult to injury, I did have Rebecca's phone, but while the photos would be on there, the phone was locked with her fingerprint. I'd stared at her old handset in frustration for a full minute, facing down the hard truth of the situation. Rebecca was gone, which meant that those memories were gone as well.

I had tried to tell myself that it didn't matter. That it was just another harsh joke grief had played on me—and a minor one in the grand scheme of things. But it had hurt. It felt like another failing on my part.

We'll get so many more.

"Come on, mate."

Before we left, I uploaded copies to the ether.

Rose Terrace Primary School was a low, sprawling building, secluded from the street behind iron railings. The main part was old and pretty: a single story with numerous peaked roofs. BOYS and GIRLS were carved into the black stone above separate entrances, although much newer signs indicated that that Victorian separation was now used to delineate different year groups instead. I'd been shown around before enrolling Jake. Inside, there was a hall with a polished wooden floor, which acted as a central hub for the surrounding classrooms. Between the doors, the walls were covered with small handprints in different-colored paint, pressed there by a selection of former pupils, with the dates they'd attended written underneath.

Jake and I stood at the railings.

"What do you think?"

"I don't know," he said.

It was hard to blame him for being doubtful. The playground beyond the railings was teeming with children, along with parents clustered together in groups. It was the first day of a new year, but everybody here—kids and parents alike—already knew each other from previous years, and Jake and I were going to be walking in as strangers to everyone except each other. His old school had been larger and more anonymous. Everyone here seemed so tightly knit that it was impossible to imagine we wouldn't always feel like outsiders. God, I hoped that he fit in.

I gave his hand a light squeeze and led him toward the gate.

"Come on," I said. "Let's be brave."

"I'm okay, Daddy."

"I'm talking about me."

A joke, but only half of one. There were five minutes before the doors were due to open, and I knew I should make an effort to talk to some of the other parents and begin to form bonds of my own. Instead, once in the playground, I leaned against the railing and waited.

Jake stood beside me, chewing his lip slightly. I watched the other children running around, and wished he'd go and make an effort to play.

Just let him be him, I told myself.

That should be good enough, shouldn't it?

Eventually, the door opened, and Jake's new teacher stood outside smiling. The children began lining up, book bags swinging. Because it was the first day of term for everyone here, most of those bags would be empty for now, but Jake's wasn't. As usual, he'd insisted on bringing his Packet of Special Things with him.

I passed him the bag and his water bottle.

"You'll look after that, won't you?"

"Yes."

God, I hoped so. The thought of it getting lost was probably as intolerable for me as it would be for him. But it was my son's equivalent of a comfort blanket, and there was no way he could have left home without it.

He was already moving over to the line of children.

"I love you, Jake," I said quietly.

"Love you too, Daddy."

I stood there, watching until he was inside, hoping he'd turn back and wave. He didn't. It was a good sign, I supposed, that lack of clinging. It showed that he wasn't intimidated by the day ahead of him and didn't need the reassurance.

I wished I could say the same about myself.

Please, please, please be okay.

"New boy, eh?"

"Sorry?"

I turned to find a woman was standing next to me. Even though the day was already warm, she was wearing a long dark coat with her hands pushed into the pockets, as though braced for a winter breeze. Her hair was dyed black, shoulder length, and she had a slightly amused expression on her face.

New boy.

"Oh," I said. "You mean Jake? That's my son, yes."

"Actually, I was meaning both of you. You look worried. Honestly, I'm sure he'll be fine."

"Yes, I'm sure he will. He didn't even look back."

"Mine stopped doing that a while ago. In fact, once we get to the playground on a morning, I might as well not exist. Heartbreaking at first, but you get used to it. It's a good thing, really." She shrugged. "I'm Karen, by the way. My son's Adam."

"Tom," I said. "Nice to meet you. Karen and Adam? I need to start learning all these new names."

She smiled. "It'll take a while. But I'm sure Jake won't have any problems. It's hard when you move somewhere new, but they're a good bunch of kids. Adam only started here the middle of last year. It's a good school."

As she walked back toward the gate, I committed the names to memory. Karen. Adam. She'd seemed nice, and I needed to make some kind of effort here. Perhaps, despite all evidence to the contrary, I really could become one of those normal adults who talked to other parents in the playground.

I took out my phone and put my headphones in for the short walk home, with something else to be nervous about now. I had been a third of the way into a new novel when Rebecca died, and while some writers might have thrown themselves into their work as a distraction, I hadn't looked at those words since. The idea I'd been working on felt empty to me now, and I suspected I was going to have to abandon the whole thing and leave it decaying on my hard drive as some uncompleted folly.

In which case, what would I write?

Back home, I turned on the computer, opened up a blank document in Word, and then saved it under the file name "bad ideas." I always did that to begin with. Acknowledging it was early days took some of the psychological pressure off. And then, since I'd always been of the mind that making coffee didn't count as procrastination, I went through to the kitchen and started the kettle boiling, then leaned against the counter and stared out of the window at the back garden.

A man was standing out there.

He had his back to me, and appeared to be rattling the padlock on my garage door.

What the fuck?

I tapped on the glass.

The man jumped and turned around quickly. He was in his fifties, short and portly, with a monk's ring of gray hair around his otherwise bald head. He was also dressed neatly in a suit, gray overcoat, and scarf, and seemed about as far away from a potential burglar as I could imagine.

I made a what-the-fuck? gesture at him with my hands and the expression on my face. He stared back at me for a moment, looking shocked, then turned and disappeared off in the direction of the driveway.

I hesitated for a moment, still thrown by what I'd just seen, then moved back through the house, determined to confront him and find out what he'd been doing.

As I reached the front door, the bell rang.

FOURTEEN

I opened the door too quickly, and found the man standing on the step outside, an apologetic look on his face. Up close, he was even shorter than he'd seemed through the window.

"I'm terribly sorry to bother you." He spoke formally, in keeping with the old-fashioned suit he was dressed in. "I wasn't sure if anybody would be home."

One obvious way to check if someone is home, I thought, *would be to ring the fucking doorbell.*

"I see." I folded my arms. "What can I do for you?"

The man shuffled uncomfortably. "Well, it's a slightly unusual request, I have to admit. But the thing is—this house. I actually grew up here, you see? Many years ago now, obviously, but I have such fond memories of the place . . ."

He trailed off.

"Okay," I said.

And then I waited for him to continue. But he just stood there, looking expectant, as though he'd provided me with enough information already and it was awkward, or perhaps even rude, of me to make him say the rest.

A moment later, the penny dropped.

"You mean you want to come in and look around or something?"

He nodded gratefully.

"It's a terrible imposition, I know, but I would appreciate being able to do so immensely. This house holds such special memories for me, you see."

Again, his tone was so ostentatiously formal that I almost laughed. But I didn't, because the idea of having this man in my house set my nerves on edge. He was dressed so *properly,* and his manner was so ostentatiously polite, that it all felt like some kind of disguise. Despite the apparent lack of physical threat, the man seemed dangerous. I could picture him stabbing someone with a sliver of a knife, looking into their eyes and licking his lips as he did so.

"That's not possible, I'm afraid."

The prissy manner faded immediately, and a hint of annoyance crept onto his face. Whoever he was, he was clearly used to getting his own way.

"What a terrible *shame,*" he said. "May I ask why?"

"For one thing, we've only just moved in. There are boxes everywhere."

"I see." He smiled thinly. "Perhaps another time, then?"

"Well, no. Because I'm also not particularly inclined to let complete strangers into my house."

"That is . . . disappointing."

"Why were you trying to get into my garage?"

"I was doing *no such thing.*" He took a step back, looking affronted now. "I was looking to see if I could find you."

"What—inside a locked garage?"

"I don't know what you think you saw, but no." He shook his head sadly. "I see this has been a regrettable mistake. What a shame, indeed. Perhaps you'll change your mind."

"I won't."

"Then I'm sorry to have bothered you."

He turned and began walking away up the path.

I followed him out, remembering the letters I'd received.

"Mr. Barnett?"

He hesitated at that, then turned around and looked at me. I stopped where I was. His expression was entirely different now. His eyes had gone completely blank, and despite the difference in our sizes, I thought that if he took a step toward me right now, I would back away.

"I'm afraid not," he said. "Goodbye."

And then he walked away, reaching the street, then heading away without another word. I followed him again, then stood on the pavement, unsure whether to pursue him down the road or not. Despite the warmth of the sun, I was shivering slightly.

I'd been so preoccupied with the inside of the house that I hadn't gotten around to looking in the garage yet. Certainly it was not the most desirable part of the property: two blue, corrugated metal doors that barely met in the middle; gray walls with a cracked window on the side. Overgrown grass wavered at the base. It seemed to be squatting at the back of the house like an old drunk, unsteady on its feet and trying not to teeter over to one side.

The doors were secured by a padlock, but the real estate agent had given me the key. The metal scraped and scratched against the driveway as I unlocked it and pulled one door open, and then I ducked slightly and stepped inside.

I looked around in disbelief. It was full of junk.

I'd assumed that when Mrs. Shearing had emptied the house after that first viewing, she'd hired a removal firm to empty out the old furniture. It was clear now that she'd saved herself that particular expense, and that it was all in here instead, smelling of mold and dust. There were piles of cardboard boxes in the center, crumpling damply under the weight of the ones above, and old tables and chairs stacked and intermingled like wooden puzzles down one side. An old mattress was leaning against the back wall, the tea-colored stains on the fabric so extensive that it resembled a landscape map of some foreign world. I could smell the blackened barbecue to one side of the door.

There were piles of crisp brown leaves around the walls. I gingerly moved a can of paint in the corner with my foot, and found the largest spider I'd ever seen. The thing just bounced gently where it sat, apparently unperturbed by my presence.

Well, I thought, looking around.

Thank you very much, Mrs. Shearing.

There wasn't much room to move about, but I stepped forward to the piles of boxes and opened the one on top, the cardboard moist beneath my fingers. I peered in to find old Christmas decorations. Faded coils of tinsel, dull baubles, and what looked like jewels on the surface.

One of the jewels flew straight out into my face—

"Jesus Christ!"

—and I nearly lost my balance, one foot skidding on the leaves behind me, my arm waving at the air in front of my face. The thing fluttered up to the roof, then bounced down and whirled around, before hitting the gray window and smacking itself repetitively against it.

Tap, tap, tap. The gentlest of collisions.

A butterfly, I realized. Not one I recognized, although admittedly my knowledge extended about as far as cabbage whites and tortoiseshells.

I edged carefully over to the window, where the butterfly was still fluttering against the glass, and watched for a few seconds until it finally got the message and settled down on the grubby sill, its wings splayed flat. The thing was as large as the spider behind me, but where that had been an ugly shade of gray, the butterfly had astonishing coloring. Yellow and green swirls played across its wings, with hints of purple at the tips. It was beautiful.

Moving back over to the box, I looked in again and saw three more, resting on the surface of the tinsel. These ones weren't moving, so perhaps they were dead, but glancing down I saw another on the side of the lowest box in the pile, its wings moving as slowly and gently as breath.

I had no idea how long they had been in here, or what their life cycle might be, but there didn't seem to be much hope for them, except perhaps as meals for that spider. I felt an urge to disrupt that particular ecosystem. Tearing off a damp square of cardboard from the top box, I made an effort at wafting one of the butterflies on the pile toward the door. The butterfly was having none of it, though. I tried the one by the window instead, but it was equally stubborn. And despite the size of them, they appeared very delicate close up, as though they might crumble to dust at the faintest touch. I didn't want to risk brushing them.

So that was that.

"Well, guys." I threw the cardboard to one side and rubbed my hand against my jeans. "I did my best."

There didn't seem any point in staying in the garage any longer. It was what it was. Clearing it out could now be added to my long list of tasks, but at least it wasn't an urgent one. What was it in here that had interested my visitor so much? It was obviously just junk. But now that the encounter had faded a little, I wondered if he might even have been telling the truth and I'd simply misunderstood what I had seen.

Outside, I clicked the padlock back in place, sealing the butterflies within. It seemed remarkable that they'd survived in there for so long in such fruitless and insubstantial conditions. But as I walked back up the drive to the front of the house, I thought about Jake and me, and I realized that was just what happens. The butterflies didn't have a choice, after all. That's what things do. Even in the toughest of circumstances, they keep living.

FIFTEEN

The room was small, but because every surface was painted white it had the sensation of infinite space. A place without walls. Or perhaps somewhere out of space and time altogether. To anyone watching on CCTV, Pete always imagined it must look like a scene from a science fiction film, with one person sitting in an endless, empty environment in which the virtual surroundings had yet to be built around them.

He ran his fingertip over the surface of a desk that completely divided the room. It squeaked slightly. Everything here was clean, polished, sterile.

And then the room was silent again.

He waited.

When there was something awful that had to be faced, it was better to face it immediately; as bad as the event might be, it would occur regardless, and at least that way you wouldn't have to endure the anticipation as well. Frank Carter understood that. Pete had visited him at least once a year since his incarceration, and the man always made him wait. There would be some petty delay back in the cell block—some manufactured incident. It was a statement of control, making it clear which of the two men was in charge of proceedings. The fact that Pete was the one who could leave afterward should have been reassuring, but it never was. He had nothing to offer Carter but diversion and entertainment. Only one of them had anything the other wanted, and they both knew it.

So he waited, like a good boy.

A few minutes later, the door on the far side of the desk was unlocked, and two prison guards entered, moving to either side of it. The doorway itself remained empty. The monster, as always, was taking his time to arrive.

There was the usual sense of unease as the moment approached. The escalation of the pulse. He'd long stopped trying to prepare questions for these meetings, as the words inevitably scattered into a jumble in his mind, like birds startled from a tree. But he forced his face into a blank expression and tried to keep as calm as possible. His upper body ached from the gym that morning.

Finally, Carter stepped into view.

He was dressed in pale blue overalls and was manacled at the hands and feet. Still sporting the familiar shaved head and ginger goatee. As always, he ducked slightly as he shuffled in, even though he didn't need to. At six-foot-five and close to three hundred pounds, Carter was an enormous man, but he never missed an opportunity to make himself seem bigger.

Two more guards followed him in, escorting him to the chair on the far side of the desk. Then the four departed, leaving Pete alone with Carter. The door closing at the back of the room seemed like one of the loudest sounds he had ever heard.

Carter stared at him, amused.

"Good morning, Peter."

"Frank," Pete said. "You're looking well."

"Living well." Carter patted his stomach, the chains that bound his wrists rattling softly. "Living very well indeed."

Pete nodded. Whenever he visited, it always surprised him how Carter seemed to be not only surviving his incarceration but thriving on it. Much of his time appeared to have been spent in the prison gym, and yet, while he remained as physically formidable as he had been at the time of his arrest, there was also no denying that the years in prison had softened him in some way. He looked *comfortable*. Sitting here now, with his legs splayed and one beefy arm resting on the chair arm, he might have been a king lounging on a throne, surveying a courtier. It was as though, outside these walls, Carter had been a dangerous animal, angry and at war with the world, but caged in here with his celebrity status and coterie of fawning fans, he'd finally found a niche in which he could relax.

"You're looking well too, Peter," Carter said. "Eating well. Keeping in good shape, I see. How's the family?"

"I don't know," Pete said. "How's yours?"

The sparkle went out of Carter's eyes at that. It was always a mistake to needle the man, but it was sometimes hard to resist, and Carter's wife and son provided an easy target. Pete still remembered the look on Carter's face as he'd listened to Jane Carter's testimony playing in the court via video link. The man must have imagined she was too scared and broken to turn against him, but in the end she had, letting Pete into the extension and retracting the alibis she'd given her husband in the months before. His expression that day was similar to the one he wore now. However comfortable Carter might be in here, the hate he felt for his family had never waned.

He leaned forward suddenly.

"Do you know," he said, "I had the most *extraordinary* dream last night."

Pete forced a smile.

"Did you? Jesus, Frank. I'm not sure I want to know."

"Oh, no, you do." Carter settled back, then laughed to himself. "You really do. Because *the boy* was there, you see? The Smith boy. At first, as I'm dreaming, I'm not sure it's him, because all those little bastards are the same, aren't they? Any one of them will do. Plus his top is all pulled up over his face so I can't see it properly, which is the way I like it. But it's him. Because, you see, I remember what he was wearing, right?"

Blue jogging pants. Little black polo shirt.

Pete didn't say anything.

"And someone's *crying*," Carter said. "But it isn't him. For one thing, he's long past the crying stage by now; that's all done with. And the sound's coming from off to one side anyway. So I turn my head, and I spot them both there—the mother and father. They've seen what I've done to their boy and they're sobbing—all their hopes and dreams, and look what I've gone and done." He frowned. "What are their names?"

Again, Pete didn't reply.

"Miranda and Alan." Carter nodded to himself. "I remember now. They were in court that time, weren't they? You sat with them."

"Yes."

"Right. So, Miranda and Alan are crying these big fat tears, and they're looking at me. *Tell us where he is.* They're begging me, you see? It's a bit pathetic, but all that does is remind me of you, and I think to myself, *Peter* wants to know that too, and he might come visit me again soon." Carter smiled across the table. "He's my friend, right? I should try and help him out. And so I look around more carefully, trying to work out where I am and where the boy is. Because I've never been able to remember that one, have I?"

"No."

"And then the most *amazing* thing happens."

"Does it?"

"*Really* amazing. Do you know what it is?"

"You wake up," Pete said.

Carter tipped his head back and laughed, then clapped his hands together as best he could. The chains rattled as he applauded. When he finished and spoke again, his voice was back to its normal volume, and his eyes had regained that familiar sparkle.

"You know me too well, Peter. Yeah, I wake up. A shame, though, isn't it? Guess Miranda and Alan and you will have to keep crying for a while longer."

Pete wasn't going to take the bait.

"Did you see anyone else in your dream?" he said.

"Anyone else? Like who?"

"I don't know. Anyone else there with you? Helping you, maybe."

It was too blunt an approach for his purpose, but as always, he watched Carter's reaction to the question carefully. On the matter of a potential accomplice, Carter had generally played it well, sometimes amused, sometimes bored, but never confirming or denying a second individual having been involved in the murders. This time, he smiled to himself, but the reaction was different from normal. Today, there was an extra edge to it.

He knows why I'm here.

"I wondered how long it would take you to come to see me," Carter said. "With that little boy going missing and all. I'm surprised it's taken you this long."

"I asked before now. You said no."

"What? Refuse to see my good friend Peter?" Carter feigned outrage. "As if I'd do that. I'm guessing that maybe the requests didn't filter through to me. An administrative error. They're next to useless in here."

Pete forced a shrug.

"That's okay, Frank. You're not actually a priority. You've been in prison awhile now, so it's safe to say that you're not a suspect with this one."

The smile returned to the man's face.

"Not me, no. But it always comes back to me for you, doesn't it? It always ends where it starts."

"What does that mean?"

"It means what it means. So what is it you want to ask me?"

"Your dream, Frank, like I said. Was there anyone else there?"

"Maybe. You know what dreams are like, though. They fade quickly. Shame, isn't it?"

Pete stared at Carter for a moment, evaluating him. It would have been easy enough for him to have learned about Neil Spencer's disappearance; it had been all over the news. Did Carter know anything else, though? He was clearly enjoying giving the impression that he did, but that didn't mean anything in itself. It could easily be just another power play. Another way for him to make himself seem bigger and more important than he really was.

"Lots of things fade," Pete said. "Notoriety, for one."

"Not in here."

"In the outside world, though. People have forgotten all about you."

"Oh, I'm certain that's not true."

"You've not been in the papers for a while, you know. Yesterday's man. Barely even that, actually—this little boy went missing a couple of months ago, like you say, and you know how many of the news reports mentioned you?"

"I don't know, Peter. Why don't you tell me?"

"None of them."

"Huh. Maybe I should start granting the interviews all those academics and journalists keep asking for? I might do that."

He smirked, and the futility of the situation hit Pete. He was putting himself through this for nothing; Carter didn't know anything. And it would end the same as it always did. He knew full well how he would be afterward—the way that talking to Carter brought everything back. Later, the pull of the kitchen cabinet would be stronger than ever.

"Yes, maybe you should." He stood up, turned his back on Carter, and walked away. "Goodbye, Frank."

"They might be interested in the whispers."

Pete stopped, one hand on the door. A shiver ran up his back, then spread down his arms.

The whispers.

Neil Spencer had told his mother about a monster whispering outside his window, but that aspect of the boy's disappearance had never been made public or found its way into the news. It could still be fishing, of course. Except that Carter had played it more triumphantly than that, like a trump card.

Pete turned around slowly.

Carter was still reclining nonchalantly in his chair, but there was a smug look on his face now. Just enough bait added to the hook to keep his fish from swimming off. And Pete was suddenly sure that the reference to whispers hadn't been guesswork at all.

Somehow, the bastard *knew*.

But how?

Right now, more than ever before, he had to remain calm. Carter would feed on any sense of *need* he detected in the man across from him, and he already had enough of that to play with.

They might be interested in the whispers.

"What do you mean by that, Frank?"

"Well—the little boy saw a monster at his window, didn't he? One that was talking to him." Carter leaned forward again. "*Talking. Very. Quietly.*"

Pete tried to fight down the frustration, but it was beginning to whirl inside him. Carter knew something, and a little boy was missing. They needed to find him.

"How do you know about the whispers?" he said.

"Ah! That would be telling."

"So tell me."

Carter smiled. The expression of a man who had nothing to lose or gain beyond the pain and frustration of others.

"I'll tell you," he said, "but first you have to give me something I want."

"And what would that be?"

Carter leaned back, the amusement suddenly gone from his face now. For a moment his eyes were blank, but then the hate flared there, as visible as two pinpricks of fire.

"Bring my family to me," he said.

"Your family?"

"That bitch and that little cunt. Bring them here and give me five minutes alone with them."

Pete stared at him. For a second he was overwhelmed by the anger and madness blazing across the table from him. Then Carter threw back his head, rattled the chains at his wrists, and the silence in the room was broken as he laughed and laughed and laughed.

SIXTEEN

"Give him five minutes alone with his old family?"
Amanda thought about it. "*Could* we conceivably do
that?"

But then she saw the look on Pete's face.

"I'm joking, by the way."

"I'm aware of that."

He slumped down in the chair on the other side of
her desk and closed his eyes.

Amanda watched him for a moment. He looked
drained and diminished compared to their first meeting after Neil Spencer went missing. She didn't know
him well, of course, and their interactions over the past
two months had hardly been extensive, but he'd struck
her as . . . well, what? A man in control of his emotions.
Excellent shape for a guy his age, obviously. Calm and
capable. He'd barely wasted a word talking her through
the old case, and had even been implacable and detached
when he was showing her the photographs taken inside
Frank Carter's extension—scenes of horror that he'd
witnessed firsthand. It had actually been quite intimi-
dating. It had made her worry about how she was bearing

up so far, never mind how she'd cope if it came to the worst.

It won't.

The sensible coppers let it go. DCI Lyons was like that, she was sure, because that was the only way to climb—with as little weight holding you down as possible. Before Neil Spencer went missing, she'd imagined she would be the same, but she was no longer quite so sure. And if she'd initially thought Pete Willis was calm and detached, then looking at him now made her reevaluate that first impression. He was just good at keeping the world at a distance, she thought, and Frank Carter was a man who could get closer to him than most.

Not so surprising, given the history they shared, and the fact that one of Carter's victims had never been found—a kid who had effectively gone missing on Pete's watch. She glanced at her computer screen and saw the familiar photo of Neil Spencer in his football jersey. His absence was an actual physical *ache* inside her, and no matter how much she tried not to think about it, the feeling of failure worsened every day. She couldn't imagine how bad it might feel after twenty years. She didn't want to end up like the man across from her now.

It won't come to that.

"Talk me through the accomplice theory again," she said.

"There's very little there, really." Pete opened his eyes. "There's a witness report of an older man with gray hair talking to Tony Smith that doesn't match Carter. And then there are some overlaps on the abduction windows."

"Pretty thin stuff."

"I know. Sometimes people want things to be more complicated than they really are."

"It's possible for him to have committed these crimes entirely alone. Occam's razor states that—"

"I know what Occam's razor states." Pete ran his hand through his hair. "*Do not multiply entities unnecessarily.* The simplest solution that fits all the facts is the one you go with."

"Exactly."

"And that's what we do here, isn't it? We get our guy, and we prove he's done it, and that's enough for us. So we tie a bow around the investigation, stick it in the filing cabinet, and move on. Case closed, job done. On to the next."

She thought about Lyons again. About *climbing*.

"Because that's what we have to do," she said.

"But sometimes it's not good enough." Pete shook his head. "Sometimes things that look simple turn out to be much more complicated, and the extra stuff ends up being missed."

"And the extra stuff in this case," she said, "could include someone getting away with murder?"

"Who knows? I've tried not to think about it over the years."

"I think that's wise."

"But now we have Neil Spencer. We have the whispers and the monster. And we have Frank *fucking* Carter sitting there, knowing something about it."

She waited.

"And I don't know what to do about it," Pete said. "Carter isn't going to tell us anything. And we've been over his known associates a hundred times. They're all clear."

Amanda thought about it. "Copycat?"

"Possibly. But Carter wasn't guessing back in that room. The whispers never made it to the press, and he knew about them. No visitors aside from me. The correspondence he receives is all vetted. So how does he *know*?"

His frustration was suddenly so palpable that she was surprised he didn't hit the table. Instead, he shook his head again and looked away to one side. At least it had brought him back to life a little, Amanda thought. That was a good thing. Fuck calm—she was a keen believer in the idea that *rage* was a good motivator, and God knew there were times when you needed something to keep you going. At the same time, she could tell that a great deal of Pete's anger was directed inward: that he blamed himself for not having been able to get to the truth. And that was no good. She was an equally keen believer in the idea that guilt was about as unhelpful as emotions got. Once you let guilt get ahold of you, the bastard never let go.

"Carter was never going to help us," she said. "Not willingly."

"No."

"The dream about Tony Smith—?"

He waved it away.

"That's just business as usual. I've heard all that before. I have no doubt he killed Tony, and that he knows exactly where he left him. But he's never going to say. Not when it's something to hold over us. Over *me*."

It was clear to her now how much going to see Carter took out of Pete. And yet, as hard as it must be, he went regardless—still put himself through the ordeal, because finding Tony Smith meant that much to him. But Carter had found a new game to play now, and they had to focus on that. While she understood Pete's turmoil, the fact remained that Tony Smith had been dead for a long time, while Neil Spencer could still be alive.

Was still alive.

"Well, he's got another hold over us now," Amanda said. "But remember something. You said that you go to see him in case he gives information away by accident."

"Yes."

"Well, he has—he *knows* something, doesn't he? That can't have happened by magic. So we have to work out how."

When he didn't reply, she thought about it herself.

No visitors. No unvetted correspondence.

"What about friends inside?" she said.

"He's got loads of those."

"Which is surprising on one level. Child killer and all."

"There was never a sexual element to the murders, which helps him a bit. And physically, he's still an absolute monster. Plus, there's the celebrity of it all—all that *Whisper Man* rubbish. He has his own little kingdom in there."

"Okay. So who's he closest to?"

"I've no idea."

"But we can find out, right?" Amanda leaned forward. "Maybe he's been passed the information secondhand?

Someone visits one of his friends. Friend tells Carter. Carter talks to you."

Pete considered that. A moment later, he looked annoyed with himself for not having thought of it himself. She felt a flush of pride—not that she needed to impress him, of course. She just needed him motivated, or at least not walking so obviously wounded.

"Yes." He stood up. "That's a good idea."

"So do it." She hesitated. "Not that it's my place to give you things to do. But that would be a way forward for us, wouldn't it? If you've got time."

"I've got the time."

But he paused at the door.

"There's another thing," he said. "You said Carter had given something away—that he knows about the whispers somehow."

"Right."

"But there's also the timing. For two months now, he's been refusing to see me. That's never happened before. And suddenly he changes his mind and wants to see me."

"Meaning?"

"I don't know for sure. But we might need to prepare ourselves for there being a reason for that."

It took a second for her to understand what he was implying, and then she looked back at the photo of Neil Spencer, not wanting to think about the possibility.

It won't come to that.

Except that Pete was right. There had been two months without a single development or break in the case. Perhaps Carter's decision to talk meant one was about to come.

SEVENTEEN

At lunch break, Jake sat by himself on a bench in the playground, watching the other children running around getting all hot and sweaty. It was very noisy and they all seemed oblivious to him. This was a new school year, but his class had all known each other for a long time, and it had become apparent that morning that they weren't all that interested in knowing anyone else. Which was okay. Jake would have been happier sitting inside drawing, but you weren't allowed, so he had to sit out here next to some bushes instead, kicking his legs and waiting for the bell to ring.

You start school tomorrow.

I'm sure you'll make lots of new friends.

Quite often, Daddy didn't know how wrong he was. Although Jake wondered if perhaps he did, because the way he'd said it had sounded more hopeful than anything else, and maybe deep down they had both known it was never going to turn out that way. Mummy would have told him it didn't matter, and she would have made him believe it too. But Jake thought that it did matter to Daddy. Jake was aware that he could be very disappointing sometimes.

The morning had *basically* gone okay, at least. They had practiced some basic multiplication tables, which were all pretty easy, and that was good. The classroom had a traffic light system on the wall for bad behavior, and everybody's name was currently on the green area at the bottom. George, the classroom assistant, was nice, but Mrs. Shelley, the class teacher, seemed very stern indeed, and Jake really didn't want to move up to yellow on his first day. He couldn't make friends, but he could at least manage that. That was really your job at school—to do what you were told and fill in the answers to the blanks, and not cause any problems by thinking up too many questions of your own.

Crunch.

Jake flinched as a soccer ball crashed into the bushes beside him. He had already memorized the names of all the children in his class, and it was Owen who came sprinting over to retrieve it. He was coming for the ball but glaring at Jake the whole time, which made Jake think the kick might have been deliberate. Unless Owen was just really bad at soccer.

"*Sorry* about that."

"It's okay."

"Yeah. I *know* it's okay."

Owen pulled the ball roughly out of the branches, still glaring at Jake as though it were all his fault, and then stalked away. Which didn't make sense. Perhaps Owen was just really stupid. Even so, it might be better to move.

"Hello, Jake."

He looked to one side, and saw the little girl kneeling

in the bushes. His heart leaped with relief, and he started to get up.

"Shhh." She put a finger to her lips. "Don't."

He sat down again. But it was hard. He wanted to bounce on the bench! She looked exactly the same as she always did, wearing the same blue-and-white dress, with that graze on her knee and her hair swept oddly out to one side.

"Just sit as you were," she said. "I don't want the other children to see you talking to me."

"Why not?"

"Because I shouldn't be here."

"Yes, you're not wearing the right uniform, for one thing."

"That is one thing, yes." She thought about it. "It's good to see you again, Jake. I've missed you. Have you missed me?"

He nodded vigorously, but then forced himself to calm down. The other children were there, and the ball was still thudding around. He didn't want to give the little girl away. But it was so good to see her! The truth was that he'd been very lonely in the new house. Daddy had tried to play with him a few times, but you could tell his heart wasn't really in it. He'd play for ten minutes and then get up and say his legs were hurting from kneeling on the floor, even though it was obvious he really just wanted to do something else instead. Whereas the little girl would always play with him for as long as he wanted her to. He'd been expecting to see her *all the time* after moving to the new house, but she hadn't been around at all.

Until now.

"Have you made any new friends yet?" she said.

"Not really. Adam, Josh, and Hasan seem okay. Owen isn't very nice."

"Owen is a little shit," she said.

Jake stared at her.

"But a lot of people are, aren't they?" she said quickly. "And not everybody who acts like your friend really is."

"But *you* are?"

"Of course *I* am."

"Will you come to my new house and play?"

"I'd like to. But it's not as simple as that, is it?"

Jake's heart sank, because no, he knew that it wasn't. He wanted to see her all the time, but Daddy didn't want him talking to her.

I'm here. We're *here. New house, new start.*

Or, at least, Jake wanted to see her all the time when she wasn't looking as serious as she was right now.

"Tell me," she said. "Tell me the rhyme."

"I don't want to."

"Say it."

"If you leave a door half open, soon you'll hear the whispers spoken."

"And the rest."

Jake closed his eyes.

"If you play outside alone, soon you won't be going home."

"Keep going."

She sounded barely there now.

"If your window's left unlatched, you'll hear him tapping at the glass."

"And?"

The word was so quiet that it might have been nothing more than air. Jake swallowed. He didn't want to say it, but he forced himself to, speaking as quietly as the little girl just had.

"If you're lonely, sad, and blue, the Whisper Man will come for you."

The bell rang.

Jake opened his eyes to see the children in the playground in front of him. Owen was there with a couple of older boys Jake didn't recognize. They were watching him. George was there too, a concerned expression on his face. After a second the children started laughing, and then headed away toward the main doors, glancing over their shoulders at him.

Jake looked to his side.

The little girl was gone.

"Who were you talking to at lunchtime?"

Jake wanted to ignore Owen. They were supposed to be writing neatly on the lines in their books, and he wanted to concentrate on that, because it was what they'd been told to do. Obviously, Owen didn't care; he was leaning over the table and staring at Jake. It was clear to Jake that Owen was one of those boys who didn't care about being told off. He also knew that telling Owen about the little girl would be a very bad idea. Daddy didn't like him talking to her, but Jake didn't think he would ever make fun of him for doing so. He was pretty sure that Owen would.

So he shrugged. "Nobody."

"Somebody."

"I didn't see anybody there. Did you?"

Owen considered the matter, then leaned back.

"That," he said, "was Neil's chair."

"What was?"

"Your chair, idiot. It was Neil's."

Owen seemed angry about this, although once again Jake wasn't sure what he was supposed to have done wrong. Mrs. Shelley had told them all where to sit that morning. It wasn't like he'd stolen this Neil person's chair on purpose.

"Who's Neil?"

"He was here last year," Owen said. "He's not here anymore because someone took him away. And now you've got his chair."

There was an obvious error in Owen's thinking.

"You were in a different classroom last year," Jake said. "So this was never Neil's chair."

"It *would* have been if he hadn't been taken away."

"Where did he move to?"

"He didn't move anywhere. Someone took him."

Jake didn't know what to think about that, as it didn't make sense. Neil's parents had taken him somewhere but he hadn't moved? Jake looked at Owen, and the boy's angry eyes were clearly full of dark knowledge that he was desperate to pass on.

"A *bad man* took him," Owen said.

"Took him where?"

"Nobody knows. But he's dead now, and you're sitting in his chair."

A girl called Tabby was also sitting at the table.

"That's horrible," she told Owen. "You don't know Neil's dead. And when I asked my mummy she said it wasn't nice to talk about anyway."

"He *is* dead." Owen turned back to Jake and gestured at the chair. "That means you'll be next."

That didn't make sense either, Jake decided. Owen really hadn't thought this through at all. For one thing, whatever had happened to Neil, he'd never sat in this *particular* chair, so it wasn't like it was cursed or anything.

And also, there was a much more likely possibility. It was one he knew he shouldn't say, and he remained silent for a second. But then he remembered what the little girl had told him outside, and how alone he felt, and he decided that if Owen could treat him like this, then why couldn't he treat Owen the same right back?

"Maybe it means I'll be *last*," he said.

Owen narrowed his eyes.

"What's that supposed to mean?"

"Maybe the bad man will take the class one by one, and they'll all be replaced by new boys and girls. So that means the Whisper Man will take you before me."

Tabby gasped in shock, then burst into tears.

"You've made Tabby cry," Owen said matter-of-factly. The teacher's assistant was making his way over to the table. "George, Jake told Tabby the Whisper Man was going to kill her like he did Neil, and she got upset."

Which was how Jake went up to yellow on his first day.

Daddy was going to be very disappointed.

EIGHTEEN

The day had gone better than I expected.

Eight hundred words might have been a relatively meager tally, but after not writing anything for months, at least it was a start.

I read it through again now.

Rebecca.

At the moment, it was about her. Not a story in itself, or even the beginning of one, as things stood, but the beginning of a letter to her, and one that was difficult to read. There were so many happy memories to draw on, and I knew that I would as I continued, but while I loved and missed her more than I could say, I also couldn't deny the ugly kernel of resentment I felt, the frustration at being left alone with Jake, the loneliness of that empty bed. The sense of being *abandoned* to deal with things it felt like I couldn't cope with. None of that was her fault, of course, but grief is a stew with a thousand ingredients, and not all of them are palatable. What I'd written was an honest expression of a small part of how I felt.

Groundwork, basically. I had an idea now of what I could write about. A man, a little like me, who had lost a woman, a little like her. And as painful as it would be to explore, I could do that, moving from the ugliness to the beauty, and hopefully some final sense of resolution and acceptance. Sometimes writing can help to heal you. I didn't know if that would be the case here, but it was something to aim for.

I saved the file, and then went to pick up Jake.

When I arrived at the school, all the other parents were lined up against the wall, waiting. There was probably strict but unspoken etiquette about where to stand, but it had been a long day and I decided I didn't care. Instead, I spotted Karen standing by herself near the gate and just went over to her. The afternoon was even warmer than the morning, but she was still dressed as though prepared for snow.

"Hello again," she said. "Do you think he survived?"

"I'm pretty sure they'd have phoned by now if not."

"I imagine so. How was your day? Well—I call it a day. How were your six hours of freedom?"

"Interesting," I said. "I finally looked in our new garage and discovered that the previous owner decided to empty out all the junk by hiding it in there."

"Ah. How annoying. But also how *cunning*."

I laughed, but only slightly. The writing had taken away some of the unease from the man calling around, but it returned to me now.

"I also had some random guy snooping about."

"Okay, that sounds less good."

"Yeah. He said he grew up in the house and wanted to look around. Not sure I believed him."

"You didn't let him in, right?"

"God, no."

"Whereabouts have you moved?"

"Garholt Street."

"Just around the corner from us." She nodded. "The *scary house*, by any chance?"

The *scary house*. My heart sank.

"Probably. Although I prefer to think of it as having character."

"Oh, it does." She nodded again. "I saw it was up for sale over the summer. It's not really scary *at all*, obviously, but Adam used to say it looked strange."

"Totally the right place for me and Jake, then."

"I'm sure that's not true." She smiled, then leaned away from the railing as the school door opened. "Here we go. The beasts are loose."

Jake's class teacher came out and stood by the door, looking over the parents, then calling over her shoulder for individual children. They came scurrying out one by one, their book bags and water bottles swinging at their sides. Mrs. *Shelley*, I remembered. She looked somewhat unforgiving. I was sure her gaze landed on me a few times, but it moved on before I could tell her I was Jake's dad. A boy I presumed was Adam joined us and Karen ruffled his hair.

"Good day, kid?"

"Yes, Mum."

"Come on, then." She turned to me. "See you tomorrow."

"You will."

After they headed off, I waited some more, until I was

the only parent still standing there. Finally, Mrs. Shelley beckoned me over. I walked across, effectively summoned.

"You're Jake's dad?"

"Yes."

Jake stepped out to me, staring down at the ground and looking small and subdued. *Oh, God,* I thought. Something had happened. That was why we'd been left until last.

"Is there a problem?"

"Nothing major," Mrs. Shelley said. "But I still wanted a word. Do you want to tell your father what happened, Jake?"

"I got put on the yellow square, Dad."

"The what?"

"We have a traffic light system on the wall," Mrs. Shelley explained. "For naughtiness. As a result of his behavior today, Jake's the first of our children to move up to yellow. So not an ideal first day."

"What did he do?"

"I told Tabby she was going to die," Jake said.

"And Owen too," Mrs. Shelley added.

"And Owen too."

"Well," I said. And then, because I couldn't think of anything more sensible to add: "We *are* all going to die."

Mrs. Shelley was not impressed.

"That is not funny, Mr. Kennedy."

"I know."

"There was a boy here last year," Mrs. Shelley said.

"Neil Spencer? You might have seen about him on the news."

The name rang the vaguest of bells.

"He went missing," she said.

"Oh, yes."

I remembered now. Something about the parents letting him walk home on his own.

"It's all been very unpleasant." Mrs. Shelley looked at Jake and hesitated. "It's not something we like to talk about. Jake suggested that these other children might be next."

"Right. And so he's . . . on yellow?"

"For the next week. If he moves up to red, he'll have to go to see the headmistress."

I looked down at Jake, who appeared utterly miserable. I didn't much like the idea of him being publicly shamed on a wall, but at the same time I was frustrated with him. It seemed such an awful thing for him to have said. Why would he have done that?

"Right," I said. "Well, I'm disappointed to hear about this behavior, Jake. Very disappointed."

His head sank lower.

"We'll talk about it on the way home." I turned to Mrs. Shelley. "And it won't happen again, I promise."

"Let's make sure it doesn't. There's something else too." She stepped closer to me and spoke more quietly, even though it was obvious Jake would still be able to hear. "Our teaching assistant saw him at lunchtime, and was a little concerned. He said that Jake was talking to himself?"

I closed my eyes, my heart properly falling now. God, not that as well. Not in front of everyone. Why couldn't things be simple?

Why couldn't we just *fit in* here?

"I'll talk to him," I said again.

Except that Jake refused to talk to me.

I tried to coax the information out of him on the way home, gently at first, but after being met by repeated stony silences, I lost my temper a little. I knew it was wrong even as I did, because the truth was that I wasn't really angry with *him*. It was just the situation. Irritation that things hadn't gone as well as I'd hoped. Disappointment that his imaginary friend had returned. Concern about what the other children would think and how they would treat him. Eventually I fell into a silence of my own, and we walked alongside each other like strangers.

Back home, I went through his book bag. His Packet of Special Things was still there, at least. There was also some reading to do, which I thought looked a little basic for him.

"I mess everything up, don't I?" Jake said quietly.

I put the papers down. He was standing by the couch, head bowed, looking smaller than ever.

"No," I said. "Of course you don't."

"That's what you think."

"I don't think that, Jake. I'm actually very proud of you."

"I'm not. I hate myself."

Hearing him say that was like being stabbed.

"*Don't say that,*" I said quickly, then knelt down and tried to hug him. But he was completely unresponsive. "You mustn't *ever* say that."

"Can I do some drawing?" he asked blankly.

I took a deep breath, moving away slightly. I was desperate to get through to him, but it was obvious that wasn't going to happen right now. We could talk about it later, though. We *would* talk.

"All right."

I went through to my office, and touched the trackpad so that I could look back over the day's work. *I hate myself.* I'd told him off for that, but if I was honest, they were words I'd thought about myself quite a lot over the last year. I felt them again now. Why was I such a failure? How could I be so incapable of saying and doing the right thing? Rebecca had always told me that Jake and I were very much alike, and so perhaps the same thoughts were going through his head right now. While it might be true that we still loved each other when we argued, it didn't mean that we loved ourselves.

Why had he said such an awful thing at school? He'd been talking to himself—but, of course, that wasn't really the case. I had no doubt at all that it was the little girl he'd been speaking with—that she'd finally found us—and I had no idea what to do about that. If he couldn't make real friends, he would always have to rely on imaginary ones. And if they caused him to behave the way he had today, surely that meant he needed help?

"*Play with me.*"

THE WHISPER MAN | 127

I looked up from the screen.

A moment of silence followed in which my heart began beating harder.

The voice had come from the living room, but it hadn't sounded like Jake at all. It had been croaky and vile.

"I don't want to."

That was Jake.

I stepped closer to the doorway, listening intently.

"Play with me, I said."

"No."

Although both voices had to belong to my son, they seemed so distinct that it was easy to believe there really was another child there with him. Except it didn't sound like a child at all. The voice was too old and throaty for that. I glanced at the front door beside me. I hadn't locked it when we got back home and the chain wasn't hooked. Was it possible someone else had come in? No—I had only been in the next room. I would have heard that, if so.

"Yes. You're going to play with me."

The voice sounded like it was relishing the prospect.

"You're scaring me," Jake said.

"I want to scare you."

And at that, I finally moved into the living room, walking quickly. Jake was kneeling on the floor next to his drawings, staring at me with wide, frightened eyes.

He was totally alone, but that did nothing for my heart rate. As had happened before in the house, there was a sense of presence in the room, as though someone or something had darted out of sight just before I arrived.

"Jake?" I said quietly.

He swallowed hard, looking like he was going to cry.

"Jake, who were you talking to?"

"Nobody."

"I *heard* you talking. You were pretending to be someone else. Someone who wanted to play with you."

"No, I wasn't!" Suddenly he seemed less frightened than angry, as though I'd let him down somehow. "You always say that, and it isn't fair!"

I blinked in surprise, and then stood there helplessly as he began stuffing papers into his Packet of Special Things. I didn't always say that, did I? He must have known I didn't like him talking to himself—that it bothered me—but it wasn't as though I'd ever actually *told him off* for it.

I walked across and sat down on the couch near him.

"Jake—"

"I'm going to my room!"

"Please don't. I'm worried about you."

"No, you're not. You don't care about me at all."

"That's *not* true."

But he was already past me and heading for the living room door. My instinct told me to let him go for now—to allow things to cool down and then talk later—but I also wanted to reassure him. I struggled for the right words.

"I thought you *liked* the little girl," I said. "I thought you *wanted* to see her again."

"It wasn't her!"

"Who was it, then?"

"It was the boy in the floor."

And then he was out of sight in the hallway.

I sat there for a moment, unable to think of what to say. The boy in the floor. I remembered the raspy voice that Jake had been talking to himself with. And, of course, that was the only explanation for what I'd heard. But even so, I felt a chill run through me. It hadn't sounded like him at all.

I want to scare you.

And then I looked down. While Jake had gathered most of his things together, a single sheet of paper remained there, a few crayons lying abandoned around it. Yellow, green, and purple.

I stared at the picture. Jake had been drawing butterflies. They were childishly imprecise, but still clearly recognizable as the ones I'd seen in the garage this morning. But that was impossible, because he'd never been in the garage. I was about to pick the sheet up and examine it more closely when I heard him burst into tears.

I stood up and ran out into the hallway, just as he emerged, sobbing, from my office, pushing past me and running up the stairs.

"Jake—"

"Leave me alone! *I hate you!*"

I watched him go, feeling helpless, unable to keep up with what was happening, not understanding.

His bedroom door slammed.

I walked numbly into my office.

And then I saw the awful things I'd written to Rebecca

there on the screen. Words about how hard everything was without her, and how a part of me blamed her for leaving me to deal with all this. Words my son must have just read. And I closed my eyes as I understood only too well.

NINETEEN

----·----·----

Pete was sitting at his dinner table when the call came through. He should have been cooking or watching television, but the kitchen behind him remained dark and cold, and the living room was silent. Instead, he was staring at the bottle and the photograph.

He had been staring at them for a long time.

The day had taken a heavy toll on him. Seeing Carter always did, but this was much worse than usual. Despite the fact that Pete had waved away Amanda's comment, the killer's description of his dream about Tony Smith had gotten to Pete. Last night he had been determined to forget about Neil Spencer, but that wasn't possible now. The cases were connected. He was involved.

But what use was he? An afternoon spent investigating visitors to friends of Carter's inside had proved fruitless—so far, at least. There were still several to look at. The sad truth was that the bastard had more friends in prison than Pete had out of it.

So drink, then.

You're worthless. You're useless. Just do it.

The urge was stronger than ever, but he could survive this. After all, he had resisted the voice in the past.

And yet the idea of returning the bottle unopened to the kitchen cabinet brought a sense of despair. It felt like there was an inevitability to him drinking.

He pressed his hand to his chin, slowly rubbing the skin around his mouth, and looked at the photograph of him and Sally.

Many years ago, in an effort to combat the self-hatred that plagued him, Sally had encouraged him to make a list: two columns, one for his positive attributes, one for negative, so that he could see for himself how well they balanced out. It hadn't helped. The feeling of failure was too ingrained to be dispelled with a list. She had tried so hard to help him, but in the end it had always been the drink he'd turned to instead.

And he could see that in the photograph. Although they both looked happy, the signs were there. The way Sally's eyes were wide open to the sun, her skin luminescent, whereas he seemed unsure of it, as though a part of him were reluctant to allow the light in. He had loved her as deeply as she loved him, but the gift and receipt of love was a language with foreign grammar to him. And because he believed he was undeserving of such love, he had slowly drunk himself into a man who was. As with his memories of his father, distance had helped him understand all that. Battles often make more sense from the sky.

Too late.

It had been so many years now, but he wondered where Sally was and what she was doing. The only consolation was that he knew she must be happy somewhere, and that their separation had saved her from a life with him. The idea that she was out there, living the life she had always deserved, sustained him.

This is what you lose by drinking.

This is why it's not worth it.

But, of course, the voice had an answer to that, just as it had an answer to everything. If he'd already lost the most amazing thing he'd ever have in his life, why put himself through this torment?

What did it matter?

He stared at the bottle. And then he felt his phone vibrating against his hip.

It always comes back to me for you, doesn't it? It always ends where it starts.

Frank Carter's words returned to him as he swept the beam of his flashlight over the waste ground, walking slowly and carefully into its pitch-black heart. The sense of sickness and foreboding in his chest was matched only by the feeling of failure. The *certainty* of it. Carter's words had seemed casual and throwaway at the time, but Pete should have known better. Nothing Carter said or did was meaningless. He should have recognized the subtle deployment of a message, one deliberately intended to be understood only in hindsight.

He saw the tent and floodlights up ahead of him, with the silhouettes of officers moving cautiously around it. The sickness intensified, and he almost stumbled. *One foot in front of the other.* Two months earlier, he had been here searching for a little boy who had gone missing. Tonight, he was here because a little boy had been found.

He remembered how, that night in July, he'd left a dinner going cold on the dining room table. Tonight, the bottle was there. If he found what he was expecting to here, then he would be opening it when he got home.

He reached the canopy and clicked off his flashlight. The beam was redundant under the strength of the floodlights positioned around it. Seeing what was lying in the center, in fact, there was altogether too much light. He wasn't ready for that yet. Glancing away, he spotted DCI Lyons standing at the side of the tent, staring back at him, the man's expression blank. For a moment Pete imagined he saw a flash of contempt there—*you should have stopped this*—and he looked away again quickly, his gaze falling on the television with the pockmarked screen. It was a moment before he realized Amanda was standing beside him.

"This is where he was taken from," Pete said.

"We can't know that for sure."

"I'm sure of it," he said.

She looked away into the darkness. The brightness and intensity of activity in front of them only emphasized the blackness of the waste ground surrounding them.

"*It always ends where it starts*," Amanda said. "That's what Carter told you, right?"

"Yes. I should have picked up on that."

"Or I should have. It's not your fault."

"Then it's not yours either."

"Maybe." She smiled sadly. "But you look like you need to hear it more than I do."

He could tell that wasn't true. She looked pale and

sick. Over the past couple of months, he'd noticed how efficient and capable she was, and he'd suspected she was ambitious too—that she'd imagined a case like this might help her career without fully understanding what else it might do. He felt a strange kind of kinship with her now. Finding the dead boys in Carter's house had broken him for a time. He knew that Amanda had worked—and hoped—just as hard as he had twenty years ago, and that right now, whatever her expectations, she must be feeling like an open wound.

But it wasn't a kinship that could be spoken of out loud. You walked the road alone. You got through it or you didn't.

Amanda breathed out slowly.

"The fucker *knew*," she said. "Didn't he?"

"Yes."

"So the question then is *how* did he know?"

"I'm not sure yet. I've got nothing on that level so far. But there's still a long list of friends inside to look at."

She hesitated.

"Do you want to see the body?"

You can have a drink when you get home.

I'll let you.

"Yes," he said.

Together, they moved under the canopy to where the boy was lying spread-eagled, close to the old television. His backpack was on the ground beside him. Pete did his best to take in the details as dispassionately as possible. The clothes, obviously: the blue tracksuit pants; the Minecraft T-shirt that had been pulled up over the boy's face, turning the design on the front inside out.

"That was never made public," he said.

Another connection to Carter.

"No real blood." He peered around the body. "Not enough, anyway—not for those injuries. He was killed elsewhere."

"Looks that way."

"That's a difference between our new man and Carter. Carter killed those children where I found them, and he kept them in his house. He never made any attempt to dump the remains."

"Apart from Tony Smith."

"That was down to circumstances. And also, this is public." He gestured around. "Whoever did this, they wanted the body to be found. And not just anywhere either. Back where it started, just like Carter told me."

You can have a drink when you get home.

"The clothes are the ones he went missing in. The injuries aside, it looks like he's been reasonably well cared for. Not obviously emaciated."

"Another difference from Carter," Amanda said.

"Yes."

Pete closed his eyes, trying to think this through. Neil Spencer had been held somewhere for two months before he was killed. He had been looked after. And then something had changed. Afterward, he had been returned to the place he'd been abducted from.

Like a present, he thought.

A present someone had been given that they decided they didn't want anymore.

"The backpack." He opened his eyes. "Is the water bottle in there?"

"Yes. I'll show you."

He followed her closer still, edging around the boy's body. She used a gloved hand to open the top, and he looked inside. There was the bottle, half full of water. Something else. A blue rabbit—a bedtime toy. That had never been on the list.

"Did he have that with him?"

"We're trying to find out from the parents." Amanda scrabbled in her pocket. "But yes. I think he had that with him as well, and they just didn't know."

Pete nodded slowly. He knew all about Neil Spencer by now. The boy had been disruptive at school. Aggressive. Already old and toughened beyond his years, the way people get when life bruises them.

But underneath all that, still just six years old.

He forced himself to look at the boy's body, not caring about the feelings it evoked or the memories it stirred. He could have a drink when he got home.

We're going to get the person who did this to you.

And then he turned around and stepped away, flicking his flashlight back on as he entered the darkness there.

"I'm going to need you on this, Pete," Amanda called after him.

"I know." But he was thinking about that bottle on the dining room table and trying not to break into a run. "And you're going to have me."

THE WHISPER MAN / 139

course through it. The act of killing had left him adrift

TWENTY

The man stood shivering in the darkness.

Above him, the blue-black sky was clear and speck-led with stars, the night a stark, cold contrast to the heat of the day behind him. But it was not the temperature that was making him tremble. Even though he refused to think directly about what he had done that after-noon, the impact of his actions remained with him, just out of sight beneath his skin.

He had never killed before today.

Beforehand, he had imagined he was prepared to do so, and in the moment the rage and hatred he had felt had carried him through. But the act had left him off-kilter afterward, unsure what he was feeling. He had laughed this evening, and he had cried. He had shaken with shame and self-hatred, but also rocked on the bathroom floor in confused elation. It was impos-sible to describe. Which made sense, he supposed. He had opened a door that could never be closed, and ex-perienced something few others on the planet ever had or would. There was no preparation or guidebook for the journey he had embarked on. No map showing the course through it. The act of killing had left him adrift on an entirely uncharted sea of emotions.

He breathed the cool night air in slowly now, his body still singing. It was so quiet here that all he could hear was the rush of the air, as though the world were murmuring secrets in its sleep. The streetlights in the distance shone brightly, but he was so far from the light here, and standing so motionless, that someone could walk past meters away without seeing him. He would see them, though—or sense them, at least. He felt attuned to the world. And right now, in the early hours of the morning, he could tell that he was totally alone out here.

Waiting.

Full of shivers.

It was difficult now to remember how angry he had been this afternoon. At the time, the rage had simply consumed him, flaring within his chest until his whole body was twisting with the force of it, like a puppet wrenched about on its strings. His head had been so full of blinding light that perhaps he wouldn't be able to recall what he'd done even if he tried. It felt like he had stepped outside himself for a time, and in doing so had allowed something else to emerge. If he had been a religious man, it would have been easy to imagine himself possessed by some external force. But he was not, and he knew that whatever had taken him over in those terrible minutes had come from inside.

It was gone now—or at least it had slunk back down into its cave. What had felt right at the time now brought little but a sense of guilt and failure. In Neil Spencer he had found a troubled child who needed to be rescued and cared for, and he had believed that he was the one to do so. He would help and nurture Neil. House him. Care for him.

It had never been his intention to hurt him.

And for two months, it had worked. The man had felt such peace. The boy's presence and apparent contentment had been a balm to him. For the first time he could remember, his world had felt not only possible but *right*, as though some long-standing infection inside him had finally begun to heal.

But, of course, it had all been an illusion.

Neil had been lying to him all along, biding his time and only ever *pretending* to be happy. And finally the man had been forced to accept that the spark of goodness he'd imagined in the boy's eyes had never been real, just trickery and deceit. From the beginning he had been too naïve and trusting. Neil Spencer had only ever been a snake in a little boy suit, and the truth was that he had deserved exactly what happened to him today . . .

The man's heart was beating too hard.

He shook his head, then forced himself to calm down, breathing steadily again and putting such thoughts out of his mind. What had happened today was abhorrent. If, among all the other emotions, it had also brought its own strange sense of harmony and satisfaction, that was horrible and wrong and had to be fought against. He had to cling instead to the tranquility of the weeks beforehand, however false it had turned out to be. He had chosen badly—that was all. Neil had been a mistake, and that wouldn't happen again.

The next little boy would be perfect.

TWENTY-ONE

It was harder than ever to get to sleep that night.

I hadn't managed to resolve anything with Jake after our argument. While I could justify what I'd written about Rebecca to myself, it was impossible to make a seven-year-old boy understand. To him, they were just words attacking his mother. He wouldn't talk back to me, and it wasn't clear whether he was even listening. At bedtime he refused a story, and I stood there helplessly again for a moment, torn between frustration and self-hatred and the desperate *need* to make him understand. In the end, I just kissed the side of his head gently, told him I loved him, and said good night, hoping things might be better in the morning. As if it ever works like that. Tomorrow is always a new day, but there's never any reason to think it will be a better one.

Later, I lay in my own bedroom, shifting from side to side, trying to settle. I couldn't bear the distance that was growing between us. Even worse was the fact that I had no idea how to stop it from increasing, never mind close it. And lying there in the dark, I also kept remembering the rasping voice Jake had put on, and shivering each time I did.

I want to scare you.

The boy in the floor.

But as unnerving as that had been, for some reason it was his drawing of the butterflies that bothered me more. The garage was padlocked. There was no way Jake could have been in there without my knowledge. And yet I'd looked at the picture over and over, and there was no mistaking them. Somehow, he'd seen them. But how and where?

It was a coincidence, of course; it had to be. Maybe the butterflies were more common than I realized—the ones in the garage must have arrived from somewhere, after all. Obviously, I had tried to talk to Jake about them too. Equally obviously, he had refused to answer me. And so, as I tossed and turned, trying to sleep, I realized the mystery of the butterflies came down to the same thing as the argument itself. I'd just have to hope it would be better in the morning.

Glass smashing.

A man shouting.

My mother screaming.

Wake up, Tom.

Wake up now.

Someone shook my foot.

I jerked awake, soaked with sweat, my heart hammering in my chest. The bedroom was pitch-black and quiet—still the middle of the night. Jake was standing at the bottom of the bed again, a black silhouette against the darkness behind him. I rubbed my face.

"Jake?" I said quietly.

No reply. I couldn't see his face, but his upper body

was moving gently from side to side, swaying on his feet like a metronome. I frowned.

"Are you awake?"

Again, there was no answer. I sat up in bed, wondering what the best thing to do was. If he was sleepwalking, should I wake him gently, or try to steer him, still asleep, back to his room? But then my eyes adapted a little better to the darkness and the silhouette grew clearer. His hair was wrong. It was much longer than it should have been, and it seemed to be splayed out to one side.

And . . .

Someone was whispering.

But the figure at the end of the bed, still swaying ever so slowly from side to side, was entirely silent. The sound I could hear was coming from somewhere else in the house.

I looked to my left. The open bedroom door gave me a view of the dark hallway. It was empty, but I thought the whispering was coming from somewhere out there.

"Jake—"

But when I looked back, the silhouette at the end of my bed had disappeared and the room was empty.

I rubbed the sleep from my face, then slid across the cold side of the bed and padded quietly out into the hall. The whispering was a little louder out here. While I couldn't make out any words, it was obvious now that I was hearing two voices: a hushed conversation, with one participant slightly gruffer than the other. Jake was talking to himself again. I moved instinctively toward his room, but then glanced down the stairs and froze where I stood.

My son was at the bottom, sitting by the front door. A soft wedge of streetlight was cutting around the edge of the curtains in my office to the side, staining his tousled hair orange. His legs were curled up underneath him, and his head was against the door, with one hand pressed there beside it. In the other, resting against his leg, were the spare keys I kept on the desk in the office.

I listened.

"I'm not sure," Jake whispered.

The reply was the gruffer voice I'd heard.

"I'll look after you, I promise."

"I'm not sure."

"Let me in, Jake."

My son moved his hand toward the mail slot in the door. That was when I noticed that it was being pushed open from the outside. There were *fingers* there. My heart leaped at the sight of them. Four thin, pale fingers, poking through among the spidery black bristles, holding the mail slot open.

"Let me in."

Jake rested the side of his small hand against one of them, and it curled around to stroke him.

"Just let me in."

He reached up for the chain.

"Don't move!" I shouted.

It came out without me thinking, from my heart as much as my mouth. The fingers retreated immediately and the mail slot snapped shut behind them. Jake turned to look up at me as I thudded down the stairs toward him, my heart hammering in my chest. At the bottom, I snatched the keys out of his hand.

Sitting like that, he was blocking the door.

"Move," I shouted. "*Move.*"

He scrabbled out of the way, crawling on his hands and knees into my office. I scraped the chain out of the lock, then tried the door handle, which turned easily— Jake had already unlocked the fucking thing with the keys. Pulling the door open, I stepped quickly onto the front path and stared out into the night.

As far as I could tell, there was nobody up or down the street. The amber haze beneath the streetlights was misty, the pavements empty. But looking across the road, I thought I could see a figure running swiftly across the field. A vague shape, pummeling away through the darkness.

Already too far away for me to catch.

My instinct took me down the front path anyway, but I stopped halfway to the street, my breath visible in the cold night air. What the hell was I doing? I couldn't leave the house open behind me and go chasing someone across a field. I couldn't leave Jake in there by himself, alone and abandoned.

So I stood there for a few seconds, staring into the darkness of the field. The figure—if it had ever been here at all—had disappeared now.

It *had* been here.

I stood there for a moment longer. And then I went back inside, locked the door, and phoned the police.

PART THREE

TWENTY-TWO

Credit where it's due, two police officers arrived on my doorstep within ten minutes of my phone call. After that, things began to go downhill.

I had to take some responsibility for what happened. It was half past four in the morning, and I was exhausted, frightened, and not thinking straight, and the account I had to give was light on detail anyway. But there was no getting away from Jake's role in what unfolded.

When I'd come back inside to make the call, I'd found him at the bottom of the stairs, hugging his knees and with his face buried in them. I had eventually calmed down enough to calm him down too, and then I'd carried him into the living room, where he'd curled up at one end of the couch. And then refused to talk to me.

I had done my best to hide the frustration and panic I was feeling. I probably hadn't succeeded.

Even when the police officers joined us in the living room, Jake remained in that same position. I sat down awkwardly beside him. Even then, I was aware of the distance between us, and I was sure it was also very obvious to the police. The two of them—a man and a woman—were both polite and made the requisite concerned and understanding faces, but the woman kept glancing curiously at Jake, and I got the impression the worry on her face was not wholly because of what I was telling them.

Afterward, the male officer referred to the notes he'd made.

"Has Jake sleepwalked before?"

"A little," I said. "But not often, and only ever to my room. He's never gone downstairs like that."

That was if he even *had* been sleepwalking, of course. While it made me feel better to think he hadn't been about to open that door out of choice, I realized I couldn't be sure of that. And Jesus, if that was true, what did it say about how much my son hated me?

The officer made another note.

"And you can't describe the individual you saw?"

"No. He was quite far away across the field by then, running fast. It was dark, and I couldn't see him properly."

"Build? Clothes?"

I shook my head. "No, sorry."

"Are you sure it was a man?"

"Yes. It was a man's voice I heard at the door."

"Could that have been Jake?" The officer looked at my son. Jake was still curled up next to me, staring off into space as though he were the only person in the entire world. "Sometimes children talk to themselves."

Not something I wanted to get into.

"No," I said. "There was definitely somebody there.

I saw this man's fingers holding the mail slot open. I *heard* him. The voice was older. He was trying to persuade Jake to open the door—and he was going to as well. God knows what would have happened if I hadn't woken up in time."

The reality of the situation crashed down on me then. In my mind's eye I saw the scene again, and realized how close it had all been. If I hadn't been there, then Jake would be gone now. I imagined him missing, with the police seated across from me for a different reason, and felt helpless. Despite my frustration with his behavior, I wanted to wrap my arms around him—to protect him and hold him close. But I knew that I couldn't. That he wouldn't let me, or even want me to right now.

"How did Jake get the keys?"

"I left them in my office across the hall." I shook my head. "That's not a mistake I'll be making again."

"That's probably wise."

"And what about you, Jake?" The female officer leaned forward, smiling kindly. "Can *you* tell us anything at all about what happened?"

Jake shook his head.

"You can't? Why were you at the door, sweetheart?"

He shrugged almost imperceptibly, and then seemed to move a little farther away from me. The woman leaned back, still looking at Jake, her head tilted slightly to one side. Evaluating him.

"There was another man," I said quickly. "He came by the house yesterday. He was hanging around the garage, acting strangely. When I confronted him, he said he'd grown up here and wanted to look around."

The male officer looked interested in that.

"How did you confront him?"

"He came to the door."

"Oh, I see." He made a note on his pad. "Can you describe him?"

I did, and he scribbled away. But it was clear that the man actively knocking on the door had made the development significantly less interesting to him. Plus, it was difficult to convey how uneasy the man had made me feel. There had been nothing physically threatening about him, and yet he had still seemed dangerous on some level.

"Neil Spencer," I remembered.

The male officer stopped writing.

"I'm sorry?"

"I think that was his name. We've only just moved here. But another little boy went missing, didn't he? Earlier this summer?"

The two officers exchanged a glance.

"What do you know about Neil Spencer?" the man asked me.

"Nothing. Jake's teacher just mentioned him. I was going to look it up online, but it was a . . . busy night." And again, I didn't want to go into the argument Jake and I had had. "I was working."

But, of course, that was the wrong thing to say as well, because work was writing, and Jake had read what I'd done. I felt him shrink slightly beside me.

Frustration got the better of me.

"It's just that I'd have thought this would be more worrying to you than it seems to be," I said.

"Mr. Kennedy—"

"It feels like you don't believe me."

The man smiled. But it was a careful smile.

"It's not a case of *not believing you,* Mr. Kennedy. But we can only work with what we have." He looked at me for a moment, considering me in much the same way his partner was still evaluating my son. "We take everything seriously. We'll log a record of this, but based on what you've told us, there's not a vast amount we can do right now. As I said, I recommend you keep your keys out of your son's way. Observe basic home security. Keep an eye out. And don't hesitate to get in touch with us if you see anyone else around your property who shouldn't be here."

I shook my head. Given what had happened—given that *someone had tried to take my son*—this response wasn't remotely good enough. I was angry at myself, and I couldn't help being angry at Jake as well. I was trying to help him! And in a minute the police would be gone, and it would just be me and him again. Alone. Neither of us up to the job of living with the other.

"Mr. Kennedy?" the female officer said gently. "Is it just you and Jake here? Does his mother live elsewhere?"

"His mother is dead."

I said it too bluntly, a trace of the anger I was feeling escaping. She seemed taken aback.

"Oh. I'm very sorry to hear that."

"I'm just . . . it's hard. And what just happened tonight, it scared me."

And that was the point when Jake came back to life,

perhaps animated by anger of his own. What I'd written. The fact I'd just said his mother was dead so brazenly. He uncurled and slowly sat up straight, finally looking at me, his face expressionless. When he spoke, it was with a raspy, unearthly voice that sounded far too old for his years.

"*I want to scare you,*" he said.

TWENTY-THREE

When the alarm went off, Pete lay very still for a moment, letting it ring on the bedside table. Something was wrong and he needed to prepare himself. Then there was a burst of panic as he remembered the events of yesterday evening. The sight of Neil Spencer's body on the waste ground. The almost frantic race to get home afterward. And the reassuring weight of the bottle in his hand.

The clicks as he'd broken the seal.

And then . . .

Finally, he opened his eyes. The early morning sun was already strong, streaming through the thin blue curtains and falling in a wedge over the covers bunched up over his knees. Sometime in the night, sweating with heat, he must have thrown them off his upper body, and the tangle of material felt ridiculously heavy now, wrapped tightly around his knees.

He turned his head and looked at the bedside table.

The bottle was there. The seal was broken.

But the contents remained, full to the top.

He remembered how long he'd deliberated last night, battling the urge again and again as it came back at him from different angles, both he and the voice refusing to relent or retreat. He'd even brought the bottle and a tumbler up here to bed with him. Still fighting, even then.

And in the end, he had won.

Relief rushed through him. He glanced at the tumbler now. Before going to sleep, he had put the photograph of Sally on top of it. Even after everything that had happened—the horrors of the evening—that photograph and those memories had still been enough to keep him clean.

He tried not to think about the day ahead of him or the evenings to come.

Enough for now.

He showered and ate breakfast. Even without drinking, he felt so worn down that he contemplated not going to the gym. A briefing had been scheduled for first thing, and he needed to be prepared for it, to be filled in on the case. But he already felt soaked to the skin in it. As dispassionate as he'd tried to be when viewing Neil Spencer's body, it was like pointing a camera without looking through the viewfinder; your mind took the photograph regardless. If anything, if he was going to be competent and professional in a couple of hours, he needed to empty some of that horror out.

He drove to the department and went to the gym.

Afterward, feeling calmer, he went upstairs. For a moment, he stared at the blissful piles of safe, innocuous paperwork in his office, then found the old, malignant bundle of notes he was going to need and headed to the operations room one floor above.

His calm faded slightly as he opened the door. It was still ten minutes before the briefing was due to begin, but the room was already heaving with officers. Nobody was talking; every face he could see looked somber. Most of these men and women would have worked this case from the beginning, and whatever the odds, each of them would have clung on to hope. By now they all knew what had been found last night. Before today, a child had been missing. Now a child was dead.

He leaned against a wall at the back of the room, aware as he did that gazes were falling on him. It was understandable. While his initial involvement in the case had come to nothing, all of them must know that his presence here now was not a coincidence. He spotted DCI Lyons sitting near the front, looking back at him. Pete met his eyes for a moment, trying to read the expression on the man's face. Like last night at the waste ground, it was blank, which only left Pete free to imagine. Was the man feeling an odd sense of triumph? It seemed unfair to contemplate such an idea, but it was certainly possible. Despite the disparity in their career trajectories since, Pete knew that Lyons had always resented him on some level for being the one to catch Frank Carter. This recent development meant the case never really *had* been closed. And here was Lyons, presiding over what might turn out to be the endgame, with Pete reduced now to the status of a pawn.

He folded his arms, stared at the floor, and waited.

Amanda arrived a minute later, stalking quickly through the assembled throng toward the front of the room. Even from the brief side view he got of her, it was obvious she was harried and tired. Same clothes as last night, he noticed. She'd slept in one of the overnight suites or, more likely, hadn't slept at all. As she took to the small stage, there was a subdued, defeated look about her.

"Right, everyone," she said. "You've all heard the news. Yesterday evening we had a report that a child's body had been found on the waste ground off Gair Lane. Officers attended and secured the scene. The identity of the victim has yet to be confirmed, but we believe this to be Neil Spencer."

They had all known it already, but still: Pete watched the slump travel around the room. The emotional temperature of the room dropped. The silence among the assembled officers, already absolute, somehow seemed to intensify.

"We also believe it to be a case of third-party involvement. There are significant injuries to the body."

Amanda's voice almost broke at that and he saw her wince slightly. Too hard on herself. Under different circumstances, it might have been perceived as weakness, but Pete didn't think it would be in this room right now. He watched as she gathered herself.

"Details of which are obviously not going to be released to the press at this time. We have a cordon in place, but the media know we've found a body. That is all they are going to know until we get a handle on what's happening here."

A woman by the wall was nodding to herself. Pete recognized it as the kind of action he had made in the deepest throes of his addiction, pining for a drink and riding out the pain.

"The body has been removed from the scene and a postmortem will take place this morning. We have an estimated time of death somewhere between three and five P.M. yesterday. Assuming this is Neil Spencer, he was found in roughly the same place he went missing, which may be significant. We also believe Neil was killed at a different location, presumably wherever he had been held. Fingers crossed that forensics will give us some clue as to where that might be. In the meantime, we'll be going over all the CCTV in the area. We'll be knocking on every door in the vicinity. Because I am simply not having this monster wandering around Featherbank undetected. I'm not having it."

She looked up. Despite the obvious tiredness and upset, there was fire in her eyes now.

"All of us here—we've all worked on this investigation. And even if we'd steeled ourselves, this is not the result any of us were hoping for. So let me be absolutely clear. It will not be allowed to stand. Do we agree?"

Pete glanced around again. A few nods here and there; the room coming back to life. He admired the sentiment and acknowledged the need for it right now, but he also remembered giving equally angry speeches twenty years ago, and while he had believed them at the time, he knew now that things not only *stood* whether you wanted them to or not, but that sometimes they followed you forever.

"We did everything we could," Amanda told the room. "We didn't find Neil Spencer in time. But make no mistake, we *are* going to find the person that did this to him."

And Pete could tell that she believed what she was saying just as passionately as he had all those years ago. Because you had to. Something awful had happened on your watch, and the only way to ease the pain was to do everything you could to put it right. To catch whoever was responsible before they hurt anybody else. Or at least try.

We are *going to find the person that did this.*

He hoped that was true.

TWENTY-FOUR

It was astonishing how quickly life could revert to normal when it had to.

After the police left, I decided there was no point in either Jake or me trying to go back to sleep, and as a result, by half past eight, I felt half dead on my feet. I went through the motions of preparing him breakfast and getting him ready for school. After what had happened, it seemed ridiculous, but I had no excuse for keeping him home. In fact, given his performance in front of the officers earlier on, a horrible part of me *wanted* not to be around him right now.

While he ate cereal, still refusing to speak to me, I stood in the kitchen, poured myself a glass of water, and downed it in one. I didn't really know what to do or how to feel. With just a handful of hours' distance, the events of the night seemed distant and surreal. Could I be sure I'd seen what I'd seen? Perhaps it had been my imagination. But no, I *had* seen it. A better father—an average one, even—would have convinced the police to take him seriously. A better father would have a son who talked to him, not undermined him. Who could see that I was just scared for him and trying to protect him.

My hand tightened around the glass.

You're not your father, Tom.

Rebecca's quiet voice in my head.

Never forget that.

I looked down at the empty glass in my hand. My grip was too tight on it. That awful memory came back to me—shattering glass; my mother screaming—and I put it down on the counter quickly, before I could start to fail in an altogether worse way.

At quarter to nine, Jake and I walked to school together, him trailing along to the side of me, still resisting any attempts at conversation. It was only when we reached the gates that he finally spoke to me.

"Who's Neil Spencer, Daddy?"

"I don't know." Despite the subject matter, I was relieved that he was talking to me. "A boy from Featherbank. I think he went missing earlier this year; I remember reading something about it. Nobody knows what happened to him."

"Owen said he was dead."

"Owen sounds like a charming little boy."

It was clear that Jake was thinking about adding something to that, but then he changed his mind.

"He said I was sitting in Neil's chair."

"That's stupid. You didn't get a place in the school because this Neil kid went missing. Someone else moved to a new house like we did." I frowned. "And anyway, they'd have all been in a different classroom last year, wouldn't they?"

Jake looked at me curiously.

"Twenty-eight," he said.

"Twenty-eight what?"

"Twenty-eight children," he said. "Plus me is twenty-nine."

"Exactly." I had no idea if that was true, but I went with it. "They have classes of thirty here. So wherever Neil is, his chair is waiting for him."

"Do you think he *will* come home?"

We stepped into the playground.

"I don't know, mate."

"Can I have a hug, Daddy?"

I looked down at him. From the expression on his face now, last night and this morning might as well not have happened at all. But then, he was seven. Arguments were always resolved in his time and on his terms. In this instance, I was too tired not to accept that.

"Of course you can."

"Because even when we argue—"

"We still love each other. Very much."

I knelt down, and the tight embrace felt like it was powering me back up a little. That a hug like this, every so often, would keep me running. And then he ambled inside past Mrs. Shelley without giving me even a backward glance. I walked back out through the gate, hoping he didn't get into any more trouble today.

But if he did . . .

Well, he did.

Just let him be him.

"Hello, there."

I turned to find Karen slightly behind me, walking just fast enough to catch up

"Hey," I said. "How are you?"

"Looking forward to a few hours' peace and quiet." She fell into step beside me. "How did Jake do yesterday?"

"He went up to yellow," I said.

"I have no idea what that means."

I explained the traffic light system. The gravity and supposed *seriousness* of it seemed so meaningless after the events of the night that I almost laughed at the end.

"That sounds fucking abominable," she said.

"That's what I thought."

I wondered if there was some nominal moment when playground parents decided to drop a certain level of pretense and swear like normal people. If there was, I was glad to have passed it.

"In some ways it's a badge of honor, though," she said. "He'll be the envy of his classmates. Adam said they didn't have much of a chance to play together."

"Jake said Adam was nice," I lied.

"He also said Jake talked to himself a bit."

"Yes, he does do that sometimes. Imaginary friends."

"Right," Karen said. "I sympathize with him completely. Some of my best friends are imaginary. I'm joking, obviously. But Adam went through that, and I'm sure I did too when I was a kid. You probably did as well."

I frowned. A memory suddenly came back to me.

"Mister Night," I said.

"Sorry?"

"God, I haven't thought about that in years." I ran

my hand through my hair. How had I forgotten about it? "Yeah, I *did* have an imaginary friend. When I was younger, I used to tell my mother that someone came into my room at night and hugged me. *Mister Night.* That's what I called him."

"Yeah . . . that's pretty creepy. But then, kids say scary stuff all the time. There are whole websites devoted to it. You should write that down and submit it."

"Maybe I will." But it reminded me of something else. "Jake's been saying other weird things recently. *If you leave a door half open, soon you'll hear the whispers spoken.* Have you ever heard that?"

"Hmmm." Karen thought about it. "It does ring a bell; I'm sure I've heard it *somewhere* before. It's one of those rhymes kids say in the playground, I think."

"Right. Maybe that's where he heard it, then."

Except not in *this* playground, of course, because Jake had said it the night before his first day. Maybe it was some common kid thing that I didn't know about—something from one of those television shows I put on for him and then zoned out without paying attention to.

I sighed.

"I just hope he has a better day. I worry about him."

"That's natural. What does your wife say?"

"She died last year," I said. "I'm not sure how well he's coping with that. Understandably, I suppose."

Karen was silent for a moment.

"I'm very sorry to hear that."

"Thanks. I'm not sure how well I'm coping either, to be honest. I'm never sure whether I'm being a good father or not. Whether I'm doing the best I can for him."

"That's also natural. I'm sure you *are*."

"Maybe it's whether my best is good enough that's the real question."

"And again, I'm sure it is."

She stopped and put her hands in her pockets. We'd come to a junction, and it was obvious from our mutual body language that she was heading on straight here while I was turning right.

"But whatever," she said, "it sounds like both of you have had a rough time of it. So I think—not that you asked for my opinion, I realize, but fuck it—that maybe you should stop being so hard on yourself?"

"Maybe."

"Just *a little,* at least?"

"Maybe."

"Easier said than done, I know." She gathered herself together, her whole body suddenly like a sigh. "Anyway. Catch you later on. Have a good one."

"You too."

I thought about that the rest of the way home. *Maybe you should stop being so hard on yourself.* There was probably some truth in that, because, after all, I was just fumbling through life the same as everyone else, wasn't I? Trying to do my best. But back home, I still paced around the downstairs of the house, unsure what to do with myself. Earlier on, I'd been thinking it would be good to have some time without Jake. Now, with the house empty and silent around me, I felt an urge to have him as close as possible.

Because I needed to keep him safe.

And I *hadn't* imagined what had happened last night.

That brought on a flash of panic. If the police weren't going to help us, that meant that I had to. Walking through the empty rooms, I felt a sense of desperation—an urgent need to do something, even though I had no idea *what*. I ended up in my office. The laptop had been left on standby overnight. I nudged the track-pad and the screen came to life, revealing the words there.

Rebecca . . .

She would know what to do right now; she always had. I pictured her sitting cross-legged on the floor with Jake, playing enthusiastically with whatever toys were between them. And curled up on our old couch, reading to him, his head underneath her chin and their two bodies so close that they looked like a single person. Whenever he'd called out in the night, Rebecca would have already been padding through to him as I was still waking up. And it had always been her he called for.

I deleted the words I'd written yesterday and then typed three new sentences.

I miss you. I feel like I'm failing our son and I don't know what to do.

I'm sorry.

I stared at the screen for a moment.

Enough.

Enough wallowing. As difficult as everything might be, it was my job to look after my son, and if my best wasn't sufficient, then I'd have to get better.

I walked back to the front door. It had a lock and a chain, but that clearly wasn't good enough. So I would install a bolt as well, too high for Jake to reach on his own. Motion detectors at the bottom of the stairs. It could all be done. None of this was insurmountable, whatever my self-doubt was telling me.

But there was something else I could do first, and so I turned my attention to the pile of mail on the stairs behind me. There had been another two letters for Dominic Barnett, both of them debt collection notices. I took them to my office, closed down Word on the laptop, and opened the Web browser instead.

Let's see who you are, Dominic Barnett.

I wasn't sure what I was expecting to discover about him online. A Facebook page, perhaps—something with a photo that would tell me whether he was the man who'd called around yesterday—or if not that, maybe a forwarding address of some kind that I could follow up in the real world. Anything that might help me to protect Jake and work out what the hell was going on with my house.

I found a photograph on the very first search. Dominic Barnett was not my mysterious visitor. He was younger, with a full head of jet-black hair. But the picture wasn't on a social media site.

Instead, it was beside a news item at the top of the search page:

POLICE TREAT DEATH OF LOCAL
MAN AS MURDER

The room receded around me. I stared at the words until they began to lose their meaning. The house had gone silent, and all I could hear was the thud of my heartbeat.

And then—

Creak.

I glanced at the ceiling. That noise again, the same as before, as though someone had taken a single step in Jake's bedroom. My skin tingled as I remembered what had happened last night—the figure I'd imagined standing at the base of my bed, its hair splayed out like the little girl that Jake had drawn. The sensation of my foot being shaken.

Wake up, Tom.

But unlike the man at the door, that *had* been my imagination. I'd been half asleep, after all. It had been nothing more than a remnant of a nightmare of the past, shaped by fears from the present.

There was nothing in my house.

Determined to take my mind off the noise, I forced myself to click on the article.

POLICE TREAT DEATH OF LOCAL MAN AS MURDER

Police have revealed that they are treating the death of Dominic Barnett, whose body was found in woodland on Tuesday, as murder.

Barnett, 42, of Garholt Street, Featherbank, was discovered at the edge of a stream by children playing in Hollingbeck Wood. Today, Detective Chief Inspector Colin Lyons revealed to the press that Barnett had died as a result of "significant" head injuries. A number of possible motives for the attack were being explored, but items recovered at the scene suggested that robbery was not among them.

"I would like to take this opportunity to reassure the public at large," Lyons said. "Mr. Barnett was known to officers, and we believe this to be an isolated incident. However, we have increased patrols in the area, and we encourage anyone with any information to come forward immediately."

I read it through again, the panic inside me intensifying. From the street name, there was no doubt that this was the right Dominic Barnett. He had lived in this house. Maybe sat exactly where I was right now, or slept in what had become Jake's bedroom.

And he had been murdered in April this year.

Trying to keep calm, I clicked back and searched for more articles. The facts, such as they were, emerged piecemeal, and many of them from between the lines. *Mr. Barnett was known to officers.* Careful phrasing, but the implication appeared to be that he'd been involved with drugs in some way, and that this was presumed to be the motive for his murder. Hollingbeck Wood was south of Featherbank, on the other side of the river. Why Barnett had been there was unclear. A murder weapon was recovered a week later, and the reports tailed off shortly afterward. From what I could find online, his killer had never been caught.

Which meant that they were still out there.

The realization brought an awful crawling sensation with it. I didn't know what to do. Call the police again? What I'd discovered didn't seem to add much to what I'd already told them. I would call them, I decided, because I had to do *something*. But I needed more information first.

After some deliberation, and with my hands shaking, I searched through the paperwork I'd kept on the house purchase, found the address I needed, then picked up my keys. The extra security would have to wait, for the moment. There was one person who would be able to tell me more about Dominic Barnett, and I figured it was time to talk to her.

TWENTY-FIVE
·-----·--·-----·

It always ends where it starts, Amanda thought.

She was looking through the CCTV footage that had been retrieved from the area around the waste ground, and couldn't help remembering that, two months ago, she'd been examining images of these exact same streets. Back then it had been in the hope of seeing someone taking Neil Spencer away. Now she was searching for someone returning the boy's body. But so far the result was the same.

Nothing.

Early days, she told herself—but that thought was like ash in her head. It was actually far too fucking late, not least for Neil Spencer himself. Her mind kept flashing back to the sight of his body, even though dwelling on the horrors she'd seen last night—on her failure to find Neil in time—wasn't going to help. What she needed to do instead was concentrate on the work. One foot in front of the other. One detail at a time. That was the way they'd eventually get the bastard who'd done those things to that little boy.

Another flash.

She shook her head, then looked toward the back of

the room, where Pete Willis was working quietly at the desk he'd been allocated. After she'd had the chance to sit down herself, she'd found herself keeping a surreptitious eye on him. Occasionally he picked up the phone and made a call; the rest of the time his attention was totally focused on the photographs and paperwork before him. Frank Carter knew something, and Pete was working through the visits received by the man's friends and associates in the prison, trying to figure out if one of them might be responsible for passing Carter information from the outside world. But it was Pete himself who fascinated her now.

How could he be so *calm*?

Except that she knew he was suffering too, below the surface. She remembered how he'd been yesterday, after visiting Frank Carter, and then on the waste ground last night. If he seemed detached now, it was only because he was distracting himself in the exact same way she was trying to. And if he was succeeding, it was simply because he'd had so much more practice.

Amanda wanted to ask him the secret.

Instead, she forced her attention back to the CCTV files, already knowing deep down that it would yield nothing, just like two months ago, when her team had slowly identified and eliminated the individuals caught on the village's meager selection of cameras. It was frustrating work. The more you accomplished, the worse it *felt* like you were doing. But it was necessary.

She picked her way through the fuzzy images. Freeze-frames of men, women, and children. All of them would have to be interviewed, even though none of them would have witnessed anything significant. The man they were looking for was too careful for that. And it would be the same with the vehicles. Her conviction during the briefing had been real, and a part of her was still cultivating that now, but she knew deep down the feeling was impotent. The fact remained that it wasn't difficult to drive around Featherbank and avoid CCTV. Not if you knew what you were doing.

On the pad beside her, she jotted that thought down. *Knowledge of camera position?*

But again, she'd made the same note two months earlier. History repeating itself.

It always ends where it starts.

She threw the pen down in frustration, then stood up and walked over to where Pete was working, so engrossed that he didn't even notice her. The printer on his desk was releasing a steady stream of photographs— CCTV stills of visitors to the prison. Pete was cross-referencing them with details on the screen and writing notes on the back. There was also an old newspaper printout on the desk. She tilted her head to read the headline.

"'Prison Marriage for Coxton Cannibal'?" she said.

Pete jumped. "What?"

"The news article." She read it out again. "The world never stops surprising me. Generally in terrible ways."

"Oh. Yes." Pete gestured at the photographs he was accumulating. "And these are all his visitors. His real name's Victor Tyler. Twenty-five years ago he abducted a little girl. Mary Fisher?"

"I remember her," Amanda said.

They had been roughly the same age. While Amanda couldn't picture the girl's face, her mind immediately associated the name with scary stories and grainy images in old newspapers. *Twenty-five years.* Hard to believe it had been that long, and how quickly people faded away into the past and were forgotten by the world.

"She'd probably have been married by now, maybe with a family," Amanda said. "Doesn't seem right, does it?"

"No." Pete took another photograph from the printer and peered at the screen for a second. "Tyler got married fifteen years ago. Louise Dixon. Unbelievably, they're still together. They've never spent a night together, of course. But you know how it can be sometimes. The allure men like this can have."

Amanda nodded to herself. Criminals, even the worst of them, often weren't short of correspondents in the outside world. For a certain type of woman, they were like catnip. *He didn't do it,* they'd convince themselves. Or else that he'd changed—or if not, that they'd be the one to redeem him. Maybe some of them even liked the danger. It had never made the slightest bit of sense to her, but it was true.

Pete wrote on the back of the photo, then put it to one side and reached for another.

"And Carter is friends with this guy?" she said.

"Carter was his best man."

"Well, that must have been quite a lovely ceremony. Who married them? Satan himself?"

But Pete didn't answer. Rather than looking at the screen, he was focused entirely on the photograph he'd just picked up. Another of Tyler's visitors, she assumed, except this one had caught his attention completely.

"Who's that?"

"Norman Collins." Pete looked up at her. "I know him."

"Tell me."

Pete ran through the basics. Norman Collins was a local man who had been questioned during the investigation twenty years ago, not because of any concrete evidence against him, but because of his behavior. From Pete's description, he sounded like one of those creepy fuckers who sometimes insinuated themselves into ongoing investigations. You were trained to watch out for them. The ones who hung around at the back of press conferences and funerals. The ones who seemed to be eavesdropping or asking too many questions. The ones who appeared too interested or just felt *off* in some way. Because, while it could simply be sick or ghoulish behavior, it was also the way killers sometimes acted.

But not Collins, apparently.

"We had nothing on him," Pete said. "Less than nothing, in fact. He had solid alibis for all the abductions. No connection to the kids or the families. No sheet to him at all. In the end, he was just a footnote in the case."

"And yet you remember him."

Pete stared at the photograph again.

"I never liked him," he said.

It was likely nothing, and Amanda didn't want to get her hopes up, but while you had to be methodical and sensible, there was also something to be said for gut instinct. If Pete remembered this man, there must have been something to cause that.

"And now he turns up again," she said. "Got an address?"

Pete tapped on his keyboard.

"Yeah. He still lives in the same place as before."

"Okay. Go and have the conversation. It's probably nothing, but let's find out why he was visiting Victor Tyler."

Pete stared at the screen for a moment longer, then nodded and stood up.

Amanda walked back across the room. DS Stephanie Johnson caught her before she could reach her own desk.

"Ma'am?"

"Please don't call me that, Steph. It makes me sound like someone's grandmother. Anything from the door-to-doors yet?"

"Nothing so far. But you wanted to know if anything had come in from concerned parents? Reports of prowlers—things like that?"

Amanda nodded. Neil's mother had missed that at first, and Amanda didn't want them to repeat the mistake.

"We had one come in early hours this morning," Steph said. "A man called us saying somebody had been outside the house, talking to his son."

Amanda reached across Steph's desk and turned the screen around so that she could read the details. The boy in question was seven. Rose Terrace School.

A man outside the front door, supposedly speaking to him. But the report also mentioned the boy had been behaving strangely, and reading between the lines it was clear the attending officers hadn't been sure the account was genuine.

She might have words with them about that.

Amanda stepped back, then walked across the room, glancing around angrily. She spotted DS John Dyson. He would do—the lazy bastard was sitting behind a pile of paperwork and messing around on his cell phone. When she walked over and clicked her fingers in front of his face, he actually dropped it into his lap.

"Come with me," she told him.

TWENTY-SIX

It was a ten-minute drive to the house of Mrs. Shearing, the woman who had sold me our new home.

I parked outside a detached two-story house with a peaked roof and a large paved driveway, gated off from the pavement by metal railings with a black mailbox on a post outside. This was a much more prestigious area of Featherbank than the one where Jake and I now lived, in the house that Mrs. Shearing had owned and rented out for years.

Most recently, presumably, to Dominic Barnett.

I reached through the railings of the gate and undid the clasp there. As I pushed the gate open, a dog began barking furiously inside the house, and the noise intensified as I reached the front door, pressed the buzzer, and waited. Mrs. Shearing opened it on the second ring, but kept the chain on, peering out through the gap. The dog was behind her: a small Yorkshire terrier yapping angrily at me. Its fur was tipped with gray and it looked almost as old and fragile as she did.

"Yes?"

"Hello," I said. "I don't know if you remember me, Mrs. Shearing. My name's Tom Kennedy. I bought your house off you a few weeks ago? We met a couple of times when I came to view it. My son and I."

"Oh, yes. Of course. Shoo, Morris. Get back." The latter was to the dog. She brushed down her dress and turned back to me. "I'm sorry, he's very excitable. What can I do for you?"

"It's about the house. I was wondering if I could talk to you about one of the previous tenants?"

"I see."

She looked a little awkward at that, as though she had a good inkling of which one I meant and would rather not. I decided to wait her out. After a few seconds of silence, civility got the better of any reservations she had, and she undid the chain.

"I see," she said again. "Then you'd better come in."

Inside, she seemed flustered, fussing at her clothes and hair, and apologizing for the state of the place. For the latter, there was certainly no need; the house was palatial and immaculate, the reception area alone the size of my living room, with a broad wooden staircase winding up to the floor above. I followed Mrs. Shearing into a cozy sitting room, with Morris cantering more enthusiastically around my ankles. Two couches and a chair were arranged around an open fire, the grate empty and spotless, and there were cabinets along one wall, with carefully spaced crystal-ware visible behind the glass panels. Paintings on the walls showed countryside and hunting scenes. The window at the front of the house was covered with plush red curtains, closed against the street.

"You have a lovely house," I said.

"Thank you. It's too big for me, really, especially after the children moved out and Derek passed, bless him. But I'm too old to move now. A girl comes in every few days to clean it. An awful luxury, but what else can I do? Please—have a seat."

"Thank you."

"Can I get you some tea? Coffee?"

"No, I'm fine."

I sat down. The couch was rigid and hard.

"How are you settling in?" she asked.

"We're doing okay."

"That's wonderful to know." She smiled fondly. "I grew up in that house, you know, and I always wanted it to go to someone nice in the end. A decent family. Your son —Jake, if I remember correctly? How is he?"

"He's just started school."

"Rose Terrace?"

"Yes."

That smile again. "It's a very good school. I went there when I was a child."

"Are your handprints on the wall?"

"They *are*." She nodded proudly. "One red, one blue."

"That's nice. You said you grew up on Garholt Street?"

"Yes. After my parents died, Derek and I kept it on as an investment. It was my husband's idea, but I didn't take much persuading. I've always been fond of it. Such *memories* there, you see?"

"Of course." I thought of the man who had called

around, attempting to do the math. He had been considerably younger than Mrs. Shearing, but it wasn't impossible. "Did you have a younger brother, at all?"

"No, I was an only child. Perhaps that's why I've always had such affection for the house. It was mine, you see? All mine. I loved it." She pulled a face. "When I was growing up, my friends were a little scared by it."

"Why scared?"

"Oh, it's just that kind of house, I think. It looks a little strange, doesn't it?"

"I suppose so." Karen had said much the same to me yesterday. I repeated what I'd said to her, even though, frankly, it was beginning to sound hollow. "It has character."

"Exactly!" Mrs. Shearing seemed pleased. "That's *exactly* what I always thought too. And that's why I'm glad it's in safe hands again now."

I swallowed that down, because the house didn't feel remotely safe to me. But, as I'd suspected, whoever the man was who'd come by, he had been lying about growing up there. I was also struck by her phrasing. Safe hands again *now*. She had wanted it to go to someone nice *in the end*.

"Was it not in safe hands before?"

She looked uncomfortable again.

"Not especially, no. Let's just say that I haven't been blessed with the best of tenants in the past. But then, it's so hard to tell, isn't it? People can seem perfectly pleasant when you meet them. And I never had any real reason to complain. They paid their rent on time. They looked after the property well enough . . ."

She trailed off, as though she didn't know how to explain what the real problems had been and would rather leave it. While she had that luxury, I didn't.

"But?"

"Oh, I don't know. I never had anything concrete I could use against them, or else I wouldn't have hesitated. Just *suspicions*. That perhaps there were other people staying there from time to time."

"That they were renting out rooms?"

"Yes. And that *unsavory* things might sometimes be going on." She pulled a face. "The house often smelled funny when I stopped by—but, of course, you're not allowed to do that these days without an appointment. Can you believe that? An appointment to enter your own property. *Advance warning,* more like it. The only time I ever turned up unannounced, he wouldn't let me in."

"This would be Dominic Barnett?"

She hesitated.

"Yes. Him. Although the one before was no better. I think I've just had a run of very bad luck with that house."

One you've passed on to me.

"You do know what happened to Dominic Barnett?" I said.

"Yes, of course."

She looked down at her hands, resting neatly and delicately in her lap, and was silent for a moment.

"Which was terrible, obviously. Not a fate I would wish on anyone. But from what I heard afterward, he did move in those kinds of circles."

"Drugs," I said bluntly.

Another moment of silence. Then she sighed, as though we were talking about aspects of the world that were wholly alien to her.

"There was never any evidence he was selling *them* from my property. But yes. It was a very sad business. And I suppose I could have searched for another tenant after he died, but I'm old now, and I decided not to. I thought it was time to sell it and draw a line. That way I could give my old house a new chance with someone else. Someone who would make a better go of it than I had recently."

"Jake and me."

"Yes!" She brightened at the thought. "You and your lovely little boy! I had better offers, but money doesn't matter to me these days, and the two of you seemed *right*. I liked to think of my old house going to a young family, so that there'd be another small child playing there again. I wanted to feel it might end up full of light and love again. Full of *color,* like it was when I was a little girl. I'm so pleased to hear that both of you are happy there."

I leaned back.

Jake and I *weren't* happy there, of course, and a part of me was very angry with Mrs. Shearing. It felt like the history of the house was something she should really have told me at the time. But she also seemed genuinely pleased, as though she thought she really had done a good thing, and I could understand her motivation for choosing me and Jake to sell the property to, instead of . . .

And then I frowned.

"You said you had better offers on the house?"

"Oh, yes—very much so, actually. One man was prepared to pay far more than the asking price." She wrinkled her nose and shook her head. "But I didn't like him at all. He reminded me a little of the others. He was very persistent, as well, which put me off even more. I dislike being pestered."

I leaned forward again.

Someone had been prepared to offer way over the asking price for the house, and Mrs. Shearing had refused him. He had been persistent and pushy. There had been something *off* about him.

"This man," I said carefully. "What did he look like? Was he quite short? Gray hair round here?"

I gestured to my head, but she was already nodding.

"That's him, yes. Always *impeccably dressed.*"

And she pulled another face, as though she had been no more fooled by that veneer of respectability than I had.

"Mr. Collins," she said. "Norman Collins."

TWENTY-SEVEN

Back home, I parked and stared down the driveway.

I was thinking—or trying to, at least. It felt like facts and ideas and explanations were all whirling in my head like birds, slow enough to glimpse but too swift to catch.

The man who had been snooping around here was called Norman Collins. Despite his claims, he had not grown up in this house, and yet for some reason he had been prepared to pay well over the asking price to purchase it. Which meant the property obviously meant something to him.

But what?

I stared down the driveway at the garage.

That was where Collins had been skulking when I first spotted him. The garage, filled with the debris removed from the house before I moved in, some of which had presumably belonged to Dominic Barnett. Had it been Collins at the door last night, trying to persuade Jake to open it? If so, maybe it wasn't that Jake himself had been in danger, just that Collins had wanted something.

The key to the garage, perhaps.

But thought could only take me so far. I got out of the car and headed to the garage, unlocking it and then pulling one of the doors and wedging it open with the can of paint from yesterday.

I stepped inside.

All the junk remained, of course: the old furniture; the dirty mattress; the haphazard piles of damp cardboard boxes in the center. Looking down to my right, the spider was still spanning its thick web, surrounded now by a few more remnants than before. Butterflies, presumably, chewed into small, pale knots of string.

I glanced around. One of the butterflies remained perched delicately on the window. Another was resting on the side of the box of Christmas decorations, its wings lifting and lowering gently. They reminded me of Jake's picture, along with the fact that he couldn't possibly have seen them in here. But that was a mystery I couldn't solve for now.

What about you, Norman?

What were you *looking for in here?*

I scraped some dry leaves away with my foot to clear a space, then took the box of decorations down and began sifting through it.

It took half an hour to work my way through all the cardboard boxes, emptying each in turn and spreading the contents around. While I was kneeling down among it all, the stone floor of the garage felt cold, as though the knees of my jeans were gathering ovals of damp.

The garage door rattled behind me, and I turned around quickly, startled by the noise. But the driveway was sunlit and empty. Just the warm breeze, knocking the door against the can of paint.

I turned back to what I'd found.

Which was nothing. The boxes all contained the kind of random debris you had no immediate use for but were still unwilling to throw away. There were the decorations, of course; ropes of tinsel were strewn around me now, their colors dulled and lifeless with age. There were magazines and newspapers, with nothing obvious to unite the dates and editions. Clothes that had been folded and stored away and smelled of mold. Dusty old extension cords. None of it looked to have been deliberately hidden so much as casually packed away and forgotten about.

I fought down the frustration. There were no answers here.

My investigation had disturbed several more of the butterflies, though. Five or six of them were crawling over the debris I'd unpacked, their antennae twitching, while another two were fluttering against the window. I watched as one on the tinsel lifted up into the air, then flickered past me, heading for the open door, before the stupid thing looped back in again and landed on the floor in front of me, on one of the bricks there.

I watched it for a moment, once again admiring the rich, distinctive colors on its wings. It crawled steadily across the surface of the bricks, and then disappeared down into a crack between them.

I stared at the floor.

A large section of the garage floor in front of me was made up of haphazardly arranged house bricks, and it took me a second to recognize what I must be looking at. An old mechanic's pit, where someone could lie down underneath a car to work on it. It had been filled in with bricks to approximate a flat surface.

Tentatively, I lifted up the one the butterfly had been on. It came out of the floor covered in dust and old webbing, the butterfly clinging obstinately to one side.

In the hole the brick had left, I could see the top of what appeared to be another cardboard box below.

The garage door banged again behind me.

Jesus.

This time I stood up and walked back out onto the driveway to check. There was nobody in sight, but in the last few minutes the sun had disappeared behind a cloud and the world felt darker and colder. The breeze had picked up. Looking down, I saw that I was still holding the brick, and that my hand was trembling slightly.

Back in the garage, I put the brick to one side, and then began to remove more from the pit, gradually revealing the box hidden underneath. It was the same size as the others, but had been sealed across the top with parcel tape. I took out my keys and selected the one with the sharpest tip, my heart humming.

Is this what you were looking for, Norman?

I drew the point across the center of the tape, then dug my fingers in to pull the seams apart. They came away at each end with a crackling sound. Then I peered inside.

Immediately I sat back on my heels, either unable or unwilling to comprehend what I had seen. My thoughts went back to what Jake had said last night after he'd been talking to himself in the living room. *I want to scare you.* That was when I'd assumed the imaginary little girl had come back into our lives.

A car door slammed. I glanced behind me and saw that a vehicle was parked at the end of my driveway, and that a man and a woman were walking toward me.

It wasn't her, my son had told me.

It was the boy in the floor.

"Mr. Kennedy?" the woman called.

Instead of answering her, I turned my attention back to the box in front of me.

To the bones inside.

To the small skull that was staring up at me.

And to the beautifully colored butterfly that had landed and rested there, its wings moving gently, like the heartbeat of a sleeping child.

TWENTY-EIGHT

Back in the day, Pete had encountered Norman Collins on several occasions, but he had never had cause to visit the man's home. He knew of it, though: it had once belonged to Collins's parents, and Collins had never moved out. Following his father's death, he had lived there alone with his mother for a number of years, and then continued to do so after she died.

There was nothing untoward about that, of course, but the idea still made Pete feel a little queasy. Children were supposed to grow up, move out, and fashion their own lives; to do otherwise suggested some kind of unhealthy dependency or deficiency. Perhaps it was simply because Pete had met Collins. He remembered him as soft and doughy, and always sweating, as though there were something rotten inside him that was constantly seeping out. He was the kind of man who it was easy to imagine might have kept his mother's bedroom carefully preserved over the years, or taken to sleeping in her bed.

And yet, as much as he'd raised Pete's hackles, Norman Collins had not been Frank Carter's accomplice.

There was some consolation to be had there. Whatever Collins's involvement right now, Pete hadn't missed him at the time. While the man had never officially been a suspect, he had been very much *suspected*. His alibis had checked out, though. If someone really had been helping Carter, it was physically impossible for it to have been Norman Collins.

So what had he been doing at the prison?

Maybe nothing. And yet Carter had to have received communication from the outside world somehow, and as Pete parked outside Collins's house, he felt a small thrill inside him. Better not to hope too much, of course. But he still had the sense that they were on the right track here, even if it wasn't clear right now where it was leading.

He approached the house. The small front garden was untended and overgrown, filled with sweeping whorls of grass that had collapsed down upon themselves. A bush close to the house was so thick that he had to turn sideways and scrape past to reach the front door. He knocked. The wood beneath his knuckles felt weak and flimsy, half eaten away. The front of the house had been painted white at some point, but so much had flaked away since that it reminded Pete of an old lady's face plastered with cracked makeup.

He was about to knock again when he heard movement on the other side of the door. It opened, but only to the limit of a chain. There had been no sound of it being applied, which meant Collins liked to keep his property nice and secure, even when he was home.

"Yes?"

Norman Collins didn't recognize Pete, but Pete remembered him well enough. Twenty years had barely changed him, beyond his monk's hair having grown bright white. The top of his head was mottled and red, like something angry that needed to be burst. And even though he was presumably relaxing at home, he was dressed almost absurdly formally, in a dapper little suit and waistcoat.

Pete held out his identification.

"Hello, Mr. Collins. I'm DI Peter Willis. You might not remember me, but we met a few times years ago?"

Collins's gaze flicked from the identification to Pete's face, and then his expression became tight and tense. He remembered, all right.

"Oh, yes. Of course."

Pete put the ID away.

"Can I come in for a chat? I'll try not to take up too much of your time."

Collins hesitated, glancing behind him into the shadowy depths of the house. Pete could already see beads of sweat appearing on the man's forehead.

"It's not the most convenient time. What is it regarding?"

"I'd prefer to talk inside, Mr. Collins."

He waited. Collins was a stuffy little man, and Pete was confident he wouldn't want the silence to become awkward. After a few seconds, Collins relented.

"Very well."

The door closed, and then opened fully this time. Pete stepped into a drab square of hallway, with stairs leading straight up ahead to a misty landing. The air smelled old and musty, but with a trace of something sweet to it. It reminded him of the ancient school desks from his childhood, where you'd open the top and smell wood and old bubble gum.

"How can I help you, DI Willis?"

They were still standing at the bottom of the stairs, far too cramped for Pete's liking. This close, he could smell Collins, sweating beneath his suit. He gestured to the open door to what was obviously the living room.

"Perhaps we can go through there?"

Again Collins hesitated. Pete frowned.

What are you hiding, Norman?

"Of course," Collins said. "This way, please."

He led Pete into the living room. Pete was expecting to be met with squalor, but the room appeared tidy and clean, and the furniture was newer and less old-fashioned than he would have imagined. There was a large plasma screen attached to one wall, while the others were covered with framed artwork and small glass display cases.

Collins stopped in the middle of the room, and then stood rigid, with his hands clasped in front of him like a butler. Something about his oddly formal manner made the hairs on the back of Pete's neck stand up.

"Are you . . . all right, Mr. Collins?"

"Oh, yes." Collins nodded curtly. "May I ask again what this is regarding?"

"A little over two months ago, you went to see an inmate named Victor Tyler in HMP Whitrow."

"That I did."

"And what was the purpose of that visit?"

"To talk to him. The same purpose as my other visits."

"You've visited him before?"

"Indeed. Several times."

Collins was still standing motionless, as if he'd been posed. Still smiling politely.

"Can I ask what you discussed with Victor Tyler?"

"Well—his crime, of course."

"The little girl he killed?"

Collins nodded. "Mary Fisher."

"Yes, I know her name."

A ghoul. That was what Collins had always struck Pete as—a strange little man, obsessed with the kind of darkness that others instinctively shied away from. Collins was still standing there smiling, as though waiting patiently for this business to be concluded and for Pete to leave, but the smile was all wrong. Collins was nervous, Pete thought. Hiding something. And Pete was aware that he had grown still himself—that there was an uncomfortable lack of movement in the room—so he walked over to one wall, idly examining some of the pictures and items that Collins had framed and mounted there.

The drawings were strange. Up close, it became apparent how childlike many of them were. His gaze moved here and there, over stick figures, amateurish watercolors, and then his attention was drawn to something more unusual. A red plastic devil mask. It was the kind of item you'd find in a cheap fancy dress shop, but for some reason Collins had encased it in a thin rectangle of glass and hung it on his wall.

"A collector's item, that."

Collins was suddenly beside him. Pete resisted the urge to shout, but couldn't stop himself from taking a step away.

"A collector's item?"

"Indeed." Collins nodded. "It was worn by a fairly notorious murderer during the crimes he committed. It cost a small fortune to acquire, but it's a handsome piece, and the source and paperwork are impeccable." Collins turned quickly to look at Pete. "All completely legal and aboveboard, I assure you. Was there anything else I could help you with?"

Pete shook his head, trying to make sense of what Collins had just said. Then he looked at some of the other items on the wall. It wasn't just pictures, he realized. Several of the frames contained notes and letters. Some were clearly official documents and reports, while others were handwritten, scrawled on cheap notepaper.

He gestured at the wall, feeling slightly helpless.

"And . . . these?"

"*Correspondence,*" Collins said happily. "Some personal, some acquired. Forms and paperwork from cases, as well."

Pete stepped away again, this time moving all the way back to the middle of the room. And then he turned, looking this way and that. As he understood what he was seeing, the feeling of unease deepened, folding over inside him, drawing the heat away from his skin.

Drawings, mementos, correspondence.

Artifacts of death and murder.

He had been aware before now that there were people

in the world who were driven to acquire such macabre things, and that there were even thriving online market-places dedicated to the activity. But he had never before stood in the heart of such a collection. The room around him seemed to be throbbing with menace, not least because this was clearly not simply a collection, but a celebration. There was *reverence* in the way these things had been put on display.

He looked at Norman Collins, who remained standing by the wall. The smile had disappeared from the man's face now, his expression replaced by something altogether more alien and reptilian. Collins had not wanted to let Pete in, and he had clearly hoped to conclude the conversation without Pete noticing his pictures and ornaments. But there was a sneer of pride on his face now—a look that said he knew how abhorrent Pete must find his collection, and that a part of him relished it. That he was even *above* Pete in some way.

All completely legal and aboveboard, I assure you.

And so Pete simply stood there for a moment, not knowing what to do, unsure if he even *could* do anything. Then his cell phone rang, jolting him. He took it out—Amanda—and then turned away, speaking quietly as he pressed the phone hard to his ear.

"Willis here."

"Pete? Where are you?"

"I'm where I said I would be." He noticed the urgency in her voice. "Where are you?"

"I'm at a house on Garholt Street. We've got a second body."

"A second?"

"Yes. But these remains are much older—it looks like they've been hidden for a long time."

Pete tried to take in what he was hearing.

"The house here was sold recently." Amanda sounded a little breathless, as though she were still trying to process all this too. "The new owner found the body in a box in the garage. He also made a report that someone might have attempted to abduct his son last night. And your man Norman Collins—it looks like he's been creeping at the property. Owner puts him at the scene. I think Collins knew the body was there."

Pete turned around quickly then—suddenly aware of a presence. Collins had magicked himself closer once again. He was standing right next to Pete now, his face near enough that Pete could see the pores of his skin and the blankness in his eyes. The air was singing with menace.

"Is there anything else, DI Willis?" Collins whispered.

Pete took a step away, his heart beating hard.

"Bring him in," Amanda said.

TWENTY-NINE

I parked a road away from Jake's school, thinking that it should have been reassuring to have a policeman in the car with me.

I'd been frustrated that the officers who called around that morning hadn't taken my nighttime visitor and the attempted abduction of my son as seriously as they should. That had certainly changed now, but there was nothing remotely comforting about it. It meant all this was actually happening. It meant that the danger to Jake was real.

DS Dyson looked up.

"We're here?"

"It's just round the corner."

He slipped his cell into his suit trousers pocket. Dyson was in his fifties, but had spent the journey from the police station silently absorbed with something on his phone, like some kind of teenager.

"Okay," he said. "I want you to behave exactly as you usually would. Pick your son up. Chat with the other parents, or whatever it is you normally do. Take your time. I'll have you in sight throughout, and I'll just be keeping an eye on the other people present."

I tapped the steering wheel. "DI Beck told me you'd already arrested the man responsible."

"Sure." Dyson shrugged, and from his manner, it was clear that he was simply following an order and going through the motions. "It's just a precaution."

A *precaution*.

That was the same word DI Amanda Beck had used at the police station. Things had moved quickly after the police arrived at my house and I'd shown them what I'd found. In the intervening time, Norman Collins had been arrested, which brought it home to me all too clearly what could have happened to Jake last night. But with Collins in custody, my son should have been safe.

So why the escort?

Just a precaution.

It hadn't reassured me at the police station, and it didn't now either. The police were a capable, powerful resource to have behind me, and yet it still felt as if Jake wouldn't be safe until he was right next to *me*. Someplace where *I* could look after him.

Dyson melted away behind me as I walked to the school, and it was surreal to think I was being covertly shadowed by a police officer. But then, the whole day had been off-kilter and unworldly. With events moving so swiftly, I still hadn't processed the fact that I'd found human remains, most likely those of a child, on my property. The reality of that hadn't hit me yet. I'd given my statement at the police station dispassionately, and it would be typed up and waiting for me to sign after I picked up Jake. I still had no idea what was going to happen after that.

Just behave normally, Dyson had told me, which was a completely impossible instruction under the circumstances. But when I reached the playground, I saw Karen leaning against the railings, hands stuffed into the pockets of her big coat, and figured that talking to her was about as normal as anything else. I walked in and leaned against the railings beside her.

"Hello there," she said. "How's tricks?"

"Tricky."

"Ha-ha." Then she looked at me properly. "Although that's not actually a joke, is it, by the look of things. Bad day?"

I breathed out slowly. The police hadn't explicitly told me I couldn't talk to anyone about the day's events, but I suspected it would be wise not to, yet. Aside from anything else, I had absolutely no idea where to begin.

"You could say that. It's been a very complicated twenty-four hours. I'll tell you about it properly some time."

"Well, I'll look forward to that. I hope you're okay, though. No offense, but you look like shit." She thought about it. "Although that probably *is* quite offensive, isn't it? Sorry. I always say the wrong thing. Bad habit."

"It's fine, I just didn't get much sleep last night."

"Your son's imaginary friends keeping you up?"

I actually laughed.

"That's closer to the truth than you know."

The boy in the floor.

I thought of the rusty-looking bones, and the hollow-eyed skull with its crest of jagged cracks. The beautiful colors of the butterflies Jake couldn't have seen, but had somehow drawn. And as much as I wanted him out here right now, I was also slightly unnerved by the prospect. Unnerved by *him*. My sensitive son, with his sleepwalking and his imaginary friends, and the way he talked to people who weren't there, who told him frightening rhymes and tried to scare him.

They scared me too.

The door opened. Mrs. Shelley appeared and then began looking at the parents and calling children's names back over her shoulder. Her gaze drifted across Karen and me.

"Adam," she said, and then moved immediately on to a different boy.

"Uh-oh," Karen said. "Looks like you're on the naughty step again."

"The day I've had, that really wouldn't surprise me."

"It can feel like you're a child again yourself, can't it? The way they talk to you sometimes."

I nodded. Although I wasn't sure I was in the mood to put up with it today.

"Anyway, take care of yourself," Karen said, as Adam reached us.

"I will."

I watched them go, then waited while the rest of the children were released. At least Dyson was getting a good chance to take *precautions,* I supposed—and the thought made me scan the faces in the playground myself. Except what was the point? A few of the parents were familiar, but I hadn't been here long enough to recognize more than a handful. To them I probably looked like a suspicious character myself.

When there was only Jake left, Mrs. Shelley beckoned me over. Jake emerged at her side, once again staring down at the ground. He looked so vulnerable that I wanted to rescue him—just scoop him up and take him somewhere safe. I felt a burst of love for him. Maybe he *was* too fragile to be ordinary, to fit in and be accepted. But after everything that had happened, so fucking what?

"Trouble again?" I said.

"I'm afraid so." Mrs. Shelley smiled sadly. "Jake was put on red today. He had to go to see Miss Wallace, didn't you, Jake?"

Jake nodded miserably.

"What happened?" I said.

"He hit another boy in the class."

"Oh."

"Owen started it." Jake sounded as though he was about to cry. "He was trying to take my Packet of Special Things. I didn't mean to hit him."

"Yes, well." Mrs. Shelley folded her arms and looked at me pointedly. "I'm not *entirely sure* that's an appropriate thing for a child your age to be bringing into school in the first place."

I had no idea what to say. Social convention dictated that I side with the grown-up here, which meant that I should tell Jake that hitting was bad, and that maybe his teacher was right about the Packet. But I couldn't. This situation suddenly seemed so laughably trivial. The stupid fucking traffic light system. The terror of Miss Wallace. And most of all, the idea of telling Jake off because some little shit had messed with him and, most likely, gotten exactly what he deserved.

I looked at my son, standing there so timidly, probably expecting me to tell him off, when what I actually wanted to say to him was: *Well done.*

I never had the courage to do that at your age.

I hope you hit him hard.

And yet social convention won out.

"I'll talk to him," I said.

"Good. Because it's not been a fantastic start, has it, Jake?"

Mrs. Shelley ruffled his hair, and social convention lost.

"Don't touch my son," I said.

"I'm sorry?"

She moved her hand as though Jake were electric. There was some satisfaction in that, even though my words had come out without any thought and I wasn't remotely sure what I was going to say next.

"Just that," I said. "You can't put him on your traffic light system and then pretend to be nice. To be honest, I think it's a pretty terrible thing to do to any child, never mind one who's obviously having problems right now."

"What problems?" She was flustered. "If there are problems, then we can talk about that."

I knew it was stupid to be so confrontational, but I still felt a small degree of pleasure in standing up for my son. I looked at Jake again, who was staring at me curiously now, as though he wasn't sure what to make of me. I smiled at him. I was glad he'd stood up for himself. Glad that he'd made an impact on the world.

I looked back at Mrs. Shelley.

"I *will* talk to him," I said. "Because hitting is wrong.

So he and I will have a long discussion about better ways to stand up to bullies."

"Well . . . that's good to hear."

"Fine. Got everything, mate?"

Jake nodded.

"Good," I said. "Because I don't think we can go home tonight."

"Why not?"

Because of the boy in the floor.

But I didn't say that. The strangest thing was, I thought he knew the answer to his own question already.

"Come on," I said gently.

THE WHISPER MAN | 207

wanted him for more than that. And no matter how

THIRTY

They've found him, Pete thought.

After all this time. They've found Tony.

Sitting in his car, he watched the CSI officers entering Norman Collins's property. At the moment it was the only activity on the street. Despite the gathering police presence, the media had yet to arrive, and whatever neighbors were home were staying out of view for now. One of the CSI team stood on the front step, put his hands in the small of his back, and stretched.

Cuffed and ensconced in the backseat, Collins was watching the activity too.

"You have no authority to do this," Collins said blankly.

"Be quiet, Norman."

In the confines of the car, Pete couldn't avoid smelling the man, but he had no intention of talking to him. As the situation was still developing, he had arrested Collins on suspicion of receipt of stolen goods in the first instance, simply because—given the nature of some of the items in the man's collection—it was a charge they could likely make stick, and also one that gave them authority to search the man's home. But, of course, they wanted him for more than that. And no matter how many questions he had, Pete wasn't about to jeopardize the investigation by interviewing Collins here and now. It had to be done at the department. Recorded and watertight.

"They won't find anything," Collins said.

Pete ignored him. Because, of course, they already had, and Collins appeared to be implicated in that. An older set of remains had been discovered. Collins had always been obsessed with Carter and his crimes; he had visited Frank Carter's friend in prison; he had been stalking the house where the second body had been found. Collins *had* known the body was there—Pete was certain of it. But more importantly, while official identification would come in time, he was also sure that the remains belonged to Tony Smith.

After twenty years, you've been found.

All else aside, the development should have brought a sense of relief and closure, because he had been searching for the boy for so long. But it didn't. He couldn't stop thinking of all those weekend searches, combing through hedgerows and woodlands many miles from here, when the whole time Tony had been lying far closer to home than anyone imagined.

Which meant there must have been something Pete had missed twenty years ago.

He looked down at the tablet on his lap.

God, he wanted a drink right now—and wasn't it strange how that worked? People often thought of alcohol as a buffer against the horrors of the world. But Tony Smith's body had been found, and it was more than possible that the man responsible for Neil Spencer's murder was in custody, sitting behind him right now, and yet the urge to drink was stronger than ever. There were always so many reasons to drink, though. Only ever one real reason not to.

You can drink later. As much as you want.

He accepted that he would. Whatever works—it was that simple. In a war, you used any weapon at hand to win an individual battle, and then you regrouped and fought the next one. And the next. And all the ones that followed.

Whatever works.

"I've done *nothing wrong*," Collins insisted.

"Shut up."

Pete clicked on the tablet. There was no avoiding this: he needed to figure out what he had missed all those years ago and why, and the house on Garholt Street where Tony's remains had been found was the place to start.

He scanned through the details. Until recently the house had been owned by a woman named Anne Shearing. She had inherited it from her parents, but hadn't lived in it for decades, instead renting it out over the years to numerous individuals.

There was a long list of those on record, but Pete presumed he could discount occupants from before 1997, when Frank Carter had committed his murders. The tenant at that time had been a man named Julian Simpson. Simpson had been renting the property for four years beforehand, and his residency continued until 2008. Opening a new tab on-screen, Pete ran a search and discovered Simpson had died of cancer that year, at the age of seventy. He clicked back. The house's next tenant was a man named Dominic Barnett, who had occupied the house until earlier this year.

Dominic Barnett.

Pete frowned. The name rang a bell. He ran another search, and the details came back to him, even though he hadn't worked the case himself. Barnett had been a minor underworld figure involved in drugs and extortion, known to police but considered small fry in the grand scheme of things. There were no convictions on file for the last ten years—but, of course, that didn't mean he'd gone straight, and nobody had been remotely surprised when he turned up dead. The murder weapon—a hammer—had been recovered with partial prints, but there had been no match on the database. Subsequent inquiries had failed to turn up a credible suspect. But the public, at least, had been reassured. Despite the lack of an arrest, the police believed it to be an isolated, targeted incident, and anybody reading between the lines of that could probably have intuited what lay behind it.

Live by the sword, die by the sword.

To the extent that Pete had paid attention, he had assumed the same. But he wondered about it now. Drugs remained the most likely motive for the murder, but Barnett had lived in a house where human remains had been kept hidden, and it seemed impossible that he would have been unaware of it. Did that suggest a different motive?

He looked up and watched Norman Collins in the

rearview mirror for a moment. Collins was staring blankly out of the window at his house.

There were three men to think about: Julian Simpson and Dominic Barnett, who had both lived at the property, and Norman, who seemed to be aware of what had been stored there. What was the connection between the three? What had happened twenty years ago, and in the time since?

Pete loaded up a map of Featherbank.

Garholt Street was on a natural route between the scene of Tony Smith's abduction and the direction in which Frank Carter had fled. At the time, forensic evidence had established Tony *had* been in the killer's vehicle—but if Carter had somehow been tipped off that his house was being searched, he could have dropped the boy's body there before going on the run. Julian Simpson had been living there at the time.

Pete didn't need to consult the case file to know that Simpson hadn't come up in the investigation at the time. All of Carter's known acquaintances had been investigated carefully. Simpson's name had not been among them.

And yet.

Simpson would have been around fifty at the time of the abductions, and that age would match the conflicting description given in one of the witness statements. Perhaps he had been Carter's accomplice. If so, there had to have been some connection between the two men, however oblique, which Pete hadn't discovered.

The sense of failure hit hard.

You should have found him sooner.

Whatever he had or hadn't done, it would still be his fault. He knew he would find a way to twist it around so that the blame rested with him. But the feeling remained.

Worthless.

Useless.

You can drink later.

His phone rang—Amanda again.

"Willis," he answered. "I'm still at Collins's house. I'm on my way back in a minute."

"How's the search going?"

"It's going."

He glanced at the house, knowing that was where his focus needed to be. The priority right now was nailing Collins for his involvement, not working out what Pete himself had and hadn't missed twenty years ago. That dissection could come later.

"Okay," Amanda told him. "I've got the home owner and his son here, and I need someone to help me with them. Sort out accommodation for them for the night. That kind of thing."

Pete frowned to himself. That was grunt work at best, and he knew the implications: Amanda would be the one handling the interview with Norman Collins. But perhaps that was better. *Cleaner.* They didn't want to risk his past history with the man coloring the investigation now. The answers to his questions would come in time, but it didn't need to be him who asked them. He started the engine.

"On my way."

"The guy's called Tom Kennedy," Amanda said. "His

son is Jake. Book Collins in first, and then they're in one of the comfort suites."

For a moment Pete didn't respond. His free hand was on the steering wheel. He stared at it, and noticed it begin to tremble.

"Pete?" Amanda said. "You there?"

"Yes. I'm on my way."

He hung up and tossed the phone onto the passenger seat. But rather than driving away, he turned the engine off and picked up the tablet again. He'd been too lost in the past to think about the present. He hadn't even considered the man who owned the property now.

Failing, as always.

He clicked through to the report, wondering if he'd misheard what Amanda had said. But there it was.

Tom Kennedy.

Finally. A name he recognized.

THIRTY-ONE

"Did they find him, Daddy?" Jake said.

I had been pacing back and forth across the room in the police station, waiting for DI Amanda Beck to bring the statement for me to sign, but my son's words brought me to a halt.

He was sitting on a chair that was far too big for him, kicking his legs slightly, an untouched orange juice box on the table beside him. The latter had been a gift from DS Dyson after we'd arrived. Allegedly there was coffee on its way for me, but we'd been here for twenty minutes now, and it showed about as much sign of imminent arrival as Beck did. Jake and I hadn't really spoken the whole time. I didn't know what to say to him right now, and my pacing had been as much about filling the silence in the room as the space.

Did they find him, Daddy?

I walked over now and knelt down in front of him.

"Yes. They found the man who came to our house."

"That's not who I meant."

The boy in the floor.

I stared at my son for a second, but he looked back

at me without any apparent fear or concern. It was astounding that he could take everything that was happening in stride, as though it were all perfectly normal—as though we were talking about a boy who had been playing hide-and-seek, not human remains that had been in the floor of our garage for God knew how many years, and which it was impossible for him to have known about.

It was something we shouldn't be talking about. Not here. My statement to the police had been honest but incomplete. I hadn't mentioned the drawings of the butterflies or told them about Jake talking to the boy in the floor. I wasn't sure why, beyond the fact that I couldn't make any sense of it myself, and because I wanted to protect my son. That all this was a grown-up's burden to shoulder, not a seven-year-old's.

"Yes, Jake," I said. "That *is* who you meant. Okay? This is serious."

He thought about it.

"Okay."

"We'll talk about the other thing later." I stood up, realizing that what I'd said wasn't quite enough, and that he deserved to know more. "But yes, they found him."

I found him.

"That's good," Jake said. "He was scaring me a little."

"I know."

"Although I don't think he was meaning to." Jake frowned. "I think he was just hurt and lonely, and that was making him a little bit mean. But they've found him, and so he won't be lonely now, will he? He can go home. So he won't be mean anymore."

"It was just your imagination, Jake."

"It wasn't."

"We'll talk about it later. Okay?"

I gave him the serious look I always attempted when I wanted to draw a line under a conversation. It usually had no authority whatsoever, and a minute later one or the other of us would end up shouting, but today he nodded. Then he swiveled on his chair, picked up the juice box, and began drinking it seemingly without a care in the world.

The door opened behind me, and I turned to see DS Dyson entering, carrying two cups of coffee. He held the door open with his back for DI Beck, who marched in past him. She was brandishing papers and looked as tired as I felt: a woman with a million things to do, determined to do each of them herself.

"Mr. Kennedy," she said. "I'm really sorry about your wait. Ah—and this must be Jake."

Still distracted by the juice box, my son ignored her.

"Jake?" I prompted. "Can you say hello, please?"

"Hi."

I turned back to Beck. "It's been a long day."

"I completely understand. This must be very strange for him indeed." She leaned down toward him, pressing her hands against her knees a little awkwardly, as though unsure how to talk to a child. "Have you ever been in a police station before, Jake?"

He shook his head but didn't answer.

"Well." She gave an awkward laugh, then stood up. "First and last time, hopefully. Anyway—Mr. Kennedy. I have your statement here. If you could just read through it, make sure you're happy with the contents, and then sign it. And your drink is here too."

"Thanks."

Dyson passed me the coffee, and I sipped it while I scanned the statement on the table. I'd explained about Norman Collins, what Mrs. Shearing had told me about him and Dominic Barnett, and the man who'd been at the door whispering to Jake last night. All of which had led me to investigate the garage, wondering what Collins might have been looking for. That was why and how I'd found the remains in there.

I glanced at Jake, who was now sucking at the end of his juice box, the liquid rattling at the bottom, and then I signed on the final page.

"I'm afraid you won't be able to go home tonight," Beck said.

"Okay."

"Possibly tomorrow night as well. Of course, we're happy to arrange alternative accommodation for both of you over that period. We have a safe house nearby."

My pen hovered over my signature.

"Why would we need a safe house?"

"You don't," she said quickly. "It's just property we have available for use. But I'll leave my colleague, DI Pete Willis, to talk you through all that. He should be here any moment, and I can leave you in peace. In fact, here he is now."

The door opened again, a new man coming in.

"Pete," Beck said. "This is Tom and Jake Kennedy."

I stared at the man, and everything else in the world seemed to disappear. It had been such a long time, and the years had been kind to him, but while he was much leaner and healthier than I remembered, adults changed far less than children did, and I still recognized him. A jolt of recognition in my heart, followed by a hundred buried memories bursting forth and blooming in my head.

And he knew me too. Of course he did. By now he would have learned my name and had time to prepare himself for this. As he approached me, professional and formal, I imagined nobody else would have noticed the sick expression on his face.

Glass smashing.

My mother screaming.

"Mr. Kennedy," my father said.

which meant it may very well be at the mercy of the evil

THIRTY-TWO

It had been a *very* confusing day, Jake thought.

He was extremely tired, for one thing—that was the fault of the thing that had happened in the night, but he couldn't remember much about that. He'd been half asleep at the time. But then he'd still been very angry at Daddy for what he'd written, and when the police were there, and Daddy had said Mummy was dead as though it were nothing, he'd lost his temper. That wasn't good, but he hadn't been able to help himself.

The anger had faded through the day, though, and that was confusing in itself. But then, sometimes arguments disappeared like mist did first thing in the morning. In the classroom, though, he'd felt lonely and had wanted to hug Daddy a lot more and tell him he was sorry, and to hear Daddy tell him that, actually, he was too.

It had felt like things might be better then.

And then Owen had done what he'd done, and so had Jake, and there had been Miss Wallace's office to face as a result. That actually hadn't been so bad in itself, except for two big reasons. One was that the Packet of Special Things was back in the classroom, which meant it may very well be at the mercy of the evil Owen, which was an unbearable thought. *Can you look at me, please?* Miss Wallace had needed to say it twice, because Jake couldn't take his eyes off the closed office door. And reason number two: he knew Daddy was going to be disappointed and angry with him for getting in trouble again, which meant that things weren't going to get better for a long time. Or maybe *ever,* at this rate.

Perhaps Daddy might even write horrible words down about *him* too.

Jake suspected that he wanted to.

But then, when he got back to the classroom, the Packet appeared to have been left untouched, and the possibility had occurred to him that maybe he should hit people more often. And at pickup time, Daddy hadn't seemed angry with him *at all*. He'd actually argued with Mrs. Shelley! Which was certainly brave, Jake thought. But! More importantly, Daddy had been on his side. Even if he hadn't said it outright, Jake could tell that he was. Even though he hadn't gotten a hug, that actually made things seem as good as if he had.

And now they were in a police station.

That had been fine at first because it was really quite interesting, especially as everybody had been very nice to him, but he quite wanted to leave now. And then the *next* thing had happened—the new policeman coming in—and everything was even *more* confusing now, because of how Daddy was behaving. He'd been fine with the other police people, but he looked pale and scared now, as though this were a classroom for him and the new policeman was someone like Mrs. Shelley.

Come to think of it, the new policeman looked uncomfortable too. When the woman police officer left, carrying the statement Daddy had signed, the door closed, and then the air in the room had felt *very strange* indeed. It was like there was some kind of glue that was holding everybody in place.

Then the new policeman walked slowly over and looked down at him.

"You must be Jake?" he said.

"Yes." This was true. "I am Jake."

The man smiled, but it was an odd one. He had a face that looked like it could be very kind indeed, but the smile right now was troubled. A moment later, he reached out his hand, and so Jake shook it, which was the polite thing to do. The hand was big and warm, and the grip was very gentle.

"I'm pleased to meet you, Jake. You can call me Pete."

"Hello, Pete," Jake said. "It's nice to meet you too. Why can't we go home? One of the other policemen told my daddy that we couldn't."

Pete frowned and knelt down in front of him, then peered into his face as though there might be some kind of secret there. Jake stared back at him to let him know he wasn't hiding anything. *No secrets here, mister.*

"It's very complicated," Pete said. "We have to do some investigation work at your house."

"Because of the boy in the floor?"

"Yes."

But then Pete looked across at Daddy, and Jake remembered that he wasn't supposed to have mentioned that. But honestly, the atmosphere in the room was so funny that it was easy to forget things like that.

"I told him what I found," Daddy said.

"How did you know that it's a boy, though?"

Daddy was just standing there, but he looked caught somehow, as though he wanted to move forward or backward but had forgotten how his body worked. Jake had the uncomfortable feeling that if Daddy *did* remember how to move properly, it would be forward—and quite aggressively too.

"I didn't," Daddy said. "I said *body*. He must have misheard me."

"That's true," Jake added quickly. He didn't want Daddy to hit anybody, especially a policeman, because right now it really looked like he might.

Pete stood up slowly.

"Okay. Well, let's deal with some practicalities. Is it just the two of you?"

"Yes," Daddy said.

"Jake's mother . . . ?"

Daddy still looked angry. "My wife died last year."

"I'm sorry. That must have been very hard for you."

"We're fine."

"I can see that."

So confusing! Jake wanted to shake his head. Now Pete didn't seem able to look at Daddy. But Pete was a policeman, and that meant he was in charge, didn't it?

"We can arrange accommodation for you, but you might not want that. Do you have any family you'd prefer to stay with?"

"No," Daddy said. "Both of my parents are dead."

Pete hesitated.

"Right. I'm very sorry to hear that as well."

"It's okay."

And then Daddy took a step forward. Jake held his breath, but now it only *seemed* like Daddy wanted to hit someone, rather than that he actually would.

"It happened a very long time ago."

"Right." Pete took a deep breath but still didn't look at Daddy. He was just staring at the wall, and Jake thought he suddenly looked a lot older than he had when he'd first come into the room. "In that case, we can arrange somewhere for you to stay in the meantime."

"That would be good, yes."

"And I'm sure you'll need some things. I can come back with you to your house if you like, and you can get some things you both might need. Spare clothes and things."

"You need to be there?"

"Yes. I'm sorry. It's a crime scene. I need to make a note of anything that's removed."

"Okay. That's not ideal, is it?"

"I know." Pete finally looked back at Daddy. "I'm sorry."

Daddy shrugged, his eyes still glittering.

"It is what it is. So let's get it over with, shall we? Jake—you'll need to think about what toys you might want, okay?"

"Okay."

But Jake looked from one of them to the other—Daddy and Pete—and *still* nobody was moving, or seeming like they knew what on earth to do next, and Jake decided that if *he* didn't do something, then none of them would. So he put the empty juice box down on the table with a loud, decisive thud.

"My drawing things, Daddy," he said. "That's all I want."

THIRTY-THREE

Small triumphs on terrible days. You had to cling to them, Amanda thought, as she sat back down in the interview room across from Norman Collins. After the horrors she had seen last night, and the failure she felt at not finding Neil Spencer in time, she was ready for a little blood. And often the small victories were as much as you ever got.

"Sorry about the interruption, Norman," she said. "Let's continue."

"Indeed. Let's bring this to a swift conclusion, shall we?"

"Absolutely." She smiled politely. "Let's do just that."

Collins folded his arms, smirking a little. Which didn't surprise her. She'd understood from the moment she set eyes on him exactly what Pete had meant about there being something *off* about the man. He was the sort of person you instinctively crossed the street to avoid. The exaggerated formality of his attire struck her as being a kind of disguise—an attempt at respectability that failed to hide the unpleasantness beneath. And it was clear from his manner that he felt removed from other people. Superior to them, even.

Twenty minutes into the interview, with an answer to every question she had offered, he'd probably had every reason to feel superior to her. But then Steph had knocked and leaned into the room, and Amanda had signaled a break. Now she reached over, turned the recording equipment back on, and ran through the preliminaries.

Across from her, Collins sighed theatrically to himself. She looked down now at the sheet of paper she'd brought back in with her. It was going to be a pleasure to wipe the smirk off the creepy fucker's face.

First things first, though.

"Mr. Collins," she said. "For clarity, let's quickly go back over some of the ground we've already covered. In July of this year, you visited Victor Tyler in Whitrow prison. What was the purpose of that visit?"

"I have an interest in crime. In certain circles, I am considered an expert. I was interested in talking to Mr. Tyler about his actions. Much the same, I'm sure, as the police have talked to him over the years."

Probably not quite the same, Amanda thought.

"Did your conversation touch on Frank Carter?"

"It did not."

"Are you aware that Tyler is friends with Carter?"

"I was not."

"That seems strange. What with you being such an expert, and all."

"One can't be expected to know everything."

Collins smiled. Amanda was sure he was lying, but the conversation between Collins and Tyler had not been recorded, and she had no way to prove it.

"All right," she said. "Your whereabouts on the afternoon and evening of Sunday the thirtieth of July this year, the evening Neil Spencer was abducted?"

"I've already told you. I was at home for much of the afternoon. Later on, I walked to Town Street and dined in the restaurant there."

"It's good that you recall so clearly."

Collins shrugged. "I am a creature of habit. It was a Sunday. When my mother was alive, we went together. Now I eat alone."

Amanda nodded to herself. The owner of the restaurant had verified this, which meant that Collins appeared to have a solid alibi for the period of time in which Neil Spencer had been abducted. And, while the search of his house was ongoing, officers had so far found nothing to suggest Neil had ever been held there. Collins, she was sure, was neck-deep in whatever was going on here *somehow,* but right now he seemed to be in the clear for the actual abduction of Neil Spencer.

"Thirteen Garholt Street," she said.

"Yes?"

"You attempted to purchase the property."

"Indeed. It was for sale. I have no idea why that's considered a crime."

"I didn't say it was."

"The house was on the market. I've lived where I do for a long time now, and it felt like time to spread my wings a little. Branch out on my own, so to speak."

"And then, when your acquisition was refused, you stalked the property anyway."

Collins shook his head.

"Absolutely not."

"Mr. Kennedy claims you tried to break into his garage."

"He is simply incorrect."

"A garage where the remains of a child have been discovered."

And Amanda had to give Collins credit then. While she had no doubt he was well aware of what had been found, he remembered to at least feign surprise. It wasn't remotely convincing, but it was there.

"That's . . . shocking," he said.

"I'm not sure I believe you, Norman."

"I knew nothing about that." He frowned. "Have you spoken to the seller? Perhaps you should."

"Right now I'm more interested in why *you* were so interested in the property."

"And I've told you: I wasn't. This Mr. . . . Kennedy, was it? He is mistaken. I've been nowhere near his house."

Amanda stared at him, and Collins stared implacably back. One person's word against another's. Even if they could arrange a lineup and Kennedy identified Collins, she wasn't sure that in itself would be enough to justify charges. The fact was that, right now, they couldn't prove he knew about the remains in the garage. And he appeared to be in the clear for the abduction of Neil Spencer. Given some of the items in his collection, they might have him on stolen goods right now, but perhaps not even that

And the smug fucker knew it.

Or thought he did.

Amanda looked down at the sheet of paper Steph had given her—the results of the search on the fingerprints taken from Norman Collins upon his arrival. And even though she was no closer to pinning Neil Spencer on him, she felt a thrill nonetheless. She lived for moments like this. She wished Pete was here to savor it with her. God knew he deserved to feel it too.

"Mr. Collins," she said. "Could you tell me where you were on the evening of Tuesday, April fourth, this year?"

Collins hesitated.

"I'm sorry?"

Amanda waited, still looking at the sheet of paper. That had gotten his attention, at least. Presumably, he'd been anticipating more questions about his activity on the day of Neil Spencer's abduction, which he thought was safe ground to go over. But Amanda knew now that *this* date was an enormous black pit beneath his feet.

"I'm not *sure* I recall," Collins said carefully.

"Let me help you, then. Were you in the vicinity of Hollingbeck Wood?"

"I wouldn't have thought so."

"Well, your fingers were. Was the rest of you?"

"I don't—"

"Your prints were found on the hammer that was used to murder Dominic Barnett there that night."

Amanda looked up, enjoying noticing the sweat bead on Collins's forehead. A fussy, superior man—but one easily thrown off course, when it came to it. It was interesting to watch him going through his options, searching for a way out, and slowly realizing that he was in much more trouble than he'd thought.

"No comment," he said.

Amanda shook her head. It was his right, of course, but the phrase had always rankled with her. *You* don't *have the right to remain silent,* she always wanted to tell people. And right now she wanted Collins to take ownership of what he'd done rather than hiding away. Because there were other lives at stake.

"It's in your interests right now to tell me everything you know, Norman." She rested her forearms on the table and tried to sound more sympathetic than she felt. "And not just *your* interests either. You say you had no involvement in the abduction of Neil Spencer. If you're telling the truth, that means there's a killer still out there right now."

"No comment."

"And unless we find him, that person is going to kill more children. I think you know *a lot more* about this person than you're telling me."

Collins stared at her, his face completely pale. Amanda didn't think she'd ever seen a man melt so fast— to collapse from smug self-confidence into a puddle of self-pitying misery with such speed.

"No comment," he whispered.

"Norman—"

"I want a lawyer."

"Well, we can certainly arrange that." She stood up quickly, not bothering to hide the anger she felt. The *disgust.* "Maybe then you'll realize how much trouble you're really in, and that cooperating with us is the best chance you've got."

"No comment."

"Yeah, I heard you the first time."

Small victories.

But as she formally arrested Norman Collins for the murder of Dominic Barnett, Amanda thought about everything she'd said. If he was telling the truth about not killing Neil Spencer, then a child killer *was* still out there—which meant another little boy might die on her watch.

Her mind flashed back to the sight of Neil Spencer on the waste ground last night, and any of the elation she might normally feel vanished entirely.

A small victory wasn't good enough.

THIRTY-FOUR

The police presence at the house had intensified in my absence. We arrived to find two cars and a van parked outside, with officers and crime scene investigators working in the taped-off driveway. The focus of the activity appeared to be the garage, but two police officers were stationed on the pavement to secure the whole property. My front door was open too—an incongruous sight to return home to, and one that felt invasive and wrong.

I pulled up after the other vehicles. My father's car drove past, then parked in front of me.

Not my father, I reminded myself.

DI Pete Willis.

There was no need to acknowledge him as anything else, was there? And with the exception of the way he'd knelt down and looked at Jake, there was no sign he wanted to acknowledge it either. That was a situation I was more than happy to go along with.

The shock had subsided a little now, but only in the way I imagined there might be a few beats of silence after an earthquake hit before the screaming started. I could still remember how it had felt at the police station, my father standing there, looking back at me, *seeing* me. My mind had immediately leaped back to the long-ago time when I'd last seen him, and I'd felt small and powerless. I had been transported. The fear and anxiety. The desire to diminish myself so that he might not notice me. But then the anger had come. He had no fucking *right* to talk to my son. And then the resentment. The fact that he got to be involved in my life—in a position of power over me, even—seemed so deeply unfair that I almost couldn't bear it.

"Are you all right, Daddy?"

"I'm fine, mate."

I was staring at the car in front of me. At the man in the driver's seat.

His name is DI Pete Willis, I reminded myself, *and he means nothing to you.*

Nothing at all.

Not if I didn't let him.

"Right," I said. "Let's get this over with."

He met us at the cordon, showed his identification to the officers there, and then led us into the house without saying anything. The resentment flowered again. I needed his *permission* to enter my own fucking home. It felt humiliating to follow him inside like a boy who had to do what he was told. And it was made worse by the fact that he seemed so indifferent to it all.

He had a clipboard and pen.

"I need to know what's yours, and what was here when you moved in that you haven't touched."

"Everything in the house is mine," I said. "Mrs. Shearing cleared all the older stuff out to the garage."

"We'll check with her, don't worry."

"I'm not worried."

We went from room to room, gathering some basic things together. Toiletries. Clothes for Jake and me. A few toys from his room. It burned me so hard that I had to ask my father each time, but he just nodded and noted them down, and in the end I stopped asking. If he cared, he didn't mention it. He barely looked at me at all, in fact. I wondered what he might be thinking or feeling. But then I fought that down, because it didn't matter.

We finished in my office downstairs.

"I need my laptop—" I started to say, but Jake interrupted me.

"Who did Daddy find in the garage? Was it Neil Spencer?"

My father looked awkward.

"No. Those remains were much older."

"Who are they of?"

"Well . . . between you and me, I think they might be from another little boy. One who disappeared a long time ago."

"How long ago?"

"Twenty years."

"Wow." Jake paused to take in such an expanse of time.

"Yes. And I hope they are, because I've been searching for him ever since."

Jake looked amazed by that, like it was some kind of accomplishment, and I didn't like that. I didn't want him interested in this man at all, never mind impressed by him.

"I'd have given up by now."

My father smiled sadly.

"It's always been important to me. Everybody should get to go home, don't you think?"

"Can I take this, DI Willis?" I started unplugging my laptop, wanting to bring the conversation to an end. "I need it for work."

"Yes." He turned away from both of us. "Of course you can."

The "safe house" was just an apartment above a news-dealer's at one end of Town Street. It didn't look like much from the street, and it looked like even less when Willis took us inside.

A staircase led up from the front door to a landing with four doors leading off it. There was a sitting room, bathroom, kitchen, and a room with two single beds, all of it minimally furnished. The only signs that it was used by the police, rather than simply rented out dirt cheap, were the security camera positioned subtly on the wall outside, the panic buttons within, and the prolif-eration of bolts on the inside of the front door.

"I'm sorry, the two of you'll have to share."

Willis walked into the bedroom carrying sheets and blankets that he'd gathered from an airing cupboard. I was unpacking our clothes and piling them on top of the old wooden dresser, having wiped away a sheen of dust first. The apartment clearly hadn't been cleaned in a long time and the air was itchy with it.

"It's fine," I said.

"I know it's small. We use it for witnesses sometimes, but it's mostly women and children." He seemed about to say something, but then shook his head. "They usually want to be in the same room."

"Domestic violence, I guess."

My father didn't answer, but the atmosphere between us heated up a notch, and I knew the hit had landed. What was between us remained unspoken but was growing louder, in the way that silence sometimes can.

"It's fine," I said again. "How long will we be here?"

"Shouldn't be more than a day or two. Maybe not even that. It's potentially a big case, though. We need to make sure we don't miss anything."

"You think the man you've arrested killed Neil Spencer?"

"Possibly. Like I said, I think the remains we've found in your house are from a similar crime. There was always speculation that Frank Carter—the killer back then—had an accomplice of some kind. Norman Collins was never officially a suspect, but he was too interested in the case. I never thought he was directly involved, but . . ."

"But?"

"Maybe I got that wrong."

"Yeah, I guess maybe you did."

My father said nothing. The knowledge that I might have hurt him again brought a kind of thrill, but it was a small, disappointing one. He seemed so beaten down and uncomfortable. In his own way, perhaps he felt as powerless right now as I did.

"Okay."

We moved back through to the sitting room, where Jake was kneeling down and drawing. There was a couch and a chair, a small table on wheels, and an old television balanced on a wooden chest of drawers with a mess of old cables behind it. The whole place felt cold and bleak. I tried not to think about what was happening in our house—our real home—right now. Whatever problems it had thrown up, it felt like paradise compared to this.

But you'll deal with it. And this will be over soon.

And Pete Willis would be out of my life again.

"I'll leave you to it," he said. "Good to meet you, Jake."

"Good to meet you too, Pete," Jake said, not looking up from his picture. "Thank you for this delightful apartment."

He hesitated. "You're welcome."

Out on the landing, I closed the door to the sitting room. There was a window here, but it was early evening now and the light coming in was dim. Willis seemed reluctant to leave, and so we stood in the gloom for a moment, his face full of shadow.

"You have everything you need?" he said finally.

"I think so."

"Jake seems like a good kid."

"Yes," I said. "He is."

"He's creative. Just like you."

I didn't reply. The silence between us was tingling now. As much as it was possible to tell in this half-light, Willis looked as though he wished he hadn't spoken. But then he explained himself.

"I saw your books in the house."

"You didn't know before?"

He shook his head.

"I'd have thought you might have been interested," I said. "Maybe looked me up or something."

"Did you look me up?"

"No, but that's different."

As soon as I said it, I hated myself for it, because it acknowledged that power balance again—the idea that it was his job to look for me, to be concerned about me, to care about me, rather than the other way around. I didn't want him to imagine that was true. It wasn't. He was nothing to me.

"A long time ago," he said, "I decided it would be best for me to keep out of your life. Your mother and I decided between us."

"That's one way of putting it."

"I suppose so. It's *my* way of putting it. And I've honored that. It's not always been easy. I've often wondered. But it's been for the best . . ."

He trailed off, suddenly looking weaker than ever.

Spare me the self-pity.

But I didn't say it. Whatever my father had done in the past, he'd obviously moved on since. He didn't look or smell like an alcoholic now. He was in good shape. And despite the weariness, there was an air of calm to him. I reminded myself again that this man and I were strangers to each other. We weren't father and son. We weren't enemies.

We were nothing.

He was looking off toward the window, toward the day slowly dying outside.

"Sally—your mother, I mean. What happened to her?"

Glass smashing.

My mother screaming.

I thought of everything that had followed. The way she did her best for me in spite of all the difficulties she faced as a single mother. The pain and ignominy of her death. Like Rebecca, taken far too young, long before either she or I deserved such a loss.

"She's dead," I told him.

He was silent. For a moment he even seemed broken. But then he gathered himself.

"When?"

"That's none of your business."

The anger in my voice surprised me—but apparently not my father. He stood there, absorbing the force of the blow.

"No," he said quietly. "I suppose not."

And then he started walking down the stairs to the front door. I watched him go. When he was halfway down I spoke again, just loud enough for him to hear.

"I remember that last night, you know. The night before you were gone. The last time you ever saw me. I remember how drunk you were. How red in the face you were. What you did. Throwing that glass at her. The way she screamed."

He stopped on the stairs and stood completely still.

"*I remember it all*," I said. "So how dare you ask about her now?"

He didn't reply.

And then he continued silently down the stairs, leaving me with nothing but the sick and angry thud of my heartbeat.

THIRTY-FIVE

After leaving the safe house, Pete drove too fast along empty roads, heading straight home. The kitchen cabinet was calling to him, and he was going to surrender to it. Now that the decision was made, the urge was stronger than ever, and it felt like his whole life depended on getting there as quickly as possible.

Back home, he locked the door and drew the curtains. The house around him was still and silent, and it seemed as empty with him standing in it as it must have been before his arrival. Because, after all, what did he add to it? He looked around at the spartan furnishings in the living room. It was the same throughout the house—every space just as ascetic and carefully organized. The truth was that he had lived in an empty house for years. The meager debris of a life barely lived, a real life avoided, was no less sad because it was tidy and clean.

Empty. Pointless.

Worthless.

The voice was gleeful in its victory. He stood there, breathing slowly, aware of his heart pounding. But he'd been here many times before, and this was the way it always worked. When the compulsion to drink was at its strongest, everything bolstered it. Any event or observation, good or bad, could be turned around and made to fit.

But it was all a lie.

You've been here before.

You can do this.

The urge fell silent for a moment, but then began to *howl* inside his head, conscious of the trick he was attempting to pull. He'd let it drive him home on autopilot, allowed it to believe that he was giving in, but now he was taking the wheel again.

The pain circled in his chest, swirling and unbearable.

You've been here before.

You can do this.

The table. The bottle and the photograph.

Tonight, he added a glass, and after a moment's hesitation, he opened the bottle and poured two fingers of vodka. Because why not? Either he would drink or he wouldn't. It wasn't how far down the road he went; it was whether he arrived at the end.

His phone buzzed. He picked it up to find a message from Amanda, filling him in on her interview with Norman Collins. They had Collins on the murder of Dominic Barnett, it seemed, but the situation with Neil Spencer was hazier, and Collins had decided to lawyer up.

You think the man you've arrested killed Neil Spencer?

Possibly, he'd told Tom—and it was clear that Collins was involved somehow. But if it wasn't him who had abducted and murdered Neil, that meant the actual killer was still out there. Any relief he'd felt after arresting Collins evaporated entirely at that thought, just as surely as it had twenty years ago when he'd seen Miranda and Alan Smith in the department's reception and realized the nightmare was far from over.

It shouldn't be his problem now. Tom was his son, albeit long estranged, and that conflict of interest meant he should talk to Amanda tomorrow and recuse himself from the investigation. He supposed it would bring relief of its own to be free from this pressure. And yet, having been dragged in this deep—having been forced to confront Carter again, and to look at Neil Spencer's body on the waste ground last night—he wanted to see this through, however damaging it might be.

He put the phone to one side, then stared at the glass, trying to analyze how he felt about seeing Tom again after so many years. The encounter should have shaken him to the core, he supposed, and yet he felt oddly calm. Over the years, he had grown numb to the fact of his fatherhood, as though it were something he had learned at school that no longer had any bearing on his life. Memories of Sally were on the right side of the pain threshold for him to bear, but his failure toward Tom had been absolute, and Pete had done his best never to think about that. It was better to have nothing to do with his son's life, and whenever he had found himself imagining what kind of man Tom might have become, he had quickly shoved those thoughts away. They were too hot to touch.

But now he knew.

He had no right to think of himself as a father, but

it was impossible not to evaluate the man he had met that afternoon. A writer. That made sense, of course. Tom had always been creative as a little boy—always making up stories Pete couldn't follow, or playing out elaborate scenarios with his toys. Jake appeared to be a lot like Tom had been at that age: a sensitive and clever child. From the little Pete had learned, it was obvious Tom had suffered hardship and tragedy throughout his life, and yet he was capably raising Jake alone. There could be little doubt that his son had grown into a good man.

Not worthless. Not useless or a failure.

Which was good.

Pete ran his fingertip around the edge of the glass. It was *good* that Tom had succeeded in overcoming the miserable childhood he had offered him. Good that he had absented himself from Tom's life before he could poison it any more than he already had. Because it was clear that he had. Even after all this time, he was remembered. His impact had been terrible enough to leave a lasting impression.

I remember the last time I saw you.

Pete could still picture the look of hatred on his son's face when he'd said that. He picked up the glass. Put it down again. That wasn't quite right, though, was it? He deserved hatred—he was more than aware of that —but hatred had to be earned. Pete had been drinking almost constantly by the time Sally and Tom left him, and his days and nights had been a blur, but he remembered that particular evening with absolute clarity. Tom's description of what had happened was impossible

Did it matter?

Perhaps not. If his son's memory was not literally true, then, like Pete's own feelings of failure, it presumably still felt true enough, and that was the kind of truth that mattered most in the end.

He looked at the familiar photograph of him and Sally. It had been taken before Tom was conceived, but Pete thought you could see the knowledge of impending fatherhood in his expression if you wanted to. The squint against the sun. The half smile that looked like it would soon disappear. It was as though the man in the photo already knew he was about to fail badly and lose everything.

Sally still looked so happy.

He had lost her a long time ago, but had maintained the fantasy that she was alive somewhere, leading a contented, loving life. Keeping up the miserable belief that his own loss had been her and Tom's gain. But now he knew the truth. There had been no gain. Sally was dead.

It felt like everything was.

Again, he picked up the glass, but this time he kept hold of it, watching the silky liquid fold over on itself. It looked so innocent until it did that—so much like water until you moved it and saw the mist hiding there.

He'd been here before. He could survive this.

But why bother?

He looked around the room, weighing again the emptiness of his existence. There was nothing to him. He was a man made of air. A life with no heft. There was nothing good in his past that could be saved, and nothing in his future that was worth trying to.

Except that wasn't true, was it? Neil Spencer's killer might still be out there. If the boy's murder stemmed from some past failing of his, then it was *his* responsibility to put it right, whatever the personal repercussions might be. Whether he liked it or not, he was back in the nightmare now, and he thought that he needed to see it through to the end, even if it broke him. There was a conflict of interest, yes, but if he was careful, then perhaps nobody would ever know. He doubted Tom would ever want their distant history aired.

That was one reason to stay sober.

And also—

Thank you for this delightful apartment.

Pete smiled as he remembered Jake's words earlier. It had been such a strange thing to say, but it was funny. He was a funny kid. A *nice* kid. He was creative. He was a character. Probably a handful to deal with too, just like Tom had been at times.

Pete allowed himself to think about Jake for a few moments more. He could imagine sitting down and talking to the boy. Playing with him, the same way he might—and should—have done with Tom when he had been a child. It was foolish, of course. There was nothing there. In a couple of days, his involvement with the pair of them would be over, and he'd probably never see them again.

But even so, he decided that he wasn't going to drink. Not tonight.

Easy to throw the glass, of course. Always easy to do that. Instead, he stood up, walked through to the kitchen, and poured it slowly away into the sink. He watched the liquid trailing away down the drain, and alongside the urge in his chest he thought about Jake again and felt something he hadn't experienced in years. There was no reason to it. No sense. And yet there it was.

Hope.

PART FOUR

THIRTY-SIX

The next morning, when I dropped Jake off at school, I was still quietly amazed by how well he'd adapted to our new circumstances. Last night in the safe house, he had dropped off to sleep without complaint, leaving me to sit alone in the living room afterward with my laptop and my thoughts. When I'd finally gone to bed, I'd gazed down at him, and his face had looked so serene that I'd wondered if he was actually more at peace here than he was in our new home. I'd wondered what, if anything, he was dreaming.

But then, I often thought that.

For myself, even as tired as I was, the unfamiliar surroundings had made it harder to sleep than ever, so it was a relief when he was well behaved and easy to manage that morning. Perhaps he was treating this all as some kind of exciting adventure. Whatever the reason, I was grateful for it. I was so exhausted, and my nerves so on edge, that I wasn't sure I'd have been up to any real challenges.

We drove to the school, and then I walked him to the playground.

"Are you okay, mate?"

"I'm fine, Daddy."

"All right, then. Here you go." I handed him his water bottle and book bag. "I love you."

"I love you too."

He walked off to the door, the bag swinging beside his leg. Mrs. Shelley was waiting there. I hadn't had the conversation with Jake that I'd promised I would. I'd just have to hope that today was a little easier for him, or at least that he didn't punch anyone.

"You *still* look like shit."

Karen fell into step beside me as I walked back out through the gates. She was still dressed up in her huge coat, despite the warmth of the morning.

"Yesterday, you were worried about offending me when you said that."

"Yeah, but it didn't, did it?" She shrugged. "I slept on it and figured it was probably okay."

"Then you slept a lot better than I did."

"That I can see." She stuffed her hands into her pockets. "What are you up to now? Fancy grabbing a coffee, or do you have to run off and be tired somewhere else?"

I hesitated. I had nothing to do. I'd told my father I needed my laptop for work, but the likelihood of me accomplishing anything in this state was pretty minimal. Today was likely to be a case of treading water and hoping some kind of land would eventually appear— killing time, basically—and looking at Karen now, I figured there were worse ways to do that.

"Sure," I said. "That would be nice."

We walked down to the main road, where she led me

past the small corner shop and village post office to a delicatessen called the Happy Pig. There were meadow scenes painted on the windowed front, and the inside was rustic and crammed with wooden tables, like a farmhouse kitchen.

"Bit pretentious." She pushed open the door and a bell tinkled. "But the coffee's acceptable."

"As long as it's got caffeine in it."

It certainly smelled good. We ordered at the counter, standing beside each other a little awkwardly while we waited and not speaking for the moment. Then we took our drinks over to a table and sat down.

Karen shrugged off her coat. She was wearing a white blouse and blue jeans underneath it, and I was surprised by how slim she looked without the armor on. Was it armor? I thought it might be. There was a scattering of wooden rings around her wrists, which rattled slightly as she reached up with both hands and gathered her hair back, tying it into a loose ponytail.

"So," she said. "What *is* going on with you?"

"It's a long story. How much do you want to know?"

"Oh, everything."

I considered that. As a writer, one of the things I'd always believed was that you didn't talk about your stories until they were finished. If you did, there was less of an urge to write them down—almost as though the story just needed to be told in some capacity, and the pressure reduced the more you did.

So with that in mind, I decided to tell Karen everything.

Almost everything, anyway. She already knew about

the junk in my garage and my visit from the man who'd turned out to be Norman Collins, but Jake's near abduction in the middle of the night made her raise her eyes. Then what I'd learned from Mrs. Shearing, and the events that had unfolded yesterday. The discovery of the body. The safe house.

And last of all, my father.

The impression I'd gained so far of Karen was that she was fairly frivolous: prone to playful sarcasm and jokey asides. But by the time I'd finished explaining, she looked horrified and deadly serious.

"Shit," she said quietly. "They haven't released any details to the media yet—just that remains had been found at a property. I had no idea it was yours."

"I think they're playing it close to their chests. From what I can make out, they think it's the remains of a kid called Tony Smith. He was one of Frank Carter's victims."

"His poor parents." Karen shook her head. "Twenty years. Although I guess they must have known after such a long time. Maybe it'll even be a relief for them to finally have some closure."

I remembered my father's words.

"Everybody deserves to go home," I said.

Karen looked off to one side. It seemed like she wanted to ask more, but wasn't sure if she should for some reason.

"This man they've arrested," she said.

"Norman Collins."

"Norman Collins, right. How did *he* know about it?"

"I don't know. Apparently he always had an interest in the case." I sipped my coffee. "My father seems to think he might have been Carter's accomplice all along."

"And that he killed Neil Spencer too?"

"I'm not sure."

"I hope so—well." She corrected herself. "I mean, I know that's an awful thing to say, but at least that way they've got the bastard. Christ, if you hadn't woken up . . ."

"I know. I don't even want to think about it."

"It's fucking terrifying."

It was—and, of course, not wanting to think about it didn't mean I could stop myself.

"I read up about him last night," I said. "Carter, I mean. A bit morbid, but it seemed like I needed to know. The Whisper Man. Some of the details were just horrific."

Karen nodded. "*If you leave a door half open, soon you'll hear the whispers spoken.* I asked Adam about that, after you mentioned it. It's a rhyme some of the kids say. He'd never even heard of Carter, of course, but I guess that must be where it originated. Passed down."

"A warning against the bogeyman."

"Yeah. Except this one was real."

I thought about the rhyme. Adam had heard it without realizing what it meant, and maybe it extended beyond Featherbank. Things like that often spread among children, so perhaps one of the kids at Jake's old school had repeated it and that was where he'd learned it.

It had to be something like that, of course. The little girl hadn't taught him it, because she wasn't real.

But that didn't explain the butterflies. Or the *boy in the floor*.

Karen seemed to read my mind.

"What about Jake? How's he handling all this?"

"All right, I think." I shrugged, a little helplessly. "I don't know. He and I . . . we sometimes find it hard to talk to each other. He's not the easiest of kids."

"There's no such thing," Karen said.

"And I'm not the easiest of men."

"And again. But what about you, though? It must have been strange seeing your father after all this time. Have you really had no contact with him at all?"

"None. My mother left with me when it all got too much. I haven't seen him since."

"Too much . . . ?"

"The drinking," I said. "The violence."

But then I trailed off. It was easier to explain it like that than to go into detail, but the truth was, that final night aside, I had no actual memory of my father being physically violent toward my mother or me. The drinking, yes, although I didn't really understand that at the time; I just knew that he was angry all the time, that he disappeared for days, that there was too little money, that my parents argued furiously. And I remembered the resentment and bitterness that would beat out from him—the sense of threat that pervaded the air, as though something bad might happen at any moment. I remembered being afraid. But actual *violence* might have been pushing it.

"I'm sorry to hear that," Karen said.

I shrugged again, feeling awkward now.

"Thanks. But yes, it was strange seeing him. I remember him, of course, but he's not like he was. He doesn't look like a drinker now. His whole manner seems different. Quieter."

"People change."

"They do. And it's fine, really. We're both completely different people now. I'm not a kid anymore. He's not really my father. It doesn't matter at all."

"I'm not sure I believe you."

"Well. It is what it is."

"That, I believe." Karen had finished her coffee and now she began slipping on her coat. "And on that note, I'm going to have to love you and leave you, I'm afraid."

"You have to go and be tired somewhere?"

"No, I slept well, remember?"

"Right." I swirled around the dregs of my own drink. She didn't seem inclined to tell me where she was going, and it occurred to me that I barely knew anything about her at all. "We spent the whole time talking about me, you realize? That doesn't seem fair."

"Because you're much more interesting than I am, especially right now. Perhaps it's something you can write about in one of your books."

"Maybe."

"Yeah, I'm sorry. I googled you." She looked momentarily embarrassed. "I'm good at finding things out. Don't tell anyone."

"Your secret is safe."

"Glad to hear it." She paused, as though there was

something else she wanted to say. But then she shook her head, clearly thinking better of it. "See you later?"

"You will. Take care."

I drained the last of my coffee as she left, wondering what she might have been about to say just then. And also thinking about the fact that she'd googled me. What did that mean?

And was it wrong that I quite liked it?

THIRTY-SEVEN

"Are you finished with that, love?"

The man shook his head, momentarily unsure where he was and what was being asked of him. Then he saw the waitress smiling at him, looked down at the table, and realized he'd finished his coffee.

"Yes." He leaned back. "Sorry, I was miles away, there."

She smiled again as she picked up his empty cup.

"Can I get you anything else?"

"Maybe in a minute."

He had no intention of ordering anything, but even though the shop was only half full it made sense to be polite and observe social mores. He didn't want to be remembered as someone who overstayed his welcome. He didn't want to be remembered at all.

And he was good at that —although it was true that people made it easy for him. So many of them seemed to be lost in the noise of existence, all but sleepwalking through their lives, oblivious to the world around them. Hypnotized by their cell phones. Ignoring the others they passed. People were self-centered and uncaring, and they paid little attention to things on their periphery. If you didn't stand out, you vanished as quickly from their minds as a dream.

He stared at Tom Kennedy, sitting two tables away.

Kennedy had his back to him, and now that the woman had left, the man *could* stare if he wanted. When she had been there, facing him, he had sipped his coffee and pretended to study his phone, making himself an unremarkable part of the shop's scenery. But listening carefully the whole time, of course. Conversations mingled around you if you let them, becoming an impenetrable background hum, but if you focused you could pull one out and follow it easily. All it required was concentration, like delicately tuning a radio until the static disappeared and you were left with a clear signal.

How right he had been, he thought now.

We sometimes find it hard to talk to each other.

He's not the easiest of kids.

Well, the man was sure that Jake would flourish under *his* care. He would give the boy the home he deserved and provide the love and care he needed. And then he himself would feel healed and whole as well.

And if not . . .

Time had a way of dulling sensations. He found it much easier now to think about what he had done to Neil Spencer. The shivers he'd experienced afterward had long since faded, and he could handle the memories more dispassionately now—in fact, there was almost pleasure in doing so. Because that boy *had* deserved it, hadn't he? And if there had been moments of tranquility and happiness in the two months beforehand, when everything had seemed good, there had also been a sense of calm and rightness in the aftermath of that final day that had been comforting in its own way too.

But no.

It wouldn't come to that.

Tom Kennedy stood up and made his way to the door. The man stared down at his phone, idly tapping the screen as Kennedy passed him.

The man sat for a few seconds more, thinking about the other things he'd heard. Who was *Norman Collins*? The name was completely unfamiliar to him. One of the *others,* he supposed, but he had no idea why this Collins had been arrested now. It suited him well enough, though. The police would be distracted. Kennedy might be less on edge. Which meant that he just needed to pick his moment, and everything would be well.

He stood up.

The greater the noise, the easier it was to slip silently in without being noticed.

THIRTY-EIGHT

I've been looking for you for so long.

Pete got out of the car and made his way into the hospital, then took the elevator down to the basement, where the city's pathology unit was based. One wall of the elevator was mirrored, though, and he looked fine. Calm, even. The pieces within might be broken, but from the outside he was like a carefully wrapped present that would only rattle if you shook it.

He couldn't remember ever feeling this apprehensive.

He'd been searching for Tony Smith for twenty years. On some level, he wondered if the boy's absence had even sustained him—if it had given him a sense of purpose and a reason to continue, albeit one that had always been kept occluded in the background of his thoughts. Regardless, however much he had tried not to think about it, the case had never been closed for him.

So he had to be present when it was.

He hated the autopsy suites in here, and always had. The smell of antiseptic never quite masked the underlying stench, and the harsh light and polished metallic surfaces only served to emphasize the mottled bodies on display. Death was tangible here—laid out and made prosaic. These rooms were about weights and angles, and clipboards scribbled with spare details of chemistry and biology, all of it so cold and clinical. Every time he visited, he realized that the most important parts of a human life—the emotions; the character; the experiences—were conspicuous by their absence.

The pathologist, Chris Dale, walked Pete over to a gurney at the far side of the suite. As he followed the man, Pete felt light and faint, and had to fight the urge to turn around.

"Here's our boy."

Dale spoke quietly. He was famed throughout the department for his brusque and dismissive manner when it came to dealing with the police, saving his respect for those he always referred to as his patients. *Our boy.* The way Dale said it made it clear that the remains were now under his protection. That the indignities they'd been subjected to were over, and that they would be looked after now.

Our boy, Pete thought.

The bones were laid out in the shape of a small child, but age had separated many of them, and not a scrap of flesh remained. Pete had seen a number of skeletons over the years. In some ways, they were easier to look at than more recently deceased victims, who looked like human beings but, in their eerie stillness, somehow *not.* A skeleton was so far removed from everyday experience that it could be viewed more dispassionately. And yet the reality always hit home. The fact that people die, and after a short amount of time only objects remain, the bones little more than a scattering of possessions abandoned where they fall.

"We've yet to do a full postmortem," Dale said. "That's scheduled for later. What I can tell you in the meantime is that these are the remains of a male child who was around six years of age at the time of his death. I can't even guess at the *cause* of death for the moment, and we might never know, but he's been deceased for some time."

"Twenty years?"

"Possibly." Dale hesitated, knowing what Pete was asking, then gestured at a second gurney beside them. "We also have these additional items, which were recovered from the scene. There's the box itself, of course—the remains were brought here in it to help preserve them. The clothes were underneath the bones."

Pete took a step closer. The clothes were old and matted with cobwebs, but Dale and his team had extracted them carefully, and they rested now in the same intact, neatly folded pile they had been stored in. He didn't need to move them to see what they were.

Blue jogging pants. Little black polo shirt.

He turned and looked again at the remains. The case had exerted such a hold on him all these years, and yet this was the first time he'd ever seen Tony Smith in real life. Until now there had only ever been the photographs of a little boy frozen forever in time. With just the slightest of differences in circumstances, Pete might have passed a twenty-six-year-old Tony Smith on the street today without ever having heard the name. He stared down at the small, broken frame that had once supported and held a human being, along with all the inherent possibilities of what it might become.

All their hopes and dreams, and look what I've gone and done.

Pete pushed Frank Carter's words out of his head, and stared down in silence for a few seconds, wanting to take in the enormity of the moment. Except he realized that it wasn't there, no more than Tony Smith himself was present in the empty shell of bones on the gurney. Pete had been held in orbit by this missing little boy for so long, his whole life circling the mystery of his whereabouts. But now that center of gravity was gone and his trajectory felt unaltered.

You search for something, and you find it, and there you are still.

"We found several of these in the box," Dale said.

Pete turned to see the pathologist leaning over at the waist, hands in his pockets, staring at the cardboard box that Tony Smith had been found in. Moving closer, Pete saw the man's attention was directed toward a butterfly stuck in the cobwebs there. It was obviously dead, but the colored patterns on its wings remained clear and vivid.

"The corpse moth," Pete said.

The pathologist looked at him with surprise.

"I never took you for a butterfly fan, Detective."

"I saw a documentary once." Pete shrugged. He'd always figured that he watched and read to kill time, and was slightly surprised himself to find some of the knowledge had stuck. "I have a lot of evenings to fill."

"*That* I can believe."

Pete dredged his memory for details. Despite its name, the corpse moth was a butterfly. It was native to the country, but relatively rare, and the program he'd watched had followed a team of eccentric men trailing through fields and hedgerows trying to catch sight of it. They'd found one at the end. The corpse moth was attracted to decaying flesh. Pete himself had never seen one, but ever since watching the documentary, he'd found himself scanning the country lanes and hedgerows he searched on weekends, wondering if their presence might provide some indication that he was looking in the right place.

His phone buzzed in his pocket, and he took it out to find a message from Amanda. He read it quickly: an update on the case. After a night in the cells, it appeared that Norman Collins had reevaluated his no-comment position and was now prepared to talk to them. She wanted Pete back there as soon as possible.

He put the phone away, but lingered for a moment, looking at the cardboard box in front of him. It was strapped with overlapping layers of brown parcel tape: a container that had clearly been sealed and reopened and sealed again many times over the years. The box would now be sent for forensic analysis in the hope of finding fingerprints. Pete's gaze moved over its surface now, imagining the invisible hands that might have touched it over the years. He pictured people pressing their fingertips against it, the cardboard a surrogate skin encasing the bones secreted within.

Prized among collectors.

For a moment he wondered if such people had imagined a heartbeat. Or if they had gloried in the absence of one.

THIRTY-NINE

Seated across from Amanda and Pete in the interview room, Norman Collins's lawyer sighed heavily.

"My client is prepared to admit to the murder of Dominic Barnett," he said. "He categorically denies any involvement in the abduction and murder of Neil Spencer."

Amanda stared at him, waiting.

"However, my client is prepared to make a full and frank statement regarding his knowledge of the remains found on Garholt Street yesterday. He has no desire for you to waste resources on him, potentially endangering another child, and he believes what he has to say may help you locate the individual actually responsible for the killing."

"Which we very much appreciate."

Amanda smiled politely, even though she knew bullshit when she heard it. Sitting mutely on the other side of the desk, Collins looked diminished and wounded. He was not a man built for imprisonment, and a night in custody had erased the smugness he'd displayed in here yesterday. The fact that he was finally going to talk brought her little pleasure, because it was clearly motivated by self-interest rather than any desire to save lives. There was no better nature in there; he'd simply had time to realize that talking to them—giving his side of the story—might do him some good in the long run. That it might look better for him if he cooperated and was seen to help.

But now wasn't the time to show disgust. Not if he really *could* help.

She leaned back. "So—talk to us, Norman."

"I don't know where to begin."

"You knew that Tony Smith's remains were in that garage, didn't you? Let's start there."

Collins was silent for a few seconds, staring down at the table between them, gathering himself. Amanda glanced at Pete, sitting beside her, and saw that he was doing the same. She was worried about him. He seemed more subdued than ever, and had hardly spoken to her after arriving at the department. It seemed like there had been something he was on the verge of telling her, but for some reason he had held it back. This was going to be hard for him, she knew. He'd come straight from viewing what were almost certainly the remains of Tony Smith, a boy he had searched for, for so long, and now he was set to hear the truth about what had happened all that time ago. The years might have hardened him on the surface, but she didn't want to think of all his old wounds tearing open again.

"I understand what you think of my interests, my hobby," Collins said quietly. She turned her attention back to him. "And I understand what many people think of them. But the fact remains that I am well respected in my field. And I've acquired a reputation over the years as a collector."

A *collector*. He made it sound benign—respectable almost—but she had seen details of his collection. What kind of individual was drawn to the material that he had spent so many years acquiring? She pictured Collins and the people like him as rats scurrying around in the dark underbelly of the Internet. Doing their deals and making their plans. Chewing at the wires of society. When Collins looked up at her now, the disgust she felt must have been obvious on her face.

"It's really no different from interests other people have," he said defensively. "I learned long ago that my hobby was considered niche by most, and abhorrent by a few. But there are others who share it. And I have proved trustworthy over the years, which has allowed me access to more important pieces than others."

"You're a serious dealer?"

"A serious dealer in serious things." He licked his lips. "And like any such dealings, there are open forums and there are private ones. My interest in the Whisper Man case was well known in the latter. And several years ago I was made aware that a certain . . . experience might be open to me. Assuming I was willing to pay, of course."

"What was this *experience*?"

He stared back at her for a moment, and then answered as though it were the most natural thing in the world.

"To spend time with Tony Smith."

THE WHISPER MAN | 269

A moment of silence.

"How?" she said.

"In the first instance, I was told to visit Victor Tyler in prison. Everything was arranged through Tyler. Frank Carter knew about it, but he had no interest in being directly involved. The procedure was that Tyler would vet the people who came to him. I was pleased to pass that particular test. Upon receipt of funds delivered to Tyler's wife, I was directed to an address." Collins grimaced. "I wasn't surprised to be sent to Julian Simpson."

"Why?"

"He was an unsavory sort. Poor personal hygiene." Collins tapped his head. "Not entirely *all there*. People used to make fun of him, but they were all frightened of him, really. The house too. It's a strange-looking place, don't you think? I remember children used to dare each other to go into the garden. They'd take photographs of each other there. Even before then—back when I was a child—people thought of it as the local scary house."

Amanda glanced at Pete again. His face was inscrutable, but she could imagine what he must be thinking. Julian Simpson's name had never come up in the case at the time. The police had known nothing of the man or his scary-looking house. And that was entirely understandable. There were people like Simpson in every community, their reputations among the young not necessarily based on anything *real,* and certainly not to the extent that adults would think anything of them.

But regardless, she knew Pete would blame himself for this.

"What happened next?" she asked Collins.

"I went to the house on Garholt Street," he said. "After paying more money to Simpson, I was made to wait in a downstairs room. After a time, he returned with a sealed cardboard box. He cut it open carefully. And there . . . there he was."

"For the record, Norman . . . ?"

"Tony Smith."

Amanda could hardly bring herself to ask the question.

"And what did you do with Tony's remains?"

"*Do with them?*" Collins sounded genuinely shocked. "I didn't *do* anything with them. I'm not a monster—not like some of the others. And I wouldn't have wanted to damage an exhibit like that even if it had been allowed. No, I simply stood there. Paying my respects. Imbibing the atmosphere. You may find this hard to understand, but it was one of the most powerful hours of my life."

Jesus, Amanda thought. He looked like a man remembering some lost love.

Of all the scenarios she had been imagining taking place, his answer was simultaneously the most banal and the most horrifying. The time spent with a murdered little boy's body had clearly bordered on a religious experience for him, and imagining him standing there, believing he had some special connection with the sad remains in a box at his feet, was as awful in its own way as anything she could have thought of.

Beside her, Pete leaned forward slowly.

Not like some of the others. Whatever toll the account

was taking on him, he just sounded weary right now—tired all the way down to his soul. "Who were the others, Norman? And what did they do?"

Collins swallowed.

"This was after Dominic Barnett took over—after Julian died. I think the two of them were friends, but Barnett didn't have the same level of *respect*. Things deteriorated under his care."

"Is that why you killed him?" Amanda said.

"Barnett wouldn't grant me access anymore—not after the last time. I had to protect the exhibit! Tony needed to be kept *safe*."

"Tell us about *the others*, Norman," Pete said patiently.

"This was after Barnett took over." Collins hesitated. "I'd visited several times over the years, but for me it was always the same. I was paying my respects, and I wanted to be on my own with Tony. But once Barnett was in charge, there started to be others there too. And they were not as respectful as me."

"What did they do?"

"I didn't see anything," Collins said. "I left—I was *disgusted*. And Barnett refused to refund me. He even sneered at me. But what could I do?"

"Why were you so disgusted?" Pete said.

"The last night I went, there were five or six other people there. All fascinated by the case. A mixture of types—you'd be surprised, honestly—and I got the impression that some of them had traveled a great distance. But it wasn't like the other times. They started . . .

touching the bones. It was completely unacceptable. I tried to intervene, but Barnett just laughed at me. He didn't care at all."

Collins swallowed.

"So you left?" Amanda asked.

"Yes. I couldn't bear it. When I'd visited in the past, it was like being in a church. It was quiet and reverential. I felt the presence of *God*. But with those people there. Not respecting Tony. Not respecting Frank's work . . ."

He trailed off again.

"Norman?"

Finally, he looked up.

"It was like standing in hell."

"Do you believe him?" Amanda said.

They were back in the incident room. Pete was leaning on his desk, staring intently down at the CCTV photographs of the people who had visited Victor Tyler in prison over the years. Her own gaze moved across them. There were men and women here. The young and the old. *A mixture of types,* Collins had told them. *You'd be surprised, honestly.*

"I believe Collins didn't kill Neil Spencer." Pete waved his hand over the photographs. "But as to this . . ."

And then he fell silent, expressing the same disbelief that she was feeling herself. In the course of her career, she had witnessed enough horror that people's capacity for cruelty was no longer shocking. She had stood at crime scenes and accidents and watched the crowds gather or the passing vehicles slow down for a glimpse of the carnage. She understood the pull of death. But not this.

"Do you know why they called him the Whisper Man?" Pete said quietly.

"Because of Roger Hill."

"That's right." He nodded slowly. "Roger was Carter's first victim. The family home was being renovated at the time, and Roger told his parents he'd heard someone whispering outside his window before he was abducted. Carter owned the scaffolding firm that was working on the place. That was what first brought him to our attention."

"Grooming his victim."

"Yes. Carter had the opportunity there, but the strange thing is, the parents of the other boys all claimed their children heard whispers too. There was no obvious connection to Carter, but they heard it all the same."

"Maybe they did."

"Maybe so. Or perhaps it's just that the name was in the newspaper by then, and it planted ideas in people's heads. Who knows? Whatever, it stuck. *The Whisper Man*. I've always hated that name."

She waited.

"Because I wanted him to be forgotten, you see? I didn't want him to have a *title*. But right now it seems to fit him perfectly. Because the whole time he's been *whispering*. And people—these people—have been listening." He spread the photographs out with his hand. "And I think one of them more closely than the others."

Amanda looked at the photographs again. He was

right, she thought. From everything Collins had said, it was clear that many of the individuals in front of her now had walked a fair distance down a path toward outright evil. It wasn't a stretch to believe that one of them—drawn ever onward by Frank Carter's whispers—had walked further down that path than others. The best of these people were evil sycophants, but one of them was something worse.

A student.

Somewhere among these people, she thought, they would find Neil Spencer's killer.

FORTY

After Jake had gone to bed that night, I sat in the living room of the safe house with a glass of white wine and my laptop.

Even though I was still attempting to process the events of the last few days, I was also aware that I did need to write. That seemed impossible under the present circumstances, but the money I had left wouldn't last forever. Even more than that, it felt important to be working on something, not just to distract myself from what was happening, but because it had always been that way. That was who I was. That was what I needed to reclaim.

Rebecca.

I deleted the rest of what I'd written and stared at her name. My idea the other day had been to begin to write down my feelings and trust that some kind of narrative would eventually emerge from the fog. But it was difficult to pin down my feelings right now, never mind attempt to translate them into something as simple as words.

My mind drifted back to what Karen had said in the café this morning. *Perhaps it's something you can write about in one of your books*. And the fact that she'd looked me up online. I knew how I felt about that now, because it brought a small flash of excitement. She was interested in me. Was I attracted to her? Yes. I just wasn't sure I was allowed to be. I looked at Rebecca's name on the screen. The excitement dissipated, replaced by guilt.

Rebecca.

I typed quickly.

I know exactly what you'd think about that, because you were always so much more practical than me. You'd want me to get on with my life. You'd want me to be happy. You'd be sad, of course, but you'd tell me that's the way life works. In fact, you'd more than likely tell me not to be so fucking stupid.

But the thing is, I'm not sure I'm ready *to let you go yet.*

Maybe it's me *that feels I shouldn't be happy. That I don't deserve—*

The doorbell rang.

I closed the laptop and headed downstairs, anxious that it wouldn't ring again and wake up Jake. At the door, I rubbed my eyes a little, grateful that I hadn't started crying. Even more so when I opened the door and saw my father standing there.

"DI Willis," I said.

He nodded once. "Can I come in?"

"Jake's asleep."

"I figured. But it won't take long. And I'll be quiet, I promise. I just wanted to give you an update on where things are at."

A part of me was reluctant to let him in, but that was childish—and anyway, he was just a policeman. When this was all over with, I'd never have to see him again. The fact that he seemed so beaten down, almost deferential, helped as well. Right now, in fact, I felt the more powerful of the two of us. I opened the door wider.

"All right."

He followed me upstairs and into the living room.

"We're finishing up at the house," he said. "You and Jake will be able to go back home tomorrow morning."

"That's good. What about Norman Collins?"

"We've charged him with the murder of Dominic Barnett. He's confirmed that the remains in the house belong to the victim of Carter's we never found. Tony Smith. Collins knew all along."

"How?"

"That's a long story. The details don't matter for now."

"Don't they? Well, what about Neil Spencer? And Collins attempting to abduct Jake?"

"We're working on that."

"That's reassuring." I picked up my wine and took a sip. "Oh, I'm sorry—where are my manners? Would you like a glass?" It was a test.

"I don't drink."

"You used to."

"Which is why I don't now. Some people can manage it, and others can't. It took me a while to realize that. I'm guessing you're a man who can."

"Yes."

He sighed. "I also guess that, with everything that's

happened over the years, it must have been hard for you. But you seem like a man who can do a lot of things well. That's a good thing. I'm pleased about that."

I wanted to fight back against that. Not just him having any right to pass judgment on me, but the words themselves. He was utterly mistaken—I couldn't do anything well, and I wasn't handling life at all. But, of course, there was no way I was going to display any kind of weakness in front of my father, and so I said nothing.

"Anyway," he said. "Yes. I used to drink. There were lots of reasons for that—reasons, not excuses. I struggled with a lot of things back then."

"Like being a good husband."

"Yes."

"Like fatherhood."

"That too. The responsibility of it. I never knew how to be a father. I never really wanted to be. And you were a difficult baby—much better when you were older, though. You were always creative. You used to make up stories even back then."

I couldn't remember that.

"Did I?"

"Yes. You were sensitive. Jake seems a lot like you."

"Jake's too sensitive, I think."

My father shook his head. "There's no such thing."

"There is if it makes life difficult." I thought about all the friends I never made, or who never made me. "And you wouldn't know. You weren't there."

"No, I wasn't. And like I said, it was for the best."

"Well, that's something we can agree on."

With that, it seemed like there was nothing left to say. He turned around, as though about to leave, but then he hesitated, and a moment later he turned back.

"But I was thinking about what you said last night," he told me. "About seeing me throw the glass at your mother before I left."

"And?"

"You didn't," he said. "That didn't happen. You weren't in the house that night. You were having a sleepover at a friend from school's."

I was about to say something, but then stopped. It was my turn to hesitate. My first instinct was that my father was lying—that he *had* to be, because I remembered that night so clearly. And that I hadn't *had* any friends. But was that really true back then? And whatever my father had once been, it didn't strike me that he was a liar now. In fact, as much as I didn't want to allow it, he had the air of somebody who had become scrupulously honest with himself about his faults. That perhaps, over the years, he'd needed to.

I turned the memory over in my head.

Glass smashing.

My father shouting.

My mother screaming.

I could see the image with absolute clarity in my head, but was it possible that I was wrong? The picture was more vivid than any other childhood memory I could think of. Was it too vivid? Could it have been more an emotion than an actual recollection? A summing up of how I felt rather than a specific event that had actually occurred?

"But actually, that *was* more or less how it happened," my father said quietly. "To my eternal shame, that was what I did. I didn't throw the glass *at her,* because the stupid thing is, it was the *glass* I was angry with. But it was close enough."

"I remember seeing it."

"I don't know. Maybe Sally told you."

"She never spoke badly about you." I shook my head. "You know that, right? Even after everything."

He smiled sadly. It was clear that, yes, he could believe that, and that it had reminded him of how much he'd lost.

"Then I don't know," he said. "But I wanted to tell you something else too, for whatever it's worth now. Not much, but still. You said it was the last time I ever saw you. That's not true either."

I gestured around. "Obviously."

"I mean back then. Your mother threw me out, and that was for the best. I respected that. I was almost relieved by it, to be honest, or at least it felt like what I deserved. But there were times afterward, before the two of you moved away, when if I was sober Sally would let me back in. She didn't want to disrupt you or cause any confusion, and I didn't either. So it was always after you'd gone to bed. I'd come into your room when you were asleep and give you a cuddle. You never woke up. You never knew. But I did do that."

I stood there silently.

Because, once again, I didn't believe that my father was lying, and his words had shaken me. I remembered Mister Night, my imaginary friend from childhood.

The invisible man who would come into my bedroom at night and hug me while I was sleeping. Even worse, I remembered how *comforting* it had been. How it wasn't something I had been frightened of. And how, when Mister Night had disappeared from my life, I'd been bereft for a time, as though I'd lost an important part of myself.

"I'm not making excuses," my father said. "I just wanted you to know that things were complicated. That *I* was. I'm sorry."

"Okay."

And then there really was nothing else to say. He started off down the stairs, and I was still too shaken to do anything but let him go.

FORTY-ONE

The next morning, I made sure Jake was ready earlier than usual, so that we had time to check back home before I took him to school. My father was already outside on the street below, waiting for us in his car. He rolled down the window as we walked over to him.

"Hello," my father said.

"Good morning, Pete," Jake said gravely. "How are you today?"

My father's face lit up slightly at that, amused by the overly formal tone my son could sometimes adopt. He matched it in return.

"Very well, thank you. How are you, Jake?"

"I'm fine. It was interesting staying here, but I'm looking forward to going home now."

"I can imagine."

"But not to going to school afterward."

"I can imagine that too. But school is very important."

"Yes," Jake said. "Apparently so."

My father started to laugh at that, but then glanced at me and stopped. Perhaps he thought interacting with Jake like this might annoy me. The strange thing was that, while it had annoyed me on that first afternoon in the police station, it didn't so much now. I liked it when people were impressed with my son; it made me feel proud of him. Stupid to think that way, of course—he was a person in his own right, not some accomplishment of mine—but the feeling was always there, and, if anything, with my father it was stronger than usual. I wasn't sure why. Did I want to rub his face in fatherhood, or was it some subconscious desire to impress him? I didn't like what either option said about me.

"We'll see you there." I turned away. "Come on, Jake."

The journey wasn't a long one, but it took time in the morning traffic. Jake spent most of it in the back of the car, kicking the passenger seat aimlessly and whistling a tune to himself. Every now and then I'd glance in the rearview mirror and see him, head turned to one side, squinting through the window the way he often did, as though confused to see a world out there but only mildly interested in it.

"Daddy, why don't you like Pete?"

"You mean DI Willis." I took the turn onto our street. "And it's not a case of not liking him. I don't know him. He's a policeman, not a friend."

"He is friendly, though. I like him."

"You don't know him either."

"But if you don't know him and don't like him, then I can not know him and like him instead."

I was too tired for such contortions.

"It's not that I don't like him."

Jake didn't reply, and I had no desire to argue the

point any further. Children pick up on atmosphere very well, and my son was even more sensitive than most. It was probably obvious to him that I was lying.

And yet, was it really a lie? Our conversation last night had stayed with me, and perhaps because of that, it was easier to identify with him now—to see him as a man, like me, who had found fatherhood difficult. Regardless, he was no more the man I remembered than I was still that child. How long does it take, and how much does a person have to change, before the person you hated is gone, replaced by someone new? Pete was someone else now. I didn't *not like* him. The truth was that I didn't know him at all.

We reached our house. There was no sign of police activity anymore—even the tape had been removed—and there wasn't the media presence I'd been concerned might greet us: just a small group of people talking among themselves. They didn't seem that interested as I parked in the driveway. Jake was, though.

"Are we going to be on *television*?" he said excitedly.

"Absolutely not."

"Oh."

Pete had been following our car the whole journey, and he parked sideways behind us now, then got out quickly. The reporters approached him, and I peered around to watch as he spoke to them.

"What's going on, Daddy?"

"Hang on."

Jake was straining to see as well.

"Is that—?" he said.

"Oh, fuck."

There was a moment of silence in the car after that. I stared at the small group that had gathered around my father, dimly aware that he was smiling politely at them, explaining things with a conciliatory shrug, and that a few of the reporters were nodding. But my attention was focused on one of them in particular.

"You said the *f*-word, Daddy."

Jake sounded awed.

"Yes, I did." I turned away from the sight of Karen, standing among the reporters, a notepad in her hand. "And yes. That's Adam's mother back there."

"Are we going to be on television, Pete?" Jake said.

I closed the front door behind us and put the chain on.

"I've already told you that, Jake. No, we are not."

"I'm just asking Pete as well."

"No," Pete said. "You aren't. Just like your daddy told you. That's what I was talking to the people outside about. They're reporters, and so they're interested in what happened here, but I was reminding them that it has nothing to do with you two."

"It sort of does," Jake said.

"Well, *sort of*. But not really. If you'd known more, or were more involved, then it would be different."

I shot Jake a look at that, hoping he'd understand from my expression that this was not the time to say anything else about the boy in the floor. He glanced at me and nodded, but wasn't about to let the matter drop quite so easily.

"Daddy *did* find him."

"Yes," Pete said. "But that's not information that's

been released to the people out there. As far as they're concerned, the two of you are not really part of the story. That's the best way to keep it for now, I think."

"Okay." Jake sounded disappointed. "Can I look around and see what they've done?"

"Of course."

He disappeared upstairs. Pete and I waited by the front door.

"I meant what I said," he told me after a moment. "You don't need to worry. The media won't want to prejudice any trial. I can't stop you from talking to them, obviously, but all they know is the remains were found here, so I don't think they'll be that interested in you. And they'll be very careful around Jake."

I nodded, feeling sick. That might be all the media *officially* knew, but I'd told Karen so much yesterday that it was hard to keep track of it all. She knew about the nighttime visitor attempting to abduct Jake. The fact that it was me who had found the body. That Pete was my father—my *abusive* father. And I was quite sure I'd said things I couldn't even remember right now.

I'm good at finding things out.

At the time, it had just been a conversation with a friend; I hadn't realized I was spilling everything to a fucking reporter. And it hurt. She should have told me. It had felt like she'd been genuinely interested in me, but now I wasn't so sure about that. On the one hand, there was no way she could have known in the beginning that I was connected to the case. But on the other, at no point in our conversation had she suggested that she really wasn't the person I should be telling everything to.

My father frowned.

"Are you okay?"

"Yes."

But I would have to check the damage from that conversation later. In the meantime, there was no way I was going to tell my father about it.

"Are we safe here?" I said.

"Yes. Norman Collins isn't going to be released anytime soon, and even if he was, there's nothing of interest to him here anymore. Not for any of the others either."

"Others?"

He hesitated.

"People have always been interested in this house. Collins told me it was the neighborhood scary house. Kids would dare each other to come near it. Take photographs and things."

"The scary house. I'm tired of hearing about that."

"That's just kid stuff anyway," Pete said. "Tony Smith's remains are gone. That was all Collins was ever interested in. Not you or Jake."

Not me or Jake. But I kept thinking back to seeing Jake at the bottom of the stairs that night, with the man talking to him through the mail slot. I couldn't remember the exact words I'd heard, but I could recall enough to know he'd been trying to persuade Jake to open the door, and I wasn't convinced it had only been the keys to the garage he was interested in.

"What about Neil Spencer?" I said. "Has Collins been charged with his murder?"

"No. But we have a number of suspects now. We're

closing in. And believe me, I wouldn't let you both come back if I didn't think it was safe."

"You couldn't stop me."

"No." He looked away. "I'd certainly argue the case, though, especially with Jake living here. Neil Spencer's abduction was opportunistic; he was out walking alone. This isn't a man who wants attention. You should obviously keep an eye on Jake, but there's no reason to think either of you are in any danger."

Did he sound convinced? I wasn't sure, but it was difficult to read him today. He looked exhausted. When I'd first seen him it had been obvious he was in good physical shape, but today he really looked his age.

"You look tired," I said.

He nodded.

"I am tired. And I have to do something that I'm not looking forward to."

"What?"

"It doesn't matter," he said simply. "What matters is that it has to be done."

This whole case must have taken a toll on him, I realized, and that was apparent in his whole demeanor right now. *What matters is that it has to be done.* Before me now, I saw a man weighed down by so much, struggling to cope with the load. He looked like I often felt.

"My mother," I said suddenly.

He looked back at me and waited, not asking the question.

"She died," I said.

"You told me that."

"You said you wanted to know what happened. She had a difficult life, but she was a good person. I couldn't have asked for a better parent. It was cancer. She didn't deserve what happened to her, but she didn't suffer for long either. It happened very quickly."

That was a lie—my mother's death had been prolonged and painful—and I had no idea why I was telling it this way. There was no duty incumbent on me to make Pete feel better, or to ease any pain or guilt he felt. And yet a part of me was still pleased to see the weight on him lift a little.

"When?"

"Five years ago."

"So she got to meet Jake?"

"Yes. He doesn't remember her. But yes."

"Well. I'm glad about that, at least."

There was a moment of silence. And then Jake came downstairs, and we both turned slightly away from each other at the same time, as though some tension between us had snapped.

"It's *exactly the same,* Daddy."

Jake sounded almost suspicious.

"We do a good job of searching through things carefully," Pete said. "And cleaning up after ourselves afterward."

"Admirable," Jake said. He turned and walked back into the living room.

Pete shook his head. "He's a character, that one."

"Yes. He is that."

"I'll be in touch about any developments." He handed me a card. "But in the meantime, if you need anything—and I mean anything at all—my details are there."

"Thank you."

I watched my father walk off down the driveway, head bowed slightly, and turned the card around in my hand. As he got into his car, I looked past him at the reporters gathered beyond it. Most of them had left now. I scanned the faces that remained, looking for Karen.

But she was gone.

FORTY-TWO

This is the last time, Pete told himself. *Remember that.*

The thought was something to cling to while he sat in the bright white interview room at the prison, waiting for the monster to arrive. He had been here so many times over the years, and each occasion had left him shaken. But after today, there would be no reason for him ever to return. Tony Smith—always the focus of these visits in the past—had been found, and if Frank Carter refused to talk about the man they were looking for now, Pete had already made the decision that he would walk out of this room and not look back. And he'd never have to suffer the crawling aftermath of being in Carter's presence again.

This is the last time.

The thought helped, but only a little. The air in the silent room felt full of anticipation and threat, the locked door on the far side throbbing with menace. Because Carter must also know this was likely to be their last meeting, and Pete was sure he would be determined to make it count. Until now the fear of these encounters had always been mental and emotional. He had never been physically afraid before. But right now he was glad for the width of the desk dividing the room and the strength of the shackles the man would be wearing. He even wondered if, subconsciously, all those hours in the gym had been spent preparing himself in case a moment like that ever happened.

His heart leaped as he heard the door being unlocked. *Keep calm.*

The familiar routine unfolded: the guards entering first; Carter taking his time. Pete steadied himself by concentrating on the envelope he'd brought, which was on the desk in front of him now. He stared at that and waited, ignoring the bulk of the man who finally approached, then sat down heavily across from him. Let the tables be turned, for once—Carter could wait. Pete remained silent until the guards had retreated and he heard the door closing. Only then did he look up.

Carter was staring at the envelope too, a curious expression on his face.

"Have you written me a letter, Peter?"

Pete didn't reply.

"I've often thought I might write one to you." Carter looked up and smiled. "Would you like that?"

Pete suppressed the shudder he felt. There was little chance of Carter discovering his home address directly, but the idea of receiving even forwarded correspondence was intolerable.

Again, he said nothing.

Carter shook his head in disapproval.

"I told you last time, Peter. That's the problem with you, you know? I make this big effort to talk to you. I go to all these great lengths to tell you things and be helpful. And sometimes it feels like you're not listening to me at all."

"*It ends where it begins*," Pete said. "I understand that now."

"A bit too late for Neil Spencer, though."

"What I'm interested in is how you knew that, Frank."

"And like I said, that's the problem with you." Carter leaned back. The weight of him made the chair creak. "You don't listen. Honestly, what do I care about some fucking kid? That's not even what I was referring to."

"No?"

"Not at all." He leaned forward again, suddenly more engaged, and Pete resisted the urge to flinch. "Hey—here's another one. Do you remember what you said about people in the outside world forgetting me?"

Pete thought back, then nodded. "You told me it wasn't true."

"That's *right*. Ha, ha! And you understand that now, I guess? You get how wrong you were. Because all along there was this whole bunch of people out there you didn't know about who have stayed *real interested* in me."

Carter's eyes gleamed at that. Pete could only imagine the amount of pleasure he must have taken over the years, knowing he had fans like Norman Collins visiting the house where Tony Smith's remains had been left, treating the place as though it were some kind of shrine. Even more, he must have delighted in holding a secret like that over Pete for all this time—knowing that while Pete had been searching incessantly for the missing child, others had been finding Tony so very easily.

"Yes, Frank. I was wrong. I know that now. And I'm sure the whole experience was very flattering for you. *The Whisper Man*." He pulled a face. "Your legend living on."

Carter grinned. "In so many ways."

"So let's talk about some of the others."

Carter said nothing, but he glanced down at the envelope and his smile broadened. He wasn't going to be tricked into talking about Neil Spencer's killer. Pete knew that if he was going to learn anything, he would have to read between the lines, and that meant keeping the man talking. And while Carter might be deliberately vague on some subjects, Pete was sure he would be more than happy to talk about the visitors to the house over the years, at least now that the secret was out.

"All right," Pete said. "Why Victor Tyler?"

"Ah, Vic's a good man."

"That's an interesting way of putting it. But what I actually meant is, why use an intermediary to arrange all this?"

"It wouldn't do much good to be accessible, would it, Peter?" Carter shook his head. "If everyone could see God, how many people would bother going to church? It's better to keep some distance. Better for *them* too, of course. Safer. I imagine you've checked my visits over the years?"

"I'm the only person you see."

"And what an honor, right?" He laughed.

"What about the money?"

"What about it?"

"Tyler was paid—or his wife was, at least. Simpson was too, and then Barnett after him. But not you."

"What do I care about money?" Carter looked affronted. "Everything I want in life is free now. Vic—like I said, he's a good man, a decent man. And Julian did right by me too. It's only fair they should get something for that. Never knew Barnett, and couldn't care less. But it's good those people paid to visit the place. They *should* fucking pay. I'm worth it, aren't I?"

"No."

Carter laughed again. "Maybe, after you arrest them all, they'll even end up in here with me. That'll be a real kick for them, won't it? They'd enjoy that, I bet."

Not as much as you, Pete thought.

He picked up the envelope and took out the photographs he had brought with him: a thin pile of CCTV stills taken of the visitors Victor Tyler had received over the years. An image of Norman Collins was on top, and he slid it carefully across the table to Carter.

"Do you recognize this man?"

Carter barely glanced at it.

"No."

A second photograph: "What about this man?"

"I don't know any of these fucking people, Peter." Carter rolled his eyes. "How many times do I have to tell you? *You don't listen.* You want to know who these people are, go ask Vic."

"We will."

In fact, he and Amanda had interviewed Tyler an hour earlier, and Tyler had enjoyed the situation substantially less than his friend Carter appeared to be doing. He was angry and refusing to cooperate. Pete supposed that was understandable, given that his wife was also implicated, but silence wasn't going to save either of them. Likewise, the visitors they'd identified—among whom Pete was sure they would find Neil Spencer's killer—were in the process of being hunted down and questioned.

All except one.

Pete slid another photograph onto the table. It showed a younger man, perhaps in his twenties or early thirties. Average height and build. Black glasses. Shoulder-length brown hair. He had visited Tyler on a number of occasions, most recently in the week before Neil Spencer had been killed.

"What about this man?"

Carter didn't look at the photo. He stared at Pete and smiled.

"This is the one you're interested in, isn't it?"

Pete didn't reply.

"You're so predictable, Peter. So *obvious*. You soften me up with two, then hit me with the one that matters so you can watch my reaction. This is your guy, isn't it? Or at least you think it is?"

"You're very clever, Frank. Do you recognize this man?"

Carter stared back for a moment longer. But even as he did, his cuffed hands reached out and brought the photograph closer to him. The movement was uncanny, as though his hands were being operated by something separate from the rest of him. His head didn't move. His expression didn't change.

Then he looked down, studying the image.

"Ah," he said softly.

Pete watched the man's huge chest rising and falling as he breathed slowly, taking in the details before him.

"Tell me about this man, Peter," Carter said.

"I'm more interested in what you know."

Pete waited him out. Eventually Carter looked up, then tapped the photograph gently with one huge finger.

"*This man* is a bit smarter than the others, isn't he? He used a false name to visit, but he had the paperwork to back it up. You've looked into it, and you know it wasn't real."

That was true. The man had provided identification at the time of his visits: his name was Liam Adams, he was twenty-nine years old, and he lived with his parents, thirty miles away from Featherbank. Officers had arrived at the property first thing that morning, only to be met with blank incomprehension—and then horror—on the faces of Liam's parents.

Because their son had died over a decade ago.

"Go on," Pete told Carter.

"Do you know how easy it is to buy a new identity, Peter? Much simpler than you imagine. And like I said, he's clever, this one. If you want to send a message to someone these days, you have to be, don't you? This right here." Carter lowered his voice. "This is a man who *takes care*."

"Tell me more about him, Frank."

But instead of answering, Carter stared down at the photograph again for a few more seconds, studying it. It was as though he were looking at someone he'd heard a great deal about and was now curious to see him finally. But then he sniffed loudly, suddenly uninterested in whatever he saw, and pushed the photo back across the table.

"I've told you everything I know."

"I don't believe you."

"And like I said, that's always been your problem."

Carter smiled at him, but his eyes had gone blank now.

"You just don't listen, Peter."

Pete didn't let his frustration out until he was back at the car, where Amanda was waiting for him. He clambered into the passenger seat and slammed the door, the photographs he was carrying spilling from his hand onto the floor mat.

"Shit."

He leaned over and gathered them together, even though only one was important. After he'd rammed the others back into the envelope, he kept that picture out, resting it on top of his knees. A man with a dead teenager's name, with black glasses and brown hair that could easily be a disguise, or have been changed by now. The man could be almost any age. He could be almost anyone.

"I am guessing," Amanda said, "that Carter was not forthcoming?"

"He was his usual charming self."

Pete ran a hand through his hair, angry with himself. *The last time,* yes, and he had survived it. But as always, he had come out of the conversation with nothing, even though Carter *knew* something.

"Fucker," he said.

"Tell me," Amanda said.

He took a moment to compose himself, and then ran through the conversation in detail. The idea that he didn't listen to Carter was rubbish; of *course* he listened to him. Every conversation with Carter seeped into him. The words were the opposite of sweat, soaking in and leaving him clammy on the inside.

When he was done, Amanda considered it.

"You think Carter knows who this man is?"

"I'm not sure." Pete looked down at the photograph. "Maybe. He certainly knows *something* about him. Or perhaps he doesn't, and he's just enjoying seeing me scrabble around, trying to make sense of his every fucking word."

"You're swearing more than usual, Pete."

"I'm angry."

You just don't listen.

"Run through it again," Amanda said patiently. "Not this visit. The last one. *That's* what he said you hadn't been listening to, right?"

Pete hesitated, then thought back.

"*It always ends where it starts,*" he said. "It started at the waste ground, so that's where Neil Spencer was always going to be returned to. Except Carter said that wasn't what he'd meant."

"So what *did* he mean?"

"Who knows?" Pete wanted to throw up his hands. "Then there was the dream about Tony Smith. But that wasn't real. He just made that up to taunt me."

Amanda was silent for a few seconds.

"But if so," she said, "he *made it up* a certain way. And you said it yourself—that's why you visit him. You've always hoped he'd give something away without meaning to."

Pete was ready to protest, but she was right. If the dream hadn't been real, then Carter must have conjured it up himself, choosing to describe it in the way he had. And it was possible some truth had slipped out through the gaps there.

He ran through it in his mind now.

"He wasn't sure it was Tony."

"In the dream?"

"Yes." Pete nodded. "The boy's T-shirt was pulled up over his face, so he couldn't see it properly. He said that was the way he liked it."

"Just like Neil Spencer."

"Yes."

"None of which was ever made public." Amanda shook her head in frustration. "And Carter was a sadist. Why wouldn't he want to see the faces of his victims?"

Pete had no answer to that. Carter had always refused to discuss his motivations. But while there had never been any apparent sexual element to the murders, Amanda was right: he had hurt those children badly, and it was clear he was a sadist. As to why he covered their faces, there were countless possible explanations for that. If you asked five different profilers—and they had at the time—you got five different answers. Perhaps it was to make the victims physically easier to control. Or to muffle sound. To disorientate them. To scare them. To stop them from seeing him. To stop *him* from seeing them. One of the reasons profiling was such bullshit was that different offenders almost always had massively different reasons for the exact same behavior, and . . .

Pete hesitated.

"All these bastards are the same," he said quietly.

"What?"

"That's what Carter told me." He frowned. "Something like that, anyway. When he was talking about which of the children it was in the dream. *All these bastards are the same. Any one will do.*"

"Go on."

But he fell silent again, trying to think through the implications and feeling that some kind of understanding was suddenly within reach. It hadn't mattered to Carter who he had been hurting. More than that, he hadn't wanted to see the victims' faces at all.

But why?

To stop him *from seeing them.*

Was that perhaps because he had wanted to imagine someone else in their place? Pete stared down at the photograph again—at the man who could be anyone— and recalled the strange look on Carter's face. Despite himself, he had been curious about the man in the photo. Once again, it had been as though he were seeing someone he had been interested in for a long time but was only finally laying eyes on. It made Pete think of something else. How he had fought so hard not to think of Tom over the years, and yet had found it impossible not to evaluate him when they had met. How even though traces remained of the boy, the man was so different from the little boy he remembered.

Because children change so much.

I've told you everything I know.

And now Pete remembered a different child. Another little boy—small and scared and malnourished, hiding behind his mother's legs as Pete unlocked the door to Frank Carter's extension.

A little boy who would now be in his late twenties.

"*Bring me my family,*" Pete remembered. "*That bitch and that little cunt.*"

He looked up at Amanda, finally understanding.

"That's what I didn't listen to."

FORTY-THREE

Just before lunchtime, there was a knock at the door.

I looked up from my laptop. The first thing I'd done after dropping Jake at school that morning had been to google Karen. She'd been easy enough to find: Karen Shaw had bylines for dozens of online articles at the local paper, including pieces that covered the abduction and murder of Neil Spencer. I'd read each of them with an increasingly sick feeling in my stomach: not just fear over what she might write next—all those private details I'd revealed to her yesterday in the coffee shop—but also a sense of betrayal. I'd allowed myself to imagine that she was genuinely interested in me, and now I felt stupid, as though I'd been conned in some way.

The knock came again: a quiet, tentative sound, as though whoever was outside was undecided if they wanted me to hear or not. And I thought I knew who I would find out there. I put the laptop to one side and went to the door.

Karen, standing on the front step.

I leaned against the wall and folded my arms.

"Are you bugged under that thing?"

I nodded at the big overcoat. She winced.

"Can I come in for a minute?"

"What for?"

"I just . . . want to explain. It won't take long."

"There's no need."

"I think there is."

She looked contrite—ashamed, even—but I remembered my mother telling me that explanations and apologies were almost always for the person making them, and I felt an urge to tell Karen she could make herself feel better on her own time. But her apparent vulnerability right now was such a stark contrast to her manner during our previous encounters that I couldn't. It looked like she was doing this because it really did matter to her.

I leaned away from the wall.

"All right."

We went through to the living room. A part of me was slightly embarrassed by the state of the place: my dirty plate from breakfast was on the couch by the laptop, and Jake's colored pencils and drawings were still scattered all over the floor. But I wasn't going to apologize to Karen for the mess. It didn't matter what she thought, did it? Before this morning, it would have—there was no point denying that now. Foolish, but true.

She stopped at the far end of the room, still wrapped up in her big coat, as though unsure whether she'd been invited in or not.

"Can I get you a drink?"

She shook her head. "I just wanted to explain about this morning. I know how it must have looked."

"I'm not really sure how it looked. Or what to think."

"I'm sorry. I should have told you."

"Yes."

"And I almost did. You might not believe me, but I was actually kicking myself yesterday morning. In the coffee shop, I mean, the whole time you were telling me all that stuff."

"You still let me, though."

"Well, you *kind of* didn't give me a chance." She risked a slight smile at that: a flash of the Karen I was more used to. "Honestly, it seemed like you had a lot to get off your chest, and on that level I was glad to be of use. It was a pain listening to it all as a journalist, though."

"Was it really?"

"Yeah. Because I knew I wouldn't be able to use any of it."

"I'm sure you could."

"Well, yes, in the sense that it wasn't officially off the record, I suppose I could. But it wouldn't be fair to you or Jake. I wouldn't do that to you. It's more about personal ethics than professional ones."

"Right."

"Which is fucking *typical,* frankly." She gave a bitter laugh. "Biggest story in the history of the area since I moved here, and I've got an angle none of the majors have. And I can't use it."

I didn't reply. It was true she hadn't used it—at least not yet. Her most recent article had been posted this morning, and it had only included the same basic details reported by all the other news outlets. What I'd told her went way above and beyond what was already out there, and it was also very obviously part of her beat. But, however tempting it must have been, she hadn't revealed any of it so far. Did I believe her now when she said she wouldn't? I thought I did.

"Have you talked to any of the others?" she said.

"No." I was about to repeat my father's line about not knowing anything, but that would have been a pointless lie under the circumstances. "The rest of them left early on. There have been a few phone calls on the landline, but I've just ignored those."

"Irritating."

"I never answer the phone anyway."

"No, I don't like phones much either."

"It's more that nobody ever calls me."

Not really a joke, but she smiled. And that was okay, I thought. The conversation had grown quieter the longer we'd been speaking, and some of the tension in the room had dissipated now. It was almost a surprise to me how much of a relief that was.

"Are they likely to keep trying?" I said.

"It depends on what happens. From experience, if they won't leave you alone, then it might be worth talking to one of them." She held her hand up. "Not necessarily me. In fact, as much as it kills me to say this, a part of me would probably prefer it wasn't."

"Why?"

"Because we're friends, Tom, and that makes it harder to be objective. Like I said, I was *kicking* myself yesterday. You do realize that I didn't take you for a coffee because I sniffed a story, right? It was a total surprise, what you told me. How could I possibly have known? But the point is, if you get an account out there once, there'll be less interest. See what happens, though."

I thought about it.

"But I could talk to you?"

"Yes, you could. And you know what? All that aside, it'd be nice to go for a coffee again at some point, wouldn't it?"

"Maybe I could get some dirt on you."

She smiled. "Yeah. Maybe you could."

I thought about it.

"Sure you can't stay for a drink?"

"Sadly, yes—I wasn't just saving face before. I really do need to get back." She was about to head out of the room, but then something occurred to her. "What about tonight? I could probably get my mother to babysit Adam. We could grab a drink or something?"

Her mother to babysit. Not a husband or partner. I supposed I'd been assuming she was single, and I wasn't sure now whether the confirmation was deliberate or accidental. Regardless, I very much wanted to say yes. Jesus, how astonishing would it be to go out for a drink with a woman? I couldn't remember the last time. But even more than that, I realized that I very much wanted to go for a drink with *her*. That I'd spent the morning feeling hurt and foolish for a fairly obvious reason.

But, of course, it wasn't possible.

"I'd probably struggle with a babysitter," I said.

"Right. I get you. Hang on a second." She reached

into her coat and produced a card. "I realized you hadn't got my details. All my contact stuff is on there. If you want it, I mean."

Yes, I wanted it.

"Thanks." I took the card. "I've not got one of my own."

"Duh. Just text me so I've got your number."

"Obviously. Duh indeed."

She paused at the front door.

"How's Jake today?"

"Miraculously well," I said. "I really have no idea how."

"I do. Like I said, you're too hard on yourself."

And then she headed off down the path. I watched her go for a moment, then looked down at the card in my hand. Thinking. It was the second card I'd received today, and both were complicated in their different ways. But, God, a drink out with Karen would be good. It felt like something people did, and that it should really be possible for me to do it as well.

Once I was back in the living room, I took out my phone and thought about the situation a whole lot more. Hesitating. Unsure.

Just text me so I've got your number.

In the end, it wasn't the first message I sent.

FORTY-FOUR

Back at the department, the operations room was alive with activity. While most of the officers were continuing with their existing actions, a small number were now focused on the key task of tracking down Frank Carter's son, Francis, and that knowledge had galvanized everyone. The renewed energy in the room was tangible. After two months of moving in circles and following fruitless leads, it felt like a new path had opened up for them.

Not that it would necessarily go anywhere, Amanda reminded herself. It was always best not to get your hopes up.

But always so hard not to.

"No," Pete said.

He added another sheet of paper to the pile on the desk between them.

"No," she replied, adding one of her own.

After Frank Carter's trial and conviction, Francis and his mother had moved away, and because of the infamy of the case, they had been given new identities—an opportunity to begin fresh lives, without the shadow of the monster they had lived with hanging over them.

Jane Carter had become Jane Parker; Francis had become David. After that, the pair of them had effectively disappeared. They were common, anonymous names, which was presumably one reason why they had been chosen. The task facing Amanda and Pete now was to find the correct David Parker out of the thousands living in the country.

Next sheet. This David Parker was forty-five years old. The one they were looking for would be twenty-seven.

"No," she said.

And so it went.

They worked through the names mostly in silence. Pete was intent on the pages before him, and she presumed that his focus was a way of distracting himself. The conversation he'd had with Frank Carter must have shaken him as much as all the others, but there was an added tension now. Pete had met Carter's son when Francis was a child. He had effectively saved the boy. Knowing Pete as she was beginning to, it was easy to imagine what was going through his head right now. He would be asking hard questions of himself. What if Pete's actions back then had planted a seed that had grown into this fresh horror? What if, despite his best intentions, this was all somehow *his fault*?

"We can't be sure that Francis is involved," she said.

"No."

Pete added another sheet of paper to the pile.

Amanda sighed to herself, frustrated by the knowledge that nothing she could say right now was going to rescue Pete from his thoughts. But what she had said was true. As terrible an upbringing as Francis Carter might have suffered, she had seen plenty of people emerge from horrific, abusive childhoods and grow into decent adults. There were as many paths out of hell as there were people, and the vast majority of them ascended.

She was also familiar enough with the original investigation to know that Pete had done nothing wrong—that he had worked the case as well as anybody could, even going above and beyond in his dogged pursuit of Jane Carter. He had followed his gut instinct, focused on Frank Carter, and eventually brought the man down. While he hadn't been able to save Tony Smith in time, it was impossible to save everyone. There would always be mistakes you never saw in time.

And thinking about Neil Spencer, she knew she needed to cling to that herself. She didn't want to believe that the things you missed—the things you never even had the opportunity to hit—could weigh you down so much that they threatened to drown you.

She turned her attention back to the paperwork, working her way steadily through the list of David Parkers.

"No."

The papers piling up.

"No."

The words formed a predictable pattern. *No. No. No.* It was only when she'd done three in a row without a response that she noticed Pete had been silent for longer than he should have been. She looked up at him hopefully, but then realized he had stopped paying attention to the forms on the table. Instead, he had his cell phone in his hands, and was staring at that.

"What?" she said.

"Nothing."

And yet it clearly wasn't. In fact, she couldn't quite believe her eyes. Because Pete appeared to be smiling. Could that *actually* be the case? It was the smallest of expressions, but she realized she'd never seen even that before. He'd always been so stern and serious—so *dark,* like a house in which the owner stubbornly refused to turn on any lights. Right now, though, a single room seemed to be illuminated. A text message, she guessed. Maybe it was a woman? Or a man, of course; after all, she knew next to nothing about his private life. Regardless, she liked seeing this unfamiliar expression on his face. It was a welcome break from the intensity she had become used to, and which made her worry about him.

She wanted this new light to stay.

"What?" She asked it more teasingly this time.

"Just someone asking if I'm free for something this evening." He put the phone on the table, the smile disappearing. "Which obviously I'm not."

"Don't be ridiculous."

Pete looked at her.

"I'm serious," she told him. "Technically speaking, this is my case, not yours. I'll stay as long as I have to, but listen, you are going home at the end of the day."

"No."

"*Yes.* And you can do whatever you want when you

get there. I'll keep you up to date with any developments."

"It should be me."

"It absolutely should *not*. Even if we find the right David Parker, we have no idea how or even if he's involved. It's just a conversation. And I think it would be better for him and for you if someone else handles that. I know how much this case means to you, but you can't live in the past, Pete. Other things matter too." She nodded at his phone. "Sometimes you've got to leave it at the door at the end of the day. Do you know what I mean?"

He was silent for a moment, and she thought he was about to protest again. But then he nodded.

"You can't live in the past," he repeated. "You're right about that. More right than you know."

"Oh, I *know* how right I am. Believe me."

He smiled. "All right, then."

Then he picked up his phone again, and began tapping a reply a little awkwardly, as though he didn't get many texts and wasn't used to sending ones in return. Or maybe he was just nervous about this one in particular. Regardless, she was pleased for him. There was that slight smile on his face again, and it was good to see. To know it was possible.

Alive, she realized, watching him. That was what it was.

After everything he'd been through, he seemed like a man who was finally looking forward to something.

FORTY-FIVE

I'd arranged with my father for him to arrive at seven o'clock that evening, and he was so prompt in his timing that I wondered whether he'd arrived early and been sitting outside until the designated time. Perhaps out of respect for me—the idea that if he was being allowed into my and Jake's life then it had to be precisely on my terms—but actually, I thought he was most likely the same with everyone. A man for whom discipline was important.

He was dressed neatly in suit trousers and shirt, as though he'd come straight from work, but he looked fresh and his hair was damp, so it was obvious he'd showered and changed first. He smelled clean too. As he followed me inside, I realized I'd checked that subconsciously. If he still drank, he would have started by now, and it wasn't too late for me to pull this whole event.

Jake was kneeling on the floor of the living room, hunched over a drawing.

"Pete's here," I told him.

"Hi, Pete."

"Could you at least pretend to look up?"

Jake sighed to himself, but put down the colored pencil he'd been using.

"Hi, Pete," he said again.

My father smiled.

"Good evening, Jake. Thank you for allowing me to look after you for a bit tonight."

"You're welcome."

"We both appreciate it," I said. "It should only be a couple of hours at most."

"However long you need. I brought a book."

I glanced at the thick paperback he was holding. I couldn't see enough of the cover to read the title, but there was a black-and-white photograph of Winston Churchill on the front. It was exactly the kind of worthy, weighty tome that I'd have struggled to force myself through, and it made me feel self-conscious. My father had transformed himself, physically and mentally, into this quietly impressive man. I couldn't help but feel slightly inadequate in comparison.

Stupid, though.

You're too hard on yourself.

My father put his book down on the couch.

"Can you show me around?"

"You've been here before."

"In a different capacity," he said. "This is your home. I'd prefer to hear it from you."

"Okay. We're just going upstairs, Jake."

"Yes, I know."

He was already drawing again. I led the way upstairs, pointing my father to the bathroom and then Jake's bedroom.

"He'd normally have a bath, but just skip that tonight," I said. "Half an hour or so, he comes up for bed. Pajamas are there on the duvet. His book's down there. We normally read a chapter together before lights out, and we're about halfway through that one."

My father looked down at it quizzically.

"Power of Three?"

"Yeah, Diana Wynne Jones. It's probably a bit old for him, but he likes it."

"That's fine."

"And like I said, I won't be out for long."

"Are you doing anything nice?"

I hesitated.

"Just grabbing a drink with a friend."

I didn't want to go into any more detail than that. For one thing, it made me feel curiously teenage to admit I was going on something that might be considered a date. Of course, my father and I had skipped that whole awkward period of my growing up, so perhaps it was natural to feel it a little now. We'd never had the chance to develop the language to talk about it, or not to.

"I'm sure that will be nice," he said.

"Yes."

I thought it would be too, and that brought another teenage sensation: butterflies in my stomach. Not that it *was* a date, of course. It would be foolish to go into the evening thinking of it as one. That way disappointment lay. And both Karen and I had kids at our respective homes anyway, so it wasn't like anything could really *happen*. How the hell did people manage that anyway?

I really had no idea. I hadn't dated in so long that I might as *well* have been a teenager.

Butterflies.

Which reminded me that I hadn't locked the front door after letting my father in. It was ridiculous, but the excitement was immediately replaced by a small flush of fear.

"Come on," I said. "Let's head back down."

FORTY-SIX

The ceiling was creaking as Daddy and Pete moved around upstairs. They were talking, Jake could tell, but he couldn't make out the exact words. It was going to be about him, though, obviously—instructions about how to put him to bed, and things like that. That was okay. He wanted to go to bed as soon as possible.

Because he very much wanted this day to be over with.

That was the thing about going to sleep. It kind of *scrubbed* things. Arguments, worries, whatever. You could be scared or upset about something, and you might think sleep was impossible, but at some point it happened, and when you woke up in the morning the feeling was gone for a while, like a storm that had passed during the night. Or maybe it was like being put to sleep before a big operation. Which happened sometimes, Daddy had told him. The doctors put you to sleep, and you missed all the horrible stuff they had to do and just woke up better again afterward.

Right now what he wanted was the fear to go away.

Except *fear* wasn't quite the right word for it. When you were afraid, it was of something specific, like being told off, but what he was feeling was more like a bird that didn't have anywhere to land. Ever since this morning, there had just been the sensation that *something bad* was going to happen, but he wasn't sure *what*. But if Jake was certain of one thing right now, it was that he didn't want Daddy to go out tonight.

But the feeling wasn't *real,* so the sooner he went to sleep, the better. He would be scared—or whatever the name for this feeling was—but when he woke up in the morning, Daddy would be back home, and everything would be all right again.

"No, you're right to be scared."

Jake jumped. The little girl was sitting beside him, her legs straight out in front of her. He hadn't seen her since that first day at school, and yet the hash of scabs on her knee still looked red and raw, and her hair, as ever, was splayed out to one side. He could tell from her face that, once again, she wasn't in the mood for playing—that *she* knew something was wrong too. She looked more scared than he was.

"He shouldn't go out," she said.

Jake looked back down at his drawing. Just like the feeling, he knew that the little girl wasn't real. Even if she seemed to be. Even if he so desperately wanted her to be.

"Nothing bad is going to happen," he whispered.

"Yes, it is. You *know* it is."

He shook his head. It was important to be sensible and grown up about this, because Daddy was relying on him to be a good boy. So he continued to work on his picture, as though she wasn't really there. Which, of course, she wasn't.

Even so, he could sense her exasperation.

"You don't *want* him to meet her," she said.

Jake kept drawing.

"You don't want your mummy replaced, do you?"

Jake stopped drawing.

No, of course he didn't want that. And that wasn't going to happen, was it? But he couldn't deny there had been something a little strange about Daddy's behavior when he was talking about what was going to happen tonight. Again, the feeling wasn't precise enough to put a name to, but everything *did* seem a little off-balance and wrong, like there was something he wasn't being told. But nobody was going to replace Mummy. And Daddy didn't want that either.

But then he remembered the things Daddy had written.

They had talked about that, though, hadn't they? Just like things in books, it wasn't real. And besides, Daddy had been so sad recently, and this was something that might help with that. It was important. Jake needed to let Daddy be Daddy, so that he could be him for Jake again too.

He had to be brave.

A moment later, the little girl rested her head on his shoulder, her hair stiff and unyielding against his neck.

"I'm so scared," she said softly. "Don't let him go, Jake."

He was about to say something else, but then he heard heavy footsteps on the stairs, and the little girl was gone.

FORTY-SEVEN

When we got back downstairs, Jake was still sitting on the floor by his picture, pencil in hand. But he'd stopped drawing now and was staring off into space. In fact, he looked as if he were about to cry. I walked over and crouched down beside him.

"You okay, mate?"

He nodded, but I didn't believe him.

"What's the matter?"

"Nothing."

"Hmmm." I frowned. "Not sure I believe you on that one. Are you worried about tonight?"

He hesitated.

"Maybe a little."

"Well, that's understandable. But you'll be fine. To be honest, I'd have thought you'd be looking forward to spending time with someone else for a change."

He looked at me at that, and while he still seemed so small and fragile, I didn't think I'd ever seen such an old expression on his face before now.

"Do you think I don't *want* to be with you?" he said.

"Oh, Jake. Come here."

I adjusted my position so that he could sit on my knee

for a cuddle. He perched on me, and then pressed his small body against mine.

"I don't think that *at all*. That wasn't what I meant."

Except, it had been. Kind of, anyway. One of my biggest fears since Rebecca's death was that I couldn't connect with him. That we were strangers to each other. And a part of me *did* feel he might be better off without me and my fumbling attempts at fatherhood—that when he walked into school without a backward glance, it was how he felt all of the time.

It made me wonder if he thought the same about me. Maybe my going out this evening had made him feel I didn't want to be with him. That I'd booked him into the 567 Club because I wanted to be rid of him. While I did need my own time and space, nothing could have been further from the truth.

How sad that was, I thought. Both of us feeling the same. Both of us trying to meet in the middle but somehow always missing each other.

"And I want to be with you too," I said. "I won't be out for long, I promise."

He tightened his grip on me slightly.

"Do you have to go?"

I took a deep breath.

The answer, I supposed, was no, I didn't have to, and I was reluctant to leave if it was going to upset him badly.

"I don't *have* to," I said. "But it will be fine, I promise. You'll go to bed soon, fall asleep, and when you wake up I'll be home again."

He was silent, thinking over what I'd just told him.

But the whole time, his anxiety seemed to be creeping into me as well. Apprehension. *Dread,* almost—the sudden fear that something bad was going to happen. It was silly, and there was no reason to think that. Even so, I *could* stay home, and I was about to tell him just that, but he nodded before I had the chance.

"Okay."

"Right," I said. "Good. I love you, Jake."

"I love you too, Daddy."

He disentangled himself from me, and I stood up. My father had been waiting by the door the whole time and I walked over to him.

"Jake okay?"

"Yes. He'll be fine. But any problems at all, you've got my cell number."

"I have it. But everything will be fine. Just strange for him, I guess." He raised his voice a little. "But we'll get along grand, Jake. You're going to be good for me, right?"

Jake, who was drawing again now, nodded in reply.

I watched him for a moment, crouched down and concentrating on his picture, and I felt an indescribable burst of love for him. But it was one that hardened into determination. We were going to get back on track, the two of us. Everything was going to be okay. I wanted to be with him, and he wanted to be with me, and some-how, between us, we would figure out a way to make that work.

"A couple of hours," I told my father again. "That's all it will be."

FORTY-EIGHT

"We're nearly there," DS Dyson said.

"I know," Amanda told him.

She'd made Dyson drive, if only to keep him off his phone for an hour. They were fifty miles away from Featherbank now, heading along one edge of a large university campus. A corner took them into what was obviously the student heartland of the city, the houses all redbrick and cramped together on thin streets. Each was at least three or four stories high: buildings where five or six people could live together in groups, or landlords could rent single rooms out, creating collections of random strangers who remained strangers. A square mile of disparate people. A place it was cheap and easy to disappear into.

And this was where David Parker, previously known as Francis Carter, had chosen to make his home.

The ID was a solid one—right age, and a close visual match for the build of Victor Tyler's prison visitor. They'd found him an hour before Pete had been due to leave, which had worried her at first, as she had been concerned he might overturn whatever arrangement he'd made earlier and insist on being involved. And she could tell that he had wanted to. But instead, he had watched quietly as Amanda made arrangements with the local force to visit the address, and when it had been time for him to leave, he had done so without complaint—just wished her luck and asked her to keep him informed on any developments. With the decision already made, she thought he might even have been relieved.

If only she could say the same—a part of her wished it were Pete with her right now. Because while everything they'd talked about back at the department remained true—they had no concrete evidence that Francis Carter was involved in the case at all, and this was going to be a routine visit in the first instance—she could feel it all the same. A tingle in her stomach, halfway between fear and excitement. It was telling her that she was close. That something was going to happen, and that she needed to be on guard and ready for it when it did.

Dyson turned down a steep hill. Each house here was lower than the one before it, so the roofs formed a black saw-blade pattern against the darkening sky. Francis Carter—or David Parker—was renting a one-bedroom apartment in the basement of a large shared house. Did that fit? It worked for her in some ways, but not in others. If Parker *was* their man, he would certainly want his own place for privacy. But at the same time, could he really have kept a child here for two months without anyone seeing or hearing? Or had Neil been kept elsewhere?

The car slowed.

You're about to find out.

Dyson parked under a streetlight that seemed to bleach the world of color, and they both got out of the car. The house was four stories high and seemed squeezed in by the properties beside it. No lights on at the front. There was a low brick wall with a rusted iron gate, which Amanda opened quietly before stepping onto the path. To her left was a messy garden, too small and wretched to have been tended by anyone, and then steep steps led up to the front door. But just past the garden, a second set of steps led down below ground level into an area barely wide enough for a single person to stand. From the top, Amanda could see a front window. The door to Parker's apartment was presumably directly underneath the main door above, obscured from view right now.

She led the way down, the garden rising up to her left, replaced by the brick wall containing it, and the air was much colder here. It felt like descending into a grave. The window was a dirty square of black, with cobwebs in the corners. Parker's front door was barely visible in the shadows.

She knocked hard and called out.

"Mr. Parker? David Parker?"

No reply.

She gave it a few seconds more, then knocked again.

"David?" she said. "Are you in there?"

Again she was met by nothing but silence. Beside her, Dyson had his hands over his eyes, staring in through the window as best he could.

"Can't see a thing." He leaned away. "What do we do now?"

Amanda tried the door handle—and was almost surprised when it turned with a creak. The door opened slightly. Immediately the thick, heavy stink of mold wafted out from the apartment.

"Not safe, that, in this neighborhood," Dyson said.

Because he wasn't close enough to smell what she could. *Not safe at all,* she thought, but perhaps not in the way he was meaning. The room within was pitch-black, and the tingling sensation in her stomach was stronger than ever. It was telling her that something dangerous was waiting in there.

"Stay alert," she told Dyson.

Then she pulled out a flashlight and stepped carefully inside, one coat sleeve held protectively over her nose and mouth, the other playing the beam slowly over the room before her. The air was so dusty that it looked like sand was swirling in the light. She moved the beam around and caught flashes of detritus: tattered gray furniture; tangles of old clothes strewn on the wiry carpet; paperwork scattered on the surface of a rickety wooden table. The walls and ceiling were mottled with damp. There was a kitchen area along the wall to the right, and as she ran the light steadily along the filthy plates and bowls there, she saw things moving, casting oversized shadows as they scuttled away out of sight.

"Francis?" she called.

But it was obvious that nobody lived here anymore. The place had been abandoned. Someone had walked out of here, closed the front door without bothering to lock it behind them, and never returned. She clicked the light switch beside her up and down. Nothing. The rent had been paid a year in advance, but apparently not the utilities.

Dyson stopped beside her.

"Jesus."

"Wait here," she said.

Then she stepped gingerly through the debris scattered around the room. There were two doors at the back. She opened one and found the bathroom, moving the flashlight back and forth and resisting the urge to gag. It stank far worse in here than it did in the living room. The sink at the far end was half full of dank water, with sodden towels lying knotted on the floor, their surfaces speckled with rot.

She closed the door and moved over to the second. This one had to lead to the bedroom. Bracing herself for what she might find, she turned the handle, pushed it open, and shone the flashlight inside.

"Anything?"

She ignored the question and stepped carefully over the threshold.

There was dust in the air here too, but it was clear that this room had not been neglected and uncared-for like the rest of the property. The carpet was soft, and looked newer than the rest of the furnishings. While there was no furniture in here, she could see imprints in the carpet where items had rested: a large flattened rectangle formed under what might have been a chest of drawers; a single square that she could only guess at; four small squares spaced out far enough that they might have been a long table against one wall. The latter were deep too—the table must have had something heavy stored on top of it.

No obvious marks from a bed, though.

But then she noticed something, and quickly moved the flashlight back to the far wall. She could tell that it had been painted more recently than the rest of the apartment, but it had also been amended. Around the base, someone had added careful drawings. Blades of grass seemed to grow out of the floor, with simple flowers dotted here and there and bees and butterflies hovering above.

She remembered the photographs she'd seen of the inside of Frank Carter's extension.

Oh, God.

Slowly, she moved the beam upward.

Close to the ceiling, an angry sun stared back at her with black eyes.

FORTY-NINE

Your daddy liked these books when he was younger.

Pete almost said that as he knelt down beside Jake's
bed and picked up the book. The light in the bedroom
was so soft, and Jake looked so small, lying there beneath the blankets, that he was momentarily transported
back to a different time. He remembered reading to Tom
when he had been a little boy. The Diana Wynne Jones
books had been one of his son's favorites.

Power of Three. He couldn't recall the contents, but
the cover was immediately familiar, and his fingertips
tingled as he touched it. It was a very old edition. The
covers were frayed at the edges, and the spine was so
worn that the title was lost in the string of creases. Was
this the actual copy he himself had read so many years
ago? It was, he thought. Tom had kept it and was now
reading it to his own son. Not just a story passed down
through time, from father to son, but the exact same
pages containing it.

Pete felt a sense of wonder at that.

Your daddy liked these books when he was younger.

But he caught himself before saying it. Not only did
Jake not know of Pete's relationship to him, it was not

Pete's place to reveal it, and it never would be. That was fine. If he wanted to claim he had changed over the years and was no longer the terrible father from Tom's worst memories, he could hardly lay claim to any of the better ones either.

If that man was gone, all of him had to be.

With a new man in his place.

"Well, then."

The light in the room made his voice quiet and gentle.

"Where are we up to?"

Afterward, he sat downstairs in silence, the book he had brought untouched for the moment. The warmth he'd felt upstairs had carried down with him, and he wanted to absorb it for a while.

For so long now, he'd buried himself in distractions: used books and food and television—ritual in general—as a way of clicking fingers to one side of his own mind and keeping it from glancing in more dangerous directions. But he didn't feel that now. The voices were silent. The urge to drink was not alive tonight. He could still sense it there, in the same way that a stubbed-out candle smokes a little, but the fire and the brightness of it were gone.

It had been so lovely to read to Jake. The boy had been quiet and attentive, and then, after a page or two, he had wanted to take over. Although his delivery was faltering, it was obvious that his vocabulary was impressive. And it had been impossible not to feel the peace of the room. However much Pete had messed up Tom's own childhood, his son hadn't passed that on.

Pete checked on Jake fifteen minutes later and found the boy already fast asleep. He stood there for a moment, marveling at how tranquil Jake appeared.

Look at what you lose by drinking.

He'd told himself that so many times while looking at the photograph of Sally, his mind skirting the memories of the life he'd lost. Most of the time it had been enough, but sometimes it hadn't, and these past months had been the toughest of tests. Somehow he had resisted. Looking down at Jake now, he was monumentally glad about that, as though he had somehow dodged a bullet he hadn't known was coming. Although the future was uncertain, at least it was there.

Look what you gain by stopping.

That thought was so much better. It was the difference between regret and relief, between a cold hearth full of dead, gray ash and a fire that was still alight. He *hadn't* lost this. He might not have found it fully yet either. But he hadn't lost it.

Back downstairs, he did read for a little while, but he was distracted by thoughts of the investigation, and kept checking his phone for updates. There were none. It felt like Amanda should have been there by now, and that Francis Carter should be either in custody or being questioned, and he hoped that was the case. Too busy to update him was too busy in the right direction.

Francis Carter.

He remembered the boy clearly—although of course Francis Carter was an entirely different person now: a grown man, formed from that boy but distinct from him. Pete had only interacted with the child on a handful of occasions twenty years ago, as the majority of the interviews had needed to be handled carefully by specially trained officers. Francis had been small and pale and haunted, staring down at the table with hooded eyes, giving one-word answers at most. The extent of the trauma he must have suffered living with his father had been obvious. He was a vulnerable child who had been through hell.

Carter's words came back to him now.

His top is all pulled up over his face so I can't see it properly, which is the way I like it.

The children had all been the same to him; any one would do. And he hadn't wanted to see their faces. But why? Could it possibly be, Pete wondered, because Carter had wanted to imagine the victims were his own son? A boy he couldn't touch without being caught, so the hatred he felt had to be acted out on other children instead?

Pete sat very still for a moment.

If that were the case, how might a child feel in response to that? That he was worthless and deserved to die too, perhaps. Guilt over the lives lost in his place. A heartfelt desire to make amends. An urge to help children like him, because by doing so he could somehow begin to heal himself.

This is a man who takes care.

Carter, talking about the man in the photograph he'd been shown.

Smiling at him.

You just don't listen, Peter.

Neil Spencer had been held captive for two months,

but had been well looked after the whole time. Someone had *taken care* of him—until something went wrong, that is, whereupon Neil had been killed and his body dumped at the exact spot of his abduction. Pete remembered what he'd thought on the waste ground that night. That it was like someone had returned a present they no longer wanted. He thought about it differently now.

Maybe it was more like a failed experiment.

Upstairs, Jake started screaming.

FIFTY

I'd arranged to meet Karen in a pub a few streets away from my house, not far from the school. It was the village local, called simply the Featherbank, and I felt more than a little awkward as I arrived. It was a warm evening, and the beer garden adjoining the street was full of people. Through the large windows, the inside seemed to be teeming as well. Just as when I'd walked into the playground on Jake's first day, it felt like I was entering a place where everybody knew one another, and where I didn't belong and never would.

I spotted Karen at the bar and made my way through the throng, packed in on all sides by hot bodies and laughter. Tonight, her big coat was nowhere in evidence. She was wearing jeans and a white top. I felt even more nervous as I arrived beside her.

"Hey," I said over the noise.

"Hey, there." She smiled at me, then leaned in to my ear. "Excellent timing. What can I get you?"

I scanned the nearest taps and picked a beer at random. She paid, handed me my pint, and then eased away from the bar and nodded for me to follow her through the crowd, deeper into the pub. As I did, I wondered if

I'd entirely miscalibrated this evening and she was taking me to meet a group of friends. But there was a door just past the bar, and she pushed through that into a different beer garden, this one secluded at the back of the pub and surrounded by trees. There were circular wooden tables spaced out on the grass, and a small play area, where a few children were making their way across low rope bridges while their parents sat drinking nearby. It was less busy out here, and Karen led me over to an empty table toward the far end.

"We could have brought the kids," I said.

"If we were *insane,* yes." She sat down. "Assuming you're not being incredibly irresponsible, I'm guessing you managed to find a babysitter?"

I sat down beside her.

"Yes. My father."

"Wow." She blinked. "After what you told me before, that must be strange."

"It's weird, yeah. I wouldn't have asked him normally, but . . . well. I wanted to come out for a drink, and beggars can't be choosers." She raised her eyebrows, and I blushed. "I mean about him, not you."

"Ha! This is all off the record, by the way." She put her hand on my arm, and left it there for a couple of seconds longer than she needed to. "I'm glad you could come, anyway," she said.

"Me too."

"Cheers, by the way."

We clinked glasses.

"So. You don't have any concerns about him?"

"My father?" I shook my head. "Honestly, no. Not on

that level. I don't know how I feel about it, to be honest. It's not a permanent thing. It's not *any* kind of thing, really."

"Yes. That's a sensible way of looking at it. People worry too much about the nature of *things*. Sometimes it's better just to go with them. What about Jake?"

"Oh, he probably likes him more than he does me."

"I'm sure that's not true."

I remembered how Jake had been just before I left, and fought down the guilt it brought.

"Maybe," I said.

"Like I've told you, you're too hard on yourself."

"Maybe," I said again.

I sipped my drink. A part of me remained on edge, but I realized now that it wasn't anything to do with spending time with Karen. In fact, it was surprising how relaxed I felt now that I was here, and how natural it was to be sitting this close to her, a little closer than friends normally would. No, the nerves were because I was still worried about Jake. It was hard to stop thinking about him. Hard to shake the gut feeling that, as much as I wanted to be here, there was somewhere else it was far more important for me to be instead.

I took another drink and told myself not to be stupid.

"You said your mum's looking after Adam?"

"Yeah."

Karen rolled her eyes and then started to explain her whole situation. She'd moved back to Featherbank last year, choosing the village mainly because her mother lived here. While there had never been any love lost between the two of them, the woman was good with

Adam, and Karen had figured the support would help while she established herself on her own two feet again.

"Adam's father isn't on the scene?"

"Do you think I'd be out with you if he was?"

Karen smiled. I shrugged slightly helplessly, and she let me off.

"No, he isn't. And maybe that's rough on Adam, but sometimes kids are better off that way, even if they don't always realize it at the time. Brian—that's my ex—let's just say that he was like your father in some ways. A lot of ways."

She took a sip of her own drink, and while the silence wasn't uncomfortable, it still felt like a natural point to leave that particular subject. Some conversations need to wait, if they even have to come at all. In the meantime, I watched the children clambering over the play sets in the far corner of the garden. The evening was settling in now. The air was growing darker, with midges flickering in the trees around us.

But it was still warm. Still nice.

Except . . .

I looked off in a different direction now. My internal compass had already worked out where my house was from here, and I wasn't even that far away from Jake: probably only a few hundred meters as the crow flies. But it seemed too far. And looking back at the children again, I thought it wasn't just that it was becoming gloomy, but that the light seemed *wrong* somehow. That everything was off-kilter and odd.

"Oh," Karen said, reaching into her bag. "I just

remembered. I've got something. This is a bit embarrassing, but will you sign it for me?"

My most recent book. The sight of it reminded me how far behind I was on any kind of follow-up, and that made me panic slightly. But it was clearly meant as a nice gesture, and also kind of a silly one, so I forced myself to smile.

"Sure."

She handed me a pen. I opened the book on the title page and started writing.

To Karen.

I paused. I could never think what to write.

I'm really glad to have met you. I hope you don't think this is shit.

When you signed books for people, some waited to read what you'd put. Karen was not one of those people. She laughed as she saw what I'd written.

"I'm sure I won't. Anyway, what makes you think I'm going to read it? This is going straight on eBay, mate."

"Which is fine, although I wouldn't plan your retirement yet."

"Don't worry."

The air around us was darker still. I looked over at the play area again, and saw a little girl in a blue-and-white dress standing there, staring back at me. Our gazes met for a moment, and everything else in the beer garden faded into the background. And then she grinned and ran toward one of the rope bridges, another little girl running after her, laughing.

I shook my head.

"Are you okay?" Karen said.

"Yes."

"Hmmm. I'm not sure I believe you. Is it Jake?"

"I suppose so."

"You're worried about him?"

"I don't know. Maybe. It's probably nothing, just that this is the first time I've been out on an evening without him. And I *am* having a good time, honestly. But it feels . . ."

"Really fucking *strange*?"

"A little bit, yeah."

"I get you." She smiled sympathetically. "It was the same for me when I first started leaving Adam alone. It's like there's something tethering you to home and it's stretching too thin. There's this *need* inside you to get back."

I nodded, even though it felt much more than that. The sensation inside me was that something was terribly wrong. But I was probably just being overdramatic about exactly what she was describing.

"And it's fine," Karen said. "Honestly. Early days. Let's just finish these and you can get back home, and maybe we can do this again sometime. Assuming you want to?"

"I definitely want to."

"Good."

She was looking at me, both of us holding eye contact, and the space between us felt weighted with possibility. I realized that this was a moment when I could lean in for a kiss, and that if I did, she would lean forward too. That we would both close our eyes as our lips met, and that the kiss would be as gentle as breath. I also knew that if I didn't, one of us would have to turn away. But the moment would have been there, and we would both know it, and at some point it would happen again.

Might as well be now, then.

And I was about to do just that when my phone started ringing.

FIFTY-ONE

It had been in the afternoon, and Jake and Daddy were coming back from school. It was usually Mummy who picked him up on that day, because it was supposed to be one of Daddy's days to work, but that wasn't what happened.

Daddy wrote stories for a living, and people paid him to read them, which Jake personally thought was exceptionally cool. And Daddy sometimes agreed that, yes, it was. For one thing, he didn't have to wear a suit and go into an office every day and be told what to do like lots of other parents did. But it was also hard, because it didn't *seem* like a job to other people.

Jake didn't know all the ins and outs of it, but he was dimly aware that this had caused problems between his parents at one point, in that Daddy was doing most of the pickups and drop-offs, and that meant he wasn't writing quite so many stories. The solution was that Mummy started picking him up more often. This had been meant to be one of her days. But then Daddy turned up and explained that Mummy wasn't feeling well, and so he'd had to come instead.

That was the way he said it. *Had* to come instead.

"Is she okay?" Jake said.

"She's fine," Daddy said. "She was just a bit light-headed when she got back from work, and so she's having a lie-down."

Jake believed him, because of course Mummy was fine. But Daddy seemed more tense than normal, and Jake wondered if his most recent story had been going less well than usual, and that having to come out to collect Jake was . . . well. What was the opposite of icing on a cake?

Jake often felt like he was a problem for Daddy. That things would be a bit easier if he weren't around.

And in the car, Daddy asked the usual questions about his day, and how things had been, and what he'd done. As always, Jake did his best not to answer them. There was nothing exciting to say, and he didn't think Daddy was really all that interested anyway.

They parked outside the house.

"Can I go in and see Mummy?"

He half expected Daddy to say no, although he wasn't sure why—maybe because it was something that Jake really wanted to do, and so Daddy would say no just to spoil his fun. But that wasn't very fair, because Daddy just smiled and ruffled his hair.

"Of course, mate. Just be gentle with her, okay?"

"I will."

The door was unlocked, and he ran into the house without taking his shoes off. That was something Mummy would normally tell him off for, because she liked to keep the place clean and tidy, but they weren't dirty or anything, and he wanted to see her and try to make her feel better. He ran through the kitchen and into the living room.

And then he stopped.

Because there was something wrong. The curtains at the far end of the room were open, and the afternoon sun was coming in at an angle, lighting up half the room. It looked peaceful, and everything was very still and silent. But that was the problem. Even when someone was hiding from you, you could usually tell that they were *there* somewhere, because people took up space and that altered the pressure somehow. The house right now didn't feel like that at all.

It felt empty.

Daddy was still outside, probably doing something with the car. Jake walked slowly across the living room, but it was more like the room was walking backward past him. The silence was so huge that it felt like he might bruise it if he wasn't careful.

To the side of the window, the door was open. It led to the small area at the bottom of the stairs. As Jake stepped closer, he could see more and more of it.

The marbled glass of the back door.

The only sound now was his own heartbeat.

The white wallpaper.

Approaching so slowly that he was barely moving.

The knotted wooden handrail.

He looked down at the floor.

Mummy—

"Daddy!"

Jake screamed the word before he was even properly

awake. Then he tucked himself down entirely beneath the covers and shouted it again, his small heart beating hard. He hadn't had the nightmare since the old house, and the shock of it had gotten a whole lot bigger while it had been gone.

He waited.

He wasn't sure what time it was, or how long he'd been asleep, but surely it had been long enough that Daddy must be home by now? A moment later, he heard steady footsteps coming up the stairs.

Jake risked poking his head out. The hall light was still on, and a shadow stretched into the room as someone came in.

"Hey," the man said softly. "What's the matter?"

Pete, Jake remembered. He liked Pete well enough, but the fact remained that Pete was not *Daddy,* and Daddy was who he wanted and needed to be walking over to him right now.

Pete was very old, but hc sat down cross-legged beside the bed in a quick, decisive movement.

"What's wrong?"

"I had a bad dream. Where's Daddy?"

"He's not back yet. Bad dreams are horrible, aren't they? What was this one about?"

Jake shook his head. He'd never told even Daddy what the nightmare was about, and he wasn't sure he ever would.

"That's okay." Pete nodded to himself. "I have bad dreams too, you know? Quite often, in fact. But I actually think it's all right to have them."

"How can it be all right?"

"Because sometimes really bad things happen to us, and we don't like to think about them, so they get buried really deep in our heads."

"Like earworms?"

"I suppose so, yes. But they have to come out eventually. And bad dreams can be our brain's way of dealing with that. Breaking it all down into smaller and smaller pieces, until eventually there's nothing left anymore."

Jake considered that. The nightmare had been even more frightening than ever, so it felt more like his mind was building something up rather than breaking it down. But then, it always ended at the same point, before he could *properly* remember seeing Mummy lying on the floor. Maybe Pete was right. Perhaps his own mind was so scared that it had to build itself up for that sight before it could begin to break it down.

"I know it doesn't make it any easier," Pete said. "But you know what? A nightmare can never, *ever* hurt you. There's nothing to be scared of."

"I know that," Jake said. "But I still want my daddy."

"He'll be back soon, I'm sure."

"I need him now." With the return of the nightmare, along with the little girl's warning earlier, Jake was more sure than ever that something was wrong. "Can you call him and get him to come home?"

Pete was silent for a moment.

"Please?" Jake said. "He won't mind."

"I know he won't."

Pete took out his cell phone, and Jake watched anxiously as he swiped through, pressed the screen, and then held it up to his ear.

Downstairs, the front door opened.

"Ah." Pete canceled the call. "I guess that's okay, then. Will you be all right up here for a minute while I go down and get him?"

No, Jake thought, *I won't.* He didn't want to spend another second up here in the darkness by himself. But at least Daddy was home now, and he felt a flood of relief at that.

"Okay."

Pete stood up and walked out of the room, and Jake heard his footsteps going back down the stairs, and then him calling out Daddy's name.

Jake stared at the wedge of illuminated hallway beyond the bedroom door, listening carefully. For a few seconds there was nothing but silence. But then he heard something he couldn't identify. Movement of some kind, as though furniture were being shifted about. And people talking, only with sounds instead of words, like when you were trying really hard to do something and the effort made you make a noise.

Another loud sound. Something heavy falling over.

And then silence again.

Jake thought about calling out for Daddy, but for some reason his heart was thudding hard in his chest again, as hard as it had been when he'd first woken up from the nightmare, and the silence was ringing so much that it felt like he was back inside it, back in their old living room.

He stared at the empty hallway, waiting.

A few seconds later, there was a new sound. Footsteps on the stairs again. Someone was coming up, but they were moving slowly and carefully, as though *they* were scared of the silence too.

And then someone whispered his name.

FIFTY-TWO

"I'm sure everything's fine."

Hurrying along behind me, Karen tried to make it sound breezy. And no doubt she was right; I was almost certainly overreacting—walking so quickly that she was struggling to keep up. She had come with me without us discussing it, but if she hadn't, I might even have been running right now. Because, while she was right, and there was most likely nothing to worry about, I still felt it in my heart. The certainty that something was terribly wrong.

I took out my phone and tried my father again. He had called me at the pub, but it had cut off before I'd had a chance to answer. Which meant that *something* must have happened. But when I'd tried to call him back, he hadn't picked up.

The phone rang and rang now.

He still wasn't picking up.

"Fuck."

I canceled the call as we reached the bottom of my street. Maybe he'd dialed by accident, or changed his mind about needing to talk to me. But I remembered how deferential he'd been earlier on, and how quietly pleased he'd seemed to be allowed to look after Jake and be allowed into our lives, in however small a way. He wouldn't have called me unless he could have helped it. Not unless it had been important.

The field to the right was thick with the evening gloom. There seemed to be nobody out there right now, but it was already too dark to see to the far side. I started to walk even more quickly, aware that I was probably coming across as an absolute lunatic to Karen. But I was beginning to panic now, however irrational it was, and that mattered more.

Jake . . .

I reached the driveway.

The front door was open, a block of light slanted out across the path.

If you leave a door half open . . .

And then I really did start running.

"Tom—"

I reached the door, but then stopped at the threshold. There were smears of bloody footprints all over the wood at the bottom of the stairs.

"Jake?" I shouted inside.

The house was silent. I stepped carefully inside, my heart pounding fast and hard in my ears.

Karen had reached me now.

"What—oh, God."

I looked to my right, into the living room, and the sight that awaited me there made no sense whatsoever. My father was lying on his side with his back to me, curled up on the floor by the window, almost as though he'd gone to sleep there. But he was surrounded by blood. I shook my head. There was blood all over the side of his body. Farther up, it was pooling around his head. He was completely still. And for a moment, unable to process what I was seeing, so was I.

Beside me, Karen took a sharp, shocked intake of breath. I turned slightly and saw that she'd gone pale. Her eyes were wide and she was holding her hand over her mouth.

Jake, I thought.

"Tom—"

But I didn't hear anything after that, because the thought of my son had brought me back to life, galvanizing me into action. I moved past her, around her, then headed straight up the stairs as quickly as I could. Praying. Thinking, *Please.*

"Jake!"

There was blood on the upstairs landing too: pressed into the carpet by the shoes of whoever had committed the atrocity downstairs. Someone had attacked my father, and then they'd come up here, up here to . . .

My son's room.

I stepped in. The bedsheet had been folded neatly back. Jake was not here. Nobody was here. I stood for a few seconds frozen in place, dread itching at my skin.

Downstairs, Karen was on her phone, talking frantically. Ambulance. Police. Urgent. A jumble of words that made no sense to me right then. It felt like my mind was going to shut down—as though my skull had suddenly opened up and was exposed to a vast, incomprehensible kaleidoscope of horror.

I walked across to the bed.

Jake was gone, but that wasn't possible, because Jake couldn't be gone.

This wasn't happening.

The Packet of Special Things was lying on the floor by the bed. It was when I picked that up, knowing that he would never have gone anywhere willingly without it, that reality hit me full force. The Packet was here and Jake wasn't. This wasn't a nightmare. It was actually happening.

My son was gone.

That was when I tried to scream.

PART FIVE

FIFTY-THREE

The first forty-eight hours after a child disappears are the most crucial.

When Neil Spencer disappeared, the first two hours of that period had been wasted, because nobody had realized he was gone. With Jake Kennedy, the investigation began within minutes of his father and his friend arriving home. At that point, Amanda had been with Dyson in a police department fifty miles away. They had driven back as quickly as possible.

Outside Tom Kennedy's house now, she checked her watch. Just after ten o'clock at night. All the machinery that rolled out when a child went missing was already in motion. The odd-looking house beside her was brightly lit and busy with activity, shadows moving across the curtains, while up and down the street officers were standing at porches, interviewing neighbors. Flashlights moved over the field across the road. Statements were being taken; CCTV was being gathered; people were out searching.

Under different circumstances, Pete himself would have been out with the search teams. But not tonight, of course. Trying to keep calm, Amanda took out her phone and called the hospital for an update, then listened as dispassionately as she could to the news. Pete remained unconscious and in critical condition. Christ. She remembered how formidable he had been for a man his age, but it appeared to have counted for little this evening. Perhaps he hadn't been concentrating, for some reason, and had been taken unawares; he had received few defensive wounds, but had been stabbed several times in the side, neck, and head. The attack had been unnecessarily frenzied—clearly attempted murder, and the hours ahead would reveal whether that attempt had been successful. She was told that it was touch-and-go as to whether he would survive the night. She could only hope that his fitness would serve him now where it had failed him before.

You can do it, Pete, she thought.

He would pull through. He had to.

She put the phone down and then quickly checked the online case file for updates. No developments as yet. Officers had already taken statements from Tom Kennedy and the woman he had been out with, Karen Shaw. Amanda recognized the name; Shaw was a local crime reporter. According to their accounts, they'd simply met up for a drink as friends. Their children were in the same year at school, so maybe that was all it was, but Amanda hoped for everyone's sake that Shaw was more trustworthy than most in her profession. Especially now.

Because she still didn't know why *Pete* had been here.

She remembered how alive he'd seemed this afternoon, reading the message he'd received and then making his arrangements. At the time, she'd suspected a date of some kind. In reality, it must have been this—and whatever *this* turned out to be, the fact remained that Pete was involved in the case and shouldn't have been here off duty. It was a breach of professionalism.

And what bothered her more was the knowledge that she'd effectively pushed him into it. She'd wanted him to be happy. If she hadn't pressed him, he would still be alive.

He is still alive.

She had to cling to that. More than anything else, she needed to be professional and focused right now. She couldn't afford to let her emotions out. Guilt. Fear. Anger. Once loose, any one of them would charge off, dragging the others along like dogs chained in a pack. And that was no good at all.

Pete was still alive.

Jake Kennedy was still alive.

She was not going to lose either of them. But there was only one that she could do anything about right now, and so finally she shut down the case file and got out of the car.

Inside the house, she stepped gingerly over the dance of dried blood at the bottom of the stairs, then walked cautiously into the living room, preparing herself for the sight she knew awaited her.

Several CSIs were at work in here, measuring, analyzing, and taking photographs, but she tuned them out, focusing instead on the overturned coffee table and, inevitably, the blood smeared and pooled on the floor. There was enough of it that she could smell it in the air. Her career had brought her face-to-face with worse than this, but knowing it had been Pete attacked in here meant what she was seeing now was impossible to accept.

She watched the CSIs for a moment. The forensic work was so somber, so thorough, that it felt like the room was already being treated as a murder scene. As though everybody in here knew a truth that she had yet to catch up with.

She went through to the spare room. The walls were lined with bookcases, with several boxes on the floor still to be unpacked. Tom Kennedy was pacing back and forth between them, following an elaborate path, the same way an animal might wear away the ground in an enclosure. Karen Shaw was sitting in a chair by a computer table, holding one elbow, her other hand at her mouth, staring at the floor.

Tom noticed Amanda and came to a stop. She recognized the expression on his face. People dealt with situations like this in different ways—some almost supernaturally calm, others distracting themselves with motion and activity—but in every case, the behavior was about displacement. Right now Tom Kennedy was panicking and struggling to contain it. If he couldn't move in the direction of his son, then he needed to be moving somewhere. After he stopped walking, his body began to tremble.

"Tom," she told him, "I know this is difficult. I know this is terrifying for you. But I need you to listen to me and I need you to believe me. *We are going to find Jake.* I promise you."

He stared back at her. It was obvious that he didn't believe her, and perhaps it wasn't a promise she could keep. But she meant it all the same. The determination was burning inside her. She wouldn't stop, wouldn't rest, until she'd found Jake and caught the man who had taken him. Who had taken Neil Spencer before him. Who had hurt Pete so badly.

I am not losing another child on my watch.

"We believe we know who's taken him, and we're going to find him. Like I said, I give you my word. Every available officer is focused on hunting this man down and finding your son. We are going to bring him home safe."

"Who is he?"

"I can't tell you that right now."

"My son is alone with him."

She could tell from his face that right now he was picturing every terrible possibility—that a reel of the worst imaginable horrors was unfolding in his head.

"I know it's hard, Tom," she said. "But I also want you to remember that, assuming this *is* the same man who took Neil Spencer, Neil was well cared for at first."

"And then murdered."

She had no answer to that. Instead, she thought about the abandoned apartment she had visited a few hours earlier, and the way Francis Carter had re-created the decorations in his father's extension. He must have seen the horrors in there as a child, and it seemed that he had never truly escaped that room—that a part of him had remained trapped there, unable to move on. Yes, he had looked after Neil Spencer for a time. But then some darker impulse had emerged, and there was no reason to think he would contain it any better with Jake than he had with Neil. The opposite, in fact—once the dam was broken, killers like this had a tendency to accelerate.

But she was not prepared to entertain that idea right now.

Tom, of course, had no such luxury.

"Why Jake?"

"We don't know for certain." The desperation in his question was also familiar to her. Faced with tragedy and horror, it was natural to search for explanations: reasons why the tragedy could not have been prevented, to help ease the pain; or ways in which the horror could have been avoided, serving only to stoke the guilt. "We believe the suspect may have had an interest in this house, the same way that Norman Collins did. It's likely he discovered your son was living here, and probably decided upon him as a target as a result of that."

"Fixated on him, you mean."

"Yes."

A few beats of silence.

"How is he?" Tom said.

Amanda thought he must still be talking about Jake, but then she realized he was staring past her toward the living room, and understood he was asking after Pete.

"He's in intensive care," she said. "That's the last I've heard. His condition is critical, but . . . well. Pete's a fighter. If anyone can make it through, then it's him."

Tom nodded to himself, as though that resonated with him on some level. Which didn't make sense, because he had barely known Pete at all. Once again she remembered how pleased Pete had been that afternoon. How suddenly alive he had seemed.

"Why was he here?" she said. "He shouldn't have been."

"He was babysitting Jake."

"Why Pete, though?"

Tom fell silent. She watched him. It was clear that he was considering what to tell her, choosing his words carefully. And suddenly she realized she had seen *this* expression before too. The tilt of Tom Kennedy's head. The angle of his jawline. The serious expression. Standing in front of her now, his hollow face illuminated by the light above, Tom Kennedy looked almost exactly like Pete.

Christ, she thought.

But then he shook his head and moved slightly, and the resemblance disappeared.

"He left me his card. He said, if we needed anything, to get in touch. And he and Jake . . . well. Jake liked him. They liked each other."

The explanation stumbled to an end, and Amanda continued to stare at him. Although she could no longer see the similarity outright, she hadn't imagined it. She could press that point, but she decided that it wasn't important—not right now. If she was correct, then the repercussions of that could be dealt with later. Right now, in fact, she needed to be back at the department, making good on the promise she'd made as best she could.

"Okay," she said. "What's going to happen next is that I'm going to leave here, and I'm going to find your son and bring him home."

"What do I do?"

Amanda glanced back toward the living room. It went without saying that Tom couldn't stay here overnight.

"You don't have family in the area, do you?"

"No."

"You can come to my place," Karen said. "It's not a problem."

She hadn't spoken until now. Amanda looked at her.

"Are you sure about that?" she said.

"Yes."

Amanda could tell from Karen's expression that she understood the severity of the situation. Tom was silent for a moment, considering the offer. Despite Amanda's reservations about the journalist, she hoped to God he said yes. She could do without the headache of finding him somewhere else to be right now. And it was obvious that he wanted to say yes—that he was a man on the verge of collapse—and so Amanda decided to give him a push.

"Okay, then." She held out her card. "Those are my details. Direct line. I'll get a family liaison out to you first thing in the morning anyway, but for now, if you need anything, you call me. I've got your number too. Any developments at all, and that includes about Pete, and you'll hear from me the same minute."

She hesitated, then lowered her voice slightly.

"The *same fucking minute,* Tom. I promise you."

FIFTY-FOUR

The day was dead and the night was cool.

The man stood in his driveway, warming his hands on a mug of coffee. The front door of his house was open behind him, the inside dark and silent. The world was so quiet that he imagined he could hear the steam rising from the cup.

He had made his home on an out-of-the-way street in an undesirable area, a few miles from Featherbank itself. It was partly for financial reasons, but mainly for privacy. One of the neighboring houses was vacant, while the occupants of the other kept to themselves, even when they weren't drinking. The hedges on either side of his small driveway were overgrown, shielding his comings and goings from view, and there was never anything in the way of traffic. This wasn't a street you came to, nor was it anywhere you would pass through on your way to somewhere else. It was, put simply, a place you avoided.

Francis liked to think that his presence here had contributed to that. That if you did find yourself driving past for some reason, you would understand on some primal level that it was not a location in which to linger.

Much like Jake Kennedy's former home, of course.

The scary house.

The man remembered that monstrosity from his own childhood. It appeared to have been common knowledge among the other children that the place was dangerous, although none of them had known why. Some said it was haunted; others claimed that a former murderer lived there. All without reason, of course—it was solely down to how it looked. If they hadn't treated Francis the same way, he would have been able to tell them the real reason the house was frightening. But there had been nobody for him to tell.

It felt like a long time ago. He wondered if the police had found the remnants of his old life yet. Even if so, it didn't matter; he'd left little behind but dust. He remembered how easy it had been—how simple it was, on one level, to become someone else if you wanted. It had cost less than a grand to acquire a new identity from a man sixty miles south of here. Ever since, he had been building a shell around himself to enable him to begin his transformation, the same way a caterpillar emerges from its own cocoon, vibrant and powerful and unrecognizable.

And yet traces of the frightened, hateful boy he had once been remained. *Francis* had not been his name in years, but it was still how he thought of himself. He could remember his father making him watch the things he did to those boys. From the look on his father's face,

Francis had understood only too well that the man had hated him, and that he would have done the same to Francis if he could. The boys he killed had only ever been stand-ins for the child he despised most of all. Francis had always been well aware of how worthless and disgusting he was.

He couldn't save the boys he'd seen murdered all those years ago, just as he couldn't help or comfort the child he had once been. But he could make amends. Because there were so many children like him in the world, and it wasn't too late to rescue and protect *them*.

He and Jake would be good for each other.

Francis sipped his coffee, then stared up at the night sky and its meaningless patterns of constellations. His thoughts drifted to the violence back at the house. His skin was still singing with the thrill of that, and he knew it was a sensation his mind should avoid. Because even though he had known in advance the evening would involve a physical confrontation, it had been surprising how natural it had been when it happened. He had killed once, and it had been easy to kill again. It was as though what he'd been forced to do to Neil had turned a key inside him, unlocking desires he'd only been dimly aware of beforehand.

It had felt good, hadn't it?

Coffee slopped over his hand, and he looked down to see that his hand was trembling slightly.

He forced himself to calm down.

But a part of him didn't want to. It was much easier

now to remember what he'd done to Neil Spencer, and he couldn't deny that there had been enjoyment in the act of killing. He had simply been afraid to acknowledge it until now. Thinking back, he could imagine that his father had been there with him.

Watching.

Nodding along in approval.

Now you understand, don't you, Francis?

Yes. Now he understood why his father had hated him so much. For being such a worthless creature. But he wasn't anymore, and he wondered what it might be like to look into his father's eyes now. Whether they could forgive each other for what they had been in the light of what they had become.

I'm like you, you see?

You don't have to hate me anymore.

Francis shook his head. *Jesus Christ*—what was he thinking? What had happened with Neil had been a *mistake*. He needed to concentrate now, because he had Jake to care for. To keep safe. To *love*. Because that was what all children wanted and needed, wasn't it? To be loved and cherished by their parents. His heart ached at the thought.

They wanted that more than anything.

He sipped the last of his coffee and grimaced. It had gone cold, so he poured the dregs into the weeds at the side of the doorstep, then went back inside, leaving the silent world out there for the silent one within.

Time to say good night to the boy.

No more mistakes.

And yet, as he headed upstairs to Jake, he kept thinking about killing Neil Spencer and how it had made him feel.

I'm like you, you see?

And he wondered if perhaps it hadn't been so terrible a mistake after all.

FIFTY-FIVE

When you woke up from a nightmare, things were supposed to be okay.

Not like this.

When Jake had first opened his eyes, he had been confused. It was too bright in his room. The light was on, and that wasn't right. And then he'd realized this *wasn't* his bedroom at all, but some other child's, and that wasn't right either. But his head was so groggy that he couldn't make sense of it, beyond feeling a tightening knot of *wrongness* in his heart. The world had swum around him when he'd sat up. And then a memory had come back to him, and the knot had tightened more quickly, squeezing panic out into his whole body.

He was supposed to be at home. And he *had* been. But then there had been the man coming up the stairs, and then into his room, and then something on his face. And then . . .

Nothing.

Until here.

That had been perhaps ten minutes ago. Since then, he had spent a short amount of time thinking that this must be another nightmare—a new one—because it certainly felt like one. But he knew, even before he pinched himself to test, that it was too real for that. The fear was too strong, and if he had been asleep it would have woken him up by now. He remembered about the man who had taken Neil Spencer and hurt him, though, and he wondered if maybe this *was* a nightmare after all, just not the kind you got to wake up from. The world was full of bad men. Full of bad dreams that didn't always happen when you were asleep.

He glanced to one side now.

The little girl was here with him!

"You're—"

"Shhh. Keep your voice down." She looked around the small room and swallowed hard. "You mustn't let him know that I'm here."

Which, of course, she wasn't—he knew that deep down. But he was so grateful to see her that he wasn't going to think about that. She was right, though. It wouldn't be okay for the man to hear him talking to anyone. It would be . . .

"Really bad?" he whispered.

She nodded seriously.

"Where am I?" he said.

"I don't know where you are, Jake. You're where you are, and so that's where I am too."

"Because you won't leave me?"

"I'll never leave you. *Ever*." She looked around again. "And I'll do my best to help you, but I can't protect you. This is a very serious situation. You know that, don't you? It's a long, *long* way from being right."

Jake nodded. Everything was wrong, and he wasn't safe, and it was suddenly too much.

"I want my daddy."

Maybe that was a pathetic thing to say, but once it was out, he couldn't stop himself. So he whispered it again and again, and then he started to cry, thinking that if you wanted something hard enough then it might come true. It wouldn't, though. It felt like Daddy was the distance of the whole world away from him right now.

"Please try not to make any noise." She rested her hand on his shoulder. "You have to be brave."

"I want my daddy."

"He'll find you. You know he will."

"I want my daddy."

"Come on, Jake. Please." Her hand tightened on him, halfway between reassuring and scared. "I need you to calm down."

He tried to stop crying.

"That's better."

She moved her hand and was silent for a moment, listening.

"I think it's okay for now. So what we need to do is find out as much as possible about where we are. Because that might tell us how we can get out. Okay?"

He nodded. He was still scared, but what she was saying made sense.

He stood up and looked around the room.

The wall on one side of the room only went up to chest height before it began sloping inward the way that roofs did, so that meant he must be in an attic. He'd never been in an attic before. He'd always pictured them as dark, dusty places with bare floorboards and cardboard boxes and spiders, but this one was neatly carpeted, and the walls had been painted bright white, with grass drawn on at the bottom, and bees and butterflies fluttering above. It might have been nice, if it hadn't been harshly lit by a bare bulb in the ceiling, giving everything an unreal quality, as though bits of the drawings might start coming to life at any moment. There was an open chest full of soft toys against the sloping wall. A small wardrobe against another. He looked behind him. The bed was decked out in Transformers sheets that looked old and worn.

So he was in some other child's room. Except it didn't feel right or natural in here, as though it had never really been meant to be lived in by a real boy.

There was a door in the opposite wall. He walked across and pushed it open nervously. A small toilet and sink. There was a towel in a circular hoop and soap on the basin. He closed the door again. Turning around, he could see there was a narrow corridor leading off from one corner of the room, but it only went a little way before there was another wall. He stepped into the space and found himself at the top of a dark staircase. At the bottom, there was a closed door.

A wooden handrail along the wall . . .

Jake stepped back quickly before he could see the bottom of the stairs properly. He ran back into the room and over to the bed. *No, no, no.* The stairs were almost exactly the same as the ones in the old house. And that meant he *must not* see what was—

His heart was beating far too quickly now. It didn't feel like he could breathe.

"Sit down, Jake."

He couldn't even do that.

"It's okay," the little girl said gently. "Just breathe."

He closed his eyes and really concentrated. It was hard at first, but then the air started to get in, and his heart rate began to slow.

"Sit down."

He did as she told him, and then she put her hand on his shoulder again, saying nothing for the moment beyond soft, reassuring hushing noises. When he was more under control again, she moved her hand, but still didn't speak. He could tell she wanted him to go down and check the door, but there was absolutely no way he could do that. Not ever. The stairs were out of bounds. It wouldn't matter even if—

"It's probably locked anyway," she said.

Jake nodded, feeling relieved—because she was right, and that meant he *didn't* need to go down there. What if the man made him, though? That was too much to think about. Too scary. He wouldn't be able to, and he didn't think this man would carry him.

"Do you remember what your daddy wrote to you that time?" the little girl asked.

"Yes."

"Say it, then."

"Even when we argue we still love each other very much."

"That's true," she said. "But this man, he isn't like that."

"What do you mean?"

"I think what you have to do here is be very, *very* good. I don't think you can afford to have any arguments here."

She was right, he thought. If he was bad here, it wouldn't be like with Daddy, where things were okay again afterward. He thought if the Whisper Man got angry with him, then things might end up very far from okay indeed.

The girl stood up suddenly.

"Get in bed. *Do it quickly.*"

She looked so frightened that he knew there wasn't enough time to ask why. He pulled the covers back and clambered in. As he lay down on the strange little bed, he heard a key turn in the lock downstairs.

The man was coming.

"Close your eyes," she said urgently. "Pretend to be asleep."

Jake clenched his eyes shut. It was usually easy to pretend to be asleep—he did it at home all the time, because he knew Daddy would keep checking on him while he was awake, and he didn't want to be difficult. It was harder here, but as he heard the stairs creaking, he forced himself to breathe slowly and steadily, the way sleeping people did, and he relaxed his eyes a little, because sleeping people didn't squeeze them shut, and then—

And then the man was in the room.

Jake could hear the sound of gentle breathing, and then felt the man as a terrible presence close by. The skin on his face began to itch and he could tell the man was right next to the bed, looking down at him. *Staring* at him. Jake kept his eyes closed. If he was asleep, then he couldn't be being *bad,* could he? There was no risk of an argument. He'd gone to bed like a good boy, without being told.

There were a few seconds of silence.

"*Look* at you," the man whispered.

His voice sounded full of wonder, as though for some reason he hadn't expected to find a little boy up here. Jake forced himself not to flinch as a strand of hair was moved out of his face.

"So perfect."

The voice was familiar, wasn't it? Jake thought so, but he wasn't sure. And he wasn't about to open his eyes to find out. The man stood up, then moved away quietly.

"I'm going to look after you, Jake."

There was a click, and the darkness beyond his closed eyes deepened.

"You're safe now. I promise."

Jake kept breathing slowly and steadily as the man went back down the stairs, and then as the door closed again and the key turned in the lock. Even then he didn't dare open his eyes. He was thinking about what the little girl had said about Daddy. That he would find him.

Even when we argue we still love each other very much.

He believed that. It was one of the reasons why it didn't really matter when they argued. Daddy loved him and wanted him to be safe, and however angry they both might get, they would always end up back in the same place afterward, as though none of it had ever happened.

But there was also a small part of him that knew he made Daddy's life very difficult indeed. That he was often a distraction rather than a help. He thought about how Daddy had gone out without him tonight. And he wondered if, wherever Daddy was right now, he might even be feeling glad he didn't have Jake to bother him anymore.

No.

Daddy was going to find him.

Finally, Jake opened his eyes. The room was pitch-black now, apart from the little girl, who was standing by the bed, perfectly illuminated. She was as bright as a candle flame, but in a way where the light didn't leave her edges and reveal anything around her.

"What are we doing, Jake?" she whispered.

"I don't know."

"What are we *being*?"

Now he understood.

"*Brave*," he whispered back. "We're being brave."

FIFTY-SIX

I lurched awake, immediately disorientated and confused by my surroundings. The room around me was dark and unfamiliar and full of strange shadows. Where was I? I had no idea, only that it wasn't right for me to be here. That wherever this was, I was supposed to be somewhere else, and that I desperately *needed* to be—

Karen's living room.

I remembered now. Jake was missing.

I sat very still on the couch for a moment, my heart beating hard.

My son had been taken.

The idea seemed unreal, but I knew it was true, and the tendrils of panic that brought were like a shot of adrenaline, knocking the leftover dregs of sleep away. How had I fallen asleep in this state? I was exhausted, but the terror humming inside me right now was already almost too much to bear. Perhaps I had been so tired and broken that my body had simply shut down for a while.

I checked my phone. It was nearly six o'clock in the morning, so I hadn't been asleep for long. Karen had gone to bed in the early hours. She'd been adamant about staying up with me to wait for news, but had also been so wiped out by the evening's events that I'd finally convinced her that one of us should grab some rest. Before she went upstairs, she'd told me to wake her up if there were any developments. There had been no messages or missed calls since. The situation hadn't changed.

Except that Jake had now been with whoever had taken him for a little while longer.

I stood up, flicked on the light switch, and began pacing back and forth across the living room. It felt like if I didn't move, then my feelings would overwhelm me. The aching *need* to be with Jake kept smacking up against the knowledge that I couldn't, and my heart was twisting and contorting inside me from the tension of that.

I kept picturing his face, the image so vivid that when I closed my eyes I imagined I could reach out and touch the soft skin of his cheek. He must be so scared right now, I knew. He would be lost and bewildered and terrified. He would be wondering where I was and why I hadn't found him.

If he was anything at all anymore.

I shook my head. I couldn't think like that. DI Beck had told me last night that they were going to find him, and I had to allow myself to believe her. Because if not—if he was dead—then there was nothing beyond that. It would be the end of the world: a hammer blow to the head of life, scrambling all coherent thought. After that, there would only ever be static.

He is alive.

I imagined he was calling out to me, and that somehow I could hear it in my heart. But it didn't feel like imagination, more like his actual voice, crying out on a station I was almost but not quite tuned in to. He was alive. There was no way I could know that, but there had been so many inexplicable events that was it really so impossible?

It didn't matter if it was.

He was alive. I could still feel him, so he had to be.

And so I formed the words in my head clearly and precisely, and then threw them out from me as hard as possible, hoping the message might reach him. That he might receive it in his own heart and feel the truth of it.

I love you, Jake.

And I am going to find you.

The house came to life shortly afterward.

Karen had told me to help myself to anything in the kitchen. I was leaning on the counter in there, drinking black coffee and watching the dawn light creasing at the horizon, when the floorboards began creaking overhead. I set the kettle to boil again. A few minutes later, Karen came down, already dressed, but still looking exhausted.

"Anything?" she said.

I shook my head.

"You've not called them?"

"Not yet." I was reluctant to. For one thing, without me bothering them, they could concentrate on finding Jake. For another, it also meant I didn't have to hear anything I might not want to. "I will, but if there'd been anything they would have called already."

The kettle clicked off. Karen spooned instant coffee into a mug.

"What have you told Adam?" I said.

"Nothing. He knows you're here and that you slept on the couch, but I haven't said anything else."

"I'll stay out of the way."

"You don't have to."

Even so, I kept to the kitchen after Adam came downstairs. Karen made him his breakfast and he ate it watching television in the living room. Outside the kitchen window the day was already brightening. A new morning. I listened half-heartedly to whatever program was playing in the other room, amazed by how life was carrying on. How it always does. You only notice how astonishing that is when a part of you gets left behind.

Karen left me a key before she left with Adam.

"What time is the liaison officer getting here?" she said.

"I don't know."

She put a hand on my arm. "*Call* them, Tom."

"I will."

She looked at me for a moment, her face sad and serious, then she leaned in and kissed me on the cheek.

"I'll take the car. I'll be back soon."

"Okay."

When the front door closed, I fell back down on the couch. My phone was there, and yes, I could call the police, but I was sure that DI Beck would have been in touch if there had been any news, and I didn't want to be told what I already knew. That Jake was still out there. That he was still in danger. And so instead I reached out for the item I'd brought with me from the house. My son's Packet of Special Things.

Even if I couldn't be with him physically, I could think of one way I could at least *feel* closer to him. I was conscious of the weight and importance of what I was holding. Jake had never told me I couldn't look inside it, but he hadn't needed to. His collection was for him, not for me. He was old enough to be entitled to his own secrets. And so, however tempted I had sometimes been, I had never violated that trust.

Forgive me, Jake.

I opened the clasp.

I just need to feel you close to me.

FIFTY-SEVEN

When Francis woke up, the house was silent.

For a while he lay very still in bed, staring at the ceiling and listening. No sound at all. No movement that he could detect either. But he could sense the boy's presence directly above him, and the house felt fuller as a result. There was a feeling of potential to it.

There is a child up there.

The peace and quiet were encouraging, because of course that was how things *should* be. It meant that Jake understood the situation and was happy with it. Perhaps he was even excited to be in his new home.

Francis thought back to how easily the boy had settled in last night—already asleep and comfortable when he had gone up to check on him. With Neil Spencer, there had been so much crying and shouting at first that, even with the neighbors he did and didn't have, Francis had been glad for the soundproofing he'd installed behind the walls of the attic. With Neil, he'd been too patient, writing that period off as a tantrum, whereas now he understood that Neil had been bad from the start, and there had been no chance of it ending any other way than it had.

Perhaps Jake really was different.

He isn't, Francis.

His father's voice.

They're all the same.

All hateful little bastards that disappoint you in the end.

Maybe that was true, but he shook the thought away for now. He had to give Jake a chance. Nowhere near as many chances as he'd given Neil Spencer, obviously, but an opportunity to enjoy and appreciate a happy home where he was looked after and truly cared for.

Francis went for a shower, which always made him feel vulnerable. With the door closed and the water loud in his ears, it was impossible to hear the rest of the house, and when he closed his eyes he could imagine something creeping into the bathroom and standing just outside the shower curtain. He sluiced the foam from his face quickly, and opened his eyes to see the water trailing away down the drain. He'd had to unblock that after dealing with Neil. He could unblock it again if it came to it.

You know what you want to do.

His heart was beating a little too fast.

Downstairs, he prepared coffee and breakfast for himself, made the phone call he needed to make, then set about getting food for Jake. He wiped crumbs off the counter with his forearm, then put two crumpets into the toaster. Both were leftovers, with speckles of mold around the rims, but that was good enough. Francis had no idea what Jake liked to drink, but there was an open orange juice box on the side, the one Neil hadn't had a chance to finish, and that would do as well.

Start as you mean to go on.

He carried the plate and carton upstairs, and then paused on the landing, pressing his ear against the door to the attic.

Silence.

But then he wasn't so sure. He *could* hear something. Was Jake whispering to someone? If he was, it was so quiet that it was impossible for Francis to make out the words. Impossible even to be sure that it was happening.

Francis listened carefully.

Silence.

Then the whispering sound again.

It raised the hairs on his neck. There was nobody else up there—nobody that Jake *could* be talking to—and yet Francis suddenly had an irrational fear that there might be. That in bringing this child into his house, he had somehow brought someone or something else with him. Something dangerous.

Maybe he's talking to Neil.

But that was stupid; Francis didn't believe in ghosts. As a child, he would sometimes go near the door to his father's extension and imagine one of the little boys standing on the other side, bright and pale, waiting patiently. There had even been times when he'd thought he could hear breathing through the wood. But none of it had been real. The only ghosts that existed were in your head. They spoke through you, not to you.

He unlocked the door and opened it, then climbed the stairs slowly, not wanting to scare the child. But the whispering sound had stopped, and that annoyed him.

He didn't like the idea that Jake was keeping secrets from him.

In the attic, the boy was sitting on the bed with his hands on his knees, and Francis was at least pleased to see that he had already dressed himself from the selection of clothes he'd provided in the drawers. Although less pleased to note the chest of toys didn't appear to have been touched. Weren't they good enough or something? Francis had kept those for a long time, and they meant a lot to him; the boy should have been grateful for the opportunity to play with them. He looked around for the pajamas Jake had been wearing, and saw they were folded neatly in a stack on the bed. That was good. He would need them when it came to returning the boy later.

"Good morning, Jake," he said brightly. "I see you've got dressed already."

"Good morning. I couldn't find my school clothes."

"I thought you could have a day off."

Jake nodded. "That's nice. Is my daddy going to be picking me up?"

"Well, *that* is a complicated question." Francis walked over to the bed. The boy seemed almost eerily calm. "And one I don't think you need to worry about for the moment. All you need to know is that you're safe now."

"Okay."

"And that I'm going to look after you."

"Thank you."

"Who were you talking to?"

The boy looked confused. "Nobody."

"Yes, you were. Who was it?"

"Nobody."

Francis felt a sudden urge to strike the boy in the face as hard as he could.

"We don't lie in this house, Jake."

"I'm not lying." Jake looked off to one side, and for a moment Francis had the odd sense that he was hearing a voice that wasn't really there. "Maybe I was talking to myself. I'm sorry if I was. Sometimes that happens when I'm thinking about stuff. I get distracted."

Francis was silent, considering the answer. It made a degree of sense. He sometimes got lost in a dream-world too. Which meant that Jake was like him, and that was good on one level, because it gave him something to fix.

"We'll work on that together," he said. "Here—I brought you some breakfast."

Jake took the plate and carton and said thank you without being prompted, which was another good thing. Presumably he'd learned some manners from some-where. But he also looked down at what he was now holding and didn't begin eating. The mold was still visible, Francis noticed. Clearly it wasn't good enough for him.

It had been good enough for Francis as a boy.

"Are you not hungry, Jake?"

"Not right now."

"You have to eat if you're going to grow up big and strong." Francis smiled patiently. "What would you like to do afterward?"

Jake was silent for a moment.

"I don't know. Maybe I'd like to do some drawing."

"We can do that! I'll help you with it."

Jake smiled.

"Thank you."

But he said Francis's other name afterward, and Francis went very still. The boy recognized him, of course, but a good home was no place for informality. A child needed discipline. There had to be a clearly delineated hierarchy.

"*Sir,*" Francis said. "That's what you'll call me here. Do you understand?"

Jake nodded.

"Because in this house we show respect for our elders. Do you understand?"

Jake nodded again.

"And we appreciate the things they do for us." Francis gestured at the plate. "I've gone to a lot of trouble. Eat your breakfast, please."

For a moment the eerie calm on Jake's face faded away and the boy looked like he was going to start crying. He stared off to one side again.

Francis's fist clenched at his side.

Just disobey me once, he thought.

Just once.

But then Jake looked back at him, the calm restored now, and picked up one of the crumpets. In the light up here, the mold was obvious around the edge.

"Yes," he said. "Sir."

FIFTY-EIGHT

It felt like a transgression as I opened the Packet and looked inside at the contents.

It was an assortment of paper, fabric, and trinkets, much of which overlapped with my own past and memories. The first thing I saw was a colored wristband, pulled taut at the plastic clasp where Rebecca had stretched it over her hand rather than cut it off. It was from a music festival we'd been to in the early days of our relationship, long before Jake had even been thought of, never mind born. Rebecca and I had camped with friends who had slowly drifted away over the years, and spent the weekend drinking and dancing, not caring about the rain or the cold. We had been young and carefree, and as I looked at it now, the wristband seemed like a talisman from a better time.

Excellent choice, Jake.

I recognized a small brown packet, and my vision blurred slightly as I opened it and tipped the contents into my palm. A tooth, so impossibly small that it felt like air on my skin. It was the first one Jake had lost, not long after Rebecca died. That night I'd slipped money under his pillow, along with a note from the tooth fairy explaining that she wanted him to keep the tooth because it was special. I hadn't seen it again until now.

I replaced it carefully in its envelope, and then unfolded a piece of paper that turned out to be the picture I'd drawn for him: a crude attempt at the two of us standing side by side, with that message underneath.

Even when we argue we still love each other.

The tears came at that. There had been so many arguments over the years. Both of us so similar, and yet failing to understand each other. Both of us reaching out to the other and always somehow missing. But God, it was true. I loved him through every single second of it. I loved him so much. I hoped that, wherever he was right now, he knew that.

I worked my way through the other items. They felt sacred to the touch, but also sometimes oblique in their mystery. There were several more bits of paper, and while some made sense—one of the few party invitations he'd ever received—much of it was incomprehensible to me. There were faded tickets and receipts, scribbled notes Rebecca had made, all so apparently meaningless that I couldn't fathom why Jake had dignified them as being *special.* Maybe it was even the smallness and apparent insignificance of them that he liked. These were adult things that he lacked the experience to decode. But his mother had cared enough to keep them, and so perhaps, if he studied them for long enough, he might understand her better.

Then a much older sheet of paper—torn from a small ring-bound notebook, so that one end was frayed.

I unfolded it and immediately recognized Rebecca's handwriting. A poem she'd written, presumably as a teenager, based on how faded the ink was. I started to read it.

If you leave a door half open, soon you'll hear the whispers spoken.
If you play outside alone, soon you won't be going home.
If your window's left unlatched, you'll hear him tapping at the glass.
If you're lonely, sad, and blue, the Whisper Man will come for you.

I read it again, the living room receding around me, then examined the writing once more to make sure. It was Rebecca's—I was certain of it. A less mature version than the one I was familiar with, but I knew my wife's handwriting.

This was where Jake had learned the rhyme.

From his mother.

Rebecca had known it when she was younger, and she had written it down. I did the math in my head and realized that Rebecca would have been thirteen years old at the time of Frank Carter's murders. Perhaps it was the kind of thing that would have caught the attention of a girl that age.

But that didn't explain where she had heard it.

I put the note to one side.

There were a number of photographs in the Packet, all of them so old that they must have been taken with a physical camera. I remembered doing the same as a child on holidays, and my mother and I had also done what Rebecca and her parents apparently had with these, writing a date and description on the back.

August 2, 1983—two days old.

I turned the photograph over, and saw a woman sitting on a couch, cradling a baby against her. Rebecca's mother. I had known her briefly: an enthusiastic woman, with a sense of adventure she'd passed on to her daughter. Here, she looked desperately tired but excited. The baby was asleep, swaddled in a yellow woolen blanket. From the date, I knew it had to be Rebecca, even if it was impossible to believe she had ever been so small.

April 21, 1987—playing Poohsticks.

This one showed Rebecca's father standing on a slatted wooden bridge with lush green foliage in the background, holding her up so she could dangle a stick over the water rushing past below. She was facing the camera, grinning. Not yet four years old, but I could already see the woman she would become. Even back then she had the smile that I could still picture so clearly in my head.

September 3, 1988—first day at school.

Here was Rebecca as a little girl, dressed in a blue jumper and pleated gray skirt, standing proudly in front of . . .

Rose Terrace Primary School.

I stared at the photograph for several seconds.

The school was familiar by now, and the photograph was certainly of Rebecca—but those two things did not go together. And yet there was no mistaking either of them. Those were the same railings, the same steps. The word GIRLS was carved into the black stone above the door. And that was my wife, as a child, standing outside.

First day at school.

Rebecca had lived here in Featherbank.

I was stunned by the discovery. How had I not known that? We had visited her parents on the south coast several times before they died, and while I was dimly aware they'd moved when she was younger, that had certainly been *home* for her: where she had thought of herself being from. All her friends at our wedding had been from there, and they'd seemed to share so much history that I'd assumed they'd grown up together. But then, maybe that was simply where, as a teenager, her life had flowered—where the friends she made and the stories she gathered were the vivid kind that people carry into adulthood. Because the evidence was right in front of me. Even if Featherbank had felt of little consequence to her as an adult, Rebecca had lived here as a child—or at least close enough to attend the school.

Close enough to have heard the Whisper Man rhyme.

I thought about how *focused* Jake had been on our new house when he'd seen it on my iPad—how all the others in the search results had become invisible to him after viewing the photographs of it online. It couldn't be a coincidence. I quickly flicked through the other photographs that he had kept. Most were snaps that had been taken on holiday, but a few of the locations were more familiar: Rebecca eating an ice cream on New Road Side. High up on a swing in the local park. Riding a tricycle on the pavement by the main road.

And then—

And then our house.

The sight of it was as incongruous as the school photograph had been. Rebecca in a place where she simply shouldn't and couldn't be. Here, she was standing on the pavement outside our new home, one foot placed backward on the driveway. The building behind, with its odd angles and misplaced windows, looked frightening, looming over the little girl who was just far enough over the threshold of the property to get the kudos for daring.

The local scary house.

The kids would dare each other to go near it.

Take photographs and things.

That was why the house had leaped out at Jake when he had seen it. Because he'd seen it before, with his mother standing in front of it.

And then I looked properly at Rebecca in the photograph. She appeared to be about seven or eight years old, and was wearing a blue-and-white-checked dress with a hem high enough that you could see a graze on her knee. And it must have been a breezy day when it was taken, because her hair was swept out to one side.

She was the same girl Jake had drawn in the window with him in his picture.

I fought back tears as I finally understood.

As ridiculous as it was, I'd almost begun to believe there was more to my son's invisible friend than his imagination alone. And I supposed that there was. Except he wasn't seeing ghosts or spirits. His imaginary friend was simply the mother he missed so much, conjured up as a little girl his own age. Someone who would play with him the way she always used to. Someone who could help him through the terrible new world he'd found himself in.

I turned the photograph over.

June 1, 1991, it said. *Being brave.*

I remembered how, when we'd first moved in, he had been running from room to room as though looking for someone, and my heart broke for him. I'd let him down so badly. It would have been hard for him regardless, but I could and should have done more to help him through it. Been more attentive, more present, less wrapped up in my own suffering. But I hadn't. And so he'd been forced to find solace with a memory instead.

I put the photograph down.

I'm so sorry, Jake.

And then, for what it was even worth, I searched through the rest of the material he'd kept. Each piece hurt to look at. Because I was certain now that I had lost my son forever, and that this was as close as I would ever be to him again, for whatever was left of my life.

But then I unfolded the last piece of paper he'd kept, and when I saw what was there, I went still again. It took a moment to understand what I was seeing and what it meant.

And then I grabbed my phone, already on my way to the front door.

FIFTY-NINE

"Slow down," Amanda said. "What have you found?"

She had been working nonstop through the night, and now—approaching nine o'clock in the morning—she could feel every minute of it. Her body was beyond weary. Her bones were aching and her thoughts were skittish and distracted. The last thing she really needed was Tom Kennedy gabbling down the phone at her, especially when he sounded as disjointed and out of it as she felt.

"I told you," he said. "A picture."

"A picture of a butterfly."

"Yes."

"Can you please slow down and explain to me what that means?"

"It was in Jake's Packet of Special Things."

"His what?"

"He collects things—keeps them. Things that have some kind of meaning for him. This picture was in there. It's one of the butterflies that were in the garage."

"Okay."

Amanda looked around the heaving operations room. It seemed as chaotic right now as the contents of her head. *Focus*. There was a picture of a butterfly. It clearly meant something to Tom Kennedy, but she still had no idea why.

"Jake drew this picture?"

"No! That's the point. It's too elaborate. It looks like something that a grown-up's done. He *was* drawing them, though, the evening after his first day at school. I think someone gave it to him to copy. Because how could he have seen them otherwise? They were in the garage, right?"

"The garage."

"So he *had* to have seen them somewhere else. And this must be where. Someone drew it for him. Someone who *had* seen them."

"Someone who'd been in your garage?"

"Or the house. That's what you said, isn't it—that there were more people like Norman Collins who knew the body was there? That the man you think took Jake is one of these people?"

Amanda was silent for a moment, considering that. Yes, that was what they were thinking. And while Kennedy's discovery probably meant nothing, the night hadn't brought much else to go on either.

"Who drew the picture?" she said.

"I don't know. It looks recent, so I think maybe it was someone at the school. It's on that thick paper they use at school. Jake brought it home after his first day, and that's why he was copying it."

The school.

In the days following Neil Spencer's disappearance, they'd talked to everyone who'd had any degree of regular contact with the boy, and that had included the teaching staff for the whole school. But there had been nothing suspicious about any of them. And, of course, Jake had only been at the school for a few days. This picture, assuming it had any relevance at all, could have come from anywhere.

"But you're not sure?"

"No," Tom said. "But there's something else too. That evening, Jake was talking to someone who wasn't there. He does that, right? He has imaginary friends. Only this time he said it was *the boy in the floor*. So how can he have known about that, along with the butterflies, unless someone talked to him about it?"

"I don't know."

She resisted the urge to point out that it could simply be a coincidence, and that even if it wasn't, there was still no reason to focus on the school. Instead, she turned to what seemed to her a far more fucking *pertinent* issue right now.

"You didn't think to mention this *before*?"

The phone went silent. Maybe it was a low blow to have delivered: the man's son was missing, after all, and some things only made sense in hindsight. Pictures and imaginary friends. Monsters whispering outside windows. Adults didn't always listen hard enough to children. But if Tom Kennedy had told them about this earlier, and if she had listened to him, then things might be different right now. She wouldn't be sitting here exhausted, with Pete in hospital and Jake Kennedy missing. It was impossible to keep the accusation out of her voice.

"Tom? *Why?*"

"I didn't know what it meant," he said.

"Well, maybe it doesn't mean anything, but . . . oh, for fuck's sake, hang on a second."

An alert had come through on her screen. Amanda opened the message. Sharon Bamber, the family liaison officer, had arrived at Karen Shaw's home but nobody was answering the door. Amanda frowned and pushed the phone against her ear. Now that Tom had stopped talking, she could hear traffic in the background.

"Where are you?" she asked him.

"I'm on my way to the school."

Christ. She leaned forward urgently.

"Don't do that, please."

"But—"

"But nothing. It won't help."

She closed her eyes and rubbed her forehead. What the hell was he thinking? Except, of course, his son was missing and so he wasn't thinking properly at all.

"Listen to me," she said. "Listen *right now.* I need you to go back to Karen Shaw's house. There's an officer— Sergeant Bamber—waiting for you there. I'm going to ask her to bring you to the department. We can discuss this picture then. Okay?"

He didn't reply. She could imagine him thinking it over. Torn between his determination to help Jake and the authority in her voice.

"Tom? Let's not make this any worse."

"Okay."

He hung up.

Damn it. She wasn't sure whether she believed him or not, but she supposed there was nothing she could do about it for now. In the meantime, she pinged a message back to Sharon, relaying her instructions, and then leaned back in her chair and tried to rub some life into her face.

Another report was delivered to her desk. She opened her eyes again to find more useless witness statements. None of the neighbors had seen or heard anything. Somehow, Francis Carter—or David Parker, or whatever he was calling himself—had walked into a house, committed the attempted murder of an experienced officer, abducted a child, and disappeared without attracting any attention whatsoever. The luck of the devil. Literally.

But not just luck, of course. Twenty years ago, he might have been a fragile, vulnerable little boy, but it was clear that the years since had seen him grow into a disturbed and dangerous man. One who was good at moving unnoticed and undetected.

She sighed.

The school, then, for what it was worth.

Let's take another look.

SIXTY

Go back to Karen Shaw's house.

For a moment, it had felt like I might. DI Beck was police, after all, and my instinct was to do what the police told me. And her words had stung me. On top of every other way I'd failed, there was too much that I hadn't told the police, and the fact I'd held back on information at the time to protect Jake didn't change the fact that I could have prevented this.

Which meant he was missing because of me.

I couldn't blame Beck for not taking me seriously in light of that, but she hadn't seen what Jake had drawn. Someone had *made* that picture for him to copy, and they had done so recently.

And why had Jake kept it?

What was so *special* about it?

I remembered what had happened after that first day. The argument we'd had. The words he'd read on my computer screen. The distance between us. I could only think of one explanation for why that picture had ended up in his Packet of Special Things, and it was that Jake had decided to keep it because someone had shown him the kindness and support that I hadn't.

And it was that thought that made my decision for me.

I made it to the school just in time. The doors were still open, and there were a few parents and children milling around in the playground. I'd been considering going to the office—and would have, if necessary—but the office had a security door that separated it from the rest of the school. Here, I could get straight in if I needed to.

I ran through the gates, my heart pounding, straight past Karen, who was just leaving.

"Tom—"

"A minute."

Mrs. Shelley was standing by the open door, the last of the children trailing in past her. She looked alarmed at the sight of me. I imagined I looked as frantic as I felt.

"Mr. Kennedy—"

"Who drew this?" I unfolded the sheet of paper and showed her the picture of the butterfly. "Who drew it?"

"I don't—"

"*Jake is missing*," I said. "Do you understand? Someone has taken my son. Jake came home with this picture after his first day of school. I need to know who drew it."

She shook her head. I was babbling too much information for her to process, and I fought down the urge to grab her and shake her and try to make her *understand* how important this was, and then I realized Karen was standing beside me, gently resting her hand on my arm.

"Tom. Try to calm down."

"I am calm." My gaze didn't leave Mrs. Shelley as I tapped the picture of the butterfly. "Who drew this for Jake? Was it another child? A teacher? Was it you?"

"I don't know!" She was flustered. I was scaring her. "I'm not sure. It might have been George."

My grip tightened on the paper.

"George?"

"He's one of our teaching assistants. But—"

"Is he here now?"

"He should be."

She glanced back, and that was all the time it took for me to move past her into the corridor beyond.

"Mr. Kennedy!"

"Tom—"

I ignored them both, glancing sideways into the cloakroom, where the children from Jake's class were hanging up their things—where *Jake* should have been—and then I started running, rounding the corner ahead and entering the main hall, which was filled with children traipsing toward the classrooms on all sides. I dodged between them, then stopped in the middle, the hall spinning around me as I looked here and there, not knowing which room might be Jake's, and where *George* might be. I was in trouble here, I knew that deep down, but it didn't matter because if I didn't find Jake my life was over anyway, and if George was here, then he couldn't be hurting—

Adam.

I recognized Karen's son putting his water bottle on a table at the far end of the hall, then walking through a door. I ran across, noticing one of the receptionists and an older man, the groundskeeper, heading down a far corridor toward the hall. Mrs. Shelley must have called ahead. An intruder in the school would warrant that, I guessed.

"Mr. *Kennedy*," the receptionist shouted.

But I reached the classroom before they did, moving quickly inside, still just about self-aware enough not to push the children in front of me out of the way. The room was a cacophony of color, the walls painted yellow and adorned with what seemed like hundreds of laminated sheets: multiplication tables; pictures of fruit and numbers; small, cartoonish figures performing tasks with their occupations written beside them. I looked across the sea of tiny tables and chairs, searching for an adult. An older woman was standing at the far end of the room, staring at me in confusion, clutching a register on a clipboard, but she was the only grown-up I could see.

And then I felt a hand on my arm.

I turned to find the old groundskeeper standing beside me, a firm expression on his face.

"You can't be in here."

"All right."

I fought the urge to shake his hand off me. There was no point—whoever George was, he wasn't here. But the frustration at that made me shake his hand off anyway.

"All right."

Outside the classroom, the groundskeeper pointedly

closed the door. Mrs. Shelley was walking toward me, her phone in her hand. I wondered if she'd already used it to call the police. If so, maybe they'd start taking me seriously now.

"Mr. Kennedy—"

"I know. I shouldn't be in here."

"You're trespassing."

"Put me on yellow, then."

She started to say something, but then stopped herself. More than anything else, she looked concerned.

"You said Jake is missing?"

"Yes," I said. "Someone took him last night."

"I'm sorry. I can't imagine what . . . obviously I understand that you're upset."

I wasn't sure she could. The panic was like a live wire inside me now.

"I need to find George," I said.

"He's not here."

The receptionist. She was standing with her arms folded, and she looked considerably less forgiving than Mrs. Shelley.

"Where is he?" I said.

"Well, I *imagine* he's at home. He called in sick a little while ago."

The alarm went up a notch. That couldn't be a coincidence. And it meant he was with Jake right now.

"Where does he live?"

"I'm not at liberty to reveal staff details."

I thought about marching straight past her and getting into the main office. The groundskeeper was standing there, blocking the way, but the man was in his sixties and I could win that fight if I tried. There would be police and charges to answer then, but it would be worth it if I had enough time in the office to search the cabinets and find the information I wanted. But not much use to me if I couldn't. And not much use to Jake if I ended up in custody.

"You'll give it to the police?" I said.

"Of course."

I turned and walked across the hall, back the way I'd come. They followed me, making sure I left. After I stepped outside, the door was closed and locked behind me. The playground was almost entirely empty now, but Karen was waiting for me by the gate, an anxious look on her face.

"Thank *fuck,*" she said. "You know you could have got arrested for that?"

"I need to find him."

"This George? Who is he?"

"Classroom assistant. He drew something for Jake to copy—a butterfly. One of the ones they found with the body in the garage."

Karen looked skeptical. And hearing myself say it out loud again, I didn't blame her. But just as with Beck, it was impossible to make other people understand. The person who had taken Jake had known about the remains, I was sure of it, so they would know about the butterflies and the boy in the floor. My son wasn't psychic. He was vulnerable and lonely, and he had to have learned about those things from someone. Someone with access to him.

Someone with access to him right now.

"The police?" Karen said.

"They don't believe me either."

She sighed.

"I know," I said. "But I'm *right,* Karen. And I need to find Jake. I can't bear the thought of him being hurt. Of him not being with me. Of it all being my fault. I *need* to find him."

She was silent for a moment, considering that. And then she sighed again.

"George Saunders," she said. "He's the only George listed on the school website. I got his address while you were inside."

"Christ."

"I told you," she said. "I'm good at finding things out."

SIXTY-ONE

"I don't think you should be drawing that."

The little girl sounded nervous. She was pacing back and forth across the small attic bedroom. Every now and then she'd stop and look down at his work. Before now, she hadn't said anything, but that was when he'd been drawing the house and its elaborate garden, the way he was supposed to, copying the intricate scene George had drawn for him. Before he'd given up and started drawing a battle scene instead.

Around and around the circles went.

Force fields. Or portals. He couldn't decide which, and maybe it didn't matter. Something for protection or something for escape: either would do. Anything that would make him safe or take him away from here, from George, from the awful presence he could feel throbbing just out of sight at the bottom of the stairs. He wasn't sure George had even locked the door when he left earlier, and he thought the little girl wanted him to sneak down and try it. No way. Even with a clear path to the front door, there was no—

"Please stop, Jake."

And he did. His hand was trembling so much he

could hardly hold the marker. He was pressing it down so hard that the portal was beginning to cut through the paper.

"I've done as well as I can," he said. "I can't do it."

George had given him four sheets to work on, and he'd used three already trying to replicate the picture of the house and its garden. But it was too complicated. A part of him suspected George had done that deliberately—that it was a test, the same way that the disgusting breakfast had been. With the tests at school, you could tell that the teachers *wanted* you to pass, but he didn't think that George wanted that at all. When Mrs. Shelley had put him on yellow that first day, Jake thought that she probably hadn't wanted to. But with George, it felt like he was looking for any excuse to put him straight onto red.

So he'd tried. He'd done his best. And there was one sheet left, so he was drawing a battle. It was good to be creative, wasn't it?

Daddy always liked his pictures.

But he didn't want to think about Daddy right now. He started drawing again. Around and around. And maybe the little girl *was* right, but he couldn't stop himself now. It was all that was holding back the panic, even though his hand seemed to be totally out of control, so maybe this *was* panic after all—

The door opened at the bottom of the stairs.

Around and around.

Footsteps coming up.

And then there was so much ink on the sheet that the paper tore. The figure popped out.

You're safe now, Jake thought.

And then George entered the room.

He was smiling, but it was all wrong. Jake thought it was like George had put on a parent costume, except it was uncomfortable and didn't fit, and what he really wanted to do was take it off as quickly as possible. Jake didn't want to see what might be underneath. He stood up, his heart trembling as hard as his body was.

"Now, then!" He walked across. "Let's see how you've done."

He stopped a short distance away. He could see the picture.

The smile disappeared.

"What the fuck is that?"

Jake blinked at the swear. As he did, he realized there were tears in his eyes. He had started crying without even noticing, and the urge to let himself—to break down and sob—was tremendous. It was only the look on George's face that stopped him. George wouldn't want real emotion. If Jake broke down, then George would simply wait until he was finished and then give him something to really cry about.

"That's not what I told you to draw."

"Show him the others," the little girl said quickly.

Jake rubbed his eyes and then pointed down at the drawings he'd been meant to be doing. *I want my Daddy.* The words were bubbling up inside him, threatening to come out.

"I did my best," Jake said. "I couldn't do it."

George looked down, examining the pictures blankly.

The room was silent for a few seconds, the air humming with threat.

"These aren't good enough."

Despite himself, the comment stung Jake. He knew he was no good at drawing, but Daddy always said he liked them anyway, because—

"I tried my best."

"No, Jake. Evidently you *didn't*. Because you gave up, didn't you? You had another sheet to practice on, and you decided to do . . . *this* instead." George waved his hand contemptuously at the battle scene. "Things in this house cost money. We do not waste them."

"*Say sorry,*" the little girl told him.

"I'm sorry, sir."

"Sorry isn't good enough, Jake. Not good enough at all."

George was staring down at him very gravely. It looked like he was struggling to control himself, because his hands were trembling. And Jake knew that the drawing was just an excuse. Deep down, George *wanted* to be angry with him. His hands were trembling because he was trying to decide if this was enough of an infringement to let his anger fly.

He made up his mind.

"And so you're going to have to be punished."

And then George became totally still. The costume came away. Jake could see all the goodness and kindness falling away from him, as though they had only ever been pretend, things that could be discarded as easily as pulling off a T-shirt. There was a monster standing in front of him. And he was alone here with it. And it was going to hurt him.

Jake retreated until the backs of his calves were against the small bed.

"I want my daddy."

"What?"

"Daddy! I want my daddy!"

George started to move closer, but then Jake jumped at the sound of an alarm somewhere in the house below, and George stopped where he was. Very slowly, he turned his head and stared back toward the staircase. The rest of his body remained angled toward Jake.

Not an alarm, Jake realized.

Someone was ringing the doorbell.

SIXTY-TWO

On the second floor, seething with rage, Francis ducked quickly into his bedroom and pulled on a white robe. He was supposed to be sick, after all. He also forced himself to calm down enough to hide the rage he felt. It was good to keep it close to the surface, though. Accessible. He might need it.

The fucking doorbell.

Still ringing. He headed downstairs. It wouldn't be the police, he decided. If anything ever brought them to his door, their arrival would be considerably less polite than this. He looked out through the peephole in the front door, the bell ringing loudly and incessantly in his ear. The glass gave a fish-eye view of the steps and garden, and he saw Tom Kennedy leaning on the bell, a look of wild determination on his face. Francis recoiled slightly. How the fuck had Kennedy found him? What could have brought *him* here but not the police?

And why would he even want his son back?

Francis stepped back from the door. There was no need to answer it—surely Kennedy would go away soon. It was madness to think the man might stay there much longer.

And yet the doorbell continued ringing.

Francis thought again about the look on the man's face, and he wondered if perhaps Kennedy really *was* insane. If that was what losing a child, even one as blatantly uncared-for as Jake, might do to a man.

Or if perhaps he'd misjudged.

He rested his forehead against the door, bare inches from the man outside now, feeling Kennedy's presence as a tingle in the front of his skull. Was it possible that Jake was loved, after all? That his father cared about him so much that his abduction had driven him to such extremes? The idea sent an explosion of loss and hopelessness through Francis. It wouldn't be *fair* if that was true. None of this was fair. Little boys didn't matter that much to anyone. He had known it all along deep down, but he was certain of it now. They were worthless. They deserved nothing but—

The bell kept ringing.

"All *right*," he called out loudly.

Kennedy must have heard him, but he didn't relent. Francis walked quickly into the kitchen, selected a small, sharp knife from the draining rack, and slid it into the pocket of the robe. Finally, the bell stopped. Francis put the feeling of loss away inside him and brought the anger back up again, keeping it just out of sight.

Get rid of him.

Deal with the boy.

Then he put on his best face and went back to the door.

SIXTY-THREE

"All *right*."

I was so surprised when I heard the voice from behind the door that I forgot to take my finger off the bell.

I'd given up expecting anyone to answer. By that point it was more that I had nowhere else to be and nothing else to do. I wasn't even sure how long I'd been standing there. I had just become intent on ringing that bell, as though by holding it down I could somehow save Jake.

I stepped back, then turned around and looked at Karen. She was waiting in the car, watching me anxiously, her phone pressed to her ear. She'd insisted on calling the police, so I'd left her with DI Beck's details. She stared back at me now, shaking her head.

I turned again to the door, with no idea what was going to happen next. I'd been running on adrenaline since looking through Jake's Packet of Special Things, and now that I was here, I had no idea what the hell I was going to say to George Saunders, or what I was even going to do.

A key in the lock.

The memory of seeing my father last night came back

to me. The injuries that had been inflicted on him. He had been a fit, capable man, and yet whoever had attacked him had overwhelmed him easily. He had been unarmed, and perhaps taken by surprise, but even so. What use was I going to be?

I hadn't thought this through well enough.

The door opened.

I expected it to be on a chain, with Saunders only half visible, perhaps peering guiltily out. But he opened it fully and confidently, and I was immediately taken aback by the sight of him. He was average-looking in every way, and while I guessed he was in his twenties, he looked much younger. There was a soft, childlike sense to him. I didn't think I'd ever seen anyone appear so harmless.

"George Saunders?" I said.

He nodded sleepily, then pulled the white robe he was wearing more tightly around him. His hair was messy and unkempt, and the expression on his face suggested that he had only just woken up, and was both bewildered and slightly irritated about it.

"You work at Rose Terrace School, right?"

He squinted at me.

"Yeah. Right."

"My son goes there. I think you might teach him."

"Oh. Well, no, I don't teach. I'm just an assistant."

"Year three. Jake Kennedy."

"Right. Yeah, I think he's in my class. But what I meant is, it's his teacher you'd need to talk to." He frowned, but more out of sleepy confusion than suspicion, as though the thought had only just occurred to him. "And at the *school* too. How did you even get my address?"

I looked at him. His face was pale, and he was shivering slightly despite the heat of the morning. He really did *look* ill. And yes, slightly perturbed by my presence, but not about it being me in particular. Just uneasy about a parent turning up on his doorstep.

"It's not really about his schoolwork," I said.

"What is it about, then?"

"Jake is missing."

Saunders shook his head, not understanding.

"Someone *took him*," I said. "Just like Neil Spencer."

"Oh, Jesus." He looked genuinely aghast at that. "I'm so sorry. When did this . . . ?"

"Last night."

"Oh, Jesus," he said again, then closed his eyes and rubbed his forehead. "That is awful. *Awful.* I haven't really had much to do with Jake, but he seems like such a nice kid."

He is, I thought. But I also noted Saunders's use of the present tense, and began doubting myself more. The evidence that had led me here was paper thin, and in the flesh Saunders looked like someone who wouldn't hurt a fly. And he seemed genuinely surprised by the news that Jake had been abducted—upset, even.

I held up the picture of the butterfly.

"Did you draw this for him?"

Saunders peered at it.

"No. I've never seen that before."

"You didn't draw this?"

"No."

He took a step back. I was holding the sheet of paper up, my hand trembling, and he was responding exactly the way anyone would when faced with a man like me on their doorstep.

"What about the boy in the floor?" I said.

"What?"

"The *boy in the floor*."

He stared at me, more obviously horrified now. It was the kind of horror that came from gradually understanding he was being accused of something, and if he was faking it, then he was a phenomenal actor.

This is a mistake, I thought.

But even so.

"*Jake,*" I shouted past him.

"What are you—?"

I leaned up against the doorframe, almost chest to chest with Saunders now, and shouted again.

"*Jake!*"

No answer.

After a few seconds of silence, Saunders swallowed. The noise it made was so hard that I could hear it.

"Mr. . . . Kennedy?"

"Yes."

"I can understand you're upset. I *really* can. But you're scaring me. I don't know what's going on, but I really think you should go now."

I looked at him. The fear in his eyes was obvious, and I thought it was real. His whole body was frozen in a flinch. He was the kind of timid man you could force down into a huddle just by raising your voice, and it seemed I was halfway there.

Saunders was telling the truth.

Jake wasn't here, and I—

And I—

I shook my head, taking a step back.

Lost now. Completely lost. It had been a mistake coming here. I needed to do what I'd been told to and get back to Karen's house before I could do any more damage. Before I could fuck things up any more than I already had.

"I'm sorry," I said.

"Mr. Kennedy—"

"I'm sorry. I'm going now."

SIXTY-FOUR

Wait here.

What choice did he have? None.

Jake sat on the bed, gripping the edges with his hands. When George had left, he'd locked the door at the bottom of the stairs. The bell had still been ringing then. The sound had continued for another minute or so before finally stopping, and so Jake assumed that George must have answered it, and was probably still talking to whoever was at the door. Otherwise, surely he would be back up here? Doing what he'd been planning to do before whoever it was called around.

Maybe not if I'm good, he thought.

Maybe if he waited here then George would like him again.

"You know that's not true, Jake."

He turned his head. The little girl was sitting on the bed beside him, and she had her serious face on again. But it was different now. She looked scared, but also full of quiet determination.

"He's a bad man," she said, "and he wants to hurt you. And he's going to hurt you if you let him."

Jake wanted to cry.

"How am *I* supposed to stop him?"

She smiled softly, as though they both knew the answer to that question. *No, no, no.* Jake looked over at the corner of the room, where the short corridor led to the stairs. There was no way he could go down there. He couldn't face what might be waiting at the bottom.

"I can't do that!"

"But what if it's Daddy at the door?"

Which was exactly what Jake had hardly been daring to think. That maybe Daddy *did* want to find him after all, and that somehow he had, and that it was him who was downstairs now.

It was too much to hope for.

"Daddy would come up and get me."

"Only if he knows you're here. He might not be sure." She thought about it. "Maybe you need to meet him halfway."

Jake shook his head. It was too much to ask.

"I can't go down there."

The little girl was silent for a moment.

Then:

"Tell me about the nightmare," she said quietly.

Jake shut his eyes.

"It's about finding Mummy, isn't it?"

"Yes."

"And you've never told *anybody* about it before, not even Daddy. Because you're so scared of it. But you can tell me now."

"I can't."

"Yes, you can," she whispered. "I'll help you. You walk into the living room, and the house feels empty.

Daddy's not there, is he? He's still outside. So you walk across the living room."

"Don't," Jake said.

"It's sunny."

He scrunched his eyes shut, but it didn't help. He could remember the angle of sunlight through their old back window.

"You walk so slowly, because you can feel that something is wrong. Something is missing. Somehow, you already know that."

And now he could see the back door, the wall, the handrail.

All revealed in stages.

And then—

"And then you see her," the little girl said. "Don't you?"

This wasn't a nightmare, so there was no way to wake up and stop the image from appearing. Yes, he saw Mummy. She was lying at the bottom of the stairs, her head tilted to one side and her cheek resting against the carpet. Her face was pale, even slightly blue, and her eyes were closed. It had been a heart attack, Daddy told him afterward, which didn't make sense because that was something that happened to older people. But Daddy said that sometimes it happened to younger people too, maybe if their hearts were too . . . and then he'd trailed off and started crying. They both had.

But that was afterward. In that moment, he'd just stood there, understanding what he was seeing in a way his mind couldn't make sense of, because the feelings were all too big.

"I saw her," he said.

"And?"

"And it was Mummy."

Just Mummy. Not a monster. The monstrous thing was how it had made him feel and what it meant. In that moment, it had seemed like a part of *him* was lying there instead, and that he would never have the words to describe the world of emotions that exploded inside him, as big as the way the Big Bang had made the universe.

But it had just been Mummy. He didn't need to be scared of her.

"We need to go downstairs now." The little girl put her hand on his shoulder. "There's nothing to be frightened of."

Jake opened his eyes and looked at her. She was still there, and somehow more real than ever, and he didn't think he had ever seen anyone who loved him so much.

"Will you go with me?" he said.

She smiled.

"Of course I will. *Always,* my gorgeous boy."

Then she stood up, and reached out, and took his hands, pulling him to his feet.

"What are we being?" she said.

SIXTY-FIVE

"I'm sorry. I'm going now."

I wasn't even sure who I was apologizing to. Saunders, I supposed, for arriving on his doorstep and accusing him, frightening him, without any real evidence. But the apology also went deeper than that. It was to Jake. To Rebecca. To myself, even. In some way or other, I'd let all of us down.

I looked back at Karen. She was still holding the phone to her ear, but she shook her head at me again.

"Look," Saunders said carefully. "It's okay. Like I said, I know you're upset. And I can't imagine what you must be going through right now. But . . ."

He trailed off.

"I know," I said.

"I'm *happy* to talk to the police. And I hope you find him. Your son. I hope this is all some kind of mistake."

"Thank you."

I nodded, and I was about to head back to the car when I heard a noise coming from somewhere in the house behind me. I stopped. Then turned back to Saunders. It was a distant hammering sound, and someone was shouting, but so indistinct that it was barely audible.

Saunders had heard it too. The expression on his face had changed while my back had been turned, and he no longer looked quite so ill or soft or harmless. It was as though the humanity had only ever been a disguise, and now it had fallen away and I was facing something entirely alien.

He closed the door quickly.

"Jake!"

I got up the step just in time to wedge my leg in. The door slammed agonizingly on the sides of my knee, but I ignored the pain and pushed against it, bracing one hand inside the jamb, and then my back against the wood, heaving as hard as I could. Saunders was grunting on the other side, pressing back against me. But I was bigger than him, and the sudden burst of adrenaline was adding to my weight. Jake was somewhere inside this house, and if I didn't reach him, then Saunders was going to kill him. He couldn't escape from this. He wouldn't try. But if he managed to keep me out, he could still hurt my son.

"Jake!"

Suddenly the resistance was gone.

Saunders must have stepped away. The door shot open, and I barreled into the living room, half barging into him, half falling. He hit me half-heartedly in the side as I collided with him, and then he tumbled backward and we landed hard, me on top of him, his head tilted to one side against the floorboards, my right forearm across his jaw. My left hand was pinning his right arm to the floor at the elbow. His body shook upward, trying to fight me off, but I was heavier than him and I was suddenly sure that I could hold him.

But then he lurched up against me again and I felt his hand at my side, where he'd hit me so ineffectively, and I registered the pain there. Not overwhelming in itself, but sickening and awful. Deep, internal, wrong. I glanced down and saw the ball of his fist still pressed against me, and then the blood that was beginning to soak into the white robe he was wearing.

The knife he was holding was somewhere inside me, and when he flopped up against me, screaming in rage, my whole world shrieked with him.

Jake!

I wasn't sure if I shouted it or simply thought it. Saunders was baring his teeth inches from my face, spitting and trying to bite me. I pressed down on him, my vision beginning to star at the edges. And then, when he lurched up again, the blade moved with him, and those stars exploded. If I let him up now, he would kill me and then kill Jake, so I pressed down harder on him, and the knife moved again, and that explosion of stars blurred into white light that gradually filled my vision. But I couldn't let him up. I would hold him down as he killed me.

Jake.

The hammering and shouting was still coming from somewhere above me. I could make out the words now. My son was up there, and he was calling for me.

Jake.

The stars disappeared as the light overwhelmed me.

I'm sorry.

SIXTY-SIX

Adrenaline had a way of waking you up.

Francis Carter, Amanda thought.

Or David Parker, or whatever he's calling himself.

Back at the department, she'd worked her way through the school's employees, looking for a male in his late twenties. There were four men working there, including the groundskeeper, and only one of them was an approximate age match. George Saunders was twenty-four years old, while Francis Carter would be twenty-seven by now, but when it came to buying a fake identity, the age only needed to be approximate.

Saunders had been spoken to after Neil Spencer went missing, and the interview hadn't sounded any alarm bells. She had read the transcript. Saunders had been erudite and convincing. He had no alibi for the exact period of the abduction, but that wasn't so surprising. No record. No warning signs at all. Nothing to pursue.

Except that a new search now revealed that the real George Saunders had died three years earlier.

Reality felt heightened as Amanda drove into the

street. She parked at the top, outside a property that appeared to be derelict, a little way back from the target house, and then a van pulled in behind her, with two more approaching from the opposite direction and coming to a stop a short distance down the hill. All of them kept away from the eyeline of the house, so that if Saunders were to look out of his window right now, he would see nothing. That was important. The last thing they needed was for him to barricade himself in and for them to end up dealing with a hostage situation.

Not that it would come to that, she thought. If he was cornered, Saunders would simply kill Jake Kennedy.

Her phone had been buzzing the whole way. She took it out now. Four missed calls. The first three were all from an unknown number. The fourth was from the hospital. Which meant there was news about Pete.

Something fell away inside her. She remembered how determined she had been last night—that she would not lose Pete, that she would find Jake Kennedy. How stupid to think like that. But she put those feelings away for now, gathering herself together, because there was only one of those things she could do something about right now.

I'm not losing another child on my watch.

She got out of the car.

The street was silent. It felt almost wholly deserted here, an area of the city that was slowly dying in its sleep. She heard the side of the van behind her rumbling open, and then the scuff of shoes on the driveway. Down the hill, officers were congregating. The plan had been that she would go first, ostensibly alone, and try to get Francis to open the door and allow her inside the property. At that point, there would be a flurry of activity, and he would be taken down in seconds.

But then Amanda noticed a car parked outside, its driver's door open. And as she walked down the street, she realized the door to George Saunders's house was ajar as well, and she began running.

"Everybody move."

Through the front garden, up the path, and then through the open door into what turned out to be a living room. There was a mess of bodies on the floor, blood everywhere, but it wasn't immediately obvious who was hurt and who wasn't.

"Help me, please."

That was Karen Shaw. Amanda moved over. Shaw was kneeling on one of Francis Carter's arms, trying to hold it still. Between them, Tom Kennedy was pressing onto Francis Carter. Carter himself was pinned in place, eyes shut tight, concentrating on moving even though the weight of the two of them together was enough to keep him in place.

From somewhere above them, Amanda could hear a hammering noise and shouting.

Daddy! Daddy!

Officers swarmed in past her, a dozen bodies overtaking the scene.

"Don't move him," Karen shouted. "He's been stabbed."

Amanda could see the spread of blood soaking into Carter's bathrobe. Tom Kennedy was completely still.

She couldn't tell if he was alive or not—if she had lost him today as well . . .

Daddy! Daddy!

That, at least, she could still do something about.

She ran to the stairs.

PART SIX

SIXTY-SEVEN

Pete remembered hearing that your life flashed before your eyes when you died.

It was true, he realized now, but it also happened while you were alive. How *fast* things went, he thought. As a boy, he had marveled at the life spans of butterflies and mayflies, some of them alive for only days or even hours, and it had seemed unimaginable. But he understood now that it was true for everything— that it was only a matter of perspective. The years accumulated quicker and quicker, like friends linking arms in an ever-expanding circle, reeling faster and faster as midnight approached. And then, suddenly, it was done.

Unfurling backward.

Flashing before your eyes, as it did for him now.

He looked down at a child, sleeping peacefully in a room barely lit by the soft light from the hall. The little boy's hair was swept back behind his ear, with one hand clutching the other in front of his face, completely still aside from the gentle rise and fall of the covers. Everything was calm. A child, warm and loved, was sleeping safely and without fear. An old book, its pages splayed open, lay on the floor by the bed.

Your daddy liked these books when he was younger.

And then here was a quiet country lane. It was summertime and the whole world was in bloom. He looked around, blinking. The hedges on either side of the road were lustrous and thick with life, while the trees reached together overhead, their leaves forming a canopy that colored the world in shades of lime and lemon. Butterflies flickered across the fields. How beautiful it was here. He had been too focused to notice that before— too busy looking without looking. He saw it so clearly now that he wondered how he could have been so distracted as to miss it then.

Here—a flash—was a scene so abhorrent that his mind refused to countenance it. He heard the nasal buzz of the flies that were darting mindlessly through the wine-stained air, and he saw an angry sun staring down at the children on the floor that were not children anymore, and then somehow, mercifully, time reversed more quickly. He stepped backward. A door swung shut. A padlock clicked.

Nobody should have to see hell even once.

There was no need to look inside it ever again.

Here was a beach. The sand beneath the backs of his legs was as soft and fine as silk, hot from the bright white sun that seemed to fill the sky above. In front of him, the sea was a froth of silver feathers. A woman was sitting so close to him that he could feel the tiny hairs on her bare upper arm tingling against his own skin. With her other hand she was holding out a camera, pointing it at them both. He did his best to smile, squinting against the light. He was so happy right then—he hadn't realized it at the time, but he was. He loved her so much, but for some reason he had never known how to articulate that. He did now; it was so simple in hindsight. When the photograph was taken, he turned his head to look at the woman, and he gave himself permission to feel the words as well as speak them.

I love you.

She smiled at him.

Here was a house. It was squat and ugly and throbbing with hatred, much like the man he knew resided within, and while he didn't want to go inside, he had no choice. He was small—a child again now—and this was his home. The front door rattled and the carpet breathed out dust beneath his feet. The air was thick and gray with resentment. In the living room, a bitter old man sat in an armchair by an open fire, his paunch pushing out so far against the dirty sweater that it rested on his thighs. There was a sneer on the man's face. There was always that, whenever there was anything at all.

What a disappointment Pete was. It was clear to him how useless he was, how nothing he did was ever good enough.

But it wasn't true.

You don't know me, he thought.

You never did.

When he was a child, his father had been a language he was unable to speak, but he was fluent now. The man wanted him to be someone else, and that had been confusing. But he could read the whole book of his father now and he knew that none of it had ever been about *him*. His own book was separate, and always had been. He had only ever needed to be himself, and it had just taken time—too much time—to understand that.

Here was a child's bedroom, windowless and small, only twice the width of the single bed.

He lay down, breathing in deeply the suddenly familiar smell of the sheets and pillow. The comfort blanket from his cot was tucked between the mattress and the wood. Instinctively, he reached out for it, curling a corner of the soft cloth in his hand, bringing it to his face, closing his eyes, and breathing in.

This was the end, he realized. The tangle of his life had been unpicked and set out before him, and he saw and understood it clearly now, all of it so obvious in hindsight.

He wished he could have it again.

Here was a door opening. An angle of light from the shabby hallway fell over Pete, and then a different man walked tentatively into the bedroom, moving slowly and carefully, limping slightly, as though he had been hurt and his body was tender in some way. The man approached the bed and, with difficulty, knelt down beside it.

After watching Pete sleeping for a time, unsure what he was going to do, the man finally came to a decision. He leaned across and embraced him as best he could.

And even though Pete was all but lost in deeper dreams by then, he sensed the embrace, or at least imagined he did, and for a moment he felt understood and forgiven. As though a cycle had been completed, or something found.

As though a missing piece of him had finally been returned.

SIXTY-EIGHT

"Are you all right, Daddy?"

"What?"

I shook my head. I was sitting by Jake's bed, holding *Power of Three* open at the last page, staring into space. We had just finished the book, and then I had gotten distracted. Lost in thought.

"I'm fine," I said.

From Jake's expression, it was clear that he didn't believe me—and he was right, of course: I was a long way from being fine. But I didn't want to tell him about seeing my father for the last time at the hospital that day. In time, perhaps I would, but there was still so much he didn't know, and I wasn't sure I had the words yet to explain any of it, or to make him understand.

Nothing ever changed on that level.

"Just this book." I closed it and ran my hand thoughtfully over the cover. "I haven't read it since I was a kid, and I guess it brought back memories. Made me feel like I was your age again a bit."

"I don't believe you were ever my age."

I laughed. "Hard to believe, isn't it? Cuddle?"

Jake pulled the sheet away, then clambered out. I put the book down as he perched on my knee.

"Carefully."

"Sorry, Daddy."

"It's okay. Just reminding you."

It had been nearly two weeks since my injuries at the hands of George Saunders, a man I now knew had once been called Francis Carter. I still wasn't sure how close I'd come to dying that day. I couldn't even remember most of it. A lot of what happened that morning was a blur, as though the panic I had been experiencing had smeared it all away and stopped me from retaining it. The first day in the hospital was much the same; my life only swam back into focus slowly. I was left now with bandages across one side of my body, an inability to put my weight down properly on that foot, and a handful of impressions that were little more than memories of a dream. Jake shouting for me; the desperation I had felt; the *need* to reach him.

The fact that I had been ready to die for him.

He hugged me now, very gently. Even so, I had to do my best not to wince. I was grateful that he didn't need me to carry him up and down the stairs in this house. After what had happened, I'd been worried he might be more scared than ever, and that the behavior might return, but the truth was that he'd dealt with the horrors of that day far better than I'd imagined. Perhaps better than I had.

I hugged him back as best I could. It was all I could ever do. And then, after he'd clambered back in, I stood in the doorway, watching him for a moment. He looked so peaceful in bed, warm and safe, with the Packet of Special Things resting on the floor beside him. I hadn't told him that I had looked inside it, or what I had found there, or the truth about the little girl. That was something else that—for the moment at least—I didn't have the words for.

"Good night, mate. I love you."

He yawned.

"Love you too, Daddy."

The stairs were hard for me right now, so after I turned off the light I went into my own room for a while, waiting for him to go to sleep. I sat on the bed and opened my laptop, turning my attention to the most recent file and reading what was there.

Rebecca.

I know exactly what you'd think about that, because you were always so much more practical than me. You'd want me to get on with my life. You'd want me to be happy.

And so on. It took me a moment to understand what I'd written, because I hadn't touched the document since that final night in the safe house, which seemed like a lifetime ago now. It was about Karen—how I felt guilty for having feelings for her. That also seemed very distant. She had come to see me in the hospital. She'd taken Jake to school for me and helped to look after him as I gradually recuperated. There was a growing closeness between us. What happened had brought us together, but it had also knocked us off a more predictable track, and that kiss hadn't happened yet. But I could still feel it there waiting.

You'd want me to be happy.

Yes.

I deleted everything apart from Rebecca's name.

My intention before had been to write about my life with Rebecca, the grief I felt over her death, and the way the loss of her had affected me. I still wanted to do that, because it felt like she would be an important part of whatever I did write. She didn't end when her life did because, even without the existence of ghosts, that's simply not the way things work. But I realized now that there was so much more, and that I wanted to write about all of it. The truth about everything that had happened. Mister Night. The boy in the floor. The butterflies. The little girl with the strange dress.

And the Whisper Man, of course.

It was a daunting prospect, because it was all such a jumble, and there was also so much I didn't know and perhaps never would. But then again, I wasn't sure that in itself was a problem. The truth of something can be in the feeling of it as much as the fact.

I stared at the screen.

Rebecca.

Only one word, and even that was wrong. Jake and I had moved to this house for a fresh start, and as much as Rebecca was an integral part of the story, I realized it shouldn't be about her. That was the whole point. My focus needed to be elsewhere now.

I deleted her name.

Jake, I typed.

There is so much I want to tell you, but we've always found it hard to talk to each other, haven't we?

I hesitated.

So I'll have to write to you instead.

That was when I heard Jake whispering.

I sat completely still, listening to the silence that followed the noise, and which now seemed to fill the house more ominously than before. Seconds ticked by—long enough for me to begin to believe I had imagined the sound. But then it came again.

In his room on the other side of the hall, Jake was talking very quietly to someone.

I put the laptop to one side and stood up carefully, then made my way out into the hall as silently as I could. My heart was sinking a little. Over the last two weeks, there had been no sign at all of the little girl or the boy in the floor, and although I was happy to let Jake be himself, I had been relieved about that. I didn't relish the possibility of them returning now.

I stood in the hallway, listening.

"Okay," Jake whispered. "Good night."

And then nothing.

I waited a little longer, but it was clear that the conversation was over. After a few more seconds, I walked across the hall and stepped into his room. There was enough light from behind me to see that Jake was lying very still in his bed, entirely alone in the room.

I moved over to the bed.

"Jake?" I whispered.

"Yes, Daddy?"

He sounded barely there.

"Who were you talking to just now?"

But there was no reply, beyond the gentle rise and fall of the covers over him, and the steady sound of his breathing. Perhaps he had just been half asleep, I thought, and talking to himself.

I tucked the covers over him a little better, and was about to head back to the door when he spoke again.

"Your daddy read that book to you when you were young," he said.

For a moment I said nothing. I just stared down at Jake, lying there with his back to me. The silence was ringing now. The room suddenly felt colder than it had before, and a shiver ran through me. *Yes,* I thought. *He probably did.* It hadn't been a question, though, and there was no way Jake could have known. I didn't even remember it happening myself. But, of course, I'd told Jake the book was a childhood favorite of mine, so I supposed it was a natural assumption for him to make. It didn't mean anything.

"He did," I told Jake quietly. "Why did you say that?"

But my son was already dreaming.

SIXTY-NINE

The letter was waiting for Amanda when she got home but she didn't open it straightaway.

It was obvious from the HMP Whitrow stamping who it was going to be from, and she was unwilling to face that right now. Frank Carter had haunted Pete for twenty years—taunting him; playing with him—and she was damned if she was going to read him gloating about that on the day Pete died. Not that Carter could have known about that when he sent this, of course— but then, the man seemed to know *everything* somehow.

Fuck him, though. She had better, more important things to do.

She left the letter on the dining room table, poured herself a large measure of wine, and then raised the glass.

"Here's to you, Pete," she said quietly. "Safe journey.

And then, despite herself, she started crying—which was ridiculous. She'd never been prone to tears. Had always taken pride in being calm and dispassionate. But the investigation had changed her. And there was nobody here to see it right now, she supposed, so she decided it was fine to let herself go. It felt good. She wasn't even crying for Pete, she realized after a while, so much as allowing all the emotion of the past few months to come pouring out. Pete, yes. But also Neil Spencer. Tom and Jake Kennedy. All of it. It was as though she had been holding her breath for weeks, and the sobbing now was a deep exhalation she had desperately needed.

She drank the wine and poured another.

Having spoken to Tom, and knowing what she did now, she imagined getting drunk probably wasn't what Pete would have wanted. But he would also have understood. In fact, she could imagine the understanding look he would be giving her if he could see her right now—it would be just like some of the others he'd given her. One that said: *I've been there, and I get it, but it's not something we can talk about, can we?*

He'd understand, all right. The Whisper Man case had taken up the last twenty years of his life. After everything that had happened, she imagined it might end up doing the same to her if she wasn't careful. Perhaps that was all right, though—maybe that was the way it was even *meant* to be. Some investigations stayed with you, sinking their claws in and hanging on, so that you would always have to drag them behind you no matter how hard you tried to dislodge them. Before this, she had always imagined she would be impervious to that—that she would be a climber like Lyons, not weighed down the way Pete had been—but she knew herself a little better now. This was something she was going to be carrying for a long time. That was the kind of cop had turned out she was. Not the sensible kind at all.

So be it.

She downed the wine and poured a third.

There were positives to cling to, of course, and despite everything, it was important to do that. Jake Kennedy had been found in time. Francis Carter was in prison. And she would always be the woman who had caught him. She had worked herself to the bone, doing everything she could, and she had not been found wanting. When the hour had come, she had filled every fucking second of it.

Eventually, she steeled herself and opened the letter. She was drunk enough by then not to care anymore what Frank Carter might have to say. What did he matter? Let the fucker write what he wanted. His words would bounce off her, and he would still be rotting where he was afterward, and she would still be here. It wasn't like with Pete. Carter had nothing to hold over her. No way of hurting her.

A single sheet of paper, almost entirely empty.

If Peter can still hear, Carter had written, *tell him thank you.*

SEVENTY

Francis sat in his cell, waiting.

He had spent these two weeks in prison in a state of anticipation, but something in the world had clicked today, and he had known that it was finally time. Past lights-out, he was sitting patiently on his bunk in the darkness, still fully dressed, his hands resting on his thighs. He listened to the metallic echoes and the catcalls of the other convicts gradually dying away around him. He stared almost blindly at the rough brickwork of the opposite wall.

Waiting.

He was a grown man, and he was not afraid.

They had done their best to make him so, of course. When he'd first been brought to the prison, on remand and still unconvicted, the guards had been professional but also either unable or unwilling to hide their hatred for him. Francis had killed a little boy, after all, and—perhaps even worse in their eyes—a police officer. The body search had been overly robust. He had been allowed to keep his own clothes, but had been confined to a single cell and not allowed to mix with the other prisoners. The latter was allegedly for his own protection, but there had been frequent bangs and clatters against his door, threats hissed and whispered from the walkway outside, and beyond the occasional call to knock it off, the guards had sounded bored and done little to stop it. Francis thought they enjoyed it.

Let them.

He waited. It was warm in the cell, but his skin was singing, his body was trembling slightly. But not with fear.

Because he was a grown man. And he was not afraid.

The first time he had seen his father was a week ago in the prison canteen. Even at mealtimes Francis was kept separate from the other inmates, and so he had been seated at a table by himself, with a guard watching over him as he ate the slop that had been provided. Francis thought they gave him the most disgusting portions they could, but if that were the case then the joke was on them. He had eaten much worse. And he had survived far harsher treatment than this. Spooning up a mouthful of cold mashed potato, he had told himself for the hundredth time that this was all just a test. Whatever they threw at him, he would endure. He would earn what—

And then he had turned his head and seen his father.

Frank Carter walked through the door to the canteen as if he owned the whole prison, ducking slightly, his presence immediately immense in the hall. A mountain of a man. The guards, most of them shorter than him by a head, kept a respectful distance. A group of other inmates flanked him, all of them wearing orange prison uniforms, but his father stood out among them, clearly the leader of the group. He did not appear to have aged. To Francis, his father seemed almost supernaturally large and powerful, as though, if he wanted, he could walk through the walls of the prison and emerge unscathed, covered with dust.

As though he could do anything.

"Hurry up, Carter."

The guard prodded him in the back. Francis ate the mash, thinking that the man could soon be made to regret doing that. Because his father was king in here, and that made Francis royalty. As he ate, he stole surreptitious glances over at the table where his father was holding court. The prisoners there were laughing, but it was too far away for Francis to tune out the other noises and hear what they were saying. His father wasn't laughing, though. And while Francis thought some of the others occasionally looked his way, his father never did. No—Frank Carter just ate quickly, occasionally dabbing at his beard with a napkin but otherwise staring straight ahead of him as he chewed, as though he had serious business on his mind.

"I said *hurry up.*"

In the intervening days, Francis had seen Carter on a handful of other occasions, and each time it was the same. He was impressed anew by the size of the man—always towering over the figures around him, like a father surrounded by children. And each time he had seemed entirely unaware of Francis. Unlike the coterie of fawning men around him, he never even looked in Francis's direction. But Francis *felt* him constantly. Lying alone in his cell at night, his father was a solid

presence, throbbing somewhere just out of reach beyond the thick door and the steel walkways.

The anticipation had built steadily until, today, he had
known the moment was coming.

I am a grown man, Francis thought now.

And I am not afraid.

The prison had fallen as quiet as it ever did. There
were still distant noises, but his own cell was so silent
that he could hear himself breathing.

He waited.

And waited.

Until, finally, he heard footsteps approaching in the
hallway outside, the sound simultaneously both cautious
and excited. Francis stood up, his heart beating with
hope, listening more carefully now. It was more than
one person. There was soft laughter followed by hushing sounds. The rattling of keys. Which made sense—
his father would have access to anything he wanted in
here.

But there was also something almost taunting about
the noise.

Outside the cell, someone whispered his name.

Fraaaaancis.

A key turned in the lock.

And then the door opened.

Frank Carter stepped into the cell, the solid bulk
of the man filling the doorway. There was just enough
light for Francis to be able to see his father's face, to see
the expression there, and—

And—

He was a child again.

And he was terrified.

Because Francis remembered the expression on his father's face only too well. It was the look he had always worn when he would come to Francis's bedroom at night and order him to *get up,* to *get downstairs,* because there was something he needed to see. Back then, the hatred he saw had been constrained by necessity and directed at others in his place. But here and now, finally, there was no longer any need for constraint.

Help me, Francis thought.

But there was nobody to help him here. No more than there had been anyone all those years ago. There was nobody to call to who would come.

There never had been.

The Whisper Man walked slowly toward him. With his hands trembling, Francis reached down and took hold of the bottom of his T-shirt.

And then he pulled it up to cover his face.

ACKNOWLEDGMENTS

I owe a huge debt of gratitude to a number of people—firstly to my fabulous agent, Sandra Sawicka, along with Leah Middleton and everyone else at Marjacq. Joel Richardson is my editor at Michael Joseph in the UK, and his patience and advice along the way have been invaluable. I would also like to thank Emma Henderson, Sarah Scarlett, Catherine Wood, Lucy Beresford-Knox, Elizabeth Brandon, and Alex Elam for their hard work and support, and Shan Morley Jones, Elizabeth Catalano, and Dave Cole for catching my mistakes. Huge thanks are due to Will Staehle and Anne Twomey in the U.S. for such a gorgeous cover, Ryan Doherty for his editorial input, and to everyone else at Celadon for their hard work on the book. I have been bowled over by each and every one of you, and I cannot thank you enough.

In addition, the crime fiction community is famous for its warmth and generosity, and I'm constantly grateful to enjoy the support and friendship of so many amazing writers, readers, and bloggers. You're all ace. I need to raise an extra-large glass—a beaker, even—to the Blankets. You know who you are.

Finally, thanks to Lynn and Zack for absolutely everything—not least, putting up with me. This book is dedicated to both of you, with so much love.

Turn the page for a sneak peek of

THE SHADOWS

Now available in trade paperback from
Celadon Books

PROLOGUE

It was my mother who took me to the police station.

The officers had wanted to drive me in the back of their squad car, but she told them no. It's the only time I can remember her losing her temper. I was fifteen years old, standing in the kitchen, flanked by two huge policemen. My mother was in the doorway. I remember her expression changing as they told her why they were there and what they wanted to talk to me about. At first she seemed confused by what she was hearing, but then her face shifted to fear as she looked at me and saw how lost and scared I was right at that moment.

And, while my mother was a small woman, something in the quiet ferocity of her voice and the strength of her posture caused both of those huge policemen to take a step back from me. On the way to the police station, I sat in the passenger seat beside my mother, feeling numb as we followed the car that was escorting us through the town.

It slowed as we reached the old playground.

"Don't look," my mother told me.

But I did. I saw the cordons that had been put in place. The officers lining the street, their faces grim. All the vehicles that were parked along the roadside, their lights rotating silently in the late afternoon sun. And I saw the old jungle gym. The ground beside it had always been dull and gray before, but right now I could see it was patterned in red. It all seemed so quiet and solemn, the atmosphere almost reverential.

And then the car ahead of us came to a stop.

The officers were making sure I got a good look at a scene they were certain I was responsible for.

You have to do something about Charlie.

It was a thought I'd had a great deal in the months leading up to that day, and I still remember the frustration it always brought. I was fifteen years old, and it wasn't fair. Back then, it felt like my entire life was constrained and controlled by the adults around me, and yet none of them appeared to have noticed the black flower rotting in the middle of the yard. Or else they had decided it was easier to leave it alone—that the grass it was poisoning didn't matter.

It should not have been left to me to deal with Charlie.

I understand that now.

And yet, as I sat in the car right then, the guilt they wanted me to feel overwhelmed me. Earlier that day, I had been walking through the dusty streets, squinting against the sun and sweating in the simmering heat, and I had spotted James right there in the playground. My oldest friend. A small, lonely figure in the distance, perched awkwardly on the jungle gym. And while it had been weeks by then since he and I had spoken, I had known full well what he was doing. That he was waiting there for Charlie and Billy.

A number of the officers at the scene turned to look at us, and for a moment I felt trapped in a pocket of absolute silence. Stared at and judged.

Then I flinched as a sudden noise filled the air.

It took me a second to realize that my mother was leaning on the car horn. The blaring volume of the sound seemed jarring and profane in the setting—a scream at a funeral—but when I looked at her I saw my mother's jaw was clenched and her gaze directed furiously at the police car ahead. She kept her hand pressed down, and the sound continued, echoing around the town.

Five seconds.

"Mom."

Ten seconds.

"*Mom*."

Then the police car in front of us began moving slowly away again. My mother lifted her hand from the horn and the world fell quiet. When she turned to me, her expression was somehow both helpless and resolute at the same time, as though my hurt were her own and she was determined to bear the weight of it for me as much as she could.

Because I was her son, and she was going to look after me.

"It's going to be okay," she said.

I did not reply. I just stared back, recognizing the seriousness in her voice and the conviction on her face, and feeling grateful that there was someone there to look after me, even if I would never have admitted it. Grateful there was someone with me who cared about me. Someone who had such faith in my innocence that the words themselves didn't need to be spoken out loud.

Someone who would do anything to protect me.

After what felt like an age, she nodded to herself, and began driving. We followed the car out of the town and left the parked police vans, the staring officers, and the bloodstained playground behind us. And my mother's words were still echoing in my head as we reached the main road.

It's going to be okay.

Twenty-five years have passed, but I still think about that a lot. It's what all good parents tell their children. And yet what does it really amount to? It's a hope, a wish. A hostage to fortune. It's a promise you have to make, and one you must do your best to believe in, because what else is there?

It's going to be okay.

Yes, I think about that a lot.

How every good parent says it, and how often they're wrong.

PART ONE

ONE

NOW

On the day it began, Detective Amanda Beck was technically off work. She slept late. Having been woken in the early hours by the familiar nightmare, she clung to the thin threads of sleep for as long as possible, and it was approaching noon by the time she was up and showered and making coffee. A boy was being killed right then, but nobody knew it yet.

In the middle of the afternoon, Amanda started out on the short drive to visit her father. When she arrived at Rosewood Gardens, there were a few other cars parked in the lot, but she saw nobody. A profound silence settled over the world as she walked up the winding path between the flower beds that led to the gated entrance, and then took the turns she had committed to memory over the last two and a half years, passing gravestones that had become familiar markers.

Was it strange to think of the dead as friends?

Perhaps, but a part of her did. She visited the cemetery at least once a week, which meant she saw more of the people lying here than the handful of living friends she had. She ticked them off as she walked. Here was the grave that was always well attended by fresh flowers.

There, the one with the old, empty whiskey bottle balanced against the stone. And then the plot covered with stuffed toys: a child's grave, that one, Amanda guessed, the presents left by grieving parents who couldn't quite allow their child to leave them yet.

And then, around a final corner, her father's grave.

She stopped and pushed her hands into the pockets of her coat. The plot was marked by a rectangular stone, broad and strong, the way she remembered her father from growing up. There was something pleasingly implacable in the simplicity of it—the way there was just his name and a pair of dates that bookmarked his life. No fuss, exactly the way he would have wanted. Her father had been loving and caring at home, but his life had been spent on the force, where he had done his duty and left his work in the office at the end of the day. It had felt right to reflect that aspect of his character in her choice of headstone. She had found something that did the job required of it—and did it well—but kept emotion separate.

No bloody flowers on my grave, Amanda.

When I'm gone, I'm gone.

One of the many orders she had followed.

But, God, it still felt odd and jarring to her that he was no longer in the world. As a child, she had been scared of the dark, and it had always been her father who came to her when she called out. Whenever he was out on a night shift, she remembered being anxious, as though a safety net had been taken away and if she fell there would be nothing there to catch her. That was the way life seemed these days too. There was a constant sensation in the back of her mind that something was wrong, something missing, but that it wouldn't last. Then she would remember her father was dead, and the stark realization would come. If she called out now, there was nobody to find her in the night.

She pulled her coat a little tighter around her.

No talking to me after I'm gone either.

Another order, so all she ever did when she visited the grave was stand and think. Her father was right, of course. Like him, she wasn't religious, and so she didn't see much point in saying anything out loud. There was nobody to hear now, after all; the opportunity for interrogation had passed. She had been left with the short lifetime of experience and wisdom her father had gifted her, and it was down to her to sift through that. To hold parts up to the light, blow dust from them, and see what worked and what she could use.

Dispassionate.

Aloof.

Practical.

That was how he had been when it came to his job. She thought often of the advice he had given her: When you saw something awful, you had to put it away in a box. The box was something you kept locked in your head, and you only ever opened it to throw something else inside. The work, and the sights it brought you, had to be kept separate from your life at all costs. It had sounded so simple, so neat.

He had been so proud of her joining the police, and while she missed him with all her heart, there was also a small part of her that was glad he wasn't around to see how she'd dealt with the last two years. The box of horrors in her head that would not stay closed. The nightmares she had. The fact that it had turned out she wasn't the kind of officer he had been, and that she wondered whether she ever could be.

And although she followed her father's instructions, it didn't stop her from thinking about him. Today, as always, she wondered how disappointed he would be.

She was on the way back to the car when her phone rang.

Half an hour later, Amanda was back in Featherbank, walking across the waste ground.

She hated this place. She hated its coarse, sun-scorched bushes. The silence and seclusion. The way the air always felt *sick* here, as though the land itself had gone sour and you could sense the rot and poison in the ground on some primal level.

"That's where they found him, right?"

Detective John Dyson, walking beside her, was gesturing toward a skeletal bush. Like everything else that managed to grow here, it was tough and dry and sharp.

"Yeah," she said. "It is."

Where they found him.

But it was where they had lost him first. Two years ago, a little boy had disappeared while walking home here, and then, a few weeks afterward, his body had been dumped in the same location. It had been her case. The events that followed had sent her career into a free fall. Before the dead boy, she had imagined herself rising steadily up the ranks over the years, the box in

THE SHADOWS | 467

her head sealed safely shut, but it turned out she hadn't known herself at all.

Dyson nodded to himself.

"They should fence this place off. Nuke it from orbit."

"It's people who do bad things," she said. "If they didn't do them in one place, they'd just do them somewhere else instead."

"Maybe."

He didn't sound convinced, but nor did he really seem to care. Dyson, Amanda thought, was pretty stupid. In his defense, he at least seemed to realize that, and his entire career had been marked by a singular lack of ambition. In his early fifties now, he did the work, collected the pay, and went home evenings without so much as a backward glance. She envied him.

The thick tree line that marked the top of the quarry was just ahead of them now. She glanced back. The cordon she'd ordered to be set up around the waste ground was obscured by the undergrowth, but she could sense it there. And beyond that, of course, the invisible gears of a major investigation already beginning to turn.

They reached the trees.

"Watch your step here," Dyson said.

"Watch your own."

She stepped deliberately in front of him, bending the fence that separated the waste ground from the quarry and then ducking under. There was a faded warning sign attached a little way along, which did nothing to stop local children from exploring the terrain. Perhaps it was even an incentive; it probably would have been to her as a kid. But Dyson was right. The ground here was steep and treacherous, and she concentrated on her footing as she led the way. If she slipped in front of him now she would have to fucking kill him to save face.

The sides of the quarry were dangerously steep, and she made her way down cautiously. Roots and branches, baked pale by the oppressive summer heat, hung out from the rock like tendons, and she gripped the rough coils of them for balance. It was about a hundred and fifty feet down, and she was relieved when she reached solid ground.

A moment later, Dyson's feet scuffed the stone beside her.

And then there was no sound at all.

The quarry had an eerie, otherworldly quality. It felt self-contained and desolate, and while the sun was still strong on the waste ground above, the temperature was much cooler here. She looked around at the fallen rocks and the clusters of yellowing bushes that grew down here. The place was a maze.

A maze that Elliot Hick had given them directions through.

"This way," she said.

Earlier that afternoon, two teenage boys had been taken into custody outside a nearby house. One of them, Elliot Hick, had been borderline hysterical; the other, Robbie Foster, empty and calm. Each was holding a knife and a book, and both were soaked almost head to toe in blood. They were being held for questioning at the station, but Hick had already told the attending officer what the two of them had done, and where they would find the results of it.

It wasn't far, he'd said.

Three hundred feet or so.

Amanda headed between the rocks, taking her time, moving slowly and carefully. There was a pressure to the silence here that felt like being underwater, and her chest was tightening with apprehension at the thought of what they were about to see. Assuming Hick was telling the truth, of course. There was always a chance there was nothing to be found here at all. That this was some kind of bizarre prank.

Amanda reached out and moved a curtain of sharp branches to one side. The notion that this was a practical joke seemed absurd, but it was infinitely preferable to the idea that she was about to step out into a clearing and see—

She stopped in her tracks.

And see that.

Dyson stepped out and stood next to her. He was breathing a little faster, although it wasn't clear if that was from the physical exertion of the climb and the walk, or the sight that lay before them now.

"Jesus Christ," Dyson said.

The clearing ahead of them was roughly hexagonal, the ground jagged but basically flat, and it was bordered on all sides by trees and tangles of bushes. There was something almost occult about the setting, a first impression that was only enhanced by the tableau laid out there.

The body was about fifteen feet away, directly in the center. It had been posed in a kneeling position, bent over almost in prayer, the thin arms folded backward along the ground like broken wings. It appeared to be that of a teenage boy. He was dressed in shorts and a T-shirt that had ridden up to his armpits, but the blood made it difficult to tell what color the clothing had been. Amanda's gaze moved over the body. There were numerous dark stab wounds on the boy's exposed torso, the blood around them pale brown smears on the skin. There was a deeper pool beneath his head, which was tilted awkwardly to one side, barely attached, and facing mercifully away from her.

Dispassionate, Amanda reminded herself.

Aloof.

Practical.

For a moment, the world was completely still. Then she saw something else and frowned.

"What's that on the ground?" she said.

"It's a kid's fucking body, Amanda."

She ignored Dyson, and took a couple of careful steps farther into the clearing, anxious not to disturb the scene but needing to make sense of what she was seeing. There was more blood on the stone floor, stretching out in a circle on all sides around the body. The pattern seemed too uniform to be accidental, but it was only when she reached the edge of the bloodstains themselves that she realized what they were.

She stared down, her gaze moving here and there.

"What is it?" Dyson said.

Again, she didn't reply, but this time it was because she didn't quite know how. Dyson walked across to join her. She was expecting another exclamation, more bluster, but he remained silent and she could tell he was just as disturbed as she was.

She counted the stains as best she could, but it was hard to keep track of them. They were a storm on the ground.

Hundreds of blood-red handprints pressed carefully against the stone.